Praise f

THERE ARE WOLV

"*There Are Wolves Here Too* delivers a powerful story about small towns and dark secrets. Howell is a writer to watch."
—SAM WIEBE, award-winning author of *Hell and Gone*

"With his follow up to his stellar debut novel, *Only Pretty Damned*, Niall Howell not only serves up yet another dazzling showcase of riveting drama told underneath a lingering cloud of criminality, but he also distinguishes himself as one of the finest fiction writers currently working in Canada. *There Are Wolves Here Too* is a mesmerizing coming-of-age masterpiece."
—A.J. DEVLIN, award-winning author of the "Hammerhead" Jed mystery-comedy series

"Niall Howell gets everything right in this swift, riveting coming-of-age noir: the complications of nostalgia with all its beauty and regret, the intense, romantic disorientation of adolescence. *There Are Wolves Here Too* draws us into its vividly realized suburban world before extracting its darkness with masterfully restrained technique. The characters live and breathe. The plot is meticulously rhythmed. The dialogue is fresh and real. Filled with haunting sadness, sharp humour, and sombre wisdom, this novel is a stunning achievement."
—MIKE THORN, author of *Shelter for the Damned* and *Darkest Hours*

"Niall Howell is fast becoming one of noir's masters of subversive voice. Robin, the narrator of this lean and bleak bildungsroman, is as complex and morally compromised a character as you'll find in crime fiction. But he's a kid. And that's what makes this novel so unique. All the signatures of Teen Comedy are here—the hot mom, the class bully, the tested friendship, the budding romance—but put in service of something much richer, and deeper, and darker: a Young Adult novel that is definitely not for young adults."
—RANDY NIKKEL SCHROEDER, author of *Arctic Smoke*

THERE ARE WOLVES HERE TOO

Library and Archives Canada Cataloguing in Publication

Title: There are wolves here too : a novel / Niall Howell.
Names: Howell, Niall, author.
Identifiers: Canadiana (print) 20210379693 | Canadiana (ebook) 20210379715 |
    ISBN 9781774390597 (softcover) | ISBN 9781774390603 (EPUB)
Classification: LCC PS8615.O942 T54 2022 | DDC C813/.6—dc23

Editor for the Press: Claire Kelly
Cover and interior design: Michel Vrana
Author photo: Cedna Portrait Stories

NeWest Press wishes to acknowledge that the land on which we operate is Treaty 6
territory and a traditional meeting ground and home for many Indigenous Peoples,
including Cree, Saulteaux, Niitsitapi (Blackfoot), Métis, and Nakota Sioux.

NeWest Press acknowledges the Canada Council for the Arts, the Alberta
Foundation for the Arts, and the Edmonton Arts Council for support of our
publishing program. We acknowledge the financial support of the Government of
Canada through the Canada Book Fund for our publishing activities.

NeWest Press
#201, 8540-109 Street
Edmonton, Alberta T6G 1E6
NeWest Press www.newestpress.com

No bison were harmed in the making of this book.

Printed and bound in Canada
22 23 24 25 5 4 3 2 1

For Rory

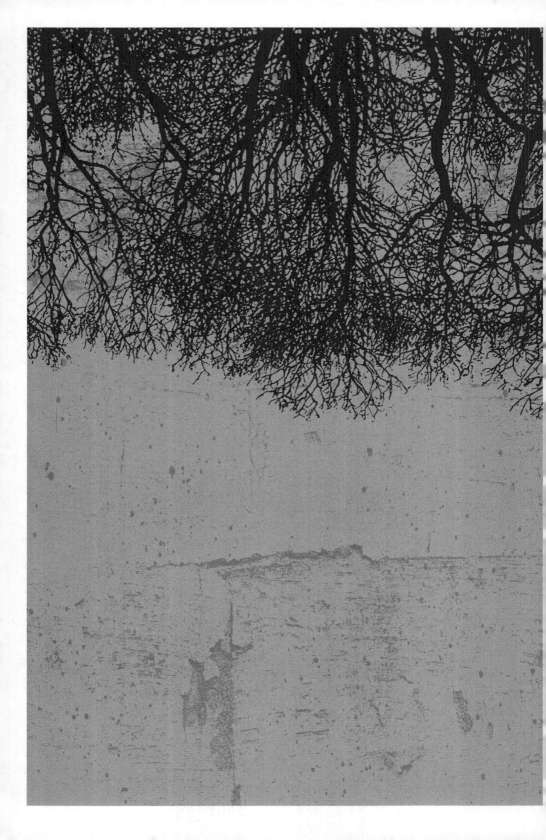

THERE ARE WOLVES

HERE TOO

a novel

NIALL HOWELL

NeWest Press

THE HARDEST THINGS TO LOSE ARE THE ONES YOU DON'T KNOW YOU CAN.
The things you don't think of as things because they seem to exist some-where beyond everything else. They're ingrained in your world, which makes them different from all that other stuff you worry about losing.

When I was a kid, I'd worry about misplacing my homework and having to redo it. Or I'd step over a storm drain and worry about my house key somehow leaping out of my pocket and diving between one of the voids in the grate, leaving me stranded in my backyard until my parents came home. I'd worry about someone breaking into my locker at the pool, reaching into the pocket of my balled-up jeans, and nabbing the ten my grandma gave me for my birthday—"Don't spend it all in one place,"—gone before I could spend any of it in any place. Before I'd lost anything real, that's what I'd worry about: stuff. Things that, when you got right down to it, were pretty meaningless, pretty replaceable.

But I'm older now, and I know better. I know that the hardest things to lose are the ones you get so used to having you don't even think about them. Like tap water. You twist the handle, water shushes out from the

7

faucet and into your glass, and you don't spend one second thinking about how lucky you are to have it at all. It feels so natural that it doesn't even warrant thought.

Time. Feelings. People. They're like tap water. You get to thinking they're somehow permanent. But you can only believe that for so long, because part of growing up is realizing that everything can be taken away. It can all dry up and vanish overnight, and the next morning when you turn on the tap and get that awful wheeze empty pipes make when they're trying too hard, you'll hate yourself for not being more grateful back when you had so much you didn't even have to think about it.

Yeah, I'm older now, and I know better. And I realize that makes me lucky. Because not everyone gets to be that. Older, I mean. Not everyone gets to be older.

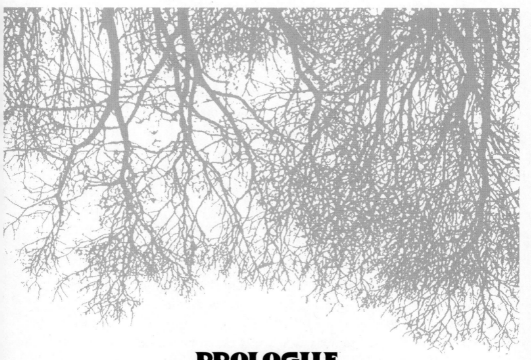

PROLOGUE

HADDINGTON SPRINGS' IDENTITY CRISIS BEGAN LONG BEFORE I WAS BORN.
"Confusion started the moment ground broke" was the often-invoked expression, usually by seniors or teachers at the beginning of a lesson on local government. On paper, it was a city. We had our own police force and we had a transit system. Both were very modest—transit was six bus routes, and no fancy CTrains like the ones that zipped passengers around Calgary like tokens on a Snakes and Ladders board—but they existed, and that counted for a couple of ticks in the city column. We also had a rec centre, a bigass mall with a bigass movie theatre in it, and our own TV station: HG Three. We only ever watched the local news, the rest was fluffy community junk and cheap ads, but we had it, so the homegrown Napoleons who kept score would take it. *Tick, tick, tick, tick.* We were a city.

But to outsiders, Haddington Springs was a town. We had our one Boston Pizza, and it was general consensus that if you slung pizzas there for more than six months, you'd be a local lifer, and you'd either be pregnant or impregnate someone before your

9

twentieth birthday. Other ticks in the "town" column included the fact that no parking meters were to be found in Haddington Springs, even on Main Street, and that our local mascot, a cowboy named Haddington Henry, was memorialized not only in bronze, but also on the gym clothes of all the students at Haddington Springs Public High School. And if you drove to the east edge of the city at night, you could just see the bright lights of Calgary glinting in the distance. They were beautiful and glamorous (by comparison), and they were just grand enough to make you feel tiny. We were our own lonely little asteroid, floating somewhere just shy of the gravitational grasp of something much bigger.

More than anything though, I think Haddington Springs *felt* like a town. And the feeling wasn't because of a lone Boston Pizza or a lack of parking meters. That feeling came from elsewhere. Part of it might've had to do with the way everyone seemed connected somehow, bound to together by sticky little threads. Like a spider's web, there were times you only saw the threads when the light hit them from the right angle. But there were also those times they couldn't be ignored, when you'd feel a strong tug from someone wiggling around on the other side of the mesh and their vibrations somehow became part of your own. It wasn't quite the case that everyone knew everyone, but it's fair to say that most people knew *of* most people, by sight at least. You couldn't go anywhere without seeing a familiar face. Not necessarily someone you knew well enough to talk to, but at the very least they'd be a recurring background extra in the movie of your life. This interconnectedness made the city feel not just closed off, it made it feel closed in. Even though there was no shortage of open space, Haddington Springs felt constricting. And I don't think it ever felt more constricting— more *suffocating*—than August of 1997, the summer that little Catherine Hillerman went missing near the ravine.

It sure felt like a small town then.

PART 1

1

AUGUST 1997

GLASSES WERE BROKEN AND BLOOD WAS SPILT. BOTH MINE, THAT DAY.

Steph lined her soccer ball up.

"Stay still," she said.

I straightened and put my hands behind my back. "I'm expecting a call from the Governor."

Steph knelt down, closed one eye and examined the angle between her ball and my head. She made a minute adjustment before nodding and standing back up.

"The Governor call is a death row thing. This is a firing squad."

"Then shouldn't I be kicking a ball too?" Dylan, leaning against a tree on the clearing's edge, asked. "I thought with a firing squad you weren't supposed to know who made the kill."

Steph gave him a look like *you've-gotta-be-kidding-me.* "Your aim sucks. If you kicked, you'd actually hit him," she said from behind a cupped hand, as if I weren't supposed to hear it.

Dylan shrugged. "Fine by me. I just thought you did things by the book."

"If it were by the book, Robin would be blindfolded. And I think we'd have to give him a cigarette."

I picked a small twig up from the ground and popped it in my mouth. "One last puff," I pleaded, trying to contain my laughter. It crunched when I bit down and the taste that leaked from it gave my tastebuds a bitter sting, so I spat it out right away, hamming up the nastiness. My friends found this hilarious.

My reason for having to face the firing squad that day was an unforgiveable offense: inviting Steph's kid brother Jeremy join her, Dylan, and I at the ravine so we could play two-on-two for once instead of triple-threat. Jeremy drove Steph *nuts*, and she took any opportunity available to get away from him. I didn't think he was that bad. Maybe a bit of a pest, but he was nine—older than any of the other siblings available to us—so I figured we could at least make do with him. I was wrong.

The invitation wasn't appreciated by Steph. When we left her house, Jeremy was standing at the door in tears, his loud cries following us nearly to the corner, where they were finally drowned by distance and the sounds of passing cars. Steph wasted no time making clear to me that it wasn't up to me to invite her brother along to anything.

Having the luxury of being entertained by the situation, Dylan snickered and told me I was "so dead," while Steph quickened her pace and walked ahead of us the rest of the way to the ravine. But not too far ahead. None of us liked to be in the ravine alone, even for a minute.

Steph took her place behind the ball. "Any last words?" she asked me.

I thought about it for a second. When nothing original came to me, I replied, "Whatever the guy in *Braveheart* said."

Dylan snickered and gave me a slow clap. Steph shook her head.

"Your last words are the same as the last words of the character in *Braveheart*? Or your last words are literally, 'Whatever the guy in *Braveheart* said?'"

"Both," I told her.

Before she wound up her kick, I leaned forward and give a big toothy smile and said, "Pepsi," because a school photographer had us say that instead of cheese back when we were getting our pictures taken in the sixth grade. We thought that was really lame, so since then, whenever the opportunity presented itself, we'd smile and say Pepsi in the most obnoxious, nasally voice we could pull off.

"May God have mercy on your wretched soul." Steph took a few steps so she could approach the ball from an angle, the way she would if it were a penalty kick, which, I supposed, in a way it was, and then she went for it. Three steps, the swing of the leg, the strike. It *looked* like her usual perfect execution. But instead of whizzing by my head like it always did when either Dylan or I were in this position, her grass-stained, Union-Jack-adorned ball smashed right into my face, shattering both of my lenses and giving me a gusher of a nosebleed. I crumpled, blood flowing from my face, painting the grass of the ravine, trickling onto thirsty soil that soaked up the crimson pools quicker than seemed possible.

Steph was beyond apologetic. My parents, I knew, would be beyond pissed.

At the time, I had no idea what had been set in motion.

× × ×

Late the next morning I didn't recognize the blur that was Dylan when he first rounded the corner, but the jangling gave him away. He had been going on about this day for months. His grandma had these three glass jars in her study. One of the jars was filled with pennies, one was a mix of nickels and dimes, and one was filled to the brim with quarters. Around last Christmas, during one of his family's visits to Calgary, Dylan was helping his grandma move a chair out of the study and he mentioned to her how that many quarters would go a long way at the arcade. His grandma, being the saint that she was, made Dylan a deal: commit to an hour of yardwork the next couple times the family visited, and the jar would be all his.

His conspirator's grin was the first thing I noticed when he came into focus. The second thing I noticed were the bulging pockets of his cargo shorts, which he was struggling to keep up around his waist. The five loonies I had on me suddenly felt much less significant than they did when I first grabbed them earlier that morning.

Dylan went to greet me with a high-five, but the instant he took his right hand away from his shorts they went lopsided. He returned his hand to the waistband, yanked them back up. "You ready to put some bad words on some high-score lists?" he asked.

I pointed to his shorts. "You're going to need both hands if you want to make it onto any high-score lists."

"If I stand the right way," He shifted so that his body angled to one side and his left foot pointed out like he was going to trip someone, "they stay up no problem." He raised his hands in the air for a rushed three count, the way you do when you're showing someone you can ride your bike with no hands, and then hurriedly returned them to his shorts before they slid off him. "This load's just going to get lighter the longer we play," he added, then he pointed with his head to the mall entrance. "Destiny awaits."

× × ×

The arcade was attached to the theatre at the Midtown Mall, one of Haddington Springs' most revered attractions. There were days when it was a toss-up between catching a movie or dumping our money into glowing red coin slots, but today was no contest. Not only did Dylan have to burn through his approximate weight in quarters, but any movie we wanted to see we were too young for, and anything else we had either already seen—*Batman and Robin, The Lost World, Men in Black*—or we felt we were too old for. If anyone from school caught the two of us going into a movie about a dog playing basketball, we'd have beats and new nicknames waiting for us on September 2nd.

We walked through the mall, past the food court, which was empty save for a table of retirees who sat in a booth against the far wall. The air around them was permeated with the stale cigarette smoke that lived in their clothing, and black coffee, steam coiling from their neighbourhood of Styrofoam cups like exhaust from factories. As we walked by, I wondered if something clicked in a person's mind once they cleared the age of seventy that made sticking enamel pins in baseball caps seem like a cool thing to do. A couple of them nodded at us and we nodded back.

We got to the theatre just as the accordion doors were being opened. To our right was a set of stairs that led to the concession area. A small group of employees—a couple of them only a year or two older than us—wore matching blue and black polo shirts and Midtown Cinema caps and stood around a man in his early twenties holding a clipboard and wearing theatre supervisor regalia: an oversized short-sleeved white dress shirt with a red tie whose knot was just slightly askew. To our left was the arcade, a vast, dark room lit by the glow of screens, the neon trim of air hockey tables, and the blinking lights of pinball machines. I put three of my five dollars into the change machine and a metallic downpour followed. I did a quick count to make sure I had what I was supposed to, and from there Dylan and I rushed over to *Mansion of the Damned*—a cheap knockoff of *House of the Dead*—which we both knew was our first stop without having to discuss it. The game was new and was really gory, which made it cool, so if it was vacant we knew we had to claim it and enjoy it while we could. Any time after noon you'd have a crowd gawking at you. The thing about arcade observers is they either offer unsolicited pointers—"Reload!" or "Watch out for the guy with the axe!"—or they bicker among themselves about whose turn is next, which is very distracting when you're trying to shoot your way through a house full of monsters.

We put our change in and removed the plastic guns from their holsters. I pressed down the blinking player-two start button, and few seconds later, after positioning his legs in a way that would keep his shorts up, Dylan pressed the player-one start button. The game was a first-person shooter, but during the opening montage you got to see your character's face. I thought player two looked like a grownup version of me. For about five seconds I got to see what I thought of as a blocky, pixelated rendering of myself fifteenish years down the road. My lanky spaghetti limbs had grown lean and muscular, so much so that the bulge of my biceps could be seen through my slick leather jacket as I fired my Magnum at an axe-wielding ghoul who was closing in on a hot brunette scientist. There was a pair of aviator sunglasses resting on my forehead, pushing back my reddish-brown hair, and I had a peppering of stubble that looked to be a couple days shy of Wolverine. I loved being player two.

"Looks like you finally grow into those ears," Dylan said, as he had every time since I had told him about the perceived resemblance.

After older me fired—gun barrel pointing directly at the screen, directly at my own face—the scene zoomed to the ghoul with the axe. His head exploded and the grateful scientist ran toward us, her movements jittery and rigid. "Thank you so much," she said. "You need to help my colleagues—they're all trapped in that mansion with those . . . *damned things!*"

"Looks like you finally grow into your boobs," I said to Dylan, which had also become part of our routine.

"Shut up," Dylan said. In the corner of my eye I could see his smirk.

A moment later the game cut to both our characters standing together. Player one, who Dylan maintained was *his* older self, had slick jet-black hair and a dark suit (not exactly prime monster-killing attire). He nodded at player two, who returned the gesture, and then the pair of them kicked the evil mansion's front door open. From there our perspective shifted to first-person and the real game began.

As we blasted our way through the first level, I was wasting a bit more ammo than normal without my glasses.

"Should've brought the bayonet," Dylan said after taking some damage from a ghoul, referring to a piece of family history that hung in his living room. The bayonet had been used by his grandpa, who, like mine, had served in World War II. After he died, Dylan's grandma gave the gun and bayonet to her only son. She said she didn't like being reminded of war and what it does to people. As far as antique heirlooms went, I couldn't think of anything cooler than that rifle, which stood out in a home that was otherwise filled exclusively with new things.

"What time do we meet Steph?" I asked, blasting a couple rounds into a ghoul's chest.

Dylan finished the menace off with one to the head. "Don't know," he said, shrugging. "What day is it?"

It was summer so I couldn't be totally sure.

"I *think* it's Wednesday," I said.

Dylan thought about it for a second. "So, that means her dad's working until two or something."

Steph's dad worked for a trucking company. He used to be a driver and would be on the road for days, sometimes weeks, at a time. Now he worked as a dispatcher because Steph's mom was dead and he needed to be around more for his two kids. For the first year or so after her mom went, Steph's grandma would look after her and Jeremy. Steph said it was sometimes hard for her grandma to look after the pair of them, because she was old and got tired easily. Her grandma also smoked all the time, and while she didn't smoke inside when her grandkids were over, her house still stunk of cigarettes, meaning the pair of them always came home cloaked in the stench of Du Maurier regulars, which her dad, an ex-smoker, didn't like. As soon as Steph turned twelve, he got her to take on babysitting duties as often as possible.

I squinted at the clock on the wall. "We still have lots of time," I said. It was only a bit after eleven.

"Good," he said. "*We* still have *lots* of quarters."

We turned and looked at one another, risking, for maybe two seconds, death by axe, or bite, or claw slash. Dylan smiled at me and shrugged, and I repeated the combo back to him, then we brought our attention back to the task at hand: expelling the forces of evil from a creepy old mansion that had been repurposed as an insane asylum. One bullet at a time.

× × ×

When our gun arms grew weak, our marksmanship lazy, we decided to let someone else take up our sweaty weapons. The arcade was getting busy, and during our last three attempts at the game's ninth level (no one seemed to know how many levels there were in total, but the arcade rumour mill said twenty-five) we had drawn a small crowd, which made the game less fun. It was like eating a meal in a full restaurant with waiting customers huddled around the table watching you chew.

We'd burned through enough quarters to allow Dylan to walk entirely hands-free, though he still jangled like Christmas as we made our way to the Orange Julius in the food court. Dylan drank his extra-large down in no time, barely even slowing when a brain freeze struck him. He was always like that. He called it "living in the now," which he probably got from one the Tony Robbins tapes his mom played in the car.

He passed the time waiting for me to finish my drink by folding his straw over and over on itself until it resembled a tiny staircase. He was trying to get it to stand when something behind me caught his attention and made his eyes bug.

I turned, squinted, and managed to make out Louis Duss and Connor Monaghan making their way down the walkway at the edge of the food court, toward the arcade. Toward us.

My eyes bugged, too.

Louis and Connor went to our school. They were part of a large group of neighbourhood kids we used to play pickup hockey with up until a couple winters ago, but for some reason when they hit the seventh grade, the pair of them turned into total assholes. They were going into the ninth grade now—a year ahead of us—and Dylan, Steph, and I avoided them as much as we could. Earlier that summer I found myself hanging out with them . . . it was *not* a good time. Louis and Connor were pretty terrible to us, but there were plenty of people who got it worse than we did. We were never forced to eat dirt like Max Kendrick and none of us had been pantsed like Brent Sinclair during sports day. My best guess was that Louis and Connor didn't consider us to be worthwhile pursuits. We didn't give the reactions that some of their more favoured targets did—tears, whimpering, begging, that whole gamut—so the two of them didn't put that much effort into harassing us. There were times I'd been thrown against a locker for no particular reason, and if I ever crossed paths with either of them when I was wearing my Canucks jersey, I'd be informed that I was a fag, but really, it could've been worse. Most times.

For some reason they always went at Dylan with the tiniest bit more malice. This was largely due to the fact that Dylan possessed something that was more valuable to the pair of them than nerd tears, or the thrill of humiliating someone in public. Dylan had resources. At school, my friend was a well-known junk food baron. Whenever he pulled his paper-bagged lunch out of his backpack Louis and Connor would close in on our little corner of the cafeteria like two xylophone-ribbed hyenas and take the most desirable item from Dylan's bag. Sometimes it was a Twinkie, other times it was a bag of chips, or a four-pack of Oreos. The pair of them operated like medieval tyrants, ruthlessly taxing their subjects into poverty. The thing with our school was that most of the subjects were already peasants. Practically no one had anything too special in their lunch. Once word got out that your parents splurged on the good stuff, you were screwed. By the end of the last school year Dylan had even stopped protesting. Louis and Connor would walk over to us, hold out their hands, and Dylan would hand over whatever he had that day. It was a completely wordless transaction.

The two of us sat frozen watching the two of them. They were close enough that we could hear their voices, though not what they were saying. I knew we were both thinking the same thing: once they found out about all Dylan's change—and make no mistake, they'd find out, guys like them always did—it'd be game over.

Connor, the more menacing of the two (although they were pretty neck-and-neck in that category) looked to be telling a story to his partner in crime. His unusually-deep-for-his-age voice echoed across the food court, amplified by the vastness of the space, making him sound like a god. A god who many people, including myself, suspected had been held back a grade, but a god nonetheless. Every couple steps he'd throw a gesture into the mix of whatever he was telling Louis. Based on these gestures—vast sweeping motions, kicks, the flailing of arms—I gathered that he was either going on about someone he'd beat up, or a particularly violent death he'd seen in a movie.

As they drew nearer, I noticed my friend nervously grabbing his straw creation from the table, bunching it up, and closing his fist around it.

Connor's voice came into range: "And he was like, 'Ahhh, fucking let go of my nips, fucker!'" Then he stopped and bent forward, hands on his knees. He was in hysterics at his own story. At first Louis looked down on his friend as if he were watching someone in the throes of madness. But then a second later, he too cracked up, giggling like a little kid.

We hadn't been noticed yet, which meant we had a small window to make ourselves scarce. Dylan got my attention with a nod of his head. "Photo booth," he said.

"No, man. They spot us sneaking in there, we're screwed. Nowhere to run. We should go to a store. They wouldn't do anything with adults around," I said, fully aware my last point was pure conjecture.

Dylan looked almost disturbed by my suggestion. He shook his head. "Fuck that. Having adults around doesn't mean anything. We're going to the photo booth."

I hadn't expected that kind of pushback from him, but before I had a chance to argue, he stood up from his chair. I followed. What else could I do?

We tiptoed through the network of tables toward the side opposite Louis and Connor, with Dylan pressing his pockets against his thighs to minimize jangle. Nearsighted as I was, I followed my friend closely, being extra careful not to bump into a chair and give away our position. There was a photo booth sitting against the far wall. It was tucked discreetly between an ATM and a giant-gumball machine. Our safe haven. I followed Dylan in and tugged the curtain closed. He had half his ass on half of the stool in the centre. I planted half my ass on the other half. We both breathed sighs of relief, but these sighs were something of a performance. Our backs were perfectly straight, our shoulders tense, our rigid arms crossed tightly across our chests. A minute went by, and then without looking at me, Dylan whispered, "That was so close," the slightest trace of laughter invading his words. I nodded but said nothing. It felt too early to speak and I didn't want to jinx anything.

After a few minutes the silence was too much, so we risked the occasional muttered word.

"Man."

"Too close."

"Yep."

"Shit."

"Man."

Eventually I stood up, deciding it was about time the both of us got back to the lives that were waiting for us somewhere outside that cramped little box.

I poked my head out and squinted to try and make out any Connor- and Louis-shaped blurs. It seemed safe. "All clear."

We both stepped out.

"Wait a sec." Dylan was rifling through his pocket. After a moment, he pulled out a fistful of quarters. I could tell by his expression that he was doing math in his head. He returned two of the quarters to his pocket. "This occasion needs to be commemor-ated." He slid some quarters into the coin slot on the outside of the booth, then motioned for me to hurry in. "Quick," he said, "there's a countdown."

The two of us returned to our previous positions, a cheek each on the stool. The countdown began beeping just as I closed the curtain behind us. We read over the instructions: wait for the ten-second countdown. Look at the X on the screen. Four poses.

We both whispered along: "...four...three...two...one." The beeping halted, and we heard a *deet-deet-deet-da-deet* from some-where behind the screen, then the flash, which felt like a supernova in the dark booth, went off, and again, and again, and again.

We killed the few minutes it took the photos to print by look-ing over the sample shots on the side of the booth, one set of which was of a beautiful red-headed girl who looked like she was trying to pull off glamour poses.

I moved close to get a clearer look at her shots. "Hubba, hubba," I said. "I hope it accidently prints hers off."

Dylan snickered. "Hubba, hubba, I want some Hubba Bubba."

"What the hell?" I laughed.

Dylan waved me off. "I don't know."

Our stupid faces looked even goofier printed than they felt being pulled, so I guess mission accomplished. I walked over to a nearby food court table, and ripped the photo strip in half. I put both hands behind my back and pretended to mix them up. "Pick," I said. After a rushed round of Eenie Meenie, Dylan gave my left shoulder a smack. I handed his prize over.

"Nice," he said, "these were the two I wanted. You look like Frankenstein taking a shit in the first one."

"You look like a penis with a face," I said, looking at Dylan in my two shots. "Not just in these photos, but in general."

Carefully, I tucked my half away in my wallet.

I still have my half.

"We should go," Dylan said, consulting the clock that stood in the middle of the food court, which was far enough away to be just a blurry white disc to me. "We still have time before we have to meet Steph, but I don't want to stick around here and risk running into those assholes."

Dylan needed to go to the washroom before we left. I kind of had to too, but I never wanted to use the mall washroom. When I was younger my mom sat me down for a stranger danger talk and told me to watch out for perverts, taking special care to specify mall washrooms. Plus, the place always stunk like the elephant enclosure at the zoo. I decided I'd find a secluded tree to use on the way to Steph's.

Dylan went in by himself, and I found a good spot on the wall to lean against. He'd been in there for a good couple of minutes, and I was trying to decide what joke to make about his extended stay when he finally came out. But then I saw Kyle and his kid sister, Catherine. The Hillermans. I gave a wave. Kyle and I were in the same grade and would sometimes work together in class, and we'd chat in the hall on the way to our lockers, but we didn't really hang out outside of school. I went to his seventh birthday party— glow-in-the-dark bowling—but everyone in our grade was invited. Kyle returned my wave and gave this sort of sheepish shrug that said "What can ya do?" which I assumed had something to do with being seen in public with his little sister. Catherine seemed to be orbiting her big brother. She paced around him, pigtails whipping at the side of her head as she talked to herself with the sort of scattered, frenzied energy little kids tap into when they're visiting another plane of existence. She moved her hands around, saying, "Oh, zank you, kint zir. Zat is very kint oof you, I vood love some, zanks, *dah*-ling, zanks," and somehow, despite the awfulness of her made-up accent, for a flash I pictured her at a glamorous dinner party, a tiara on her head, pearls on her neck, an elegant black gown, mingling with royalty, and a handful of fantasy creatures in formal attire. She paused for a second—it really couldn't have been more than that—smiled at me, then went back to her imagination.

"Hey," Kyle said to me.

"Hey."

"No glasses?"

I touched the bridge of my nose to confirm what I already knew. "Nope. They got broken. Soccer ball."

"That sucks," Kyle replied. "I'm supposed to take her to a movie." Kyle gestured toward Catherine.

"What movie?" I asked.

"Don't know yet. She's only six though, so it's gotta be G. That usually means we have a maximum of two choices."

I warned him: "Me and Dylan were just up there. I hate to break it to you, but I'm pretty sure you only have one choice."

"So really no choice. Nice."

"There's a choice," I said. "Option one: see the only G movie. Option two: don't."

"I guess that's true," Kyle conceded. The three of us stood for a moment before he told me they should get going.

"Hope you like dogs playing basketball," I said. Kyle shrugged and smiled and Catherine gave me a transient wave, fingers fluttering.

'Ta-ta, *dah*-ling,' she whispered.

At the time, it didn't feel there was anything special about our brief interaction. When Dylan came out, wet hands slapping up and down his shorts, all I bothered to say about it was, "I ran into Kyle Hillerman and his kid sister," which he responded to with "Cool." If I'd known what would happen, I would've paid closer attention. I would've committed every little detail to memory. I don't know if there was anything there to remember, but later, I wished I had something—anything—more to give.

2

IT MAY HAVE BEEN A FEW YEARS SINCE BRUCE, STEPH'S DAD, MANNED A BIG rig, but he wasn't going to let that stop him from looking the part. He answered the door wearing one of his usual flannel shirts—this one a faded blue that looked like it had lived through some serious trauma—unbuttoned, exposing his relic '88 Olympics souvenir shirt. His dark mustache, whose bulk and shape always made me think of a bat's wings, covered most of his mouth. It shifted up and down as he chomped on a bagel, as if it had a life of its own. "Hey, guys," he said after force-swallowing a bite, "I'll get her. Come on in."

Dylan and I stepped inside. The screen door clicked closed behind us. Bruce called his daughter's name and a second later we heard the familiar sound of her feet pattering upstairs from the basement, where the family's TV was. She breezed past her dad, giving him a quick smack on the arm as she went by, and came to us. She motioned that we should scooch over so she could get her runners from the closet we were blocking.

"Steph, repeat offenders get grounded," Bruce called from the kitchen. "Maybe leave the soccer ball here today?"

Steph smirked at that. "Right," she muttered, shaking her head, because there was just no way.

"And, Robin, did you tell your parents I'll pick up the tab for your new specs?"

"Yeah. They said they appreciate it, but they'll get them because it was my fault for being careless," I replied, having to raise my voice a little, which made me cringe. My voice was just starting to change, and anytime I had to speak up I felt bummed because I could really hear myself and who wants to sound like Kermit the Frog?

Steph sprung up from tying her shoes fast enough to let her hair (the same inky shade as her mother's) experience zero gravity for an instant before falling back in to position. Her wavy bangs were parted like an open curtain across her forehead. She hooked a couple loose strands behind her ears, gave us a nod indicating she was good to go, then grabbed her soccer ball and slipped it into the crook under her arm.

"Bye, Dad!" she called, nudging the screen door open.

I called, "Bye, Bruce," but Dylan kind of mumbled his good-bye because he came from a family that insisted on always using "Mr." and "Mrs." when it came to talking to adults. He'd tried Mr. Sheldon with Bruce once, but was quick to learn that wouldn't fly.

× × ×

Around us, gas lawnmowers roared and impact sprinklers blasted across lawns like machine guns while we recounted to Steph our near run-in at the mall. Steph listened patiently as we added embellishment on top of embellishment while she dribbled her ball up the sidewalk.

"Throw salt on them next time you see them," she said of Louis and Connor. "It's supposed to work on demons."

She'd been into stuff like that for as long as I'd known her. Stuff that I didn't know how else to classify other than weird. Demons, UFOs, cryptozoology. It was cool, but odd, because she seemed too mature for that kind of thing.

"Yeah, I'll make sure to grab extra packets next time I'm at Mickey Dee's," I replied, then added I'd seen Kyle Hillerman at the mall after Dylan and I dodged Louis and Connor. Steph stopped in her tracks and made a gagging face.

"When our class did valentines last year, he wrote me this really long card that had an acrostic poem of my name, and his *phone number* in it."

"You two would make a cute couple," Dylan said with fake sincerity.

"Shut up," Steph told him. And he did.

My stomach fell into my runners. "Did you call him?" I asked. It was the first I'd heard of this. She didn't say anything, she just gave me a look like I had dicks for eyebrows. It was all the answer I needed.

We ended up at the field at Saint Phillip's school. Whenever I think back to that day, I can't help but dwell on our choice to go there instead of the ravine. I don't remember even having a discussion about it. There were certainly perks to Saint Phillip's: the field was well maintained, and there were real goal posts with real nets, an upgrade from what we used for goal posts in the ravine, which was usually any combination of a hoodie, a water bottle, or a large rock. But the ravine, with its unkempt grass and its spindly trees, whose branches overlapped each other like a tangled catch of rickety veins, was where we almost always went. You'd never set foot in the ravine alone, but it was *the* coolest place to go as a group. In the ravine, you could say shit and fuck as loud as you wanted without having to worry about a parent at the nearby playground scolding you for exposing their child to such disgusting language. In the ravine, if you had to pee, you could just step into the woods and go. Sometimes you'd see older kids smoking, or drinking, or making out—we'd seen condom wrappers on the ground there on more than one occasion—which made the place cool. The ravine had secrets, and if you went there, you got to be part of one. Whether you wanted to or not.

But we didn't go to the ravine that day, we went to the field at Saint Phillip's. And because we were unaware that would be the last carefree day we would have in a while, we spent our time there the same way we would have any other afternoon. We played triple-threat soccer. We went over to the baseball diamond on the opposite end of the field and drew pictures and wrote bad words in the gravel with our feet. We walked to the 7-Eleven down the street and got Slurpees and taquitos, which gave us enough fuel for a little more soccer.

While we were finishing up, Dylan quietly suggested a sleepover to me before saying louder, "I think I have to head home." Both Dylan and I had tapped out, but Steph was still juggling her ball, hacking it with her ankles and bouncing it off her knees. "I need to hit ten," she told us, not missing a beat as she bounced the ball off her forehead.

"I'll ask, but I'm pretty sure my parents will be okay with it," I replied, equally quiet to Dylan. But I felt like a dick making plans like that, whispering to one another while Steph stood distracted a few steps away. But that didn't stop us, because we knew Steph couldn't be included in our plans because she was a girl. There had been a couple of times when we were younger—usually on birthdays—when some parents were willing to host a mixed-gender sleepover. I remember staying the night at Steph's place once, when her mom was still alive. Dylan was there too, and a few other kids from school. Her mom had arranged it so that the guys slept in the basement and the girls slept in Steph's room. We had a strict eleven o'clock curfew. Apart from someone Cheeto-barfing on the carpet (the culprit never came forward, and theories about who'd done it outnumbered those of the Kennedy assassination), the night was incident-free. But once we all cleared twelve years of age, mixed overnights were repeatedly kiboshed.

Finally, on her third attempt, Steph hit ten. She caught her ball and walked over to us. "Good to go," she said, then blew a lock of hair out of her eyes. "We should go to the pool."

"Today?" Dylan asked.

"No, not today, dumbass. It's too late to go today." Steph did a mock throw at Dylan's head. "On the weekend."

Shielding himself, Dylan said, "Careful with that thing. I don't have nerd goggles to protect me. Haven't you learned your lesson, Stef-*uh*-nee?"

I booted Dylan in the ass. The leftover change jangled. "You don't need glasses because you can't read," I said. The kick pushed him closer to Steph, so she gave him a good one—revenge, no doubt, for saying her name the way the bullies at school did. *Jangle.* I thought her kick might set Dylan off. He'd stormed away the week before in a huff saying we were both teaming up on him, but that day Dylan giggled. His signature giggle was shrill and giddy. We heard it almost daily, but I suspected he put it on sometimes because he knew how funny we found it. Steph and I called it the Mickey Mouse.

"Ha-*ha*," Steph mocked, going extra high on the second ha.

I gave it my best go. "Ha-*ha*. Ha-*ha*. I bet my voice wouldn't be this high if Walt hadn't got me neutered. Ha-*ha*. Poor Minnie. Ha-*ha*."

"Wait," Dylan said, rubbing both of his tenderized ass cheeks, "are males neutered? Or spayed?"

"Ask Bob Barker," Steph said.

Before Dylan and I parted ways with Steph, we all agreed that the pool was too busy on weekends, so we'd shoot for Friday morning. The catch was, since it was a weekday, Steph would need to bring her brother, Jeremy, which she, after thinking for a moment, decided was a fair trade-off for not having to wait in the high dive line for a month. We said our goodbyes, neither Dylan nor myself mentioning our potential sleepover, and then Steph dropped her ball to the sidewalk and turned the corner to her street. I knew that ball, which still had a few dots of blood on it from my gusher at the ravine two days before, would be dribbled all the way home.

3

WITH MY BROTHER, PETER, IN THE MIDST OF A RITALIN BREAK, MY PARENTS needed minimal convincing to let me sleep over at Dylan's. I tossed some pyjamas and my toothbrush in a backpack, and Dylan and I walked the four blocks to his house carrying my sleeping bag and pillow.

Compared to most of the homes in our area, Dylan's house was majestic. It wasn't a borderline mansion, like the houses on the other side of the overpass, but next to the '50s bungalows that populated much of Haddington Springs, the Mayer family home—comparatively new, two storeys tall—stood out. Dylan and I walked past the thick laurel hedge that bordered the front yard, then up the steps and inside, where we were immediately greeted by Mrs. Mayer. "Hey, boys, good timing," she said from the hallway that led to the kitchen, standing in a snapshot pose: leaning against the wall, arms crossed, one leg bent behind the other. "Are you guys taking the basement or living room tonight?"

"Living room," Dylan said. The obvious choice.

"Why don't you put Robin's things downstairs for now and you guys can get setup after dinner. It'll be ready in a few minutes."

"'Kay," Dylan called, already taking the stairs that led to the basement carrying my pillow. As I hurried to wiggle my shoes off, I looked at Mrs. Mayer and gave her what I'm sure was a very awkward smile. She smiled back, which made my face heat up a little.

Mrs. Mayer was different from other parents. She was more laid-back and a bit younger than everyone else's mom and dad. Enough that you noticed, especially when she stood next to her husband, who was in his fifties and looked it. And she always seemed more put together, more composed, than any other mom I knew. Even at her most casual, she managed to exude a strange knee-weakening radiance I hadn't encountered anywhere else. With her dark, shining hair, her long neck and cosmic eyes, her thin brushstroke smile and the perfect teeth her lips opened up to, she seemed like she belonged somewhere more glamorous than Haddington Springs. Like she'd be more at home strutting through some European museum, or sipping wine on a rooftop restaurant, than she did at the Canada Day picnic they had at Memorial Park every year, surrounded by yee-hawing Molson drinkers and children with ketchup-stained shirts. Everyone noticed her. On many occasions, I had a front-row seat to witness otherwise unmalleable men reduced to bumbling messes who couldn't maintain eye contact to save their life. When Mr. Mayer was around, I sometimes got the sense he liked it, that he was proud to see other men drooling over his wife. There were exceptions, of course, when it went beyond a distant admiration and became more vulgar, unclean. Like the time we all went to Calgary for the Cannons game. At the end of the third inning, Mrs. Mayer got up to go to the bathroom and one of the sloppy drunks sitting behind us nudged his friend and whispered, "They're real, and they're *spectacular!*" loud enough for everyone to hear. I didn't get the *Seinfeld* reference until catching the rerun a couple years later, but Mr. Mayer whipped around and stared the guy down, using his eyes to pin him to his seat. He didn't say anything and didn't need to. I still remember the shade his face turned, the same red as the fire engines I'd see parked at the fire station a couple blocks from my house.

"Are you guys going to party all night? Do we need to warn the neighbours?" Mrs. Mayer asked me, her eyebrows doing a quick jump.

"Oh yeah," I said. "It's gonna be wild."

She laughed, then spoke over her shoulder to her husband. "Ken, you hear that? We're going to need to get the earplugs out tonight."

"What's that?" Mr. Mayer's voice sounded from the kitchen.

"Robin tells me they're going to be wild tonight. I said I guess we should get our earplugs out if we want to get any sleep."

Mr. Mayer responded with a disinterested wordless sound, which was followed by the clanging of dishes.

Enthusiasm dampened just a bit, she turned back to me. "We'll call you guys up when dinner's ready."

As I headed to the stairs, I heard her hushed tone and Mr. Mayer grumble something in response. The only thing I caught over the hum of the stove fan and the bubbly rumble of pots climbing to a boil was Mrs. Mayer saying in a pointed voice, "Well he asked *me*, and *I* said it was all right. Let them have their fun, Ken."

"You don't have to say yes to everything," her husband said.

The faucet started gushing then, and I headed downstairs, feeling like a bit of a snoop.

"Are your parents cool with me staying the night?" I asked Dylan.

"Yeah. Why wouldn't they be?" Dylan took my sleeping bag from me and tossed it in the corner of the room next to my pillow.

"Just want to make sure," I assured him, seeing for an instant a flash of that same look he'd given me at the mall earlier when I suggested we go running to adults for safety. Disturbed, almost disgusted by the suggestion. *Fuck that. Having adults around doesn't mean anything.*

Dylan snarked, "You're *so* polite. That's why my mom likes you so much."

"She thinks I'm polite?"

"Yeah," he grinned. "I told her you were really a dick, but she wouldn't buy it."

"*Puh*-lease. You wouldn't say *dick* in front of your mom."

"Yeah, I would," he insisted.

"Okay, then. How about I say it at dinner. 'Pass the salt, *dick*.'"

"*No!*"

He laughed, then rushed toward me and punched me in the arm. I swung back, but missed. "Don't worry, I'll be polite when I say it."

Dylan was about to go in for another shot at me when Mrs. Mayer called from upstairs instructing us to come up and wash our hands.

The table was set for five. I don't want to make it sound like I was over for dinner every night, but I had my own spot, just as Dylan did at my house. I went to my usual seat, next to Dylan, my back to the sliding screen door that opened onto the backyard. Mrs.

Mayer took her seat at the end of the table closest to the kitchen, and her husband took his, which was opposite her. On the other side of the table sat Emily, who at six years old was forever the family baby. Dylan had an older brother, Adam, but he was away at university, which was fine with me not only because I got his seat, but because Adam was kind of a jerk. Emily and Dylan had gotten all the decent genes divvied up between them. It was a sixty/forty split, but if Dylan were ever to ask me, I'd tell him it was eighty/twenty in favour of Emily.

Spaghetti, meat sauce, and parmesan cheese circulated. Mrs. Mayer had also made lemonade—the real deal. Dylan, Emily, and I all got a glass, while both parents went for red wine. While we ate, Dylan recounted our time at the mall, leaving out our near run-in with Connor and Louis, and told his parents about going to Saint Phillip's field with Steph. Only Mrs. Mayer seemed to be listening. Mr. Mayer, I noticed, was preoccupied with Emily, who was having a bit of trouble managing her spaghetti. She used her fork like her pasta was struggling prey, bringing it straight down on her plate and twisting it like a dagger. Once she'd accumulated enough spaghetti on the fork, she'd lift it to her mouth and at the same time turn her head to make the transaction more manageable. Mr. Mayer, who hadn't touched his own food yet, watched her with an affectionate smile. Any other time I'd been over for dinner, he would've been up from his seat, standing behind Emily and coaching her, sometimes reaching in with his own hands and correcting the way she was holding her utensils. But not that night. That night he just looked on lovingly at Emily—his tiny, adorably gnomish little girl with her short, braided pigtails that always stood out like she'd been shocked by lightning—as if watching her navigate a plate of spaghetti was the most mesmerizing sight in the world.

"You're not hungry, Ken?" Mrs. Mayer asked.

Mr. Mayer snapped out of his trance with a little jolt. He looked at his watch, then to his wife. "What's that?" He took a gulp of wine.

"I asked if you were hungry. You've hardly touched your food."

It took Mr. Mayer a moment to process this information. "I'm . . . I had a late lunch at work."

For a second, the two of them locked eyes, then Mrs. Mayer shrugged before turning to me. "Robin, how are your parents?"

I told her things were pretty much business as usual: my mom was taking shifts here and there, my dad was working, Peter existed. She nodded along, going "uh-huh, uh-huh," and then told me I'd have to say hi for her.

Then the phone rang. Mrs. Mayer put down her fork and was about to stand. But Mr. Mayer beat her to it, rising from his chair and hurrying to the kitchen. "I got it."

"Who calls at six?" Mrs. Mayer said to the three of us remaining with her at the table. Then, over her shoulder, "If it's a telemarketer you better let 'em have it, Ken. They should know better than to call at dinnertime."

We heard the click of the cordless coming out of its cradle, followed by the beep of the talk button being pressed and Mr. Mayer saying "Hello?"

It seemed an unwritten rule that no one except the person who answered it spoke while the phone was in use. A call during dinner wasn't just an interruption, it was an event. Mrs. Mayer's ear was cocked to the kitchen. Even Dylan had paused his chewing. Only Emily was too lost in her spaghetti to care.

"This is he," Mr. Mayer said from the kitchen. "Who am I speaking to?" A lengthy pause. "Are you kidding me?" Pause. "So you call *now*?" Pause. "Well, of course we're home—everyone's home, we're all eating dinner. It's fine. Yes. Okay. He'll return it." He hung up without a goodbye and came back into the dining room.

"*GoldenEye?*" Mr. Mayer said, his eyes boring into Dylan, whose half-full mouth had dropped open.

"Huh?" Dylan managed.

"*GoldenEye,*" his dad repeated.

Dylan rolled his head back and groaned. "Shit. Sorry."

"*Excuse* me?" Mrs. Mayer said. "Language, Dylan!" She mimed slapping her son in the back of the head. He winced as if contact had actually been made.

Dylan apologized to his mom, who shook her head and gestured at Emily. "Sorry about the bad word," he told his sister.

Emily let her shoulders rise and fall. She wasn't as bothered as Steph's little brother Jeremy—the Haddington Springs' One-Man Swear Task Force—would've been.

Mr. Mayer returned to his seat. He took a sip of his wine like he really needed it. "Our son rented a movie and never returned it," he explained to his wife. "Dylan, you realize if you were to add up the amount of money you—or, realistically, *I*—spend on late charges, you could *buy* a bunch of the movies you seem compelled to rent over and over again."

Dylan nodded. He looked over at me for a second. I thought I'd join the side that seemed to be winning, so I shook my head at him and made a disappointed face. He smirked at me.

"It's not funny," Mr. Mayer said, yanking Dylan back to attention. "Take some responsibility."

"Sorry. I'll bring it back right away."

"I know you will. You don't have a choice."

"Robin and me were going to go rent a movie for tonight, so I'll take it back right after dinner."

I nodded, doubling his credibility.

"All right," Mr. Mayer agreed, then, turning to his wife, said, "Maybe you can give them a lift over?"

"They can walk," Mrs. Mayer said. "It's summer."

"Yeah, Dad, we can walk."

Mr. Mayer waved off the idea. "No," he said. "The walk is at least twenty-five minutes each way. By the time you go there, choose a movie—and get snacks, I presume?"

We both nodded.

"There you go. Get snacks, come back, by the time you do all that it'll be too late."

I could tell Dylan was about to ask why it mattered if we were a bit late, but his mom got there first. "Ken, they'll be up all night anyway."

"Well," Mr. Mayer said, "if you let me finish, Diane, I was going to say that not only will it be late, but I'd like a movie picked up for us, too."

"You're going to watch a movie on a weeknight?" Mrs. Mayer asked her husband, making no attempt to mask the skepticism in her voice.

"Not tonight. But for Friday."

"Then why not rent it on Friday?"

Mr. Mayer was not prepared for his suggestion to be met with such intense scrutiny. He put down his knife and fork, then closed his eyes and pinched the area between them. "Diane," he said, frustration seeping into his words, "Blockbuster is always packed on Friday. It'll save us a trip. I don't see why—look, I'd take them myself, but I'm expecting a call from work." He looked at his watch again. "The whole shebang will take you half an hour, tops. And if you take the boys, *you* can pick our movie, and you won't even have to listen to me whine if you choose something like *The English Patient*."

That seemed enough to entice her. She smiled at the rich prospect of movie-pick autonomy. "I'm going to choose something *really* awful, then," she said, her eyebrows doing a triplet of mischievous jumps. The tension having evaporated, the two of them laughed like the whole thing was much funnier than it actually was.

× × ×

The Blockbuster Video on Chester Street was our cathedral. Walking through the front door and seeing its altar, the New Releases section—the sharp blue lettering of its sign popping out from a wall painted a cartoonish canary yellow—gave me a feeling of near weightlessness every time. The New Releases wall was always our first stop. Even if I knew the chosen movie featured on the wall was the sort of flick I'd have no interest in watching until I was fifty, I'd still float over and gawk at the spectacle that was—or at least what seemed like—one hundred copies of the same movie case, mint, lined up in symmetrical rows of ten. I always loved seeing how many copies of the featured New Release were checked out, regardless of whether the movie appealed to me or not.

Someone at school, whose older sister used to work at there, once told me that employees got unlimited free rentals. And since hearing of this potential perk, I vowed to get a job there as soon as I was fifteen, which was the minimum age to work in a video store, unless you worked at the VHQ on Carrington, where they had a porno section in the back so you had to be at least eighteen.

Together, Mrs. Mayer, Dylan and I approached the wall. The featured new release was called *The Devil's Own*. I picked up a copy and looked over the cover. The movie starred Harrison Ford, who I knew from *Star Wars*, *Indiana Jones*, and nothing else, and Brad Pitt, who I knew from people saying he was good-looking. Dylan grabbed a case too and scanned the synopsis. "This looks meh," he determined after a few seconds. We began working our way around the perimeter of the store, where we could check out the other new releases under the comforting sounds of trailers playing on a loop. Mrs. Mayer did the same, but she moved at a much slower pace than Dylan and I, stopping, it seemed, to consider nearly every movie on the shelf.

From there we moved to our three go-to sections: Action, Horror, and Comedy. We'd come to this Blockbuster so many times, often just to loiter, that everything in these sections was all very familiar to us. Each section had certain staples that we'd rented multiple times, but that night Dylan and I agreed to go for something new. We lingered in Horror and Action a little longer than Comedy, nervously looking over our shoulders for Mrs. Mayer as we scoped covers to find movies that looked like they might contain nudity. Drama and Foreign were also good sections for this, but she'd have known something was up if she'd spotted us in either of those aisles. Dylan's parents didn't have an age restriction placed on his card, so he could rent anything up to R, meaning only the NC-17 stuff was a no-go. We'd normally rent one appropriate-looking movie, nothing that looked to sleazy, that we'd be able to show his parents when they asked what we picked out, and one movie that the parents wouldn't be all right with, like *The Slumber Party Massacre*, which we'd hide down the front of one of our pants when we returned to the house. But with Dylan's mom with us, it'd have to be a one-movie night. After some deliberation, we settled on *Friday the 13th Part 3*. We walked up to the checkout, where Mrs. Mayer was waiting with a movie called *Emma*, and together we entered the line, which was bordered by tall shelves of impulse-buy junk food. My parents had given me a ten earlier that evening when I went to get my things, and Dylan still had like two pounds of change jangling in his pockets, but anyone with half a brain knew that the snack prices at Blockbuster were a rip-off. Mrs. Mayer had agreed to drive us to Perry's Pantry after to buy supplies: a gigantic bag of Doritos, two one-litre pops, and, if we had enough cash, Twizzlers.

When we reached the front of the line, Mrs. Mayer turned to Dylan, who fully expected to pay the *GoldenEye* late fee on his own, and pointed to our rental. She nonchalantly said, "I'll get it," and went to take our choice from her son's hands.

"But, uh, there's the late fee, too," he reminded her.

Mrs. Mayer waved him off and walked up to the till, where Allison, without a doubt the most attractive girl working at any Blockbuster in the world, took Mrs. Mayer's membership card and began to ring her through. Allison—who must have been around twenty—always made me nervous. The couple attempts at small talk I has previously tried were so brutally awful that the last few times I'd come in, I prayed she wouldn't be my cashier. I always enjoyed admiring her from a far-off corner of the store, though, or from the safety of the line with a two-or-three-person buffer between us. She, in all her blue-and-yellow polo-shirted loveliness, was a regular star in my dreams. Her place of business, a regular location of those dreams.

It was close to eight when we returned from Perry's Pantry. On the ride home, Mrs. Mayer reminded us to pace ourselves. "If you need to puke it's crucial you make it to the bathroom," she emphasized. I felt that the comment was directed more at Dylan than myself. He didn't believe in moderation, and his mom sure knew it.

We walked up the steps behind Mrs. Mayer. She went to open the front door but found it locked and had to fish out her keys. "Hi, hon," she called as she stepped inside, returning the key ring to her purse. Dylan and I followed her in. There was no response. "Ken?" she called.

The foyer was dark, but the living room at the end of the hall lent some of its glow. Dylan and I kicked off our shoes, and Mrs. Mayer bent down and took hers off and placed them neatly against the wall. She flicked on the light and began walking toward the living room where music could be heard coming from the TV. When she was about halfway down the hall, Emily stepped into view. "Mommy," she exclaimed, throwing her hands in the air and running to greet her.

"Hi, Em-Gem," Mrs. Mayer said, pulling her daughter in for a one-arm hug. She continued making her way down the hall with Emily attached to her waist. "Where's your dad?"

"He's in his office. On the phone." Emily made a phone with her hands and held it up to her ear.

I heard a gasp as Mrs. Mayer entered the living room. "Emily, what are you watching, honey?" On the screen was a racy music video playing on the family's fifty-eight-inch TV set. I knew it's exact size because Dylan mentioned it all the time. *Yeah, but just think how awesome that'll look on our fifty-eight-inch! Multiplayer mode is the best on our fifty-eight-inch!*

"I wanted to see if my song was on," Emily said. Her song was "Say You'll Be There," by the Spice Girls. She was obsessed. I wasn't sure what the video playing at the moment was, but it definitely wasn't the Spice Girls. It featured a stoic man in sunglasses fanning himself with American money while girls in their underwear danced around him. The few seconds I caught of their gyrating was enough to make me feel it.

"Sweetie, you have your music video on your tape," Mrs. Mayer said while she searched for the remote, which she found wedged between two couch cushions. She quickly turned the TV off like someone expelling a demon from her home. "Yuck," she muttered, tossing the remote aside like she might catch something from it if she held it too long. She turned to Emily, looking set to deliver a lecture on unsupervised evening channel-surfing, when the sliding door of Mr. Mayer's office opened. In one hand he held the cordless phone, in the other an almost empty glass of red wine. He looked like he had just woken from a deep sleep and was still coming to terms with reality.

"Do you know what she was watching?"

Mr. Mayer didn't respond right away. He looked from his wife, to his daughter, to Dylan. He lingered on me for a moment, then went back to his wife. "I . . ." he started, then blinked hard, as if to reset himself, and said, "I'm sorry. I just got off the phone with Greg. Things went a bit south with the developer today."

Mrs. Mayer let her shoulders rise and fall. "Okay," she said, truly sympathetic. "But while you were on the phone with Greg, Emily had found her way to some trashy music video. You know you've got to keep an eye on what she's watching, especially at this time of night, Ken. I mean, it's either that or we start blocking certain channels."

The prospect of blocking TV channels lit a spark in Dylan. "Mom! No way," he protested. "That would be *so* unfair."

Both parents shot him a look. He crossed his arms and stared at the floor. "It *would*," he muttered.

× × ×

We changed into our pyjamas. The UBC shirt my cousin Megan brought me last time she visited was a favourite of mine and I wore it with pride. We brushed our teeth, which was pointless with the harvest of junk we'd brought home, but sometimes things need to be done for the sake of appearances. I lingered in the bathroom for a minute after I finished brushing. My stubborn baby tooth always felt off after brushing. I stood in front of the mirror and hooked my index finger onto my cheek and tugged to one side. When I angled my head the right way, the light hit the tooth. I nudged it a couple times with my tongue and it moved roughly the same amount it had last time. My dentist appointment was more than a week away, but I thought the tooth would've come out on its own by now. Dr. Towne said it wasn't necessarily common to have a baby tooth stick around this long, but it wasn't that weird either. He might have just been saying that to make me feel better. I nudged the tooth back into its comfy spot with my tongue and reminded myself that when we opened the Doritos, any serious chewing would need to be done on my left side.

When I returned to the living room, the coffee table had been moved against the wall so we had more room. Both Mr. and Mrs. Mayer were in the kitchen behind us. They had been talking in hushed tones, but stopped when they noticed us unrolling our sleeping bags. Mr. Mayer was probably in deep trouble still. He was working on another drink. Mrs. Mayer smiled when she saw us.

"Ready to party, boys?"

"Oh yeah, Mom, we're sure gonna party," Dylan said. "Robin brought over a case of beer and once you guys go to sleep, we're gonna get drunk and throw the TV out the window."

I nodded, confirming that Dylan spoke the truth, and his parents rolled their eyes.

"As long as you're paying for the new TV, go for it," Mr. Mayer said.

Both Dylan and I assured him that we definitely had that kind of cash.

"I don't doubt it." He grabbed his wine glass off the counter and made his exit. "Night, guys."

Mrs. Mayer leaned into the granite island, her fingers splaying on its surface. She stared at the smooth slab, its creamy lines and dots swirling across the shiny blackness that dominated, mesmerized by the galaxy in front of her. Then she sighed and smiled at something neither Dylan nor I were privy to. She turned to the cupboard and got a wine glass for herself. "Well, I don't think it's fair if you two are the only ones who get to party tonight."

Dylan pointed to the three-quarters-empty wine bottle on the counter at the other end of the kitchen. It was a different bottle than the one that had been at the dinner table earlier that night. "I think Dad's partying, too."

Mrs. Mayer's pause was so brief that I nearly missed it. But it did happen. "All the more reason," she said. She poured the remainder of the wine bottle into her glass, filling it almost to the rim, and said goodnight to us, kissing her son on the top of his head and giving me a wink. She took a couple steps then paused and twisted back around. Her brimming glass in one hand, she took her free arm and hugged it tightly around her torso, which caused her breasts to shift beneath the navy blouse she was wearing. She regarded us for a second, then said, "Look at you two. You're not little kids anymore, are you?"

Dylan punched me in the shoulder and did an awful Woody Woodpecker laugh. "Nope," he said. "We're super mature now."

I punched him back and showed him a proper rendition of the laugh. Then he flicked my ear, which he knew I hated, and by the time we had settled down, Mrs. Mayer was at the far end of the hall that led upstairs.

"Don't kill each other," she called without turning back.

× × ×

It was Dylan's brother Adam who first let us in on the secret that vodka was the best thing to drink if you wanted to avoid detection. He said it was basically odourless. Given Adam's track record with alcohol and all things sketchy, we trusted him. The Mayers locked their liquor cabinet, but the key was kept in the drawer. With Adam gone, neither parent made any attempt to hide it anymore. And why would they? Dylan and I were good kids.

I was given the task of standing at the threshold of the living room and keeping watch while Dylan funnelled vodka into our Pepsi bottles. Stealing from your parents' liquor cabinet was all about maintaining balance. You had to take careful note of the levels in the bottles and determine how much could be taken without it being obvious if anyone were to check. And your parents had to be regular drinkers so that the bottles and levels were changing regularly. This meant that Dylan and I were both drinking different kinds of vodka. Fortunately, there was no shortage of choices. The plan was to watch the movie, get a good buzz, and channel surf for Live Links ads—so many local singles in our area who wanted to stay in and chat. They were willing to talk about "whatever we wanted," so the least we could do was watch their commercials and hear them out.

I popped *Friday the 13th Part 3* into the VCR and hit play, and we got comfy on our separate couches with our snacks and our drinks. The movie got off to what I thought was an okay start, but we had to pause it about fifteen minutes in so Dylan could rant.

"What the hell's wrong with these people?" he said, pointing at the dopey teenagers paused on screen, thin lines of static running across them like threads. "First, they said they know some bad stuff happened at Crystal Lake. Then they drive by these paramedics carrying body bags out of a store. *Then*, this crusty old hobo who's just sitting on the road playing with a fucking *eyeball* warns them to go back where they came from . . . and they're *still* going to go to Crystal Lake?"

I sipped my vodka-enriched Pepsi, considering this. "Maybe there's something about Crystal Lake," I said. "Maybe it summons people to it. Or pulls them in. There's got to be something special about it if Jason Voorhees keeps coming back to life there. They've made like fifty of these movies, and they all take place there, right?"

Dylan shook his head, somehow seriously annoyed at my horror-movie logic. "That's dumb," he said.

I took a longer drink this time and offered up my second explanation, one that didn't feel as *right* to me but that might make

Dylan put the movie back on. "If they didn't go to Crystal Lake, the movie would only be like ten minutes long."

Dylan seemed hesitant to press play, like he was enjoying the power. He decided we should take a quick break to strengthen our mixes—both of us agreeing they lacked the kick we were looking for—before continuing to watch.

The movie got better when we returned. It had a ton of jump-scares. A couple of close calls—one where I almost spilled my drink, another when Dylan nearly choked on a mouthful of Doritos—forced us to time our junk food intake very carefully. In a horror movie, there are really no safe moments, but there are certain types of scenes where you know you're at least less likely to be startled. Busy daytime locations are usually safe, so when Vera and Shelly go to buy groceries and have to deal with the rude cashier and the trio of angry bikers, we knew we were good to indulge. Music cues are important too. In any *Friday the 13th* movie, as soon as you hear that *shh-shh-shh-shh . . . ah-ah-ah-ah,* it's time to put the snacks down.

For most of movie's remainder, we sat tense on the couch, our arms, even our legs, crossed inside our sleeping bags, bracing for impact. I felt extra vulnerable without my glasses. Even though I was nearsighted and could see the TV all right, there was the faintest bit of fuzz, just enough to make me feel disoriented. The vodka didn't help. My face felt warm. My limbs light. Dylan and I had both been lulled into a wobbly state of captivity. And I remember feeling even more focused than normal and thereby more scared for the characters on-screen. Oh, if only they knew what was waiting for them! At least we were safe in the living room, and if any masked killers showed up, Dylan's grandpa's antique bayonet was close by, hanging above the mantel, its still-sharp point glinting light from the corner lamp.

We were about an hour in when Dylan reached for the remote and hit pause. At first I was worried he had another complaint, but then he said, "I have to take a piss, and based on how this movie's going, I think it's better if I go now, of my own free will, instead of during the next scare, in my sleeping bag."

He got up, steadied himself, and walked to the nearby bathroom. I grabbed myself a Pull 'n' Peel and turned it into a cat-o'-nine-tails. After eating a couple strands, I realized I also had to go to the bathroom. I waited a couple minutes, then, recalling the '80s boobs the movie had treated us to earlier, realized that Dylan could be doing any number of things behind the bathroom door. I decided to slip upstairs and use the bathroom there.

On tiptoes and vodka legs, I moved down the hall as silently as I was able to. The floor was hardwood, so with each step came the potential of a creak. I wasn't worried about waking Dylan's parents but I didn't want to wake Emily. Plus, I didn't want the Mayers to figure out there was something . . . off about me. One phone call to my parents is all it would take. They'd ship me off to a gulag if they found out I'd been drinking.

I felt safer once I made it off the hardwood and onto the stairs where my steps were cushioned by the same smooth ash-coloured carpet that covered the whole top floor. Dylan's room was at one end of the hall, his parents' room on the opposite end. Between the two were Emily's room and the bathroom. My eyes hadn't adjusted to the dark, but the scant light from the master bedroom at the end helped guide me. When I shuffled toward the bathroom, I saw Dylan's parent's door was open a crack. I could tell the TV was on. I heard their voices, and I don't know why, but I paused when I reached the bathroom and stared ahead, down the hall, into their room. I squinted and saw the edge of their bed, where Mr. Mayer's bare feet rested on top of their flannel duvet cover. Mrs. Mayer, off-screen, said something. Even though I was closer now, I still couldn't hear her words, but she sounded sad.

I *swear* I was right about to enter the bathroom when her figure appeared in the void between their ajar door and the wall. She was wearing only a pair of shorts and a black bra that struggled to contain her. A high-voltage bolt of panic zapped my heart. I went to move, but she noticed me, her searchlight eyes freezing me where I stood. My brain barely registered the red-alert signal my bladder fired up to it, and for a split second I actually thought I was going to piss myself before immediately dropping dead from embarrassment. At first, Mrs. Mayer looked startled. Then she turned her gaze down to herself, as if she had suddenly become aware of her body and felt the need to appraise all she had. Slowly, she craned her neck back up and looked at me again, her lips curving into what I thought was a smirk. Then she softly closed the bedroom door, leaving me alone in the dark hall.

I stayed there processing what I had just seen. What I thought I had seen. To this day, I question whether or not it really happened. I wasn't wearing my glasses. It was dark. I was kid with an overactive imagination, hopped up on sugar and vodka and whatever the hell Doritos are made of. I don't think I actually know if I saw what I saw.

After a moment I returned downstairs, I took a long drink. My Pepsi packed even more of a punch than it had earlier. "Mine tasted weak again, so I added more for both of us," Dylan said, grinning at me. From there on, *Friday the 13th Part 3* might as well have been steady static.

PART 2

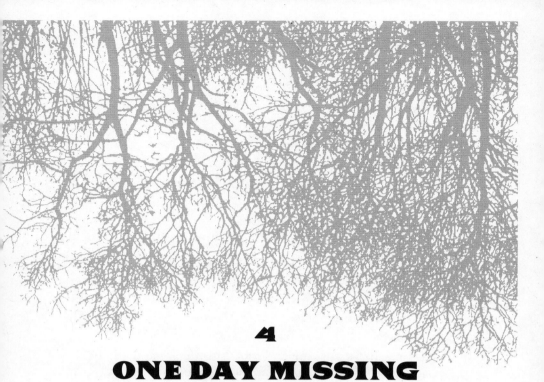

4

ONE DAY MISSING

MOUTH GAUZY FROM VODKA, MIND FOGGY FROM A DREAM I COULDN'T remember, I was drifting in and out of sleep when she came in.

"Guys? You awake?"

I sat up, rubbed my eyes, and reached for my glasses before remembering I had none. I leaned over and nudged Dylan. The first nudge did nothing. The second nudge got a miniscule response. The third nudge—more of a punch, really—got him up.

"What the hell?" he whined.

Mrs. Mayer walked over to the couch he lay parallel to, sat down, and tightened the embrace of her robe. I glanced at the VCR clock. 7:05 a.m. Dylan pushed himself into a sitting position.

"Sorry to wake you guys up," Mrs. Mayer said. Her voice had a slight wobble to it. "I . . . your father left early for work. I couldn't fall back asleep so I put the radio on in our bedroom. They said a little girl's gone missing. She's the sister of that boy in your grade—Kyle Hillerman. His sister—Catherine, right? The newscaster said she was last seen at Midtown Mall. I thought of you two, and . . ." She looked for a moment as if she were about to become untethered and drift away, but then something inside her clicked in time for her to tighten the knot on her rope to reality. "You guys always stick together when you're out, right?"

Dylan and I both assured her we did.

"Did you see anything weird yesterday at the mall?"

"No," Dylan said.

I nodded without really thinking.

Mrs. Mayer reached over and tousled her son's already messy hair. "I'm sure she's all right, that she just went to a friend's place without telling her parents. It's just . . . it's scary. This is why I always get cranky when you complain about having to walk Emily somewhere. Strength in numbers. She . . . the news said she's six. The same age as your . . ."

Dylan reached across me and took his mom's hand. He held it for a second, gave it a squeeze, then let go and rolled back onto the floor. I didn't move at all. I was trying to process what we'd been told, but my mind, a brick-dry sponge floating on top of a puddle, was taking its time absorbing the information.

Mrs. Mayer rose and headed toward the kitchen. Dylan looked over at me. "That's freaky, man." He wiggled a little to straighten his sleeping bag.

I got up and walked to the kitchen. Mrs. Mayer stood at the coffee maker, spooning Nabob grounds into the filter.

"*I saw her,*" I said. It came out a whisper.

She stopped what she was doing and turned to me. "What was that, Robin?"

I cleared my throat. Louder this time: "I saw her."

× × ×

My parents had to be present for the interview. Mrs. Mayer said it was the law. She called them first and and Dad rushed over, bringing Peter with them. They beat the police by about ten minutes. Peter was sent to play with Emily, who was only mildly frazzled from being dragged out of bed early. He was a year younger than her, but she welcomed him in a sisterly way, slinging an arm around him and escorting him to her bedroom.

Mom and Dad were freaked out. I sat on the couch, sandwiched between them. Mom rested her hand on my back and left it there. Dad shook his head and kept muttering "Jesus Christ" at what seemed like thirty-second intervals. He repeatedly tapped me on the knee. It was as if by maintaining physical contact my parents were assuring themselves that I wouldn't vanish into thin air, like Catherine Hillerman had.

Mrs. Mayer brought out coffee for my parents. Dylan and I got hot chocolate so we felt included. When they arrived, Detective Purser and Detective Hennig, as they'd introduced themselves, had their own coffees. Purser, who looked the most like a detective of the two, appeared as though he hadn't slept in a couple days. The pouches under his eyes were edged with a purple tint, and he had a head covered in thick, swooping brown hair and a blocky mustache that was mostly a coppery colour. But it had a couple of frosty spots, which reminded me of Bolland, our long-dead calico cat. He took a small recording device out of his pocket and placed it on the coffee table, then gave a thumbs up to Detective Hennig, who seemed to be the leader of the duo.

Detective Hennig had dark, pointed eyebrows that looked like the tips of an archangel's wings. Her long hair was tied into a tight ponytail, and she wore a stern expression that was almost enough to mask the softness of her face. Her wide coffee-coloured eyes made me want to talk to her. "It's standard procedure that we record these interviews," she said. "Is that all right, Robin?"

I knew my input on the matter wasn't really necessary, but I appreciated her asking. I nodded.

My dad added, "Whatever you need."

As Detective Purser went to turn the recorder on, my mom leaned forward, her hand raised like a student in an elementary classroom. "Before we start, can I ask . . . to clarify, you think she's been taken by someone?"

"Yes," Detective Hennig said without hesitation. "At this point, that's what we believe to be the case. But that information doesn't leave this room."

With that, she nodded at her partner, who pressed a button on the recorder's side. "This is Detectives Purser and Hennig. The date is Thursday, August 14th, 1997. Current time is . . ." he flicked his left wrist, ". . . 7:46 a.m. The interview being conducted is with Robin Murphy, age thirteen. The subject's mother and father are present and have consented to their son taking part in this interview."

Dad muttered, "That's right," which prompted Mom to reach across and poke his arm to shush him.

Detectives Purser and Hennig asked me to tell them all I remembered from my brief encounter with Catherine and Kyle at the mall. I told them about Catherine talking in her funny made-up accent and how she seemed to be playacting an imaginary character. I told them how Kyle told me that they were going to a movie, and that meant he had to see to one that was G-rated, and that I'd said they could only see *Air Bud*. While I spoke, Detective Purser made notes. He managed to do this without looking down at his note-pad. Once I'd gone over my interaction with the Hillermans twice, Detective Hennig asked, "Was there maybe someone you noticed watching you while you talked to Kyle and Catherine?"

I felt my heart rate speed up. It was the first question I didn't immediately know the answer to. I tried responding but had a couple of stuttery false starts. Noticing my nervousness, Detective Hennig leaned forward and lowered her head so she could meet my eyes. "It's okay," she assured me. "Take your time. You're not in trouble. We just want you to try your best."

I nodded, closed my eyes, and tried to make a short trip back in time. I had no trouble playing back the conversation, no trouble seeing myself with Catherine and Kyle outside the washrooms. As far as anyone else, though, I truly didn't know. I mean, it was the mall, so of course there were other people walking around. And it wasn't that I couldn't remember people walking right past us, but no matter how hard I tried, I couldn't remember much detail about anyone else who was there. I recalled that there was a couple holding hands and some parents and kids, but as soon as Kyle and Catherine showed up, I stopped noticing other people. No one was remarkable. They were all part of the background, faceless blurs, there one second, gone the next. I wanted to explain this to the detectives, but I just said, "I can't remember anyone else who was there."

"He didn't have his glasses," Mom interjected. Then, almost defensively, she added, "I'm taking him to get new ones today."

Purser nodded. "That's all right," he assured her. Then he turned his attention back to me. "We just need you to try, that's all."

"Yes, and you've been very helpful so far," Detective Hennig added.

I noticed both of my parents looking at me with pride I didn't feel I deserved. I hadn't done anything to help.

Hennig said, "Is there anything else you remember, Robin? Even if it doesn't seem important to you, it might be something that can help us."

I thought for a second, then shook my head.

The detectives, who I was beginning to suspect operated with some level of telepathy, nodded in unison. Purser flipped his note-pad shut, placed his pen in the coiled loop on the side of it, and returned both to his coat pocket. Hennig turned off the recorder. The pair of them thanked me, my parents, and Mrs. Mayer for our time, and then all the adults stood up and shook hands. Hennig gave my parents and Mrs. Mayer her card. "We'll be in touch again, but don't hesitate to call us if anything else comes up."

Before the detectives could make their exit, Dylan chimed in from the step that marked the border between living room and kitchen, "What about Louis and Connor?"

The detectives shared a glance.

"Who?" Purser asked. He fished his notepad back out, removed the pen from its loop, clicked it.

Dylan cleared his throat and straightened up. "It might not be important, but Louis and Connor were at the mall too. They go to our school. We saw them before Robin ran into Kyle and Catherine. They're older, and . . ." he paused for a second, looked over to me, then back to the detectives, "they're kind of assholes."

Mrs. Mayer—whose look of disgust at her son's choice of words was on par with that of someone who had woken up to a surprise orgy in their living room—opened her mouth to scold, but Dylan was a millisecond faster. "Sorry, Mom," he said, raising his hands in a hold-your-horses gesture.

Mrs. Mayer didn't have time to say anything as Detective Purser pulled the recording device back out, and history repeated itself. First asking for permission from Mrs. Mayer, Purser stated, with the recorder running, the date, the time, and the fact that the interviewee's mother had consented to questioning. Dylan told the detectives about us spotting Louis and Connor and fleeing to the photo booth because we knew they'd take our arcade money if they found us.

When Dylan finished, Hennig thanked him and asked one follow-up question. "Dylan, do you think that Louis and Connor would know Kyle and Catherine?"

"Maybe not Catherine, but definitely Kyle," Dylan said. "They'd have known him from school. But not because they're friends or anything. If Kyle saw them, he'd probably try to avoid them too."

The detectives shared another look. They both nodded as if they'd read each other's minds, and then Purser turned the recorder off.

Finishing up for a second time, Detective Hennig confirmed Louis's and Connor's last names—Duss and Monaghan—and assured us that the pair wouldn't find out we had anything to do with them being questioned, provided, Hennig said, they got questioned at all.

They opened the door to leave, but just before they could, I blurted out, "*I'm sorry.*"

Hennig's eyes met mine, and once her tractor-beam gaze locked onto me, I was unable to look away from her. "Robin," she said in a voice that was a swirling mix of concern and confusion, "what on earth do you have to be sorry for?"

"That I forgot about seeing those two. That I forgot about Connor and Louis."

She took a step toward me. "You've been nothing but helpful."

I mumbled some indistinct syllable of agreement and Hennig shifted her attention back to the adults, freeing me. She said goodbye, and the two of them made their way back to the world.

× × ×

My parents were never really close friends with the Mayers. That's not to say they disliked them. There was always an exchange of pleasant chatter whenever either of my parents picked me up from Dylan's place, or vice versa. And Mrs. Mayer would always ask my mom about how things were going at the assisted living centre she worked at. Or she'd instigate gossip about the teachers at our school, and my mom always asked her about the aerobics and pottery classes she sometimes took in the hours that weren't occupied by homemaking. Mr. Mayer and my dad would sometimes talk about their jobs, but mostly they'd talk about how different things were now from when they were younger. Every one of their conversations seemed to feature the catchphrase, *Hey, you remember when. . . ?*

But since we lived so close to each other and weren't little kids anymore, parental pickups had become rare. And when they did happen—late at night, or during a spell of nasty weather unfit for man, beast, or teenager—pleasantries were usually exchanged just inside the door. Almost always, there would be a polite offer of coffee, or a quick drink, but apart from maybe two or three times ever, the offer would be respectfully declined. That morning, though, the status quo got a bit of a shakeup. The strangeness of sitting with my parents in the Mayers' living room hadn't dawned on me initially, because of the distraction of the detectives interviewing me about a missing person. But once the they'd left and Mrs. Mayer invited my parents back in for *more* coffee and they accepted, it occurred to me that the circumstances had given way to an unlikely situation.

Dylan and I were still standing in the foyer, observing the three adults when he turned to me and asked, "What do you think happened to her?"

"Who?" I responded, realizing the instant I formed the word what a ridiculous question it was. I shook my head, surprised by my spaciness.

Dylan grinned at me. He went to flick my ear but I managed to swat his hand away.

"Try again, dumbass," he said.

I thought about it for maybe a second, then shrugged. Not an I-don't-care shrug, but an I-seriously-have-no-clue shrug. "How would I know?" I replied. "If I did, I would've told the police, right?"

"Dude, I'm not trying to be a dick about it. I just mean, actually, what *could* have happened? Between the washroom and the theatre? There doesn't really seem like that many possibilities between point A and point B."

Dishes clattered in the kitchen. "Dylan, do you boys want some cereal?" Mrs. Mayer called.

"No," Dylan shouted back without breaking eye-contact with me. He looked like he was trying to read the faint impression of just-erased words on a sheet of paper.

"Go ask your sister and Peter. They might want some," Mrs. Mayer called.

Dylan called up to my brother and his sister.

Upstairs a door creaked open. "What?" Emily called.

"Food!"

"'Kay."

The two kids stampeded down the stairs and breezed past us. They moved so quickly that the only way I knew for sure that one of them was my brother was by the way he swatted at my stomach as he went by.

"It didn't necessarily happen at the mall," I reminded Dylan.

"That's true," he said, "but they seemed super interested in what went on outside the washroom." I'd noticed that too, and wondered if my mom's stranger danger lecture had been right in that detail.

"Yeah, but they're detectives. It's like in movies, they have to make a big deal out of every little thing before they can figure it out. They've probably got a million more people to talk to. I bet there's someone at the mall who saw more than I did."

"Or at least *noticed* more than you did."

I slugged Dylan in the shoulder. "Fuck off, man."

"Shit, I didn't mean it like that. I mean, when you were talking to Kyle, it's not like your eyes were going all over the place and you were looking for a kidnapper, or a pedo, or whatever. You were just talking to someone from school—why would you be looking at anything else? But if there was a guy working at the food court and he didn't have any customers to deal with, maybe he was just watching people. Maybe he saw something."

I agreed with Dylan and apologized for the punch.

He rubbed his shoulder and made a pouty face, then laughed. "If Connor and Louis find out that we told the cops about them they're gonna beat the shit out of us."

I laughed back. Because it was funny, and because it was true. But the laughter felt wrong when I thought about what might be happening to Catherine.

5

NOTHING ABOUT THE DISAPPEARANCE WAS IN THE MORNING PAPER. IT HAD been too late to make the printer, I guess. But as we drove home— my parents in the front, Peter and I in the back of our family ship, a '95 Mercury Villager—Catherine Hillerman's vanishing was all the local radio stations wanted to talk about. After a quick scroll through the FM dial my mom switched the radio to CBC, because she said they didn't sensationalize as much and were more credible than the others.

The reporter gave a description of Catherine. He started by saying that she was a six-year-old Caucasian girl, stood 1.1 metres tall, and weighed approximately twenty-five kilograms. Hearing these stats was the sort of reminder that showed up every once and a while outside of math class: a reminder that while movies and comics and sports stats had conditioned me to think in feet and pounds, when it came to stark reality, the metric system reigned supreme. After the reporter described Catherine in strictly clinical terms, he moved on to what she was wearing. There were details that I remembered, and details that were new to me. When she was last seen, her hair was in pigtails and she was wearing a purple short-sleeved dress with a cartoon cat on it (that part I had told the police about, and when the radio reporter mentioned the dress my mom turned to me with a proud smile). They said she was wearing black runners with glittering silver stars and had a neon blue bracelet on her right wrist. These were details I didn't recall, but as soon as they were mentioned, they inserted themselves seamlessly into the mental picture of Catherine I was doing my best to preserve. The reporter said, "A photo of Catherine will be broadcast throughout regularly scheduled programming on all local and provincial television stations. Police urge anyone with information on the whereabouts of Catherine to call 911 immediately." As always, the end of the news was marked with the sounding of a familiar tune made up of four notes. The program was followed by a call-in show whose topic of the day was dog park etiquette.

× × ×

My mom turned on the radio as soon as we got in the house, which meant a gap of only about thirty seconds in my knowledge on the type of vaccinations my non-existent dog needed before I let him socialize at the park. Both my parents again reminded me that I had done a great job talking to the police. My dad patted my shoulder and said we could get pizza for dinner. Hearing this, Peter did a lap around the house in order to prevent himself from exploding from excitement.

Dad then said that circumstances aside, the late start was nice, but he had to head into work. "Kirby Luxury Mattresses isn't going to assistant-manage itself," he said in the cardboard tone he used whenever work was being discussed.

My mom gave him a kiss on the cheek. They stared at each other for a moment, but the connection broke when Peter raced by yelling, "Pizza!" and starting on another lap.

"*Jesus*," she whispered to my dad. "That girl, she's only one year older than our little dynamo."

"They'll find her," Dad said. He sounded confident, but I remember thinking, *How do you know?*

× × ×

Every summer, our mom had her status at work changed to "casual." This meant she'd work the occasional night shift when the assisted living centre needed her, and she'd pick up the odd weekend day, but otherwise she was at home with us. When Peter and I were in school, she'd switch back to full-time days. Despite the dip in income, she liked summers because she got to see more of my brother and I. Peter was young enough that he got plenty of hang out time with her, and even though I was a busy teenager with places to go and people to see (a maximum of two people, sure, but people nonetheless), I still saw my mom every morning when I woke up and every evening when I came home, provided, of course, I wasn't crashing at Dylan's.

Mom sat on the couch in the living room, nursing a cup of tea (her daily threshold of two coffees had already been crossed) and staring out the window while Peter and I inhaled Frosted Mini-Wheats at the dining-room table. Every now and then she'd shake her head.

"Are you okay?" I asked between mouthfuls, sounding as if I'd just finished a sprint.

"Yeah, mom, are you okay?" Peter echoed. I glared at him and he mimicked the glare back at me.

Without turning to face us, she replied, "I'm okay, boys. I'm just thinking . . . Robin, what's the clock say?"

I turned and squinted at the glowing green digits above our kitchen stove. "It's, like, nine forty," I reported.

"It's *like* nine forty, or it *is* nine forty?"

I squinted again. "It is precisely 9:42 a.m. August 14th, 1997, AD."

My mom smiled slightly. "Your attention to detail is appreciated."

"When is the news on again?"

"They do the news at the beginning of each hour, so pretty soon."

"Do you think they'll know anything more?"

She shifted to the end of the couch closest to the dining room and leaned into its plush arm. The couch, which looked to have been made from Paul Bunyan's hand-me-downs, had been in our family longer than I had. The corner she was sitting in was the choice spot, so it had a bit of a slope to it. She took a sip of her tea, and said, "I don't know, Robin. I'm not the police and I'm not the news. But I sure hope they'll have more to tell us."

On any other day, unless I was eating or reading the daily comics, there really wasn't any reason for me to linger in that part of the house. My PlayStation was downstairs. And my comic books were in my room. But on that day, even though I was full of cereal, had caught up on *FoxTrot* and confirmed that Garfield still loathed his loser of an owner, I stuck around, waiting with my mom for ten o'clock to arrive. It's the first time in my life I can recall actively following a news story.

They opened with Catherine. This time, the words "suspected abduction" were used. The reporter ran through the exact same details as he had an hour earlier. When Catherine's story ended, the reporter got as far as "Government officials in . . ." before my mom reached over and turned down the volume, reducing the broadcaster's baritone to a background hum. The update, if you could call it that, had been a letdown. I didn't think they'd found her yet or anything. Still, didn't they have something—*anything*—more?

I stood up to leave. "Where are you off to?" Mom asked.

"I'm going to call Steph and Dylan."

She considered this for a moment, then said, "All right, but if you guys get together, it'll have to be at someone's house. I"—she paused, blinked hard, and exhaled deeply—"I don't want you guys out roaming around like you always do. If you want, I'll take you all to rent a video game, or you can play in the yard here. I just—I think parents should know where their kids are today."

My first thought was to protest. To tell her that it wasn't fair, and that it was summer, and remind her of the difference between a six-year-old girl and a thirteen-year-old boy. But out of a maturity I didn't know I had, I stopped myself.

× × ×

As it turned out, my mom wasn't on her own when it came to precautionary parenting. "My dad called and said we have to stay in," Steph said over the phone. "Even when he gets back this afternoon, he wants me and Jeremy home, or at least with him. He said he'll take us to Dairy Queen, which means he definitely means business." I recalled my own dad's promise of pizza. It wasn't that rare of an occurrence—my family loved pizza—but we'd had Chinese takeout a few days back, and two takeout nights that close together was extraordinary.

"Hey, maybe you could come with us," Steph said.

"Yeah, maybe," I replied. "That'd be cool."

"Oh, wow, Robin, you're hi-larious." There was a steamrolled flatness to her voice.

"What?"

"Going to Dairy Queen would be *cool*. Ba-dum-chh."

She then told me she'd give me a call when her dad was home, then she switched gears to Catherine's disappearance. "I wonder if a pervert took her."

I was about to say something pointless, like *I hope they find her*, when it occurred to me that I hadn't told Steph about my being interviewed Purser and Hennig.

"I forgot to tell you—you're not gonna believe this—but as of right now, I'm one of the last people to have seen her. Two for-real detectives talked to me this morning. Dylan, too. It was just like a movie."

"*Holy shit*," Steph replied, and I heard the voice of her brother Jeremy in the background saying he was telling. As usual, she was quick to dismiss him. She hissed a shush at him and returned to the receiver. "Were you able to tell them anything that would help? Did you, like, have a flashback when they questioned you?"

"I don't think so. Not really."

Enthused, Steph blurted out, "But that's so cool, it's like *Unsolved Mysteries*." She was quick to gain her composure, though. "I mean, it's not cool that she's missing. That's frickin' terrible—*no, Jeremy, frickin' isn't a swear*—but, well, you know what I mean. It's not every day you get interviewed by detectives. Cool isn't the right word, but you know what I mean, right?"

"Yeah, I know what you mean."

Often, when Steph and I ended a phone conversation, our initial goodbye would be followed by each of us waiting for the other to hang up. *Are you still there? No, you hang up first. Okay, we both hang up on three. One . . . two . . . three. Are you still there? Hang up, dammit!* I had once asked Dylan if Steph did the false hang up with him. He said she didn't. I remember him seeming almost annoyed with

67

me asking him about it, the way he'd said an unenthused "Weird" before immediately changing the subject. That morning there were no games from either Steph and I though. We'd both said bye to each other and ended it at that.

I returned the cordless to its cradle on the wall and was about to head downstairs when Mom called me from the living room. "Yeah?" I called back, staying in the kitchen.

"What do you say we head over to the mall?" She must have anticipated me asking why, because before I got the first sylla-ble out, she followed herself up with "I think it's time we replace those glasses."

6

FOR TWO DAYS IN A ROW, I'D HAD THE HONOUR OF BEING AMONG THE FIRST customers at Midtown Mall. On the drive over in Mom's Saturn, I received a lecture that I knew was coming. It was part of a series. I needed to be more careful with my glasses, and how Steph was really only partially to blame, because they're my glasses. Oh, and money, it turned out, wasn't grown—not on trees, or on vines, or in carefully tended soil. Peter had a smile plastered on his face the entire time.

We parked at the mall's south entrance, which was where Dylan and I had left from the day before, right after I'd seen Kyle and Catherine. I thought at first that Mom might have done this intentionally. Maybe she thought that going to the same entrance might trigger my memory, that I might have one of those flash-backs Steph was asking about and recall some crucial detail and, *poof*, Catherine Hillerman would be returned home. Safe, sound, not a hair on her head or a thread in her purple cat dress disturbed. But we only made it a few steps from the car when it occurred to me that the south entrance was where my mom, a true creature of habit, always parked.

We pushed through the mall doors and were greeted by the alluring smell of freshly baked cookies, wafting over from Carol's Cookie Cabin. Mom guided Peter and I toward the stand.

The only thing cabiny about Carol's was the lacquered log pan-elling that surrounded the counter. There were two employees work-ing that morning, a guy and a girl who were both in their late teens. The girl had dyed-black hair and heavy eyeshadow, and her nails were painted in alternating black and metallic blue. If she teased her hair a little and swapped her red apron and white polo out for a Marilyn Manson *Smells Like Children* T-shirt, she would've been the perfect poster girl for one of those cringy "Have You Talked to Your Child About Depression?" ads you see on busses. The guy, on the other hand, looked like the type who refused to work Sundays because of church. His hair was neatly parted in the middle. And he looked like someone who had a stick up his ass, didn't like it, but had come to terms with its placement. Beneath his apron, his polo was buttoned right to the top. I thought back to Dylan's comment about how maybe someone working close by might have noticed something I hadn't. I stared at the odd couple behind the counter, trying to recall if I'd noticed them at all yesterday, but they didn't look familiar. They might have been there. But I wasn't sure.

The guy straightened up when he greeted us. "Good morning. What can I do for you folks today?" His name tag read "Douglas."

"My guess is they want cookies, Doug," the girl, who was leaning with her back against the sink, offered.

Doug forced a smile. Perhaps unconsciously, he straightened his name tag, which, like his posture, didn't really need straightening.

"She's bang-on," Mom said, smiling at the both of them. "What are you thinking, boys?"

Peter had made up his mind long before the question was asked. He pointed at the transparent display case and threw his head back. "Double chocolate!" he shouted, as if he were outing the cookies as witches. Knowing Peter as I did, I was sure it was the word double that pushed him toward that particular cookie. If Dylan were with us, he would've gone the same route.

"I like this kid," the girl behind the counter said.

"Yeah, so we'll get one of those, and . . . Robin?"

"I'll get chocolate chip."

Mom repeated my order. "One chocolate chip. And I'll have . . ." She surveyed the display counter, landing on white chocolate macadamia, a grown-up cookie if there ever was one.

"All righty," Doug said. He punched our order into the register and each cookie's name made a brief appearance on the black LCD screen in blocky alarm-clock lettering. The girl grabbed a pair of tongs and three wax-paper bags as thin as envelopes. After she bagged the cookies, she reached over the display case—where I couldn't help but notice her breasts rested—and handed me the bags.

"Enjoy," she said. Her name tag read "Angie." Before she moved away from the counter, she took the tongs and snapped at Doug's arm with them, making him jump and almost drop the change he was handing my mom.

The three of us started to leave, but then Mom stopped, turned, and walked back to the counter. "I'm sorry," she said, "but were either of you two working yesterday morning?"

Doug and Angie exchanged a quick glance, then Angie said, "I was."

"I wasn't," Doug added.

My mom nodded. She reached her arm around me and pulled me close. "I don't suppose you recall seeing this guy here yesterday morning, do you?"

Angie looked me up and down. Her gaze lingered on my face for a moment before returning to my mom's face. "Sorry, for me to remember him he'd need to have, like, an eye patch or a hook for a hand or something." She zeroed back in on me. "Does junior need an alibi?" she asked, smirking.

Mom laughed. "Oh no, nothing like that. I only ask because—"

"Is this about the missing girl?" Doug interrupted.

"Actually, it is," Mom replied, seeming somewhat surprised by Doug's interjection.

Angie said, "The police already talked to us when we opened. I told them everything I remembered."

"Was it Hennig and Purser you spoke with?"

"Who?"

"The detectives."

"Oh, no. Or, I'm not sure if they were detectives. How do you tell? They looked like any other cops. They're probably still here. They said they were talking to, like, the whole mall. All I told them was I remembered seeing—"

Again, Doug interrupted, "You're—I don't think you're supposed to share the information with random people."

Angie rolled her eyes and shook her head. "Whatever, Doug. And they're not random, they're valued customers. *Any*way," she shot Doug an irritated glare, "I told them the only thing that really stood out from yesterday was that there was an old guy sitting on the bench over there." She pointed, and everyone—me, Mom, Peter, and even Doug, who was now leaning against the sink, sulking—turned to look at the cushy bench sandwiched between two Jurassic-sized potted plants. It was directly across from the washrooms. When we brought our attention back to Angie, she shrugged and said, "It probably wasn't even worth mentioning, but they said 'anything you remember,' so I told them this dude was sitting there for like half-an-hour."

Mom thanked them both and the three of us left for LensCrafters, each of us diving right into our still-warm cookie of choice. We passed the spot where I had stood the previous day, where I talked with Kyle while Catherine paced about, her speaking in that made-up accent to guests at the royal dinner party she was attending in her own head.

Zanks, dah–ling, zanks.

× × ×

In front of the mirrored wall, Mom encouraged me to try some new frames, something fun. But I've always taken after my dad, an if-it-ain't-broke-don't-fix-it kind of guy. I chose the pair of glasses that were closest to my last pair. No thick, funky frames, no crazy colours, just the usual, please: thin, rounded, black. Nothing fancy. I figured if I hated wearing glasses in the first place, why get a pair that stood out? The lady who rang us through said turnaround was quick and I should have my new glasses in just a few days. Before we left, she suggested buying a hockey visor for the next time I played soccer.

"I think that's a great idea," my mom said, and I rolled my eyes.

We spent about an hour meandering around the mall, following Mom from store to store. Normally she'd give Peter and I a few bucks and let us go off on our own for a bit, but not that day, of course. The thought that a kidnapper—if that's what it was—would strike two days in a row seemed ridiculous, but I couldn't blame Mom for being cautious. I thought back to my conversation with Steph, how her dad had insisted she and Jeremy stay in, and how instead of a carrot, there was a DQ Blizzard at the end of the stick. And I considered the warm cookies Peter and I were just finishing, and the pizza we were promised later for dinner, and I figured that a little junk food was a good enough trade-off for a parent's peace of mind.

After lingering in Talbots, a store my mom liked to browse but never bought anything from, we made our way to Jack's Toys, which Peter referred to as Toys"R"Us, because all toy stores were Toys"R"Us to him. I was glad to get out of the women's clothing shops, not only because there was nothing there for me, but because each time we passed an underwear display I thought of Mrs. Mayer.

To get to Jack's Toys we passed through the food court, where the air was smeared with competing greasy smells. I spotted the table where Dylan and I had sat the day before, when we had noticed Connor and Louis and were forced to take refuge in the photo booth. I wondered if those two had been questioned by the police, and if so, had they figured out we'd been the ones who gave their names to the cops. They probably hadn't. Likely a couple randoms would end up taking a pounding on behalf of Dylan and I.

I could live with that.

Annoying as Peter could be sometimes, it was fun being in a toy store with him. He was so excited, running from aisle to aisle, picking up packaged toys, gasping. After a bit though, I headed to the tiny video game section, then browsed an *X-Men* action figure display. I felt too old for action figures, but still liked to look. Mom let us kill almost half an hour in the store. When we left, everyone in a twenty-kilometre radius knew what Peter wanted for his birthday, which was only ten short months away.

On our way out, we walked back past Carol's Cookie Cabin, and the bench where an old man who may or may not have mattered sat for half-an-hour. Outside, a police cruiser idled in the fire lane. Two uniformed officers sat inside. The one in the driver's seat was talking into his hand-held radio. We crossed in front of the car and Mom looked at the cop and nodded. He nodded back and waved without missing a beat in the conversation he was having. No more than a second after we passed the car, its siren blasted to life. The piercing sound startled us and we all jumped. We stood in the middle of the road as the cruiser peeled away from the curb and tore out of the lot. I found what seemed to be only cloud in an otherwise clear blue sky and tried to send a prayer, or a thought, or a hope up to it.

7

BRUCE STAYED QUIET AS I EXPLAINED MY MEETING WITH THE POLICE. IN the time I had known him, which was six years, he had always been thrifty with his words. He was the sort of person who had an ocean inside his head. Most of him was kept internal, but while his surface was often stoic, there was a frenzy of movement going on beneath. I told him, Steph, and Jeremy, who was half-listening at best, about the questions I had been asked, and what I remembered about seeing Catherine.

While Steph had some sort of reaction to everything I said, Bruce remained placid, nodding along and occasionally shovelling a mouthful of his kingdom-come-sized Rolo Blizzard into the mouth he kept somewhere beneath his mustache. When I finished, he shook his head and added, more to himself than anyone else, "That's awful."

"It is," Steph said, "but I still think it's so cool you got to talk to the cops."

"Steph," Bruce, said, looking up from his excavation, "there's nothing 'cool' about it."

Steph scoffed and gave a world-class eye roll, with her spine mimicking the same movement of the eyes, as if the motion took extreme physical effort. For a moment Bruce stared. He had this look, like he'd only just then realized in that moment that he was raising a teenage girl by himself, but then he blinked the look away and returned to his snack. "Just don't say something like that's 'cool,'" he said in a soft voice mottled by ice cream, caramel, and chocolate.

"Dad, I *obviously* don't mean that Kyle's sister going missing is cool. I mean talking to the cops is cool." Then Steph sighed and dove back into her Mint Oreo Blizzard.

Jeremy and I got Mint Oreo too. Because Jeremy had a peanut allergy, Bruce had requested that we all avoid his Kryptonite. He even went as far as supervising the kid making the Blizzards

75

to make triple-sure the mixer was sanitized and didn't have any traces of peanuts. I always thought it was random, that a little thing like a peanut could kill certain people. It seemed like a half-assed Achilles heel thought up by the same person who decided Green Lantern could be hurt by the colour yellow.

Steph pointed at me with her long, red plastic spoon. "What kind of glasses did you order?"

"Pretty much the same as my old ones. They come in a couple days."

"*So* adventurous, Robin."

"Why mess with a good thing?"

"Exactly," Bruce agreed. "You know what you like."

"Yup."

Bruce narrowed his eyes. "I still feel we should have picked up the tab on those."

"My mom *insisted* it was my fault."

Bruce considered this for a second, then said, "All right. But I think it's only fair that you come to our place, choose one thing from Steph's room, and smash it to pieces. Eye for an eye, you know?"

"Dad!" Steph protested. She sounded offended, but the corners of her mouth were curving into a smile. I saw, for a flash of a second, her mint-tinted tongue, the chewed-up bits of Oreo stuck to her teeth. I wasn't grossed out one bit.

We'd gone the rest of our DQ experience without further talk of Catherine Hillerman. I knew that when I got home, it would be right back to CBC Radio, and then the six o'clock news, and it was nice to get a break. But then I thought about how Catherine, wherever she was, sure wasn't getting a break. And neither was Kyle, or the rest of their family. Not only was I next to no help to Detective Hennig and Detective Purser, but here I was, sitting in a Dairy Queen, comfortably full of ice cream while somewhere in this city (was she still in this city?) a little girl was separated from her family, lost and afraid.

Lost and afraid *at best*.

Maybe that night I'd have a dream that would trigger a forgotten memory—something small, but crucial—and I could rush to the police station and share the pinprick-sized detail with the two detectives, and it would be just what they were looking for. The proverbial missing link. And just like that, everything would come into focus. That's how it works, right?

Bruce hung a left at the T that led to my house when I remembered to ask, "Oh, I forgot: are we still going to the pool tomorrow?"

Jeremy, who was riding shotgun, whipped around and looked at Steph and I in the back seat. "The *swimming* pool?" he asked.

"No, Jeremy," Steph said, "the cesspool. We're all going to the cesspool tomorrow. You included."

"What's a—"

Before Jeremy could finish, Bruce jumped in. "I don't think the pool's a great idea tomorrow. With all that's . . . Maybe hold off, okay?"

Steph let her dad's response hang there for a second, then she nodded her head and, to my surprise, said, "All right. That's fair." She looked over at me, her palms turned up to say, *Well, isn't it?*

× × ×

We watched the news that evening, my parents sitting on the couch, leaning against one another like two halves of a drawbridge reuniting, and me sitting in the chair in the corner, a big tartan-patterned old thing that was cushy and wide and always made me feel like I was sitting in a fortress. The opening montage, a hurried blend of previews from the evening's stories played over music that sounded equal parts epic and urgent, promised new developments in Catherine's case, which still held the honour of top story. But after the music faded and after Trish Nadel, who co-anchored the six o'clock news with Ray Huang, had finished shuffling the papers in front of her (a task that seemed never-ending), I quickly learned that "new developments" was, by and large, another way of reporting the same story but amplified. "The search continues for six-year-old Catherine Hillerman," Trish Nadel said. I had seen Trish's face so many times on the sides of busses and on the big billboard that towered over Ninth Avenue that I felt I knew her. A photo of Catherine appeared in the top corner of the screen, next to Trish's head. It was a school picture. You could tell by the blotchy-blue backdrop. Her smile wasn't the big toothy grin you often got in school photos from children that age. It was more of a smirk, like she was up to something. Or maybe, more likely for Catherine, recalling a private joke to herself. "Catherine was last seen at Midtown Mall just over twenty-four hours ago," Trish continued as they cut to a shot of the mall, the same entrance I'd used earlier that day with Mom and Peter. Catherine's photo remained on-screen. "Police have interviewed a number of witnesses and are requesting the help of the public in locating the missing girl."

A man who looked like a thumb with a face appeared on-screen and was introduced as Police Chief Kitrosser. He wore the same uniform as the officers we saw in the cruiser outside the mall, but he had insignias on his shoulder—including a red-and-gold crown, which made him seem sort of royal—and had some of those coloured badges over his heart, the kind that looked like the colour bars that came on TV stations when there was no signal. He spoke into a microphone that poked sneakily into frame from the bottom corner. "We are pursuing every lead," he said. The line was the cop equivalent of *we're gonna give it a hundred and ten percent and play to the best of our ability*. He leaned slightly closer to the mic. "But we also need the public's help. We've set up a hotline, and we urge anyone with information to come forward and help us bring this little girl home."

From there, the show went back to Trish Nadel and Ray Huang in the studio, Catherine's hotline number glowing white at the bottom of the screen.

I made it through a few more minutes of the news before I decided to leave the living room and head downstairs to play *Mortal Kombat 3*. Peter followed. I wasn't supposed to let him watch *Mortal Kombat 3*. Usually I'd play *Crash Bandicoot* if Peter was around. He loved that game. And I'd always start off by letting him play, but after he walked off a cliff five or six times, I'd politely offer to "help" him, which was code for taking over completely. For Peter, though, it was still a team effort, even after I took the reins. He'd sit close to me, cheering me on.

But that night, *Crash* stayed in its case. To my surprise, Peter didn't make a peep of protest. He grabbed a pillow, hugged it, and inched back from the TV so that he was sitting at a safe distance and wouldn't have to worry about getting any pixelated blood on him. I don't remember how long I played, but I do remember that it swallowed up a good portion of the evening and that during that time, Peter went from fearful onlooker to engaged supporter, no longer hiding behind his pillow shield. His excitement wasn't as vocal as when I played *Crash*, but as I slugged buckets of blood out of a cornered Baraka, I noticed in my periphery that Peter was mimicking my character's punches. I felt a glimmer of pride—I'd introduced the kid to the wonders of video game gore, a brotherly rite of passage if there ever was one. When I finished the round, Peter told me I did a good job killing "the vampire." And I don't know why I felt the need to push this corruption further, but I got the urge to tell Peter a joke I'd heard from a ninth grader last year at the school Halloween party. I paused the game. "Hey, Peter," I began. "Listen to this. Two vampires walk into a bar—"

"Where?"

"Huh?"

"Where?"

"It doesn't matter where. It's a joke."

"Oh. That's funny."

"No . . . that's not . . . Just listen. Okay. Two vampires walk into a bar. They sit down, and one of them orders a pint—like a cup—of blood from the bartender. The bartender asks the second vampire if he wants one too. The second vampire just asks for a mug of hot water. The first vampire asks the second one why he ordered hot water and the second vampire pulls a used tampon out of his cape pocket and says, 'I'm *hawwvink* tea.'"

Peter stared at me like he was expecting something. "Then what?" he asked, after a moment.

"That's it," I said. "That's the whole joke." As the words came out, and my lips curved into a sicko's grin, I realized how dumb I was, trying to get a six-year-old to wrap his head around a risqué joke.

Peter looked down at his lap. He fidgeted with the string on his pyjama bottoms. "I don't get it," he said, disappointed.

"That's okay," I told him. "Forget about it, it's a dumb joke. I told it wrong."

He untied the string from his pjs, and then tightened it and tied it back up, as if practising how my dad had taught him to tie his shoelaces a few months before. Like every kid who was new to the world of loop tying, he was very slow and methodical. When he finished with the bunny ears, he looked up at me. "Did a vampire take that girl?"

It took me a second to grasp what he was asking. "No," I said once the question sunk in. "It wasn't a vampire that took Catherine. And you don't know, she might have just got lost or something."

Peter's eyes fell back to his pyjama string. He tugged at one of the loops. "I don't think she got lost," he whispered.

"Me neither," I said. "But whatever happened, it isn't a vampire. *If* someone took her, it was just a person." I nudged his shoulder. "Don't be scared of vampires, Pete. They're not real. They're fake."

Peter considered this for a moment, then nodded. "Okay," he said. "I'll only be scared of people."

× × ×

In the moments before I fell asleep, snapshots of the last couple of days whirred through my mind like a jerky View-Master disc. The disc lingered on some moments for a bit longer than others, like Blizzards with Steph and her Mint Oreo mouth. And the siren from the police cruiser that made us all leap out of our skins while we crossed the mall parking lot. The last thing I remember thinking of before I dozed off was Mrs. Mayer spotting me outside her bedroom, her swelling chest and the smirk that was probably nothing more than a cruel trick of the light. My world dimmed and she turned to mist.

× × ×

I'm in my room, lying on my bed. I don't know if I've just woken up, or if I've been lying there awake, but the first moments feel normal.

Then I'm standing beside my bed. I'm already dressed. And as I make my way to the door, I hear the scraping of chairs and my parents' voices coming from somewhere above me. This is what tips me off: there *is* no above me. At our house, everyone's room is on the same level. I can't understand what my parents are saying— not with their having to contend with the ruckus of wooden legs being pushed across the floor—but I recognize their familiar tones. Though it sounds like they're arguing.

I'm in the hallway. Our home looks the same but different. Everything's wider, and the colours are all mottled like they've been filtered through a greasy piece of wax paper. Moving towards the staircase, I notice that large tree roots are growing out of the walls. I run my fingers over them. They have a strange claylike texture that makes me nauseous. I pull my hands away and stuff them in my pockets.

At the top of the stairs, Ms. Mayer is waiting for me with another beautiful woman I've never seen before. The mystery woman is a bit younger than Ms. Mayer. She has red hair, dark eyes, and a wide smile. She looks like she should be in commercials. Maybe she is. Both of them are wearing green bikinis and have lit sparklers sticking out from their breasts like darts from a bull's eye. I step past them onto the stairs, which are suddenly wide enough to accommodate all three of us, and the two women start clapping for me while we all descend together, chanting my name, "Rob-*in*! Rob-*in*! Rob-*in*! *Wooooo!*"

The coloured flames from their sparklers crackle, sending embers flying onto my bare arms.

81

When I reach the bottom of the stairs, both women lean in and give me a kiss, one on each cheek, and then turn and leave in opposite directions. I try to follow Mrs. Mayer but my foot catches a massive tree root sticking out from the floor. I trip and careen into the kitchen, where I thud into the wall. There are even more roots climbing the wall here. I don't want to, but for some reason I can't help but touch them. The texture—it's so disgusting! And they stink too. Burnt . . . what? Styrofoam? I've never smelt anything like it. And . . . what was that? Did one of them just *move?!*

I step back from the wall and furiously wipe my hands off on my pants. I don't want that smell on me.

Robin? Can you bring me the milk?

Peter is sitting at the table. His pale skin has a blue tint to it, and his hair, jet-black here, is slicked straight back. He wears a vampire's cape and a puffy, white pirate shirt. His eyes have no irises or pupils.

Did you hear me? Peter demands.

I can't answer.

I asked you to bring me the fucking milk. He points at the bowl sitting in front of him. It's filled nearly to the brim with colourful Flintstone vitamins. *I can't eat this shit dry.*

I retrieve the milk from the fridge, place it on the table.

Peter pours the milk and starts eating. I tiptoe to the back door. The knob sticks and I have to fiddle with it. The click prompts Peter to look up. He stares at me with his dead white eyes and says, *Don't worry, Robin. Vampires aren't real.* Then he flashes me a smile that reveals a set of needle-like fangs and laughs so hard that the vitamins he's been chewing start shooting out of his nose.

The house dissolves away with the closing of the door. I'm outside and it's nighttime. I'm standing in a recently ploughed field, the ravine looming at the far end. The roots from its trees stretch out towards me. They writhe on the ground like jittery stop-motion snakes. There must be hundreds of them.

Hands clamp onto my shoulders. Dylan and Steph, one on each side of me, are robed like judges, blazing torches in hand. For a brief moment—I don't know how long—time doesn't exist; I'm gripped by a suffocating terror. But then I notice I'm a judge too, and my terror lifts, is replaced with a sense of joy. I belong here.

The three of us link arms and march across the field to the ravine. Tree roots squirm at our feet, but we don't trip over them. Now they move around us, accept us in their midst.

When we approach the threshold, Steph and Dylan stop. I stop as well—I figure I'm supposed to—but then Dylan shakes his head and gestures for me to keep going.

I go in alone? I ask.

Dylan nods.

I look to Steph, hoping for more guidance. *Why me? Why alone? What am I supposed to do in there?* Steph doesn't speak. She hands Dylan her torch, then plucks one of her fingernails off and flicks it onto the ground. An arc of blood blasts from the opening on her finger as she raises her hand and points to the ravine. *Go*, she mouths.

I realize then that I have no choice but to follow the spraying stream of Steph's blood to the cusp of the ravine. When I get there, I turn and take one last look at my friends as the trees open up and stretch around me. Dylan is waving the two torches back and forth like an air traffic controller. Steph continues to point, blood geysering from the opening in her finger. She waves goodbye with her other hand.

Wood cracks and pops as the trees fold shut around me. It's so loud, and I suppose it has to be, a forest moving like that. But somehow over the noise I hear the melody of a piano, the clinking of glasses, the clamour of friendly chatter and laughter. A dinner party is happening somewhere inside the fortress of trees, somewhere I can't see.

A voice carries from it.

Zanks, dah-ling. Zanks.

I move in toward the voice, but stop abruptly when I notice the ledge right in front of me. It's a steep drop into blackness. The plunge to oblivion. Before I can step back to relative safety, a cold burst of breath from over my shoulder kills my torchlight like a candle on a birthday cake. I realize then that a large hand is resting on my back. And I don't know how I know, but I *do* know it: the hand is connected to nothing. It thrusts me forward, and over . . .

I fall. And the last thing I remember before I wake up is being struck with the horrible certainty that there is no bottom waiting to end me.

8

"I THINK IT'S A BIT OF A RIDICULOUS REQUEST, BUT IF YOU'RE WORRIED, I'M not going to say anything to the Mayers about it. I just don't see what's wrong with *our* place."

"Mom, stop," I pleaded. "I get it." Hunched forward, arms crossed, glaring out the passenger window, I must have looked like a parody of a surly teen. *Have you talked to your child about depression?*

When the phone had rung around ten that morning, I knew it was Dylan without having to look at our caller ID. That was when we always called each other. I answered, and without saying hi back, Dylan asked, "Whose house?" On a normal day, we'd usually meet somewhere outdoors, like Saint Phillip's field, or outside Perry's Pantry, or on the street across from the ravine. But it seemed that all parents wanted their kids to stay off the streets. We decided at first that Dylan would come to my place. But in the few seconds it took me to hang up and walk to the edge of the kitchen, the phone beckoned me back. It turned out that before Mr. Mayer had left for work that morning, he'd insisted to Mrs. Mayer that Dylan and Emily stay at their house.

"Sorry, but my mom flipped when I said I was going to your place. I guess Dad really wants me and Emily to stay here."

Before we hung up for a second time I heard Mrs. Mayer protest in the background, "I did not *flip*, Dylan."

As Mom pulled to a stop in front of the Mayers' house, Peter, who had been singing "The Song That Doesn't End" from *Lamb Chop's Play-Along* for most of the drive, asked if he could come with me.

"Uh . . ." I said, glancing at Mom for backup.

Mom looked into the rear-view to meet Peter's eyes. "You get to come with me and run *errands*." By the way she said "errands," you'd think they were an event on par with going to Disneyland. Peter pouted and then started up with his song again, but this time it was deflated and sad, like he was singing the death-row version of the kiddie show tune. I thought back to when I was Peter's age, and how I couldn't really pin down exactly what errands were, but I knew I was in for a long boring day filled with endless lineups and lists—there were *always* lists.

Mrs. Mayer had told me numerous times that I was like one of the family and didn't need to knock before I came in, but it still somehow felt wrong to enter without permission. I had tried it once, pressing down on the handle of their heavy wooden door and stepping in unannounced. Nothing bad happened, but I'd felt like an intruder, so I was reluctant to try it again.

That day Emily opened the door. She looked up at me, squinting in the morning sun that hung behind my head, and sneezed. Some of her spray skittered onto my arm.

"Gross," I said.

"Sorry." She plugged one nostril with the knuckle of her pointer finger and sucked in through the other one, creating a wet sniffling sound that made me gag. This wasn't the peppy, Spice Girls-loving Emily from a couple nights ago. This Emily was pale, mellow, and looked beyond exhausted. She moved aside to let me enter and then croaked, "Dylan, your boyfriend's here!"

In the kitchen, over a bowl of Doritos left over from the other night, we took turns saying we were up for whatever, but as soon as something was suggested, the other would immediately veto the idea. At one point, after it felt like everything we could do had been rejected, I asked Dylan if he and his family saw the news story on Catherine Hillerman the night before. But as soon as I brought her up, Dylan signalled for me to cut it out. I didn't understand why at first, but then he gestured at Emily, who was sitting nearby in the living room working on a colouring book.

"My parents told me not to talk about that around Emily. She gets scared," he whispered from behind a cupped hand.

We eventually migrated to the living room, having decided with bulletproof logic that a little TV would help us think. We flipped between *Maury Povich* and baseball highlights. At one point, Mrs. Mayer came down and said hi and asked after my family. She normally did this right when I walked in the door, but, like Emily, she was a little off that day.

From the doorway of the living room, she asked me if I'd been sleeping okay. At first I didn't know what she meant and I tensed up, but then she added, "Dylan was up all night whimpering after you guys watched that charming Jason Voorhees movie."

Ever the cool mom, I was impressed, but not at all surprised, she got the character's name right.

"God, Mom, I was *not!*" He shook his head fiercely and Mrs. Mayer laughed and shot me a grin. I returned the grin, and it felt for a second like we were sharing an inside joke.

"Jesus Christ," Dylan muttered. His tone reminded me of his dad.

Mrs. Mayer got herself a Diet Coke from the fridge and vanished upstairs without acknowledging her son's moodiness. A moment later, Emily also left the living room and padded her way to her bedroom. Dylan flipped back to *Maury Povich*. When Emily had been there with us, he'd only stay on *Maury* if she seemed sufficiently distracted by her colouring book. The second she looked up at the screen—a movement that was normally triggered by someone on the show screaming, or the audience booing—he'd flip back to baseball. *Maury* wasn't *Jerry Springer*, but it wasn't kid stuff either. With Emily out of our hair, we got to find out if, in the case of four-year-old Jenna, Todd was indeed the father. After a drawn-out argument between Todd and his ex-lover, Lisa, plus a quick commercial break, Maury took out a DNA test from an official *Maury* envelope, and Todd was revealed to be the sperm donor. Lisa did a victory lap of the studio, high-fiving audience members as she went. Todd yelled insults at the audience from his chair on the stage.

"What a tool," Dylan said, chuckling.

"I pity the tool," I said, doing my best Mr. T.

Dylan let me know what he thought of my impression by whipping a pillow at me. The floral-pattern cushions that sat in the corners of the couch were exclusively decorative, and I had often seen Dylan scolded for having the audacity to use one of them *as* a pillow and once more firmly for tossing one. His defence that it was called a "throw pillow" didn't hold up for long. As I deflected his attack, I was remined of how much of a punch a cushion that was designed for anything but comfort packed. "Hey, fucknut, I don't want another nosebleed!" The pillow thudded to the floor.

Dylan held a shushing finger to his lips and pointed above him. It was a reminder that, just because his mom might allow us to watch R-rated movies, it didn't mean we could talk like we were in one.

"Sorry," I said in a whisper, then, at a pitch barely audible to my own ears, repeated myself: *"Hey, fucknut, careful, I don't want another nosebleed."*

He laughed, flipped me off, and returned his attention to the TV. Looking at him from across the room, I recalled how, a little over twenty-four hours earlier, I sat on that same couch with my parents as two detectives interviewed me. The memory was still fresh, but it surfaced with a blurry haze to it, as if my mind's eye had a layer of gauze stretched over it. I wondered what Detective Purser and Detective Hennig were doing at that moment. Were they following a lead? Was Purser cuffing some scuzzy creep—an either too-fat or too-thin man with a wispy mustache and out-of-date glasses, like you see on TV—while Hennig told him anything he said could and would be held against him in a court of law? Or were they at the morgue, doing rock, paper, scissors to decide which of them had to make the worst phone call you could ever have to make?

Maury had moved on to another potential father when Dylan got up from the couch. "This is lame. I'm going to ask my mom if she can take us somewhere." He went upstairs while I went to the kitchen for something to drink. As I filled my glass, the phone rang. And rang. I stood there sipping my water waiting for someone to pick up the receiver. Dylan's parents had a phone in their bedroom. Why wasn't Mrs. Mayer picking up? I walked to the edge of the kitchen. The phone kept going.

"Should I . . ." I started to call up the stairs, but stopped when I heard the muffled voices of Dylan and his mom arguing. I waited for a moment, then walked back to the kitchen and grasped the receiver.

"Uh, hello?"

"Jesus Christ. What took you so long?" Mr. Mayer sounded pissed.

"I . . . I didn't know if I—"

"Dylan? Is that you?" The way the words rushed out of him, it was as if he were right there in the kitchen with me, shaking me by the shoulders. *Out with it, dammit!*

"N-no," I stammered. "Sorry. This is Robin. Dylan's upstairs with Mrs. Mayer. I didn't know if they could hear it, so I answered."

Mr. Mayer sounded pained as he inhaled and let out a sigh. Wounded by my idiocy—picking up a ringing phone, how stupid of me. "You didn't know if they could—Robin, we have three phones in the house, I'm sure they . . . You know what, never mind. It's fine. Normally, when you pick up the phone at someone else's house you say, 'Mayer residence,' or whoever's house it . . . Never mind. It's fine. Would you mind getting Diane for me?"

In all the years I'd known Dylan and his family, I only needed one fingerless hand to count the number of times Mr. Mayer had referred to Mrs. Mayer by her first name while talking to me.

"Yeah," I said. "One sec."

When I turned around, Dylan and Mrs. Mayer were standing behind me. Mrs. Mayer said, "Thanks, Robin," and held out her hand. I passed her the phone and she walked into the dining room with it. "Hi, Ken."

Dylan met eyes with me for a second, then looked away. He turned toward the dining room, shaking his head, irritated. "Now it's gonna be a no," he muttered, knowing his mom was way more easy to sway than his dad.

"That sucks."

He held out his hand, displaying a thumb and index finger that, at most, had the height of an ant between them. "She was this far away from saying yes."

"I don't get it," I said. "You'd think it'd be okay if you and me went somewhere together. Like to Saint Phillip's, or, you know, somewhere open, where people could see us." I knew my mom would have let us if we were at my house.

Dylan shrugged. He opened his mouth to say something but stopped when his mom walked into the kitchen.

"Okay," she said in to the phone, "see you tonight." She ended the call, then returned the phone to its charging cradle. "I'm sorry, guys. You've got to stay here. You don't have to stay inside—you could go do something in the yard—but it's got to be here." She punctuated her message by crossing her arms and leaning back against the counter, a gesture that told us the argument was closed.

Dylan knew how to cross his arms too. He took a deep breath in, exhaled a forceful sigh, and muttered something under his breath.

"*Dylan.*" Mrs. Mayer's tone had a sharp point to it. "Your father—your father and *I*—have made a decision for your own good. You might not like it, but you have to respect it."

"But why do we have to stay in just because one little kid's missing? She's less than half our age, and she's the only one, and—"

"*She,*" Mrs. Mayer started, her voice spiking in volume, her eyes widening with what might have been anger, "is not one little kid. *She* is Catherine Hillerman, a member of our community, and the sister of a boy in your grade. A sister, who happens to be the exact same age as your own sister, young man."

As though the condescending use of "young man" was her cue, Emily sniffled, announcing her presence in the room. We all turned, and she looked up at us, her eyes drifting from person to person. Maybe it was Mrs. Mayer's mentioning that Catherine Hillerman was Emily's age that put the thought in my head, I'm not sure, but in the second Emily's eyes locked on mine, I saw Catherine for a quick flash.

Emily sniffed again, but a cough interrupted it midway through. Mrs. Mayer knelt down and put her arm around her daughter. She rubbed Emily's back as the cough persisted, causing her little shoulders to bounce up and down. The cough sounded rusty as it scraped up her throat.

"I don't think she's contagious. It's probably something left over from the bronchitis she had," Mrs. Mayer said. "It never really went away." She stood up and took the stutter-coughing Emily by the hand, and together they walked out of the kitchen and towards the stairs. "You guys will have to find something to keep yourselves busy here. There's the yard, there's TV, there's video games, board games, and don't forget about those imaginations you're supposed to have," Mrs. Mayer called to us as she climbed the stairs, her voice becoming fainter with each suggestion.

Dylan shook his head. "Jesus," he muttered.

"Let's just go outside, man. We can do one-on-one soccer. Or play Pickle, or something."

Without saying anything more, we slipped on our shoes, and Dylan grabbed his Expos hat from the peg it lived on and placed it on his head backwards. I was, and will forever be, jealous of my friend's ability to rock a backwards cap without looking like a total tool.

The Mayers' yard looked like a two-page spread from one of those home and garden magazines. It had lush green grass and a big colourful garden and was bordered by a high wooden fence that ensured maximum privacy. I remembered when the fence was being built a few summers before—it was done by contractors, but Dylan and his dad handled the staining—and Mrs. Mayer had said she wanted it as high as code would allow, so that no one would able to see her sunbathing. This was a fact that popped into my head whenever we played out back. The deck, which was also a contractor's creation, was furnished with a wicker couch, two matching chairs, and a table with an umbrella poking through its centre. The only condition to us playing back there was that we keep the ball the hell away from the garden. One time, when we were trying to see how long we could keep the ball in the air between the three of us, a sloppy header from Steph sent it smack dab into the middle of a bunch of flowers that I didn't know the name of because they weren't roses or daisies. Dylan took the blame and got real shit for it. Parents are always harder on their own kids.

After years of experimentation, we discovered using a tennis ball for Pickle instead of a football made the game more exciting. We played five decent rounds and decided to call it during the sixth, when we kept forgetting what letter we were on and the game began to melt into anarchy. We finished our afternoon sitting on the deck, Dylan on the couch, me on the chair across from it, which was blanketed in shade. I told him about DQ with Steph.

"*Oooh*, a date," he said, grinning. I felt my cheeks redden. Dylan noticed, his smile grew. "Yep, definitely a date," he confirmed pointing at me.

"Yeah, dumbass, it was a date all right. Me, Steph, who I'm not into *at all*, and her dad and brother. Super romantic, hey? It was basically that scene from *Lady and the Tramp*, but with Blizzards instead of spaghetti."

"So you admit it," he said, a giggle escaping. When Dylan knew he was annoying someone, he'd sometimes get worked into a frenzy. It was like he was high or something. He'd feed off the irritation like the Incredible Hulk fed off anger, so the more you told him he was annoying, and the more you told him he wasn't funny, just lame, the more worked up he'd get. Sometimes so much that he'd start to choke on his own laughter: Mickey Mouse drowning. It usually took physical violence to snap him out of it and for him to shrink back to his Bruce Banner self. I got up from my chair and rushed him. He held out his hands in defence, but the fact that I was attacking only fuelled his laughter, which made it hard for him to keep up. I distracted him with one hand going for the stomach, and then reached to the side of his head with my free hand and flicked at his earlobe. Then, I made like I was going to repeat that move, but once he covered his ears, I went for the area just below his ribs, jabbing with two pointed fingers on each side. As his laughter started to wind down, mine started to wind up. When we met somewhere in the middle, I ended the assault and collapsed back into my chair.

Dylan made a kissy face, but when I started to get up again, he raised his hands in submission. "Okay, okay," he pleaded, expelling one final bout of laughter from his system.

"It wasn't a date, asshat," I said.

9

WHEN THE SUN WENT DOWN, THE HILLS LOOMING IN THE DISTANCE MELTED into one mass, creating a silhouette that could have been a backdrop from one of the old movies Channel 36 played on Sunday afternoons. Grave faces, misted eyes, hands clutching Mason jars with flickering tea lights inside them. Everyone at the vigil listened to Mayor Baynes, who stood with a microphone at the base of the Eternal Sentry statue. The statue was a tribute to the Canadian soldiers who fought in the World Wars, its stony soldier brandishing a bayonet that looked like a large-scale version of the heirloom that hung in the Mayer living room. When I was younger, I used to imagine the Eternal Sentry and our local mascot, Haddington Henry, coming to life and duking it out. Like our very own version of *Godzilla vs. King Kong*. But I wasn't thinking that then. The mood was too sombre. Standing to the left of the mayor were Kyle Hillerman, and his mom, Barb. Barb Hillerman kneaded her son's shoulders nervously as the mayor spoke. Her face was a ghostly mask.

"While our police force is working tirelessly to ensure young Catherine returns home to her family, I am proud, but not at all surprised to see the way that Haddington Springers have come together in the wake of this emergency. We're a city with the heart of a small town, and when something happens to one of us, it happens to all of us."

During the six o'clock news, more information was revealed about Catherine's disappearance. It turned out, she was not *last* seen at Midtown Mall. She'd been there, of course, but had later been spotted walking down Wyckham Road, alone. Wyckham Road was one of the streets that ran from the mall to her house. It was also one of the streets that bordered the ravine.

Why was she alone? I found my eyes drawn to Kyle and his mother while Mayor Baynes spoke. Had Kyle ditched her? Or had she snuck off for some reason? Kyle's face twisted in pain, and I tore myself away as a lump swelled in my throat. I felt so awful, knowing the guilt that must have been gnawing at him. Nothing eats at you like guilt. Noticing my agitation, Mom placed a hand on my shoulder. Her other hand rested on Peter's back, and I can only imagine how much physical contact with both her boys must have comforted her at that moment.

My dad, along with Kyle's dad, Gil, and so many others, was off helping with the search. The police had people sweeping across the city. Dad was part of a group that started at Saint Phillip's and worked its way toward Century Park, a sportsplex that was home to two hockey rinks and a field used for rugby and soccer. There were a lot of whispers about Gil Hillerman before the vigil started. Most praised him for joining the search for his daughter, but some said he should be here, with the rest of his family, to comfort them. Watching Kyle cry as the mayor handed the microphone over to Father Fabares, who was our pope or whatever, I couldn't disagree that his family sure needed him. But I also couldn't blame him for joining the search. I don't know how anyone could.

After Father Fabares made a plea to God to return Catherine to her family—as if God had stashed her away somewhere and was simply waiting for the right person to ask—he called upon the crowd to join him in a round of Hail Marys. My family sometimes went to church on Christmas Eve, but only sometimes. We went on Easter one year too, when I was in kindergarten. It only took a couple rounds of the prayer to jog my memory, and by the third I was confident enough to whisper along. It was weird saying the *at the hour of our death* part. I looked over at Steph, who was standing with her family nearby. Her grandma was with them. She clutched a shell-pink rosary and prayed with her eyes closed. Steph didn't pray; I don't think she knew the words. Her grandma had made her attend church with her a few times when she was younger, after her mom had died, but it was a short-lived thing, and Steph never really took to it. Her dad, his face locked into a serious, alert expression, like he was bracing for something, was also not praying. His big Frankenstein arms were wrapped around Jeremy, who wore a vacant look.

When Father Fabares was done, he turned things back over to Mayor Baynes. "We need to stay strong. We need to stay vigilant," he said. A few people cheered at this, but it was brief. It wasn't really the sort of gathering suited to applause. The mayor went on: "As we continue working to bring Catherine home, I want to remind everyone to keep their eyes open, and to report anything you see. The RCMP has lent additional manpower to help with the search. So many of you have volunteered—you've helped with the hotline, joined the search parties. I thank you for that, and I encourage you all to continue to aid your community in this time of need. I know . . ." He paused for a moment and bowed his head, then moved the microphone away from his mouth, but not before the sound of an amplified sob came through the speakers. He breathed a deep breath and rubbed his eyes and looked back up at the crowd, at his people, who, for three consecutive terms had given him land-slides. "Excuse me," Mayor Baynes said, then cleared his throat. "I know that if we all continue to work together, it's only a matter of time before we bring our missing daughter home."

Everyone nodded in agreement, myself included. And I was ashamed the instant I thought it, but the first thing that came to mind after the mayor spoke those words was, *Yeah, but in what condition?*

× × ×

We walked toward the parking lot together with Steph's family. She and I tailed my mom and Peter, who walked with the rest. We all still had our candles lit, and with my hood up, I felt like I belonged to a procession of Druids. I wondered, if I started to chant, would it catch on? Would we all begin to sing the same ancient song as we marched as a unit toward some giant stone monument? The only place in Haddington Springs where I could imagine such a thing taking place was at the heart of the ravine. I shivered at the thought.

Just as we neared the edge of the parking lot, Dylan and Mrs. Mayer approached us. Everyone stopped and turned to them. "Hi, Diane," my mom called, the flame of her jarred tea light casting a jittery glow across her face. Mrs. Mayer and Dylan joined us. She said hello and gave all the adults a hug. This wasn't normal—our parents not only together, but hugging. It shouldn't have, but that struck me as the most surreal part of the evening. Dylan came and stood with Steph and I. He gave a subdued wave to us, and we returned the greeting, matching his energy level.

While the adults spoke, Steph, Dylan, and I made what I suppose was the thirteen-year-old version of small talk. There were no jokes, nothing about movies or video games or sports, and no plans were made. It felt wrong to have any enthusiasm. That night, as we stood on the border between park and parking lot with what seemed like our entire city moving around us, it felt like the end of a funeral.

"Where's Ken tonight?" I heard my mom ask during a lull. "Is he out with one of the search groups?"

"No," Mrs. Mayer replied. "No, he's at home." She hurried to tack on, "With Emily. She's got some sort of virus lingering from the bronchitis she had last month."

"Oh, poor thing," my mom said. "Well, it's a good idea keeping her in. It's chilly." Steph's dad and grandma agreed, and the group of them moved onto talking about the weather, showing us amateurs how small talk was really done.

The three of us stared up at the night sky, at the stars that had come out in full force to lend their twinkling light to the vigil. I thought about my cousin Megan. She went to school in Vancouver, but her parents lived in Calgary, and sometimes when she was done for the year, she'd come visit us on her drive home. I don't think it was her last visit, but maybe the one before that, when she brought me the UBC T-shirt. It was late at night and we were sitting on the deck in the backyard. Ours wasn't as grand as the Mayers' deck, but it was a nice enough spot. My parents, who rarely drank, had polished off most of a case between the two of them. From outside I could hear them in the kitchen, giggling and flirting as they clanked dishes into the dishwasher and tidied up from the barbecue we'd had earlier. Peter, who must have been three then, had already gone up to bed, and it was just Megan and I left outside. The bottle of beer she sipped from was probably her second of the evening, and never much of a drinker, she savoured it like it was the last of its kind. That night, we spent what seemed like forever stargazing. It was probably just a few minutes, but it's easy to think in forevers when you're staring up at the stars. I remember Megan telling me how lucky we were to live in a small place like Haddington Springs, because in big cities like Calgary and Vancouver, you're lucky to see half as many stars on any given night.

The smoke twisting out of Dylan's Mason jar writhed like a snake being charmed from a basket. He made a goofy, stunned face at the drifting smoke, like his mind had been blown out with the flame. His expression was all it took for me to come out of vigil mode for about two seconds.

"Way to go, numbnuts," I whispered so that none of the adults could hear me. "Not even that flame can stand to hang out with you."

Dylan's mouth curved into a grin. He had a comeback loaded and ready to go, but I'll never know what it was. Because just as he went to speak, I noticed Steph look past me, her face a blend of sadness and uncertainty, causing Dylan and I to stop what we hadn't really started yet. When I turned, I immediately met eyes with Kyle Hillerman, who was passing by. He was heading toward the parking lot with his mom. Up close, she was even more ghostly than she had been standing next to the mayor. Kyle nodded at me in recognition, then turned away, embarrassed, which made me feel embarrassed, so I looked away too.

"Kyle, we're so sorry," Steph finally said, holding her hands out in front of her, fingers laced tightly together around her Mason jar.

"Thanks." Kyle didn't look at her when he replied.

"And I know she'll come back," Steph said after a moment, her voice a little louder this time. Snared by Steph's words, Barb

Hillerman, the phantom mother, stopped walking. She didn't say anything in response, just turned to Steph with pained eyes, as if her hopeful words were some sort of unthinkably cruel attack.

Steph stammered.

Noticing his daughter struggling and the fact that Kyle and his mom were standing close by, Bruce walked over to the Hillermans. "Hey, Barb. Kyle."

Kyle's mom nodded at Bruce, who placed his hand on her shoulder. The muscles of his hand flexed slightly as he gave her what must have been the lightest squeeze a man of his stature was capable of. "Anything you need . . ." He left the words hanging, and that must have been the right thing to do, because she nodded at that too. Barb Hillerman then closed her eyes. She closed them tightly, the way you do when you're watching a horror movie and you need to make sure that there's no cracks for anything to sneak in through. The only difference, I thought as I watched her tilt her head back, probably trying to stifle the progress of oncoming tears, was that Barb Hillerman wasn't watching a horror movie. She was in one. Closing your eyes doesn't do anything when you're in one.

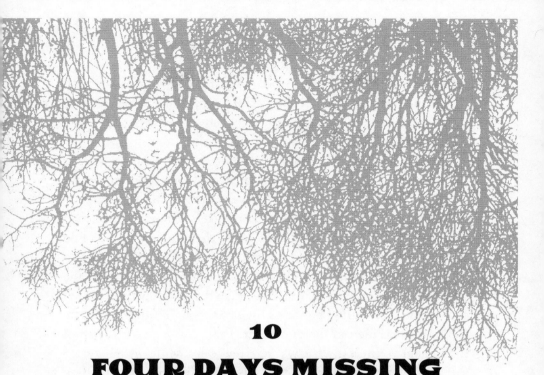

10

FOUR DAYS MISSING

THE QUESTION OF WHETHER OR NOT CATHERINE WAS ALIVE MUST HAVE been on everybody's mind since day one, but the first time I heard it posed was on the news. Trish Nadel—her bright, commanding eyes staring holes through the camera lens—was the one who first asked it.

"As the search continues, we hope and pray that Catherine Hillerman is returned to her family alive and well. We'll be right back after this."

Watching the nightly news had become routine. And despite the grim circumstances, I have to admit I enjoyed the routine on some level. My mom had stopped picking up even occasional shifts at work, so every night her, my dad, and I would watch together after dinner. They'd both drink iced tea, and I'd drink a monster of my own design, the Choco-Volcano: one cup of milk with three tablespoons of hot chocolate powder, unstirred. That was key: you couldn't stir it, you had to eat the clods of powder as you encountered them while sipping, which meant at least two or three coughing fits per Volcano. The three of us would watch the news start to finish, while Peter wandered in and out of the room, asking at nearly every commercial break how many minutes were left of what he called "the most boring show ever."

By day four, when Trish Nadel dropped those two rattling duos "hope and pray" and "alive and well" on every living room in the city, very little new information had been uncovered. But that's not to say there wasn't anything to report. For starters, extended Hillerman family from out of province had pooled their money and offered up a reward of ten thousand dollars for any information that led to Catherine's return. And more than one witness had called the hotline to report seeing a mysterious man driving down the stretch of Wyckham Road that bordered the ravine roughly an hour before Catherine was seen in the same spot. There was a police sketch of this person of interest, as he was referred to—a white male between the ages of twenty-five and thirty-five, medium build, dark hair, stubble—but the drawing looked like a rough draft awaiting finer details. The description of his car was as murky: a silver Ford Escort or Chevy Cavalier with either Alberta or BC plates, depending on who you asked.

Dad was continuing to help with the search. After the evening news he'd drive down to Memorial Park and, under the unblinking eyes of the Eternal Sentry, would meet up with the other volunteers. From there, a small team of officers would divvy them into groups of ten or so and assign each group an area to sweep. Most groups worked inside the city, but Haddington Springs was only so big, so some of the groups were sent to places on the fringes of the city limits, like McIntee River, which sliced through the southwest corner like an X-ACTO cut made with shaky hands. My dad said that he'd seen Detectives Purser and Hennig at Memorial Park a couple times, but they weren't part of any particular search group. "They probably drift back and forth, overseeing everything," he told me when I asked why they were there. "It's their show. They've gotta run it."

Steph, Dylan, and I would speculate too.

If she fell into the river, she'd be dead by now, obviously. You think she's been treading water this whole time?

She could be in another city by now. Another country.

What if she's close by but she's hidden? Chained up in someone's basement or something?

Steph had the most insight when it came to trying to piece it all together. She had been raised on true crime TV, and her *Nancy Drew* novels had an entire shelf, packed two deep, dedicated to them. I'd been given a guided tour of the collection. A chunk of them, the old hardcovers with vertical cracks running down their faded yellow spines, were her mother's when she was a girl. Her dad bought her the new ones. Their spines were soft, and the Nancys painted on the covers looked less wholesome teen detective and more hot university student. Steph would never admit to this, but the way her eyes would light up when we'd toss around theories about Catherine there was no hiding it: she thought we might be able to figure the whole thing out. Crack the case. A Nancy Drew and Hardy Boys team up, if you were able to buy Dylan and me as the Hardys, that is. Maybe the low-rent version.

On the news, Police Chief Kitrosser was encouraging kids under twelve to stay inside. Kids over twelve were told to travel in groups whenever they left the house without an adult. By day five, our parents allowed us to spend time outside of our homes, but they demanded we stay together. And they'd organized rides so none of us would be the odd one out, walking the last few blocks home alone.

My mom drove us that day. She picked Steph up and took us both to Dylan's. Bruce—probably realizing that Steph was in danger of going stir-crazy being at home with Jeremy all day, every day—pawned the kid off on their grandma to let his daughter get a breather.

From Dylan's house, the three of us left for Saint Phillip's. And it had to be Saint Phillip's, or some other wide-open public space. All five of the parents we had between the three of us made us promise that.

Dylan wasn't ready when Steph and I got there, so her and I had to wait in the foyer while he rummaged through the laundry room in search of socks. In the few minutes it took him, I got the sense that Mr. Mayer wanted to change our minds about going out. He had taken the day off work because, the way Dylan told it on the phone, between a sick kid (Emily's virus wasn't getting any better) and all the Catherine Hillerman stuff going on, Mrs. Mayer was within spitting distance of a full-blown meltdown and needed some relief.

"Dylan, did you show your friends the new game you got?" Mr. Mayer asked as Dylan pulled his mismatched socks on and rushed to tie his Reebok Pumps. He was referring to *Turok: Dinosaur Hunter*, which he'd bought for his son on a whim on the way home from work a couple days earlier.

"I'll show them later. And it's one-player anyway," Dylan said, already opening the front door. We got out of there before Mr. Mayer had time to make another transparent attempt to keep us indoors.

Everyone was in favour of a quick stop at Perry's Pantry on the way to Saint Phillip's. Steph opted for her usual bag of five-cent candies. Whenever you bought five-cent candies at Perry's, the guy who worked the register (everyone called him Perry, but we really had no idea if that was his name—or if there even *was* a Perry?) would take a small metal tray out from under the counter, pour out the contents of your miniature plastic bag, and count each individual candy with a pair of tongs to confirm that when you said a dollar twenty-five, you didn't actually mean a dollar thirty. He was always pleasant about it, but it was an odd thing to do. We figured he must have been burned *really* bad once. How many five-cent candies do you have to lose before your business implodes?

Dylan, being Dylan, went big: Cool Ranch Doritos (something savoury), a king-size Mars bar (something sweet), and a litre of Barq's Root Beer (his version of a palate cleanser). I had opted for Cherry Blasters and a Coke, the ghosts of canker sores past coming back to haunt me.

That afternoon, day five, was when I first noticed it. All those eyes staring at us from the windows of houses, from moving cars, and the persistent glances of people walking down the street.

Dylan radiated anxiety. "The hell, man?" he said. "Look at them. Why are they fucking staring at us?"

"They're probably concerned," Steph said, her candy bag twirling in her hand.

Dylan shook his head, took a bite of his Mars bar, and snickered like Steph's reply was the most ridiculous thing he'd ever heard. "They're not *concerned*," he said as he chewed, the thick texture of the Mars bar causing his cement mixer mouth to work twice as hard to get the words through. "They think we *did* something."

"*What?*" It was Steph's turn for a laugh now. "You think they think *we* kidnapped Catherine Hillerman? Why? So we could, like, finally play two-on-two soccer in our secret underground stadium without having to invite *Jeremy?*"

Dylan didn't have anything to say to that, at least not anything verbal, anything beyond rolling his head back and closing his eyes like he was in pain. The gesture was what he did when the person he was talking to Just. Didn't. Get It. His noticeable irritation didn't stop Steph from enjoying her jab, though. For the rest of that block, the only sounds made between the three of us were smacky chewing noises as we worked through our candy—my Cherry Blasters, so sugary they tasted like TV static—and Steph's soft laughter. There were few people who appreciated a good Steph joke more than Steph herself.

It was overcast that morning, and the faintest chill hung in the air. Not a cool day, but one of those reminders you get every now and then in late August that September is waiting eagerly to tag in.

As we neared the entrance, Steph tossed her ball over the chain-link fence. If, before she did this, Dylan or I had turned our heads slightly to the left, in the direction of the small asphalt basketball court outside the school's back doors, we would have screamed for her to hang onto the ball, and then all three of us would have turned and hauled ass. But we didn't, and so just as the ball rolled to a stop, it was booted back toward us courtesy of nobody's favourite teenage caveman, Louis Duss. We all jumped as the ball, which seemed to be travelling at roughly the speed of a comet, crashed into the fence in front of us, causing the metal to quake.

"Free ball! Fuck yeah!" Connor hollered. His wide-leg jeans somehow caused no wind resistance and didn't seem to slow him down at all as he ran to catch up with his friend.

Louis—in his frumpy Ecko hoodie that appropriately had the silhouette of a rhino on it—charged at the ball as it rebounded towards him. He made like he was going to boot the ball again, and Steph, Dylan, and I, all fearing that this time the comet would blast clear through the fence and turn us to dust, braced for impact. Instinctively, I turned my head away and held my hands out in front of me. I still didn't have new glasses to protect, but there was something to be said for keeping my face out of harm's way.

"Psych!"

With my one squinting eye, I saw Louis stop just shy of making contact with the ball. He flipped us all the bird and bent down and picked up Steph's most prized possession. He flashed his demon grin at us. "Happy birthday to me," he said.

Connor caught up with him a moment later, and Louis tossed the ball to his friend. Having worked up a sweat, he took off his hoodie to reveal his prized bouncer T-shirt. A Calgary transplant, Louis had been given the shirt by his dad, who apparently used to work the doors in a strip club in the city. Louis had proudly rocked the hand-me-down at school many times, and used to tell people that if you got close enough you could still "smell the snatch." This came to an end the day he said the vulgar line within earshot of our principal, who proceeded to forbid him from ever wearing the shirt at school again.

"So, shouldn't you guys be inside where it's safe?" Connor asked, tossing the ball in the air and catching it. "I hear there's a pedo on the loose. He's looking for defenceless, little kid victims, so the three of you are in serious danger of getting kidnapped and boned to death out here."

"They don't *know* it's a pedo," Steph said.

Connor hung onto the ball. He smirked at Louis, then turned to Steph. "You sure about that, Kristi Yamaguchi?"

"First off," Steph began, accentuating her point with a raised middle finger, "Kristi Yamaguchi is Japanese. I'm part Chinese. Don't be ignorant. Second off," her lone middle was then joined by an index, "Yes, I'm sure. They would have said so on the news. The only new lead they have is the man on Wyckham Road. They never said anything about a pedo."

"Wow. Thanks for that," Connor said. "But they don't tell you everything on the news. You ever consider that? That there's people who might know more than you? Like me, for example." He raised his eyebrows, smiled, and poked his tongue between his teeth, turning into a demented gargoyle for a second before tossing the ball back to Louis. "Don't believe me?"

"No," Steph said. "Somehow I don't."

Connor walked over to us, stopping a few feet from the fence that, thankfully, stood between us and him. The scenario reminded me of the Timber Wolf enclosure at the Calgary Zoo. How on a school field trip, one of the fearsome canines took notice of me and stalked right up to the barrier. And it took a second to click, but when I realized only a wall and a short distance separated us as we stared at each other and breathed the same air . . . well, it was kind of a terrifying feeling.

"What if I told you I talked to the cops?" Connor said.

A feeling of unease surged in my chest as I recalled Dylan's words with the detectives. *They're older, and they're kind of assholes.* Without turning my head, I shifted my eyes toward Dylan. His fists clenched, his posture rigid, he'd frozen where he stood, placed in a state of suspended anticipation by Connor's remark.

Steph, lured by intrigue and unaware that Dylan had pointed the finger, said, "What? Are you kidding? Why would the cops talk to *you*?"

"They talked to me too," Louis called from behind Connor. "My dad was fuckin' pissed."

Ignoring his friend, Connor spoke. "They thought we knew something," he said, shrugging. "We saw Catherine and her faggot brother at the theatre. Gave him a hard time because, well, because he was hanging out with his fuckin' baby sister." Connor shrewdly glanced at me, gestured with his chin. I knew what was coming, and felt my face flush. "You know how he's always doing that, don't you, Daredevil?"

"Daredevil? I thought we decided his name was Errand Bitch," Louis said.

Steph half-turned to me. "What are they talking about?" she asked.

"I don't know," I lied.

Connor waited a moment to see if I'd spill. When it became clear I was staying mute, he continued with his story about seeing Kyle and Catherine at the mall. "We said some shit to him, and he got all pouty and stormed off. He"—Connor paused, shook his head, giggled—"he was all whiny, and when he ran away from us, he was holding her *hand*. It's like, you do stuff like that, you're asking me to make fun of you. So, two detectives came by my house and Louis's house the next morning, asked us a bunch of questions."

"My dad had to come home from work," Louis, chimed in. Then, doubling down in case no one had heard him earlier, added, "He was *so* fuckin' pissed."

Connor shook his head. "So, Kyle, baby that he is, obviously snitched. I was thinking of kicking his ass next time I saw him, but you know what? I actually kind of feel sorry for him, because his best friend is gone."

He stood staring at us, like he was expecting something. Time dripped like molasses for a few long seconds, then Steph finally broke the long, unnerving silence: "Could I have my ball back, please?"

Connor screwed up his face like he was giving the matter deep thought. "Sure," he beamed. He tossed the ball underhand, and for a sliver of a second, I thought we were going to get it back and walk away scot-free. But then he added, "Oops," and jumped to catch the ball mid-air, before tossing it behind him.

"*Fuck*," Steph muttered, as Louis, hysterical, ran at the ball and kicked it to the far end of the field, leaving us still standing on the other side of the fence.

We watched them for a bit, hoping that our understated reactions would leave them bored, and that they'd ditch the ball (they surely wouldn't return it, but ditching wasn't beyond the realm of possibility) and move on, probably to torturing a small animal or pissing down a playground slide. Something like that. For a good minute, the two of them booted the ball back and forth, the power of their kicks producing taut thuds that we never got when we kicked it. Every couple of passes, Louis would turn his demon grin at us, while Connor, the more composed sadist of the pair, carried on without so much as acknowledging our existence.

Deciding that his regular old monster kicks weren't getting the necessary reaction out of us, Louis picked up the ball and drop-kicked it to Connor. "Happy birthday to *me!*" he shouted as the ball arced through the air, this time higher than it had any time before.

That did it for Steph. She sighed, muttered, "Dicks" under her breath, and began walking to the gap in the fence. On instinct—certainly not self-preservation, but it must have been *some* instinct—Dylan and I followed.

Connor and Louis stopped the second we, the fresh meat, stepped into their cage. They approached slowly, like our entering was too good to be true, Connor dribbling the ball as he walked, his feet moving in sloppy, exaggerated motions. "I don't know what your problem is," he said. "Sharing is caring. Don't you remember that from kindergarten?"

Steph didn't reply. Just glared at the two of them with a level of intensity that suggested she was gifting them each a telekinetic aneurysm.

"Or, hey, here's an idea," Connor said. "What if we all play together? We'll even make it easy. Us two versus you three. That's fair."

"No," Steph said. "We don't want to play with you guys. I just want my ball—my property—back." Her words had sharp tips, but they only served to encourage the pair.

"Do you have a boyfriend?" Connor asked. The way he said it, all smug, his eyes closing halfway, made my skin crawl. "And I don't mean one of these homos. A penis is required to be considered a boy."

"Look, we just want the ball back," Dylan said.

Of the three of us, Dylan was their target of choice at school, and I could only imagine what it took for him to muster up the courage to speak those words. Feeling like I should say something, I offered my best support. "Yeah, come on, guys," I said, the words coming out even flimsier than I knew they would.

Connor winced. "God, you sound like such a little queer. If that's the best you can do—fuck. We should probably keep this ball as a favour, that way you can go pursue hopscotch or some shit."

"Give the ball back." Steph's voice had a spark to it now, metal dragged across concrete.

"But it's my birthday," Louis replied, in a mock-pouty voice. "Don't you want me to have a happy birthday?"

Steph, I'm sure, had something to say to that. Standing right next to her, I could almost hear the drip as her small reserve of snowball patience melted to a puddle. I waited for her to lose it and rush at the wolves in their own cage. But she never had the chance to, because what happened instead was that Dylan—my oldest friend who, at school, handed over whatever was being demanded of him by these two goons time and time again—issued our death warrants.

"Do failed abortions celebrate birthdays?"

During the silence that followed—which lasted somewhere between two seconds and two lifetimes—the world's gravity dial spun to eleven, and everyone but Dylan's jaw dropped to the not-quite-freshly-cut grass. Steph, Connor, and I flicked our eyes back and forth at Dylan and Louis, waiting. It seemed that, despite their heft, my friend's words were taking their time to sink into the tofu-y crevices of Louis's brain. But you could tell when they hit with a thud, like an anchor smacking the floor of the ocean.

And then the sound of the world filtered back in, as Louis growled, "I'm going to kill you." He said this in a way that was so matter-of-fact you'd have to have a screw loose not to believe him. "I'm going . . ." He started to repeat himself, but shook his head. He then tossed the ball in front of himself and booted it right at Dylan. I saw Dylan's hands reach to cover his nuts, but too late. The force of the blow sent him flying backwards, where he landed flat on his ass, his hands cradling his bits, his face a mix of pain and shock.

Steph gasped. I *think* I said something.

Wanting to get in on the action, Connor picked up the ball. He tossed it in front of himself, the same way his friend had just seconds before. The difference this time was that Dylan's face was now at the same level that his nuts had been moments earlier. Connor's swinging foot met the ball, and I wondered if I'd have to shoulder the burden of explaining the decapitation of their son to Mr. and Mrs. Mayer.

But then there was Steph. In the instant before the ball made contact with Dylan's head, she got there. My mind raced back to science class, where Mrs. Clyne taught us about Isaac Newton. And I think I decided then and there to never again ask my teachers, *When are we gonna use this stuff in real life?* Because Isaac Newton and his laws were in motion right in front of me.

Every action has an equal and opposite reaction.

Yes, Mr. Newton, it sure does.

Steph, her slender leg outstretched, reached the ball with her foot, sending her most prized possession rocketing straight into Connor's face. Having recently experienced the force of one of Steph's kicks, I had an idea of the pain he felt. His head whipped back, the ball ricocheting off his nose. And, just as it had with me, the gusher started immediately.

"Fuuuuuuuck . . ." he groaned, cupping his beak, blood leaking from between his fingers.

"Bitch!" Louis yelled.

"Go!" I shouted.

Realizing that, cracked nuts or not, we had maybe two seconds to get moving, Dylan shot to his feet, and the three of us broke into a lunatic stride toward the opening in the fence.

We hadn't made it far before Louis called for pursuit. "Come on, man!" he shouted to his bloodied friend. "Let's go! Let's get 'em! Don't be a pussy!"

The sound of them huffing and puffing—in Connor's case, huffing, puffing, and wetly sniffling—reached my ears as I cleared the opening, just a few paces behind Steph, and a few more in front of Dylan. We ran onto the street and charged up the block, toward the four-way stop where Walnut Drive met Wyckham Road. I didn't dare look back. I kept my eyes on what was immediately in front of me: the intersection, Steph's bouncing hair, hopefully a long life that ended in me dying painlessly in my sleep just after my hundredth birthday. Behind me I heard the scrape of loose gravel.

"Shit!" Dylan yelled.

I turned to look. Dylan had tumbled as he rounded the corner, landing on his knees near the curb. He started to examine the damage, but I stopped him. We didn't have time. Connor and Louis, bounding after us with more grace than you'd expect from cavemen, were closer than I thought. I grabbed Dylan by the wrist, catching a quick peek of one of his bloodied kneecaps, and yanked him to his feet. "Fucking *go!*" I screeched.

He limped for his first few strides, but then cut back into a full-on run. Steph, who was now half a block ahead of us, was jogging backwards, watching. Once she saw that we were on track again, she turned back around and resumed her sprint. A stitch knifed at my side. The saliva in my mouth grew thick and stringy. I spat. Some of it hit the lawn to my right, some of it ended up on my shoulder.

"You faggots might as well just stop!" Louis called, his voice close enough to produce chills. "We might even go easy on you!" His lie pushed us further. I forced my legs to move warp speed, causing my side stitch to press deeper. The staccato gasps of Dylan's breath started doing double time as the slap of his Reeboks quickened. If only he'd had the foresight to give them a few quick pumps before all this, I thought. Up ahead, Steph was closing in on the next intersection. I didn't know where she was running to or, really, if there was a destination at all, but as she neared the next four-way it occurred to me that she had three options: she could turn right and head down the next street, which was Wendell, so more houses; she could turn left on Wendell, but crossing the street seemed like it would allow Connor and Louis to get too close; or she could keep going straight, bypassing Wendell and continuing on Wyckham, taking us to where the ravine lived.

She didn't slow as she approached the stop sign. Left? Right? Straight? Left? Right? *Straight.* Dylan and I crossed behind her, still a short distance back. As we hopped onto the sidewalk, I felt the pangs of exhaustion setting in and questioned how much longer we could do this. I pushed on, but envisioned myself collapsing somewhere near the end of the block, where, no doubt, Louis and Connor would swarm on me, beat me, and probably eat me, leaving only my head to keep as a trophy.

Then: *"Dude!"* Connor, his voice wet and nasally from the blow from Steph's ball. Tires screeched. A car horn blared. We all turned and saw the pair of them standing in the street in front of a red hatchback. Both the driver and passenger glared at the two boys, as Connor and Louis, seemingly too stunned to move, just stood there. The driver's window slid down and the man behind the wheel poked his head out. *"What the hell is wrong with you?"*

Connor, his shirt stained with blood, stared down at the ground. Louis, on the other hand, looked the man dead in the eyes. But neither spoke.

The man held his hand out the window, his thumb and pointer almost touching in a pinch. "That close," he said. "You get that? You were *that* close to being run over."

A hand on my elbow startled me. Steph. "Now would be a good time to sneak away," she whispered.

"Sneak where?" I asked.

Steph bit her lower lip and took in our surroundings. Dylan hustled over and stood with us. His knees were both scraped up. One of them wasn't dripping much but it looked like it stung like hell. The other had a few pieces of gravel stuck in it, and a thin trail of blood had worked its way down to his sock. He noticed I was staring, but before he took a look for himself, Steph spoke.

"The ravine," she said.

"The—are you kidding?" Dylan stammered.

"No."

"But we're not supposed to go anywhere near there."

"I know, Dylan, but what else do we do? You think this guy," she pointed at the hatchback, where the driver was in the midst of lecturing Louis and Connor on road safety, "is going to stick around much longer? We need to go now."

"What about your ball?" I asked.

"We need to go, *now*."

With that, she turned and walked through the trees that bordered the ravine, vanishing, it seemed, the second the threshold was crossed. I looked at Dylan, who met me with anxious eyes, and shrugged. He took one quick look at the exchange happening in the intersection. "Fuck it," he muttered, and went in too.

What choice did I have?

11

THE BRANCHES OF THE RAVINE'S SENTINEL TREES STRETCHED WILDLY IN every direction. They wrapped and twisted around each other, becoming entangled, which made the forest permanently shaded and noticeably cooler than the world outside it. The ravine had its own atmosphere. As I weaved my way between the trees, trying to keep up with Steph and Dylan a short distance in front of me, I could feel hives developing on my ankles and calves from the high grass and handsy branches brushing against them. I stumbled down the incline, over protruding roots and uneven ground, my feet sinking into patches of soft moss.

There were a number of paved paths throughout the ravine. They all snaked and sloped through the field around the river that was at the heart of the ravine, where they all intersected. We were far from any path, though. Knowing that our would-be execution-ers were probably done being chewed out by the driver, we rushed through the thick as quickly as we could, doing our best not to let any head-level branches kebab our eyeballs. I figured we'd either find our way to one of the paths or we would find a good spot among the trees to hide out for a bit.

I think that if we'd fled into the ravine at any other time, it would have felt like a haven. Mysterious, yes. Creepy? More than a little. But *mostly* safe. Any other time, yes, but this time, when we'd all been specifically told to stay away, and with all the talk about pedos and child killers floating around, it felt like we had traded one peril for another. *Had it happened here?* It seemed to me that this would be the perfect place for someone to disappear. But did Catherine set foot in these woods at all? Was she lured in, perhaps by the mysterious man depicted in the police sketch on the news? The man who somehow looked like almost anyone and almost no one at the same time—did he get her here? Or did he nab her off the street right outside the forest, dragging her kicking and screaming into that Ford Escort that was also a Chevy Cavalier and then off to God knows where to do God knows what? Twenty-five to thirty-five, medium build, dark hair, stubble. Had anyone really seen him at all? As I staggered on, I imagined the 2-D mystery man reaching out from behind each tree and dragging me away, one filthy hand clamped over my mouth to keep me quiet as my friends continued forward, oblivious. I wondered if maybe he wasn't a man at all. Maybe the thing that got Catherine was just a shadowy humanoid shape, a *thing* that haunted the ravine. Or was a part of it.

But would he—*it?*—want me? A thirteen-year-old boy? Feelings of relief and shame poured in, one just a little behind the other. Relief that somehow—and I didn't quite understand how—I was safer than someone like Catherine Hillerman. And shame for feeling relief at such a selfish thought.

Steph's voice brought me back to the moment. "Earth to Robin. You still with us?"

"Huh?"

"I said, we're gonna stay here for a bit, okay?" She and Dylan stood a little bit ahead of me in a small open patch within the forest.

"Yeah," I said, stepping sideways between two trees to join the two of them.

The area was much too small to be considered a clearing. Dylan and Steph took a seat on the softening remains of a fallen tree trunk that lay across the little shaded patch. I took a seat on the end, at the same time swatting at a mosquito taking a drink from the back of my neck, its cassette motor whine sounding near my ear as it left. The trunk looked like it had fallen long ago, and its smoothness told me we weren't the first to use it as a bench. We were surrounded by a number of skinny trees that stood in a circle around their larger fallen brother. In some spots, the grass and bramble had been trampled down by the feet of other visitors. I squinted and scanned the ground for empty bottles and condom wrappers, staples that no trip to the ravine was complete without, but I didn't spot anything, which was strange. Maybe the groups looking for Catherine had tidied while searching.

"Fuck. My nuts, man. And my *kneeees*. They sting like *hell*." Dylan bent forward and got a close-up of the damage from his fall. He made a cringing noise then looked over to Steph and I. "There's gravel in one of my knees. Like, actually *in* there."

Steph leaned over to see. "Yick," she said, wincing.

Trusting the diagnosis of *Yick*, I opted not to take a peek.

"Maybe it's one of those things that isn't as bad as it looks," Steph told Dylan. "Like, you'll have to get the gravel out, which will be gross, but there's only a few pieces. Once it's out you've just got to put Polysporin on and it'll heal up."

Dylan nodded. "My mom has a Costco-sized tube of that stuff at home. When she took it out of the bag, Dad asked her if she knew something the rest of us didn't."

"I've never used Polysporin," I said.

Dylan turned to me. "*What?*"

"Never needed to," I told him. "I have a mutant healing factor." I shrugged offhandedly.

"Do you have adamantium claws too?" Dylan asked. "Because if you do, we could've used those a few minutes ago."

Steph raised her eyebrows into a curious arch. "If you have a mutant healing factor, was the nosebleed I gave you last week just for show?"

"Pretty much," I said.

"Speaking of nosebleeds—Steph, what a geyser!"

"I didn't mean to," Steph said, sounding defensive and genuinely concerned. "I was just trying to deflect the ball."

"Well, mission accomplished," I said.

Dylan burst into his Mickey Mouse laugh, and for a second he forgot about his skinned knees and, go figure, slapped them, before grimacing, which got Steph and I going. It was a luxury to be able to laugh after cheating death like that. We rode the wave a few moments before Steph raised her hands, then brought them down in a hushing motion. "They could be looking for us," she whispered through sputtering giggles. "*Shh*. You guys . . . seriously, we . . . need to keep it down."

It took Dylan and I a bit longer, but I was impressed that we were able to rein it in as quickly as we did. We stayed silent, listening to the forest, for sounds of our pursuers, out of their cage and into the wild. Hungry, hungry, hungry. A car from the street outside could barely be heard. Its engine noise filtered through the thick trees, making it seem farther away than it actually was. I stared into the forest, not the way we'd come in, but the other way, the way we were heading before we stopped. The woods seemed to get thicker the farther in you went.

Steph surveyed the ground around our bench.

"What are you looking for?" I asked her.

"Anything," she said, and I knew that she was thinking about the same thing I was trying not to. *Anything* meant clues of Catherine's disappearance. Evidence. Something that had been missed. I wondered if this was the downside of reading too many *Nancy Drew* novels: you thought if you just looked, clues would present themselves. Like they were elves or fairies that needed you to believe in them before they'd materialize.

Dylan took another look at his knees and gave a theatrical shudder. "How long do we have to wait here?" he whispered. "Asking for a friend who's worried about gangrene."

Steph looked at me, I shrugged, and she shrugged back. "Fifteen minutes?" she said.

"Okay, sure. But why fifteen minutes?"

She thought about it for a second, turning her head reflectively and tapping her pointer finger against her chin. "It was the first number that came to mind," she said.

That was reason enough as far as I was concerned.

The three of us sat on that dead, old tree trunk in relative silence for the first couple minutes. Then Dylan started it. The infectious laughter that comes from nowhere and only takes hold when you're not supposed to be laughing, like in church or during a school assembly. At first it was small and contained, but when I noticed it growing, I shoved my elbow into his ribs, which only made it worse. It spread, first to me, then to Steph, and went on long enough to get us all teary-eyed and, at least in my case, to leave me feeling like I'd almost drowned, but in a good way. When we finally got a hold of ourselves, fifteen minutes had passed and we agreed that it was safe enough to move. We headed back the way we came in, deciding that once we were near the edge of the forest, I'd poke my head out (Dylan had been a martyr and Steph had been a hero, the least I could do was be a scout) and make sure it was safe before we headed back to Dylan's house.

As we neared the boundary, warm rays of daylight from outside the ravine spotted my shirt and face. I turned and glanced at Steph and Dylan. Steph noticed me. She smirked, but then looked away, turning her focus to the trees surrounding her. Dylan kept his eyes on the ground in front of him, probably nervous about falling and further ruining his already shredded knees. During those last few strides in the forest surrounding the ravine, I wondered something that I don't think I'd ever wondered up until then. I wondered if friends like Dylan and Steph were the sort that a person got to keep for their whole life. Until the end.

12

THEY WERE ARGUING LOUDLY. WE COULD HEAR IT FROM THE FRONT WALK,
through the door. Dylan was pissed. To come home to *this*? In front
of your friends? After what we just went through? He didn't even
try to mask his frustration as he cut ahead of Steph and I and jogged
up the steps to his house. When he reached the top, he indicated
with a wave of his hand that he wanted us to wait, and then opened
the door a crack, allowing the argument to spill out at full volume
for about one second before he slipped through and quickly yanked
the door shut behind him. Steph and I exchanged a look. The arguing continued, and then the sound of Dylan's pleading voice joined
the mix. Once he said whatever his piece was, the voices of both
parents got louder, then suddenly stopped. A short silence followed
before I heard just Mrs. Mayer's voice. It was muffled and soft. In
my periphery, I noticed that Steph was doing the same thing as me:
staring at the front of the house expectantly, as if it were a theatre
screen and the snare drum hits of the 20th Century Fox intro had
just started up. When both parents started speaking again, I could
tell that they knew they had an audience. When they stopped after
a few moments, the sudden sound of footsteps came rolling toward
the front door, causing us to snap out of our gawking trance and try
to make it look as though we were in the middle of a conversation
and hadn't actually been listening in.

"No, totally, that sounds cool. I'll have to check that out," Steph
improvised. "What did you say the movie was called again?"

It took me longer than it should have to process the question
and realize that all I needed to do was name a movie—any movie,
really—for the charade to work. I clued in right as the door opened.
"Uh, *The Lion King*?"

Steph shot me a look of disbelief and confusion. I almost spoke
up to defend my rushed choice, but stopped myself when I realized
that doing so would compromise our already flimsy improv routine.

"Hey," Dylan said from the steps above us. "You guys can come in now." He muttered an unnecessary apology as he turned and sulked back into the house.

We got inside in time to hear Mr. Mayer's office door roll shut. The padding steps of Mrs. Mayer's feet followed. A soft swish across the kitchen linoleum, then a muted shuffle as she appeared at the end of the hall, walking toward us with a mug of coffee in her hand and what must have surely been a fake smile on her face. The counterfeit was pretty convincing though.

She stopped where the hall opened up. "Well," she said, "how was the great outdoors?"

Steph and I both gave brief and unspecific rave reviews. Dylan didn't say anything.

Mrs. Mayer's lips drew into a smile. "You're a tight-lipped bunch," she said, then sipped from her mug. She motioned with her head for us to come in. "I'll stay out of your hair if you want to play Nintendo or watch something. I'd invite you two to stick around for dinner, but with Emily the way she is, it's not the best idea."

"She's still not feeling well?" Steph asked.

Mrs. Mayer shook her head. "No. She's about the same."

Steph's gaze shifted from Mrs. Mayer to the top of the stairs, where Emily's room was. "At least she's getting lots of rest. My dad says when you've got a bad bug, sleep makes all the difference," Steph said.

"Yes, I think so too." She took another sip of her coffee and added, "Thanks for asking, sweetheart."

I had polite going for me, but Steph was always better at talking to adults, especially about real-life stuff like sickness. She knew how to listen and how to empathize in a way that seemed so far beyond her years. And she made it look so easy. The one time I asked her how she did it, she told me to read a book and called me a Troglodyte.

We kicked off our shoes and followed Dylan and Mrs. Mayer down the hall. When we reached the kitchen, she grabbed a half-full bag of pretzels from the cupboard and dropped it on the table.

She took one out and said, "I can't have these in the house. You three have your work cut out for you." Just as she was about to pop the pretzel in her mouth, her gaze fell on Dylan's knees. "Oh my God, Dylan—what happened?"

Dylan looked down as though he'd forgotten himself. "I took a spill," he said.

"I can see that." Mrs. Mayer crouched down to inspect the wounds. "This looks awful."

Steph opened her mouth to speak, but only got one syllable out before Dylan shot her a look.

"The ball went over the fence at Saint Phillip's. I chased it across the street, and tripped on the way back," Dylan told his mom.

Mrs. Mayer moved her face closer to her son's knees. They weren't really bleeding anymore. It was mostly just surface ooze that was taking its time drying. "This happened on the *street*? Please don't tell me you were running across the street without looking."

"I *wasn't*," Dylan insisted.

"Then how—" She was cut off by the sound of Emily coughing upstairs before she could notice that none of us had a soccer ball. Dry, hacking, it was the kind of cough you knew came from a raw, throbbing throat. Mrs. Mayer stood up. "I need to check on her, but as soon as I'm done I'm cleaning *that* for you."

With the kitchen to ourselves, the three of us huddled around the bag of pretzels like witches around a cauldron. Dylan took fist-fuls. I normally would've taken them from the bag in twos and threes, but with Steph there I felt I ought to match her pace, so it was one at a time for me. Dylan, a tangle of pretzel tusks protruding from his mouth, went and got a glass from the cupboard and poured himself some water from the Brita pitcher in the fridge. He gulped it all down in one go.

"Oh, man, good idea," I said, my hand covering my mouth. "I'll grab a glass, too."

Dylan came back to the table and grabbed some more pretzels. He paused as he brought them to his mouth. "You *know* where they are. Get it yourself."

Steph and I exchanged a quick glance. "I wasn't asking you to get one for me. I was just saying."

Dylan didn't bother to respond. He chomped away on pretzels and kept his eyes down. I walked to the cupboard, grabbed a glass, and took a second one out and held it up to Steph, who gave me a thumbs up. Then I filled them both and returned to the table. Steph mouthed *thanks*. No one spoke. We chewed and sipped.

The bag was nearly empty when Mrs. Mayer returned to the kitchen with her first-aid kit. "The doctor will see you now."

A nod from Dylan. He grabbed another pretzel and followed his mom out of the kitchen, leaving Steph and I behind.

After an appropriate amount of time had passed, Steph whispered, "That was kinda weird."

"No kidding. What the hell? I mean, I wasn't asking him to be my servant. I was just telling him I was *also* going to get a—"

Steph held a shushing finger to her lips and, with a nudge of her shoulder, gestured to Mr. Mayer's office door. I'd forgotten he was in there. Or that he was home at all. It was a Tuesday afternoon, and normally he didn't come home until five thirty at the earliest. Dylan had told us why he was there: Mrs. Mayer needed help with Emily before she went bonkers. It was totally reasonable, but Mr. Mayer being home on a Tuesday afternoon just felt plain off. It was like seeing a teacher outside of school, at a grocery store or something, wearing a baseball hat and jeans. It made sense, sure, but it wasn't what you were used to. I was very used to Mr. Mayer being at the house—it was, after all, *his* house—but only during certain hours, or on weekends, which had a different feel to them altogether.

Steph glanced at the glowing green digits on the oven clock. It was just after two. "Should we call your mom?"

I looked back to Mr. Mayer's office, then down the hall in the direction that Mrs. Mayer had taken Dylan. "We could."

"I mean, we don't have to, but . . . I don't know. Doesn't it feel kind of like we're intruding?" She whispered *intruding* like it was a four-letter word.

I thought about it for a moment, then nodded. "Yeah," I said. "Yeah, I think you're right. I'll call." As I crossed the kitchen toward the cordless on the counter, I remembered the last time I'd used the phone at the Mayer house, or *residence*, as Mr. Mayer had corrected. I lifted the phone from its cradle, but hesitated to press the talk button.

Noticing my pause and, no doubt, the nervous expression my face had melted into, Steph shot me a quizzical look.

I lowered my head, held up one finger, and tiptoed toward Mr. Mayer's office. The sliding door had been opened slightly. From where I stood, I could see part of his desk. Piles of papers—what must have been reports, bills, officey things like that—stacked neatly, a cup stuffed with pens and pencils, a Hawaii calendar tacked to the wall. But I didn't see Mr. Mayer. And before I pressed the talk button, which felt about as dangerous in that moment as the red button that triggers a nuke launch, I needed to see him and confirm that he wasn't on the phone. Parallel to the door, but keeping my distance from it, I inched a little farther along the carpet. All I needed was confirmation, and all that required was a glimpse.

The memory of looking into a room that I wasn't supposed to pushed its way to the front of my mind. That night—*the* night— when I stood in the dark upstairs hallway, staring at that barely open door. That void that Mrs. Mayer—bra, yes, shorts, yes, but more than anything: skin—had emerged from. Real or not, I'd been thinking about it often, replaying it over and over in my head at night. She'd taunt and haunt me, and she wouldn't go away until I did something about it. I'd imagined what Dylan would say if I told him. Those conversations never ended well. Even in my mind, my fantasy land where anything should've been possible, they never ended well. I supposed that in part this was because having such a conversation with *anyone* would be difficult, but lately with Dylan, it was as though any topic of discussion had the potential to set him off. I could never tell what would cause him to react.

The squeak of a chair from inside the office brought me back to my current espionage mission, but I didn't register it as what it was until a second or two after it happened, and by then it was too late. The sound the office door made when it slid open—rolling, clattering, loud—made me think of a world of gears and tracks and swinging metal bits, like the one the terrifying War Amps robot danced through in that commercial. Compared to everything else in the Mayer house—which, bayonet aside, was sleek and new—the door sounded ancient, and I nearly jumped out of my skin as it opened in front of me.

"Robin," Mr. Mayer said, as though confirming my name to himself. His reading glasses, which I only rarely saw him wear, rested on the bridge of his nose, and he had a couple days' worth of stubble dotting his face. It was next to nothing, really, but for a guy who was *always* clean-shaven, it may as well have been Gandalf's beard. Walking past me, he said, "Excuse me, bud."

I stepped aside and watched him go into the kitchen. He greeted Steph with a nod. "Miss Stephanie," he said in a tone that was significantly more playful than the one I'd gotten.

Steph returned a greeting.

Mr. Mayer pulled open a drawer and took out a small stack of papers, then adjusted his glasses and started flipping through them. "Your dad still liking things down at Shapland?"

"Yeah," Steph said. "I think so. He's been there since I was two, so I guess he must like it enough."

"He works hard," Mr. Mayer said. And there was something in his voice, maybe a fleck of pity, or something not far from it, that made me just a little bit angry at him.

When he found what he was looking for, he returned the rest of the stack to its drawer and headed back to his office. Just shy of the door, he stopped in his tracks as a flurry of rushing footsteps sounded from the staircase down the hall. A moment later, Dylan landed at the bottom of the stairs with a thud that caused dishes to rattle in their cupboards.

"Dad!" he called as he came into view, fresh fabric bandages stretched across both his kneecaps. "Dad, it's Emily!"

"What?" Mr. Mayer tossed the papers into the office with a carelessness I'd never seen from him. He rushed toward Dylan. "What's wrong?"

"She—Mom said we have to take her to the hospital. *Now*. She started coughing, but then she puked, and there was blood in it, and—"

Mr. Mayer pushed past his son and charged down the hall and up the stairs. Dylan turned and looked at Steph and I. His eyes were wide with panic. Steph stood in the corner, her hands cupped over her mouth. Seconds later came the sound of feet thudding down the stairs. Mrs. Mayer came down first. She flung open the door of the front closet, took out her runners, and and slipped into them, leaving the laces untied. "Let's go, Ken!" she called. Before she had finished saying his name, Mr. Mayer was making his way down the stairs too. My heart sunk. Cradled in his arms, her small face looking white as paper against her vibrant pink-and-purple pyjamas, was Emily. While her father manoeuvred his feet into his shoes, Emily turned and looked in our direction with half-lidded eyes. She looked so sick—so *out* of it—that I wonder if she saw us standing there at all.

Dylan went to his family. "I'm coming too," he said.

There was no argument from either parent. "Then get your shoes. Hurry," Mrs. Mayer said, fishing her keys out of her purse. When she noticed Steph and I walking towards them, she held up her hand, halting us, then took a breath and composed herself. "No," she said. "No, I'm sorry. You two will have to wait here until you're picked up. Just"—her eyes shifted frantically for a moment and then rested back on us—"just make yourselves at home."

We both nodded.

Dylan opened the door and Mr. Mayer walked out with Emily. "Dad," Dylan called, "should we call an ambulance?"

"No!" Mr. Mayer barked back. "We'll get to the hospital faster."

With that, Dylan left the house. Mrs. Mayer flung her purse over her shoulder. She thrust her hands into its open mouth. "Shit, shit, shit," she muttered. She dug around for a few seconds, then: "*There* it is," she took out a green-and-white Alberta Health card. Mrs. Mayer shot one last glance at Steph and I. We must have looked terrified, because before she left, she said, "Don't worry, she'll be fine." I don't know how she managed to sound as calm as she did just then, but her words were so reassuring that, for a second, it felt as though Steph and I were the ones she was really worried about.

"Okay." I nodded. Because I believed her.

× × ×

We took a seat in the living room, me on the couch and Steph in the cushy reading chair in the corner. I picked up the TV remote, pointed at it, shrugged. Steph looked at it for a second, then shook her head. She said, "Nah," and I felt like a dick for suggesting it in the first place. It wasn't the time for trash TV.

"Should you try calling your mom?" Steph asked, running her finger up and down the arm of the chair.

"Yeah."

After five rings, the answering machine clicked on, followed by my dad's voice. Whenever I heard the recording, which wasn't very often, I remembered the night he taped it a few years back. My mom, Peter, and I couldn't stop laughing. He had written something like six different scripts for himself, and the whole process—rehearsals, edits, voting (we all agreed it should come down to majority rule since the message represented all of us), and take after take of recording—went on for something like an hour. The final version was the simplest: "Hi, you've reached the Murphys. We're can't come to the phone right now. You know what to do at the beep."

"She's not home," I told Steph from the kitchen.

Steph got up from her chair and walked over to where I stood by the phone cradle, stopping right in front of me and crossing her arms. Our eyes met. Steph's eyes were dark and bottomless and looking right into them made my heart speed up. I turned my gaze to the floor and pretended to clear my throat. It was then I realized I was alone in a house with a girl, and that girl was one of my best friends, and I'd known her for so long that I hardly ever thought of her as a girl, but she was one, and maybe when I actually took a step back and thought about it, she was kind of a beautiful one too.

My eyes still grounded, I faked another throat clearing—actually pronouncing *ahem!*—then took a step back and looked at Steph again. She was smiling now.

"I can try again in a bit," I said.

Steph nodded. "Sure. If not, we could always wait until my dad gets home."

"Yeah," I said. "Or, really, we could just walk home. I mean, would it be that big of a—"

"We would get in *so* much shit if either of our parents found out we walked home. Like, I know we'd probably be fine, but if we got caught . . ."

We'd be grounded for life. And we'd already broken one promise today by going into the ravine. Though that was an act of self-preservation, so my conscience excused it. But if the two of us walked home from the Mayers, we'd be together for half of the way, but there was a stretch between Steph's house and mine. I could just imagine someone, like Vicki Donovan, who worked with Mom and lived on our block, spotting me while I walked alone down the street. She'd be the type to wait outside our house to catch my mom on the way in and tell her the news, and that'd be it for my freedom.

"All right," I said. "But what do we do in the mean time?"

Steph walked past me and into the hall. An idea had been sparked. "Let's look at the Evolution of Dylan," she said. She was referring to a series of wallet-sized school pictures in a frame shaped like an old school house. The frame sat on a small corner table that was also home to a bowl of potpourri and a family Christmas photo from a few years back, when Emily was just a toddler and before Adam had moved away for university. Dylan *hated* the Evolution of Dylan series, but Steph and I sure loved it. She snatched up the frame and took a seat on the small couch that sat against the wall in the front sitting room. Her laugh was already revving up when I took a seat next to her. There were spots for thirteen pictures in the frame. Her and I used to joke that the thirteenth slot allowed wiggle room for Dylan to fail one grade, but he was always quick to remind us that "there's a thing called kindergarten, dumbasses." We also used to joke about how much fun it would be to replace the first photo with a photo of a baby monkey from National Geographic and see how long it would take anyone to notice. But neither of us had the guts to actually follow through with that.

"Now," Steph said, "let's see if we can come up with an order of Dylans. From best Dylan to worst Dylan."

The next few minutes were spent debating the pros and cons of each iteration of Dylan. We both agreed that grade-one Dylan deserved the top spot because of the missing front teeth and clip-on bow tie combo. And kindergarten Dylan's buggy alien eyes and bowl cut earned him a high ranking too. The obvious last place spot went to grade-five Dylan, who Steph said looked like he had been forced to have his photo taken at gunpoint, and grade-seven Dylan's zipper polo shirt and failed attempt at a cool-guy look landed him near the bottom as well. There were a couple of final rankings that I argued with Steph over, not so much because I disagreed with her but because she got hilariously intense when you challenged her on something she was passionate about. Like the time I insisted that Nancy Drew's *Clue of the Broken Locket* was actually called *Mystery of the Smashed Locket*.

When I conceded to her final ranking (which only took her cocking her fist and ensuring me she was "honest-to-God not screwing around"), Steph returned the picture to its place on the table, shaking her head and muttering about me being a contrarian. When I asked her what that meant, she told me to read a damn book.

She lingered at the table for a moment, then she grabbed up the family Christmas photo and brought it over to the couch. "Poor Emily," she said to herself.

"I know," I said. "But, you know, they'll figure it out at the hospital. She'll be fine. I'm sure she will."

"How can you be sure?" she asked without looking up from the picture in her hands.

I didn't have a response. Not for Steph, who had probably heard that hollow comfort a dozen times when her mom lay in the hospital, tubes in her nose, IV in her arm, her bald head wrapped tight in the green-and-blue paisley bandanna that Steph now kept in her room. *She'll be fine. Don't you worry.*

"Which era of Dylan is in that photo?" I asked her.

"It looks like grade four."

The picture was taken in front of the Christmas tree at Edmunds Park, where they had a big fair every year on the weekend before Christmas. It was a pretty big deal in Haddington Springs. Most families in town went. Just looking at the photo made me crave the hot chocolate they sold at the stand right inside the gates. It had a layer of marshmallows on the surface and came with a hunk of cinnamon bark, and it is still the best hot chocolate I've ever tasted. Dad used to tell Peter and I that was because it came directly from the North Pole.

The family in the photo looked Kodak good. Even Adam, who was usually causing some kind of trouble, had a beaming smile on his face. It looked genuine. Christmas brought that out in people. My eyes moved to Mrs. Mayer and hovered over her for a moment and then, feeling the beginnings of something, I quickly moved my gaze elsewhere. Boner—AKA the last thing I needed while I was sitting next to Steph—averted.

In the photo, Mr. Mayer still had his beard, and in his arms, he held bundled-up little Emily, who appeared to be more snowsuit than little girl.

The resemblance between father and sons stood out. When it came to Dylan, I was used to seeing this. I'd spent so much time around him and his family that I could pick out the individual features he'd gotten from each parent. Most of his face was from his dad, but he had his mom's eyes. With Adam, who I hadn't seen in person for a while, the resemblance to Mr. Mayer was clear, but there wasn't much of his mother to be found in his face. He looked like a clone of his dad, the only noticeable difference his hair and eyebrows, which were a couple shades darker than Mr. Mayer's.

"Robin," Steph said, frowning at something that had just occurred to her. "What was with the nicknames Louis and Connor called you?"

I cleared my throat. "Daredevil?"

Steph nodded.

My answer arrived so quickly it surprised me. I wondered if it'd been hiding away in some forgotten corner without my knowing. "They were making fun of me being blind without my glasses. You know, like Daredevil from comics? He's blind. *So* clever, right?"

Steph nodded slowly. Her expression didn't change. "But, after Connor called you that, Louis said, 'I thought we decided his name was Errand Bitch.' How does that work with Daredevil? Those two names have nothing to—"

We both jumped at the shrill noise that came from right outside the door. It cut Steph off with a *creeeeeeeeak* that sounded like a pterodactyl death scream, and for a moment we both sat frozen, staring at each other with matching expressions of surprise. But then came the metallic clank, followed by the footsteps of a rushing mail carrier, and we both unthawed and fell back against the couch laughing.

"Jesus. Jumpy much?" Steph said, her hand resting on her chest, over her thudding heart.

"Holy shit. I had no idea what that was at first."

"Me neither." She tilted her head back, sighed. "We must still be wound up from earlier."

"Cheating death does that, I guess."

"Yeah, and come on, Mayers, spray some WD-40 on that thing. How is a mailbox that loud?"

We stood up from the couch at the same time. I picked up the Christmas photo and returned it to the corner table, and Steph began walking toward the front door.

"I guess the least we could do is bring in their mail," she said.

She opened the door and a look of confusion washed over her face. I hurried to join her at the door. The envelope hadn't been placed in the mailbox the way a mail carrier would deliver it. It was poking out from between the box and the lid like a tongue, and was scrunched with multiple folds. Steph plucked it out.

I locked the door after she closed it, and together we walked back to the couch and sat down on cushions that had our still-warm imprints waiting for us. Steph held the envelope out before her. It was the same basic white business envelope you'd see anywhere, but it didn't have any sort of address printed on it. No stamp either, or really any indication that it had been sent through Canada Post. All it had on it, written in messy block printing was: KENNY BOY/ ANDY.

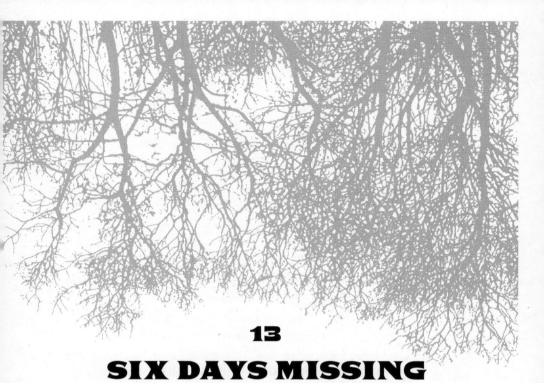

13

SIX DAYS MISSING

I'D NEVER BEEN INSIDE THE HILLERMANS' HOUSE BEFORE. A QUEASY FEEL- ing spread through me as we approached. I didn't want to go in there. I liked Kyle, but going over unannounced with my mom and an unsolicited mountain of food felt weird. Like we thought they needed charity, which I guess it was, but not in the same way a Christmas hamper is charity. No, this was much different. *Sorry the most vulnerable quarter of your family is missing. Here's a chicken casserole and a blueberry pie. You'll want to preheat your oven to 350 degrees* . . . This type of charity was in a galaxy of its own.

But the awkwardness mattered very little to me. Most of my attention was being pulled elsewhere. For what was the first time in my young life, there were too many shitty/weird/weirdly-shitty things happening at once, and I found myself having to push some things aside to make room for the other, needier things. It was a balancing act, and I'd never been very coordinated.

Pushed to the sidelines was the fear that someone else I knew was going to get kidnapped by the roving pedo child killer, who

I, like most people, was convinced was still prowling our streets looking for fresh meat. In my mind, he had now become a shadowy silhouette. He had no face, but he had bright yellow eyes and a crooked smile. A thing born of the ravine, and sent forth by it for some dark reason. This fear was still present, but it was no longer hogging the spotlight.

The same went for Louis and Connor, two guys who would assign extra beats for me if they knew I had the nerve to push them to the sidelines of my mind. I knew the two of them had probably come up with a hundred unique ways to torture and kill Dylan, Steph, and I for what we did at Saint Phillip's, but I couldn't delegate any more mental real estate to them. For now.

The third item that had been benched bothered me the most. Sitting next to the mysterious shadow man and the two bullies was little Catherine Hillerman. I still thought about her, her funny put-on accent, her purple cat dress, and her pigtails. I prayed for her at night. I prayed harder for her than I did anything else—health, forgiveness, the return to the way things were. I wished on entire constellations for her. But her being gone had started to feel normal. It's the kind of thing that should never, ever feel normal, but it did.

With this trio off to the sides, the Mayer family moved to the front.

Dylan, his parents shouting at one another. Their voices blasting through the closed door while Steph and I waited outside. His pleading with them to stop, to please just stop. And Emily, pale, coughing, groggy and limp in her father's arms as she was rushed to the hospital. *She puked, and there was blood in it . . .*

There was also the matter of the letter, or note, or whatever. And the way it had been delivered. Something about handling it felt . . . wrong. Inappropriate. Above our pay grade, as my dad would've said. After examining the envelope and tossing a couple of stupid theories around, Steph and I decided it would be best if we returned it to the mailbox. But when we left the Mayer house, I could tell Steph was still fixated on it. And her fixation was contagious.

The Mayers were still out when my mom came to pick us up from their house. And I hadn't heard from Dylan that night. When I went to call, my mom told me to give them space, and that Dylan would call me with an update as soon as he had one. And he would call, wouldn't he? Yes, of course he would. Maybe he was trying to call at that very moment and was instead talking to my dad, who'd barely had time to kick off his shoes after work before Mom pawned Peter on him and said she and I were going to ambush the Hillermans with food.

"I think this is them," Mom said, pointing at a townhouse. She pulled over in front of the neighbouring fence, squinted at the place, and nodded in affirmation. "Yeah," she said, "eighty-six, that's it."

There were a few apartment complexes in Saddler, but most of the homes were townhouses like the Hillermans': tall, skinny, bordered by either a chain-link or picket fence, and painted light blue, or beige, or some other bland colour. Lots of the houses had shingles that were so curled and crumbly it looked like you could scrape them off like frost on a windshield. I remember Mrs. Mayer calling the neighbourhood dumpy one time when we drove through there. I can't remember why we were driving, but Mr. Mayer, who was behind the wheel, had told her the neighbourhood looked nicer than he remembered it. "Lipstick on a pig," Mrs. Mayer had responded. "And I can say that, because I grew up here."

I joined my mom outside the car. "Can you grab the pie?" she asked, reaching into the back seat and removing the lid to her casserole to take a quick peek. She nodded in approval and put the lid back on. I grabbed the pie. "Careful, Robin. Don't tilt it, otherwise—"

"I know, I know."

"Well, if you knew you wouldn't have—"

"Mom, *please*," I said, louder and squeakier than I meant to. Out came cringy Kermit the Puberty Frog.

The Hillermans' fence had scabby spots, and the rust from a few of the nailheads had bled onto some of the boards. But it was in decent shape compared to many of their neighbours', which were mostly stripped of paint, or had missing pickets, making them look like a neglected set of teeth. Their gate had been propped open with a brick, an invitation, as if they had been expecting their missing daughter and sister to return at any moment and wanted to ensure that even the tiniest of obstructions had been cleared from her path.

At the top of the stairs, my mom took a deep breath and then, after hesitating a few seconds, pressed the doorbell. Its sharp *ding* could be heard from where we stood, and in what couldn't have been more than two seconds, hurried footsteps sounded from inside.

Barb Hillerman's gaze began on my mom's waist. She had been hoping for someone shorter to be waiting on the other side of her door. As her eyes moved up to meet my mom's—stopping on me for a second on their way—she put on a smile. She had a pretty smile, but it wasn't enough to hide her disappointment. She opened her mouth to say something. Nothing came out at first, but then she cleared her throat and said, "I'm sorry. Hello."

"Hi, Barb," my mom began. She looked down at the casserole in her hands, then back up at Barb. "I . . . I mean, *we* . . . " She didn't get any further than that. I couldn't see Mom's face, but the look on Barb's face told me what I was missing. Barb shut her eyes tightly and bowed her head. The beginnings of a whimper escaped her, but she cut it off quick, then exhaled, and looked back up at my mom. A tear wobbled in the corner of one of her eyes. It didn't fall. She wouldn't let it.

"No need for that just now," she said, composing herself. Then, with a faint laugh that sounded only a bit put on, she added, "I've been doing too much of that lately. If I lose any more fluid, they'll have to give me an IV."

My mom exhaled a trembly laugh. I almost laughed too, but my mouth wouldn't co-operate. My whole face felt frozen.

"You didn't have to do that," Barb said, gesturing at the dish in my mom's hand. Noticing the pie I was carrying, she added, "Oh, Lord. We've got out work cut out for us," then she stepped aside so we could enter.

Barb told us we could keep our shoes on, but neither of us did. As my mom bent down and unlaced her Keds, I stepped out of my Gazelles and swept them against the wall with one foot. When I looked up, I noticed Kyle was sitting on the stairs. He forced a brief smile and gave a wave in my general direction, like he was addressing someone just beyond me.

"Hey," I said.

"Hey."

Barb walked down the hall. "I was just about to make another pot of coffee," she said. My mom called after her. "Oh, Barb, I don't want you to go to any—"

"I'm not," Barb called back, her words rushed. "It's no trouble at all."

Mom placed her shoes against the wall next to mine. For a moment, she stared down the hall that Barb had just walked down, then she breathed deeply, composing herself, and turned to Kyle on the stairs. He looked away as her gaze fell on him, letting his eyes land on his lap. Something about the way he sat made me so sad. I didn't know if I'd ever seen someone look so ashamed. And someone who had no reason to be. God . . . it hurt to look at him, sitting there like that.

"Kyle," my mom said, resting a hand on his shoulder, "you're doing so great. You stay strong, okay?"

Kyle nodded without looking up. He muttered, "Mm hmm." His mouth, which I could just barely see, was clamped into a hard, straight line, like a stressed seam holding back far too much.

"And you better help eat this pie," my mom said to Kyle, adding a bit of a sparkle to her voice. "It came out too big."

Kyle exhaled a short laugh. It sounded like a relief. He sniffed deeply, then looked up to my mom, his eyes only a little glassy. "Yeah," he whispered, "I will."

The three of us walked down the hall together, Mom in the lead, Kyle and I trailing next to each other. I wanted to say something to him, but I had no idea what. The hallway felt longer than it looked. It was crammed and creaky. The walls were lined with framed photos. I'm sure they were all family pictures. I couldn't bring myself to look.

The scent of coffee hit me as I stepped into the kitchen. Barb was spooning grounds of Nescafé instant into the four mugs steaming on the counter. I did the math. Kyle and I were having coffee too. I'd only tried coffee once, and hated it. But that was a couple years ago, and besides, I'd always loved the smell, so maybe it was time to give it another chance.

"Smells delicious," my mom said, her arms crossed tightly, eyes drifting to the antique English tea tins that sat in a row on a shelf above the sink. Like most nurses, she was a proud caffeine addict, and I could recall a number of times she had ranted about the evils of instant coffee. *Imposter Roast*, she'd called it. But now clearly wasn't the time or the place to be picky.

Ribbons of steam floated from the mugs and mingled with one another in the air above. Barb shuffled over to the fridge, keeping her back to us the whole time. "Cream and sugar?"

"Yes, thanks. And I imagine the boys are a yes, too."

"Yeah," I said. Mom shot me a look. I got the idea fast. "Yes, *please*," I said, then added, "thank you," for good measure.

Cream and sugar were added and stirred into to every mug except Barb's, who took hers black. Barb handed my mom the third mug. "I'll leave the cream and sugar out if you . . . if you . . ." She couldn't finish. Her mug clattered against the counter, sending a spray of steaming hot coffee onto the white tile backsplash as she raised her hands to her face and began weeping.

"Oh, Barb," my mom said, setting her coffee down and putting her arm around the grieving woman's trembling shoulders, the corners of her words crumbling as she spoke.

"I can't . . . keep . . . this . . . up . . ." Barb whimpered in a shrill staccato.

From next to me, I heard Kyle begin to breathe heavily. Hearing him, Mom whipped around. "Robin, you and Kyle go outside," she said sternly. When I didn't respond, she added, "*Go.*"

And we went. Mugs in hand, through the mudroom and out the back door, which I shut on Barb's crying.

Kyle walked to the far end of the yard, where a tree stood with a knotted climbing rope dangling from one of its branches. There were a couple of plastic little kid chairs in front of the tree. They were both blue and looked like they had been outside for decades. He leaned against the tree trunk and gave the rope a swat. "Fuck," he muttered, really leaning into the *ck*, like the word was still sharp, still new to him. "Sorry, man."

"Oh. No. You don't have to be sorry. That's . . . Don't worry about it, really."

He closed his eyes and took a breath. For a moment I thought he was about to tear up, but when his eyes opened a second later, clear and, for the first time since I'd arrived, focused, I realized I was wrong. "If you guys showed up half an hour ago, you would've been here at the same time as the detectives."

"Yeah?" I said. "Hennig and Purser?"

Kyle shot me a sidelong glance. "You know them?"

"Yeah. They came and saw Dylan and me the morning after your sister . . . the morning after it happened."

Kyle sipped his coffee and nodded at the ground, looking kind of like he was doing an impression of an adult. "What did you tell them?" he asked.

It occurred to me that I maybe shouldn't tell Kyle about the specifics of our conversation with the detectives. That maybe I wasn't allowed to, or that some of the information might stress him out or somehow make things worse. But his stare had hooks at the end of it, and once they dug into me, I cracked.

His face showed no emotion while he listened to my account. I could only imagine what was bubbling below the surface. How close he'd been with his sister. Closer than most siblings I knew, including Peter and I. I told him about how Dylan and his mom were there for the questioning too, and so were my parents. How I told the detectives about running into him and Catherine outside the bathrooms, and Catherine's made-up accent, and that he was taking her to a movie. I told him they asked me more than once if I'd noticed anyone sketchy watching us, and how I hadn't. And I told him about what Dylan had said to the detectives before they left, how we'd seen Louis and Connor and how Dylan had said they were assholes.

"They *are* assholes," Kyle said when I finished. "And I—me and Catherine—we did run into them." He blinked, and his eyes came back a little glassy. "Robin, those guys are so fucking shitty. They . . ." He paused for a second, then shook his head and began again. "I messed up. They're shitty, but *I* messed up."

I stopped myself from asking him what he meant. I didn't know if I wanted to know. If I could handle it.

But eyes glinting with tears, he told me.

"They saw us waiting in line to buy snacks. She . . ." He smirked and shook his head, like he was watching the memory play out in front of him. ". . . She said she wanted Milk Duds. She always wanted Milk Duds. I used to tease her that the only reason she went to the movies was for Milk Duds. Connor and Louis, I heard them before I saw them. One of them—I'm not sure which—said, 'There's *another* faggot from our school.' Then the other one asked if there was a convention in town or something. They came over and stood next to us. They asked me what movie we were seeing, and I didn't answer. They asked again."

I noticed then that the mug in my hand kept tipping forward, almost to the point of spilling. I'd been clutching it so hard that it's handle had become slick with sweat. I tightened my grip on it even more to keep it in place. I felt so awful. About everything that'd happened at the mall. About everything that'd happened before it. Fucking Daredevil Robin. Errand Bitch Robin.

Kyle didn't seem to notice the anxiousness radiating from me as he continued his story. "I kept treating them like they were invisible, but Catherine, she spoke up. She . . . she's a bright kid. I told the detectives that. I told them that even though she probably doesn't know a lot of bad words, she could probably tell from their tone that they were assholes and just wanted them gone. So, Louis and Connor asked again, and she told them, 'My brother is taking me to *Air Bud*. Now please leave.' And those dicks, they just thought that was the funniest thing in the world. They started laughing like hyenas, and eventually . . . Robin, I got so *pissed*. I took Catherine's hand, and we walked off. They followed us for a bit, calling me a dipshit and queer and whatever. I didn't know where to go, so I took us into the first store I saw, the one closest to the theatre. Some clothing store."

"Cooke's," I said. "My dad goes there sometimes."

He stopped for a second, wiped his eyes on his bare arm, then took a sip of his coffee. "They followed us in there. I tried to ignore them, I pretended I was looking for something. You know how some teachers and parents tell you that bullies just want to get a reaction out of you? And how if you ignore them, they'll eventually go away? Well, that's bullshit. I kept trying to ignore them, but they only got worse. Next thing I know, Catherine is yelling at them. She's calling them dummies and jerk heads and all these little kid insults, which, of course, they find hilarious. Finally, the lady working there comes over, because they're being so loud. She tells them to get out or she'll call security, and one of them—I think it was Louis—he calls her a bitch. So she goes to the desk and picks up the phone and actually calls security, and the two of them run out, laughing their stupid heads off."

He kicked absently at the ground and stared off. The look on his face couldn't have been anything but pure disgust.

"After that," he continued, "well, they were gone, and Catherine obviously still wanted to go see the movie. But I was so pissed at them and I took it out on her. It was the second time this summer they'd given me shit, and I let it get to me." Tears flowed freely now, snot dripped from his nostrils. Kyle didn't let any of it interrupt his story. I could feel my hand grasping the mug's handle so hard it cramped now. "I went to the theatre and I bought her a ticket for the dog movie, and I bought a ticket for a different movie for myself. I don't even remember what I saw—something about baggage. I bought her Milk Duds, and I told her to meet me at the arcade entrance once her stupid movie was done. And she . . . she knew what I was doing was wrong. That I wasn't supposed to ditch her, but she didn't protest. She didn't say anything. She could see how pissed I was, so she just went along with it. 'Okay, Kyle,' she said, and then she pointed to the arcade. 'Right there.' And she went her way, and I went mine . . . That was the last time I saw her."

× × ×

It was raining when we left. The kind of light rain that people always call *spitting*, which grossed me out because I imagined a group of giants peering over the edge of a cloud, laughing it up as they sprayed their saliva down on us all.

Mom didn't speak much during the drive. She had whispered "Jesus Christ" after we'd both closed our doors, but the jittering sound of the van coming to life as she turned the key in the ignition had drowned out much of her taking the Lord's name in vain.

The radio was turned off now. I had gone mute too. My hands were shaky, probably some of it from the coffee, but surely not all of it. Mom was telling me, as we slipped on our shoes and said our goodbyes to the teary but thankful Barb Hillerman, that tomorrow Kyle would come to the pool with me and my friends. He needed a distraction, both moms decided. Kyle didn't have a say in this arrangement. He was lying on the couch in the other room while it was being planned. After he'd spilled his guts to me about the day his sister went missing, he went . . . hysterical? Yeah, that was the word for it. He fell down to his knees and started bawling. I didn't know what to do, so like a helpless idiot, I just stood there and watched it like it was a show. But then his breathing got all weird, so I bolted inside and got our moms. It took a while to get him to calm down, to stop hyperventilating. It was hard to watch, and harder to not be able to help. I knew it was the sort of thing I'd remember forever, no matter how hard I'd try not to.

14

"*PNEUMONIA*," MY DAD SAID, A SECOND TIME. "*AMMONIA* IS AN INGREDIENT in toilet bowl cleaners, Robin."

"Robin, *you're* a toilet bowl cleaner," a grinning Peter said, poking his head out from around the corner. The collar of his T-shirt under his chin was rumpled and damp from constant chewing. I'd gone through a similar phase when I was his age.

"How did she get it?" I asked Dad, ignoring what I knew my little brother considered to be comedy gold. Peter lingered for a moment giggling, and then vanished down the hall. "Doesn't it need to be cold out to catch pneumonia?"

Dad shook his head and force-swallowed a mouthful of toast he'd been munching on when Mom and I got home from the Hillermans. But before he could answer, Mom, the household authority on all things medical, got to the question first. "It's sometimes viral," she said.

"So, you can catch it?"

"That's what viral means," Dad answered. Smiling, he reached out and tousled my hair. "He called about five minutes after you left, by the way."

I groaned. "I was watching the phone like all day and he calls right when I leave."

"A watched pot never boils."

"You sound like your dad, Bill," Mom said as she hung her keys on the cattail hook inside the front closet.

"The wisdom is hereditary," he said to her. Then, turning his attention back to me, he added, "Robin, you should have some of it by the time you finish puberty. Mind you, the genes from your mother's side will dilute it a bit."

I rolled my eyes, which only made Dad appreciate his joke more. He savoured it for a moment, finishing his last bite of toast, then took on a more serious tone. "How were things at the Hillermans'?" he asked Mom.

"Difficult," she said. "For both of us. They're doing as well as can be expected, I guess."

"So not well at all?"

She shook her head. "Maybe fill us in on Emily first."

And that's what Dad did. His arms crossed, his eyes moving back and forth between Mom and I, he told us all he had learned from Dylan when he'd called earlier in the evening looking for me. Dylan had said that the doctors at the ER figured it for pneumonia almost right away. She was coughing up all sorts of terrible things and running a high fever. Fluid had to be drained from her lungs. She was in a lot of pain, but the doctor said that by morning her numbers were looking better than they had been when she first came in. When I asked what numbers, Dad said he didn't know, but when the doctors say the numbers are good you always count it as a blessing.

"Did Dylan sound like he was doing all right?" Mom asked.

Dad shrugged. "He sounded like he was holding up okay. I mean, considering. The whole family spent the night, but Ken had to go to work this afternoon, so it's Dylan and Diane there with her now. She should come home tomorrow morning if those numbers of hers keep looking up, they said."

"*Hmmph*," Mom muttered. "And Ken *had* to go to work,"

× × ×

The TV trays had belonged to my grandparents. Mom wasn't a fan of the trays, but they had sentimental value for Dad, whose family, I think, ate most of their dinners in front of a screen. We only ever used them a few times a year, like New Year's Eve or the Stanley Cup finals, when my parents would make loaded nachos with little bowls of salsa, sour cream, and guacamole, which Peter called gecko-moley, on the side. It felt weird using the trays in summer, even if it didn't look much like summer outside, the sky full of swelling dark clouds that looked like smudged pencil and the rain escalating from spitting to full-on showers.

The only reason Mom had given the okay to eating in front of the TV was because of the six o'clock news. We all loaded up our plates with casserole and took a seat on the couch together, except for Peter, who sat in the comfy tartan chair with a Franklin the Turtle book on hand to keep him occupied while we watched. The casserole we ate was the same as the one we'd given to Kyle and his family, and as the opening credits wrapped and Trish Nadel told viewers that it had been six days since anyone had seen Catherine, I wondered if Kyle and his parents were eating the same meal in front of their TV at the exact same time.

I was getting so used to seeing Trish and co-anchor, Ray, on a nightly basis that I found myself noticing little changes in their appearances. She was wearing a different shade of lipstick than the night before. This one had a pink tint to it. He had gotten a haircut that was too short for his wide face.

We all watched in silence as Trish reported the day's new information on Catherine, which, unsurprisingly, wasn't much. There was a reminder about the car, and the vague twenty-five-to-thirty-five-year-old driver. The news then cut to Police Chief Kitrosser. He stood on the front step of the police station, with Detectives Hennig and Purser behind him for credibility.

"While we are keeping in close contact with RCMP and police officers in other municipalities, we urge local residents to remain vigilant. We ask that the citizens of Haddington Springs continue to be on the lookout for suspicious behaviour, and not to hesitate to contact authorities if they have *any* information that they think might be helpful." He paused, breathed deeply, and looked directly into the camera, directly at me. "Let's bring Catherine home," he said. My goosebumps were instant.

The camera lingered on his stare for a long second, and then cut back to the studio. Trish Nadel nodded at something off-screen, then glanced at the camera and said, "Now we go live."

What followed caught both Mom and me off guard. We gasped in almost perfect unison, causing Peter to set his book down. He peered at us for a second, then picked it back up and opened it to the first page again. On-screen, the Hillermans' front step. Kyle and Barb were as we had left them just an hour ago. The word "LIVE" glowing in the top-right corner of the screen answered my question about whether or not Kyle's family was enjoying their casserole. Kyle's dad, Gil, was with them now. He stood between his wife and son with his arms around them. Of the three, Gil was the only one looking into the camera. A reporter I didn't recognize stood in front of them, his back to the family.

"I'm here with the Hillerman family at their home in Saddler. With young Catherine missing for six days now, the family wanted to come forward to make a plea to the public."

The camera zoomed in slightly, putting Gil in the centre of the frame.

"We need Catherine back," he said. "Whoever's got our daughter . . . we need Catherine. We . . ." His voice broke a little, then he closed his eyes and came back firmer. "There's a reward," he said. "Ten thousand dollars. You bring Catherine back, it's all yours. And if that's not enough, well, dammit, we'll get you more. You hear me? We'll find a way to get more if that's what it takes. All we want is our girl, our Catherine back."

He looked away then. Not down, like Kyle and Barb, but off to the side. Then he took a deep breath and said, "I swear to God, if she's been harmed in any way . . ." The sentence wasn't finished. It didn't need to be. I was afraid to look at my parents, but I did. Both of their faces were wet with tears. I realized then that I had teared up too, though I didn't know exactly when in the broadcast it'd happened.

Barb Hillerman got the last word in before they cut to commercial break. "I know someone knows something and they're not coming forward with it. If that's you, you're just as much to blame as whoever took her. You're just as much to blame for our misery." She shook her head. "Someone knows."

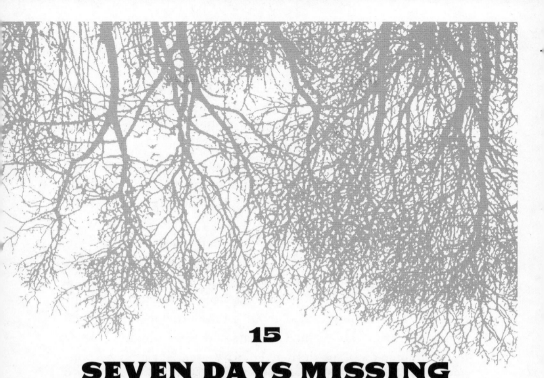

15
SEVEN DAYS MISSING

STEPH AND I TOOK THE SEATS AT THE BACK. PETER WAS UP FRONT WITH Mom, who held off on making her usual "I forgot to wear my chauffeur's cap" joke until we were a couple blocks away from Steph's house. Steph laughed politely and Peter asked again what a chauffeur was. When Mom told him, he corrected her. "You mean a butler, Mom. Like Alfred."

Making this afternoon's activity happen had required some strategizing. It all boiled down to supervision, Mom said. Could she ensure that none of us would be left alone while changing into our suits? When she'd explained the solution the parents had come up with, I was reminded of the premise of a math problem we'd had to do back in grade four, where, for some unknown reason, a human, a goat, a wolf, and some cabbage had to be transported in a small boat in a limited number of trips. In our case, it was decided that Dylan, Kyle, and I would be fine in the men's change room together; there was strength in numbers. We weren't to dawdle. We would wear our trunks underneath our pants so we could quickly strip down, lock up, and get to the pool. At the same time, Mom Peter, and Steph could all change in the women's room. Age-wise, Peter was pushing it a bit being in there, but Mom figured people would understand given what was going on. She also assured me that as soon as we got out of our respective change rooms, her and Peter would stick together and the rest of us could go off and "be annoying teenagers," as she'd put it. "Your style will remain uncramped," she'd said.

For the duration of the drive, Peter was in charge of supervising the get-well card Mom had picked up for Emily. He wanted to lick the envelope right after it had been signed by everyone at our house, but Mom wouldn't let him because she wanted Steph to sign it too. He'd grumbled about it for a bit, but it never went to a full tantrum. He seemed content now to be the one holding the light-blue envelope during the drive over. "It's a big responsibility," Mom had told him. "Not the sort of thing that I'd trust just anyone with."

The radio was tuned to a music program on CBC. I don't know what I'd classify the music as, other than just boring. Peter waved his arms along with the music like a conductor, the envelope his baton. I noticed Steph watching him, her eyes fixed on the dancing envelope.

When the music got a bit louder, she turned to me. "Hey, you remember that thing the other day?" she asked in a whisper.

"Huh?"

I followed her gaze as it moved to the front of the van, to the rear-view mirror. Mom was wearing sunglasses, but I could tell she wasn't looking back at us. "You know," Steph said, her voice even quieter now, "the envelope . . ."

"*Oh*," I said, but then Steph let me know with her eyes I was being too loud. I nodded.

"That was weird, right?"

"Yeah, like, who leaves a letter like that?"

"And it's not like the mailman delivered it. Someone ran up the steps, put it in the box, and left right away."

I looked out the window. My new glasses had come in, and everything was sharp and crisp. It was like I'd been watching a scrambled cable channel and then upgraded and got the real thing. The road curved and rose on a slight incline. A little way ahead, pointed treetops rose like they were being moved by an off-stage pulley. We were approaching the ravine.

"But we both agree that it's weird?" Steph asked.

"Well, yeah," I said, wanting to be done with it. I'd had enough of secret messages that summer.

"I'm not saying it's like, Catherine Hillerman weird," Steph said, the name fragile on her lips, like saying it the wrong way would break it. "I'm just saying it's weird for the Mayers."

I considered it for a moment. "Maybe it was one of Mr. Mayer's buddies leaving a joke note or something," I offered.

Steph gave me the same look she'd given me that time at the HMV listening posts when I'd told her Savage Garden was actually a real cool name for a band.

"*Seriously*, Robin? Like that's a thing people do?"

"Well, I don't know," I said.

"And what's the joke? Who's Andy? Mr. Mayer's alter-ego? Explain."

"I don't know," I told her, speaking a little louder than I needed to. Both of us looked back up to the front. My mom caught us in the rear-view, smiled, then turned her attention back to the road.

"Okay, yeah, sure, it was a bit weird." I could give her that. "But it wasn't even the weirdest thing *at* the Mayers' that day. Like, what about the fighting? That was nuts. They hardly ever fight. And you know what?" I began, but then stopped. From some far-off corner of my mind, an insect-sized voice told me that I shouldn't go any further with what I was going to tell her. I heard the insect voice out. It was reasonable, but Steph was staring into me with those inquisitive Nancy Drew eyes of hers. I'm only human. "When I slept over there the day we saw Kyle and Catherine at the mall, Mr. and Mrs. Mayer seemed like they were pissed at each other. Like, he seemed really on edge."

Steph's eyes widened.

"He was really grumpy during dinner and he drank a bunch of wine, more than usual. I don't think she was too happy about it."

I hadn't even finished, but Steph's mind was buzzing. She tugged at her hair, which had been tied into a ponytail for the pool, twisting it around and around at her shoulder like she did sometimes during a really hard test at school. I was just about to tell her about the other thing, the thing I didn't know if I'd seen or not when I went upstairs to use the bathroom, when she offered a theory. "Maybe he's having an *affair*," she gasp-whispered, her words the white-hot of scandal. "*Maybe that's who Andy is.*"

I covered my mouth with my hand. Would Mr. Mayer be the type to do something like that? An affair. Thinking that anything would be a downgrade from Mrs. Mayer, I asked Steph, "You think he would?" from behind a leaky wall of fingers.

Steph considered it for a moment. "He might. I don't know. That kind of stuff does happen. You hear about it all the time."

"But Andy? Isn't a name like that more . . ."

"He *could* be having an affair with a man, but, yeah, it doesn't seem likely. Unless he's a real good actor. But I think that's a stretch."

"But why would a note that's for someone named Andy be sent to their house? Whoever he is, Andy doesn't live there."

Neither of us spoke for a bit. I could tell from Steph's face that she was untangling a knotted ball of possibilities. In her head, she was probably inches away from figuring out what was going on with the Mayers, and probably the same distance from finding Catherine Hillerman safe and sound. I bet she was also on the cusp of cracking the Zodiac case too (this was one of her favourite cases, and she had a new suspect every couple months).

While I waited, my mind drifted back to Mrs. Mayer. Her shorts, her bra. Her eyes shining from that extra-tall glass of wine she'd had before bed. The way she'd looked down at her body almost like she was surprised, as if she hadn't realized until just then what a babe she was. The smile she sent me. *Had it happened at all?*

I started again. "Another thing happened that night. It was weirder than anything el—"

"*Jesus!*" Mom screamed, her foot slamming down on the brake, making us all jolt forward in our seats. We bumped something. Something so small I barely felt it, but definitely something. Peter screamed. My new glasses slid off my face and onto the floor between the two front seats.

"*Shitshitshit!*" Mom undid her seat belt and reached for Peter. "You okay, honey?"

Peter couldn't speak. His breathing was rapid and deep.

"*Are you hurt?*"

Peter didn't respond. The intense breathing continued.

"*Peter!*"

Peter must have shaken his head then, because my mom breathed a sigh of relief. "Oh, thank Christ," she whispered.

She turned and checked the back seat. Steph and I looked at each other, then back at her. "We're fine," Steph replied. I nodded, and again Mom thanked the man she normally only visited on his birthday.

Mom opened her door and stepped out. The car started going *bing bing bing* because the key was still in the ignition. "Oh no," I heard her say from outside.

I picked my glasses up off the floor and gave them a quick look over. They seemed fine. I opened my door and hopped out too. Steph followed. From inside, Peter asked, "What is it?"

"Stay inside, Peter," Mom commanded.

The cat was the colour of marmalade. He was lying on his side in front of the driver's side wheel. He hadn't been run over, but he'd been hit, and that had been enough to do it.

Steph shuddered and turned away, covering her mouth with folded hands.

Shaking her head, my mom told us to get back in the van. "I'm so sorry," she said. "You don't need to see this."

"Robin, what *is* it?" Peter asked as we climbed back in. Steph scooched back to her seat.

"It was a cat, Peter."

"Oh no!" Peter bellowed. "No!"

Mom shot me a look for telling him. I leaned into the space between the driver's seat and the passenger's seat to give my brother the best hug I could from that awkward angle.

"Is it dead?"

"Yeah," I said, and then, before he had time to process, added, "but don't worry, cats have nine lives, right?"

Peter, on the edge of tears, considered this for a second. "How do you know this wasn't its last life?" he asked.

"Once you get older you can tell how many lives a cat has," I told him. "You just look at one and you can tell right away."

We all watched Mom as she walked toward the sidewalk that bordered the ravine, her back to us, the cat in her arms, out of view. I told Peter to look away as she knelt down to place the marmalade—and now raspberry jam—cat on the grass.

"When will its next life start?" my brother asked.

"It takes seven minutes." I don't know why seven was the number I went with. It seemed to fit. "And they never come back if there's people around, so he needs to be alone for a full seven minutes."

My brother took note of the digits on the van's clock. Silently, he added seven on his fingers, then said, "Eleven . . . five-six."

"You got it, Peter," Steph said. Then she added, "That is, if we leave right now. Like your brother said, the seven minutes starts once the cat's alone." The reassurance in her voice was convincing.

"No collar, no tattoo in either of his ears," Mom said as she pulled away from the curb. "I hope he didn't belong to anyone."

We pulled away from the curb and continued down the block. The streets on all sides of the ravine were playground zones. Mom wouldn't go a notch over thirty under normal circumstances, but now she was driving even more cautiously, as if there were a whole society of cats waiting to dart out from the trees on to the road.

Peter asked Mom about the seven minutes extra life thing. She didn't know what he meant at first, but Steph jumped in and brought her up to speed, and my mom had no trouble playing along from there.

"Oh, yeah, *that*," she said. "Yes, that's exactly what happens. After seven minutes they come back to life." Naturally, Peter had a follow-up question for every one of Mom's facts about feline revival. And she had an answer for everything he threw at her. She was smooth and straightforward, and as I listened from the back seat, I thought that it was no wonder that her and Dad kept me believing in Santa until the fourth grade.

On the radio, the DJ told us they had time for one more performance before the news came on. Instinctively, my mom flipped to a different station. We came in a few notes into Sarah McLachlan's "Building a Mystery." We still had to pick up Dylan before getting Kyle, so any update on his sister would have been long over by the time he got in the van, but I guess Mom didn't even want the residue of news lingering in the vehicle.

I looked out the window at the ravine. Bad things happened there. My glasses broke and my nose bled. Catherine Hillman vanished. Bloodthirsty Louis and Connor had chased us. Now a cute little marmalade cat had died. The ravine always had a darkness to it. Something I didn't understand emanated from it. The ravine pulled things in. Like an unseen current, you wouldn't realize you were being dragged. You'd just end up there. Because it lured you.

My mind went back to the cat, who'd run out like he was trying to escape. And he'd almost made it, but something about the ravine stuck to him. Like a curse. The second he got out he died, and then his body was brought back to the ravine. Like a blood sacrifice to an angry god.

In a whisper, I told this to Steph. She thought for a moment, then said, "Maybe the ravine needed blood to appease it, and now that it got some from the cat it'll return Catherine."

"Yeah," I said, "or maybe or maybe Catherine's wasn't enough."

× × ×

155

At least in one way, the natural order of the universe had been restored: it was a Tuesday and Mr. Mayer was at work.

We all stood on the Mayers' professionally landscaped front lawn waiting for Dylan, who was rummaging around inside trying to find his beloved Expos hat. A sympathetic look on her face, Mom listened intently, nodding along as Mrs. Mayer brought us up to speed on Emily.

"Once the antibiotics started doing their thing she started improving quickly. She was so glad to get out of the hospital. She absolutely hated it there. Now it's just bedrest and finishing the run of her meds and she should be in the clear."

"That's such a relief," Mom said. "If they've let her come home, I'm sure the worst is over."

Mrs. Mayer nudged a pine cone with her barefoot. It seemed like the only thing on the pristine lawn that wasn't supposed to be there. "I sure hope so. God, Jenny, the scare she gave us."

"I can only imagine."

Mrs. Mayer's shoulders perked. "Now it's all up to Dr. Mom," she said.

The conversation shifted and Steph and I walked away and stood at the base of the steps that led to the open front door. We both looked at the mailbox. Right away Steph turned to me and did a thing with her eyebrows, as if the mailbox just by being there proved something. I shook my head.

"You're right, Robin. Maybe it was one of those really popular 'joke notes' that've been going around."

"Har-de-har."

"Maybe it's a chain letter. Very common for men in their fifties, right?"

Sometimes Steph was infuriating.

"Okay, fine. It was weird. You win, okay? It was weird. Happy?" I said.

"Yes, actually."

"Mom! Mo-om!" We all turned and looked at Peter, who stood at the bottom of the sloping lawn. He was pointing across the street.

"Look," he said. "That cat, it's orange, too. Is that the one we hit? Did it come back to life and follow us here?"

Sure enough, there was a cat sitting on the steps of the house across the street, staring at us judgingly, as cats tend to do. It was smaller than the one we'd hit, and its fur had more white than it did marmalade, but I could see why my brother thought it was the same one. There are no coincidences when you're a child.

Both moms exchanged a look like Peter had just said the most adorable thing ever. Mrs. Mayer touched her hand to her chest and made a pouty face as Mom told her about our feline speedbump.

"I think that's the Weber's cat, honey," Mrs. Mayer called to Peter. "He lives next door, but he'll sit on anyone's step like he owns it."

Mom walked to the edge of the lawn and knelt down next to Peter. He continued pointing at the cat and the two of them started talking. It was then I noticed Steph was making her way toward Mrs. Mayer. She wasted no time putting her talent for talking to adults to use.

"I'm so glad to hear Emily is on the mend, Mrs. Mayer. We were really worried about her. My dad sends his best too. He's keeping Emily in his prayers."

Touched, Mrs. Mayer reached out and rested her hand on Steph's shoulder. "That's so kind, thank you, sweetheart. You can tell your dad the prayers seem to be working, so keep sending them our way."

The thought of Bruce praying made me smirk. This was the guy whose go-to joke to someone with a crucifix necklace was "What's the t stand for?"

Steph assured Mrs. Mayer she'd pass the message along to her dad. What a bullshitter. "And thanks for letting Robin and I stay here while we waited for our ride too," she added.

"Oh, you don't need to thank me for that, Stephanie. You know you both are always welcome here."

Mrs. Mayer turned slightly and looked to my mom and Peter, who were still talking at the edge of the lawn. Peter was no longer pointing at the cat, who stood so motionless I wondered for a second if he might be ornamental, but he remained fixated on the little guy.

"I was going to ask," Steph said, pulling Mrs. Mayer back, "did you get your mail?"

Mrs. Mayer gave a puzzled look. "Yes?" she said, as if she wasn't sure it was the right response or not. "I think we've been getting all of our mail. Why do you ask?"

"Oh, just while Robin and I were waiting to be picked up, we heard someone at the front door putting something in the mailbox. I realized when we left that I should have brought it in—you know, I felt like we were watching the place, and I kind of dropped the ball there. There's been the odd time that we've actually had stuff stolen out of our mailbox, so I wanted to make sure you got whatever was in there."

"I'm sure we did. Ken's always on top of that, which is fine by me. It's mostly bills." She laughed and Steph laughed too. I felt like I was watching two girlfriends chatting. I wondered how long before Steph was offered a glass of wine, or a cocktail with one of those little toothpick umbrellas in it.

Before she could go any further with her gentle digging, Dylan appeared in the doorway. Expos hat in hand, he leapt down the steps, landing on my level. "Salutations," he said, addressing all of us. "A fancy way of saying hello."

"You been watching *Charlotte's Web*?" Steph called.

Dylan whipped the hat onto his head. "Maybe," he said, cranking the brim to the back of his head.

Laughing, Mrs. Mayer walked over to her son. "*Charlotte's Web* is Emily's favourite whenever she's sick. It's either that or *The Little Mermaid*," she told Steph. "But between us girls, I hid that tape the second we got home from the hospital. If I hear 'Under the Sea' one more time, you'll have to come visit me in the psych ward."

× × ×

On the drive over to Saddler, Mom gave us a rundown on how we were supposed to behave. We were told not to ask Kyle how it was going. Or mention the dead cat, or anything sad for that matter. We were to make sure that he felt welcome and not like he was merely tagging along. "Not that I think you would," she added. "But just do your absolute best to make him feel like you want him to be there."

"Well, we do," Steph said, indicating the cringy Valentine she'd received from Kyle was not even floating in the water beneath the proverbial bridge, his cheesy acrostic poem had long since eaten up and shat out by minnows.

"I know, hon," Mom said, slowing to a stop for an old couple at the crosswalk. "I just want to make sure we're doing all we can to take his mind off things, even if it's only for a few hours."

We drove under the Kirby Street footbridge, which, up until the concrete had been covered with a mural of colourful candy-like swirls a year ago, had HONK IF U LOVE ACID spray-painted on it for as long as I could remember. The only graffiti on it now was a small and sloppy "CLASS OF 97 RULEZ" on one of the pillars. I thought about when my friends and I would graduate. 2002. It took me from the footbridge to the intersection at Kirby and Fourth Street to do the math. I sucked at math. The calculation would have taken Steph or Dylan about two seconds. 2002. Surely, we'd all being wearing silver one-piece suits and cruising the streets on hoverboards by then. I started to calculate when Catherine Hillerman would graduate, but stopped when I realized it might further jinx her already grim circumstances.

"My mom used to live around here," Dylan said as we turned from Fourth onto Saddler Way, the neighbourhood's main artery. "Somewhere over that way. With my grandma." He pointed out his window down one of the side streets as we drove past. I thought about Mrs. Mayer's words from that time we drove through here. *Lipstick on a pig. And I can say that because I grew up here.*

"Did your grandma move?" Peter asked from his co-pilot position.

"No, she's dead," Dylan said.

Peter let that sink in for a second, then turned and looked back at Dylan. Knowing Peter, I figured he was about to ask if she came back after seven minutes, like the cat we hit, but then he said, "Me and Robin have two grandmas."

Dylan nodded. "That's cool. I just have one now. But she's really nice."

Peter responded with "Oh."

Kyle was waiting on his front step, fiddling with a strap on his backpack when we pulled up. His mom stood behind him on the other side of the screen door, the layer of mesh making her look like she was a trick of the light, a mirage. She waved when she saw us.

Mom got out of the van and walked to the gate. She stopped when it was clear that Barb Hillerman wasn't opening her door any further.

"You're a saint, Jenny," Barb called down through the mesh.

Mom raised a hand and shielded her eyes from the glaring sun that loomed overhead. "I wouldn't go that far," she said.

Barb smiled. "I would. You'll have him back by four?"

"Not a minute later."

Barb nodded and called goodbye to her son. Kyle didn't turn to her, didn't say goodbye back. Just waved dismissively as he walked away from the house, the arches of his parted hair, a deflated McDonald's M, bobbing as he walked. Steph slid the van's side door open and we all greeted Kyle with a bit too much enthusiasm. Kyle climbed in, squeezed past Steph and took a seat in the back with Dylan. As Kyle tugged his seat belt across his chest, Dylan went for a fist bump.

"What up?"

Kyle clicked the belt into the buckle and with some uncertainty bumped the fist waiting for him. "Huh?"

"No," Dylan said. "When I say 'what up?' you say 'word.'"

"Why?" Kyle asked.

"You just do," Dylan said. "Now: what up?"
"Word?" Kyle shrugged.
"There ya go."
"That makes no sense." Kyle laughed.
"Who says it has to?"

× × ×

Running the Wiener Gauntlet. That was Dylan's term for the walk from the locker area to the swimming pool. He'd coined the term last summer. Once he explained it to me, I thought it was hilarious. See, Tollcross Recreation Centre had no shortage of older men sauntering around completely nude in the change room. Guts out, nuts out, they'd walk around like they were in no hurry at all to dry off and get on with their lives, like they wanted everyone to get an eyeful of their discoloured turkey-vulture appendages. What made Tollcross different from the giant pools they had in Calgary was the stretch you had to walk from the lockers to the shower area. This stretch—the Weiner Gauntlet—was a narrow one, and there was always two-way traffic. Plus, it was bordered by rows of lockers, which meant sometimes someone would just walk out in front of you. Whenever we locked our clothes up and were ready to head to the pool, Dylan would look at me and say "The Wiener Gauntlet awaits" in what I think was supposed to be Vincent Price's voice. He kept it to a whisper now, because there was one time he shouted it at full volume and a lifeguard came and talked to him about the importance of maturity in the locker room.

We quietly explained the history of the Gauntlet to Kyle as the three of us popped our quarters into the coin slots on our lockers, twisted our keys free, and clipped them to our trunks. Kyle found it kind of funny, but clearly not as funny as Dylan and I found it. Or, I should say, Kyle didn't find it as funny as it so clearly was.

× × ×

Bodies shivering from icy pre-swim showers, arms tightly crossed, the sounds of our wet slapping feet echoing off the tiled walls around us, we made our way to the pool. While we walked, I noticed that the scrapes on Dylan's knees looked to have fully scabbed over. I smiled to myself because there was little-to-no danger of running into our tormentors at Tollcross Pool—Connor couldn't swim. This piece of schoolyard gossip seemed too good to be true when I'd first heard it. Like nothing more than a rumour, but then one day at lunch I was one of many spectators who got to look on as he beat the shit out of Trevor Fadden for announcing that during their recent phys ed trip to the pool, Connor had to sit out because he couldn't stay afloat without water wings. So, like a Tyrannosaurus rex, he may have been one of the most fearsome creatures in all of existence, but he couldn't do it all.

The smell of chlorine enveloped us completely as we emerged from the change room. It hung so thick that even with the shielding of my glasses—I hated swimming without them—my eyes stung in anticipation of the redness to come. But at thirteen, you don't worry about that. Fun now always trumps comfort later.

Kyle walked ahead of us and sat down at the edge of the pool, dipping his feet in. He turned to us. "It's not that cold," he said, through chattering teeth. He was a bit skinnier than me, an accomplishment in itself. I couldn't help but stare at his pointy shoulder blades, which poked from his back like wings about to sprout. We sat down next to him and dipped our feet in, too. The unspoken rule was that you didn't go all the way into the pool until everyone was there, so we took in our surroundings while we waited for Steph, and my mom and Peter, who'd promised to pull a vanishing act as soon as they hit the water.

The last time Dylan and I came here was on a scorching hot day in July, and the pool had been so crowded that at times it seemed more flesh than water. I recalled having to wait for an opening before I first jumped in, and hesitating after I'd found a spot because I was worried it would close up right after I jumped and I'd end up crowd-surfing. Steph came that day too, but as soon as we got there, she got all weird and said she didn't feel well and that she didn't think it was a good idea for her to go in the pool. I didn't understand why she'd go all the way there only to turn around without going in. But I get it now.

Today wasn't dead, but it was a far cry from the usual late-August busyness. The shallow end had a scattered group of little kids with their parents. The smaller ones had water wings on and wore mixed expressions of either delight or horror. There was one kid who, in retrospect, I can only describe as looking like Gollum, who had the talent to wear both at once. The older kids in the shallow end, who looked to be around Peter's age, clung to flutter boards and kicked wildly while somehow managing to not move in any direction at all.

The real action began where the shallow end sloped into what we called the medium end. In this free-for-all area, kids around our age and older splashed and slapped water at each other. They did underwater handstands, they wrestled, and they had two-on-two piggyback battles. The three of us winced at the pancake-slap of one kid's belly flop. You weren't allowed to jump into the medium end, so when the flopper came up from the water and pulled himself out of the pool, red-gutted and laughing like he meant to do it, there was a disappointed lifeguard ready to ream him out. The kid's smile dropped right off his face as the university-aged lifeguard lectured him in a way that reminded me of a highway cop tearing a strip off a speeder.

"Busted," Dylan snickered.

Kyle snickered too. He started to say something but cut himself off when a girl who was probably eighteen or nineteen walked by us. She wore a pink bikini and her movements were musical. Kyle, who probably had no clue how much he looked like a caricature of a horny teenager, gawked openly at her as she strutted behind us. When a little splash of water fell from her body onto his shoulder, he gasped, and I'd bet my PlayStation he popped one right then and there. I took a look at her too, but I was stealthier than Kyle. My technique, which I'd developed sometime in the seventh grade, was to look where the girl was *going* to be. That way, she just walks into your field of vision and you spare yourself being betrayed by a bunch of jerky head movements.

Beyond the medium end of the pool was the deep end, where you were allowed to jump in, as long as you didn't dive. The diving tank sat parallel to the deep end. The pool had two diving boards, one that was quite low and had a good bounce to it so you could do killer flips off it, and a high dive, which seemed like the scariest thing in the world to me until Steph peer pressured me into jumping off it a few summers before. I still got butterflies whenever I went up there, but I'd learned that's what made it fun to jump off of. I say "jump," because to say I ever dove off it would be an insult to dives. And what was the fun in diving anyway? Why dive when you can jump like Spider-Man, pretending to shoot webbing from your wrists as you rushed to the surface of the water. Or when you could do a Macho Man Randy Savage elbow drop, yelling *Oooh-yeah!* all the way down and twisting at the last moment to ensure you don't land on your side and crack a row of twiggy teenage ribs. Or when you can spin around and around, not knowing what direction you'll be facing when you finally hit? No, there was no reason to *dive* off the diving board. Diving was for dweebs.

We had just watched an older kid leap off the high dive and do a tail grab with his feet when Steph, Mom, and Peter showed up.

"Nagano '98!" the kid yelled as he plummeted, prompting a chorus of howls from his friends, who hung onto the ledge proudly rocking their matching frosted tips.

Steph rolled her eyes. "Everyone just *loves* snowboarding all of a sudden."

Her mom had been an avid skier, and even though Steph had only gone a handful of times herself (and never since her mom died), she was fiercely loyal to the sport. Since it had been announced that snowboarding would be in the upcoming Winter Olympics, Steph took every opportunity available to remind Dylan and I that, as far as she was concerned, it wasn't a real sport and was only for stoners who couldn't cut it skiing. We'd learned not to argue the point.

Mom reminded us—again—to stay together and then rushed off to the shallow end with a protesting Peter. I stole a glance at Steph. The shower had slicked her inky black hair to her forehead in cosmic swirls. Standing in her navy one-piece, she was shivering like the rest of us and had her arms crossed tightly across her chest, although I wasn't clueless enough to think her being cold was the only reason for this position. Feeling a rush of butterflies for having noticed Steph's awareness of her own body, I quickly suggested we all head to the deep end. Dylan indicated yes by giving his belly two slaps. The others nodded, and off we shuffled, unanimous.

Kyle was the weakest swimmer of the group. He wasn't in danger of drowning or anything, but I could tell he'd spent a lot less time in the water than the rest of us. His technique was a kind of frantic scurry where each of his limbs looked as if they were being operated by four separate brains that all had very different opinions about what the best course of action was. It seemed to work, but man, did it ever look weird. He treaded water with the same uncoordinated frenzy, breathing double time, his chin and mouth constantly dipping below the surface of the water. But what he lacked in skill he made up for in enthusiasm, and from the moment he first hit water, he'd been smiling ear-to-ear. This Kyle seemed a far cry from the boy I'd seen the day before.

When the time came to take our first breather from jumping and treading, we went to the wall and hung onto the ledge where we could watch people jump off the diving boards. An older, chubby kid inched along the high dive like he was walking a pirate's plank over shark-infested waters. While he walked, a cluster of kids standing at the base of the ladder that led to the board started chanting: *"Bel-ly flop! Bel-ly flop!"*

They might have been his buddies, but if that was the case, he needed to consider new friends. There was a note of cruelty in their incantation, like they actually wanted him to get hurt. But their words didn't seem to faze him. He walked right to the end and then right off, and as he flailed toward the surface of the water—much to the disappointment of the group of chanters—he didn't do a belly flop. At the last second, he found his form: cannonball. The impact was awesome, and the mushroom cloud of water that followed made us all cheer.

"That's so cool," Dylan said.

We all agreed. After watching a couple more jumps, none of which had the same atomic impact, Kyle pushed away from the wall, took a deep breath, and bobbed below the surface, seeing if he could pencil his way to the bottom. Steph, seeing a sleuthing opportunity in his absence, told Dylan she sure was glad Emily seemed to be doing okay.

"Yeah." Dylan nodded, his eyes staying focused on the high dive and following the descent of every jumper. "We were all pretty scared."

"So were we," Steph assured him.

Dylan didn't say anything in response. Then, after Kyle resurfaced and repeated his bob, he said, "On the bright side, it got my parents to stop bitching at each other for a bit."

Steph perked up a little. She was getting somewhere.

"Oh," she said, surprised. "Have they been fighting?"

Dylan sighed. "Come on, like you didn't notice. It's their favourite activity lately."

"Is it about money?" Steph offered. "When my mom was around, whenever my parents fought it was always about money."

"I don't think so. My parents don't usually fight about money. They don't have to. I don't know what they were fighting about. Probably something stupid, because that's what most adults fight about. Stupid stuff."

His indirect suggestion that if Steph's parents were fighting about money, it was because they *did* have to was probably accidental. Every now and then he'd say something inconsiderate like that, but I don't think it was ever on purpose. He'd just forget that he came from a family that had more than a lot of other families did. And knowing how his parents could be, with their perfectly manicured lawn, their high-end everything, their comments about neighbourhoods like Saddler, it was easy to see where he got it, so I could usually cut him some slack.

If Steph was bothered by his comment, she didn't show it. She waited a beat, hooked a squiggly tendril of wet hair behind her ear, and said, "Well, your mom seemed fine when we saw her today, so maybe things are all good now."

Dylan shrugged. When he didn't offer anything further, Steph pushed.

"Hey," she said, "did you guys hear that thing on the news about weird letters going around?"

I winced. The question was painfully transparent to me, but then I knew the motive behind it. I watched Steph, who watched Dylan, studying his reaction.

"No," Dylan said, sounding genuinely disinterested. "The news is never on at my house. My dad only watches TSN."

The high dive shuddered as a girl in a turquoise bikini dove from it, graceful as a swan. Kyle returned from the depths, took a breath, pencil-bobbed back down.

Steph continued, "My grandma was telling us about it. She said she the news said these weird letters are going around town, and—"

"What's weird about them?" I asked, my words sounding rehearsed. Steph shot me a look and I shot one right back. I was just trying to do my part, like a good sidekick.

"I'm not sure, *Robin*." She said my name with the same chilly tone an angry teacher uses when you're whispering during class. "But my grandma said they don't know who they're from because there's no return address on them, and the writing on the envelopes is always kind of sloppy."

Dylan scrunched up his face. "That's it?" he asked. "How did something like that even make the news?"

I flashed a smirk at Steph. She ignored me and gave it one more shot.

"No kidding," she agreed. "So, neither of you guys got one at your house?"

"Nope," I said.

"Sure didn't," Dylan replied.

This time, it was Steph who shot me the look, her famous *told-ya-so* face, as if Dylan's not knowing about the letter proved something. Maybe it did, but I sure wasn't smart enough to know what.

An older kid who'd just landed a sloppy dive pulled himself out of the water and his bathing suit came down a bit at the back, exposing his ass and lighting the fuse to Dylan's Mickey laugh. There was a very short powder trail between us, so my detonation was almost instant too, although not nearly as loud. Dylan's laughter bounced off the tiles on the wall and ceiling and quickly travelled to Mr. Ass himself, who had just tugged his trunks up. He turned to us, shook his head, and flipped us off.

"Fuckheads!" he called, then quickly looked to the lifeguard's elevated chair to make sure he wasn't going to get in trouble himself (the pool had a policy about vulgar language that was written on a sign in capital letters, so you knew it was serious). The lifeguard was chatting up the girl in the turquoise bikini and couldn't have cared less about any profanity. By my guess, there was at least a five-year gap between the lifeguard and the girl.

As our laughter fizzled out, Dylan took one chlorine-steeped hand out of the water and wiped it down his face. "Too good," he muttered to himself. He looked at Steph, who hadn't laughed. "Steph, did you see that?" he asked her, as if it seeing this stranger's ass was the most spectacular thing that could've happened.

"No, Dylan, I didn't," Steph said.

"Well, it was hilarious, and you missed out. Right, Robin?"

Noticing, from the corner of my eye, how unimpressed Steph looked, I shrugged. "Yeah, it was funny, but . . . you know, we can move on."

"Man," Dylan said, "I hate it when you do that."

"Do what?"

"Fucking act like you're all mature and shit. You're not *Steph*."

Dylan dipped his head below the surface of the water before Steph had a chance to respond. He and Kyle, who was returning from what must have been his fifth attempt to touch the bottom of the pool, popped back up at the same time. Kyle gasped for air and swam over to the ledge with the rest of us, his eyes closed tightly like a mole-person who had just made it out of his subterranean home.

"Guys," he said, his breathing laboured, "I did it! I touched the bottom."

"Cool," Dylan said with amplified disinterest. "So did I. When I was six."

Kyle's expression sunk. His one-float parade had officially been cancelled due to shitty weather.

"It's always hard for me to touch too," I reassured. "When you're scrawny, you really have to work to get there."

Kyle nodded and smiled partially. Behind him, Steph glared at Dylan with scolding eyes, but Dylan was making a point of not looking at her. When Steph's razor glare persisted, Dylan placed both hands onto the concrete deck and lifted himself out of the water. The quickness of his exit came with a little splash that dotted the lenses of my glasses, which pissed me off because, up until then, I'd been doing a pretty decent job of keeping them pristine as possible. Without a word, he began walking to the diving boards. Kyle looked back and forth between Steph and I, like one of us might have something to offer about what was going on. Steph shook her head, mumbled something I didn't hear, and climbed out after Dylan. Kyle waited for me as I placed my glasses in the folds of my towel that I'd placed out of the splash zone, then we both went to catch up with Steph and Dylan, doing that speed-walking thing to not get yelled at by the lifeguards.

We passed a trio of scurrying kids who were testing the edges of the no running on the deck rule, and I tried to wrap my head around the way Dylan was acting. He'd been pissy on and off lately, which was kind of understandable with his parents fighting about whatever and his sister being sick. But Emily was getting better—Mrs. Mayer had said so. And a lot of people's parents fought with each other. Granted, I only saw a sliver of what went on at the Mayer house compared to the people who actually lived there full-time, not just part-time, like me, but there was no way things were *that* bad. They were the Mayers. A catalogue family brought to life. They took portraits where everyone was wearing the same pastel shade and gave full-size chocolate bars to trick-or-treaters. There was no way.

"Robin! Look!"

Peter's voice pinballed off the tile and concrete. I stepped away from the low dive line and looked to the shallow end, squinted, and made out the fuzzy forms of him and Mom. Peter was attempting to climb onto one of the red flutter boards floating around while Mom watched him. He thrust one knee to the surface of the board, and as he lifted the other knee shouted, "I'm gonna do no hands!" Which, of course, was the last thing he said before the board rocketed out of the water. He emerged a second later. Then he grabbed the board again and began his reattempt.

If this had happened on any other day, I'd be annoyed with Peter for calling this sort of attention to me, for announcing to everyone in the pool that even though I was a cool thirteen-year-old hanging with my cool friends, I was still here with my mom and kid brother. But it was hard to think like that with Kyle there with me. I raised my arms and gave Peter two big thumbs up, which I think he returned, and which caused him to fall off the flutter board again. I walked back to the line for the diving boards, where Steph and Kyle had saved my space for me. Somewhere behind me, a couple of twerpy kids muttered about me being a budger. When I turned and faced them, they didn't have anything more to say.

Dylan, standing ahead of us, was up next. He climbed the three-step ladder and charged down the length of the board. Not slowing down as he reached the tip, he bounced once, the sound of the vibrating plank and springs reminding me of the slam of a WWF ring after a powerbomb, and flew into the air. When he reached the arc of his jump, he flailed his arms and legs wildly and yelled, "WAAAAAAA!" and then, as he fell, he reined in his limbs to ensure maximum depth.

Once Dylan surfaced, Kyle hopped up the ladder. He moved quickly down the board, but it wasn't quite a run, more of a senior citizen's jog. At first when he jumped it looked like he was going for a flip, but somewhere around the halfway point he lost confidence and the move turned into a sort of sideways roll. He landed with a smack, but when he popped up from the water, the first breath he took was spent on laughter. So it couldn't have hurt too bad.

Steph perked with excitement when it was her turn. She looked at me over her shoulder and raised her eyebrows like she was about to do something wild. Of the three of us, Steph needed the least amount of psyching up to jump off the high dive, so jumping off the low dive wasn't a big deal for her. But high or low, she just liked to jump. I did my best not to gawk at her figure as she tiptoed down the board. When she reached the edge, she turned and positioned herself so that she had her back to the water. She'd done this jump before, even off the high dive a few times, and told me it was fun, but freaky. How there was something cool about falling backwards through the air, about not really knowing where you'd land. "It messes you up," she'd told me. "Scary, but cool." This had been enough to get me to try it once, but only once. When it came to swimming, Steph's nerves were steel, mine were aluminum at best.

"Hey," she called to me. I met her eyes. "Pepsi!" she shouted, then added to the callback by mugging for the invisible camera and, with that, closed her eyes and leapt backwards into the water.

Once I hoisted myself up the steps, I checked to make sure the coast was clear. Steph had resurfaced and was paddling toward the edge to join Dylan and Kyle, who were both watching to see what my jump of choice would be. Another unwritten pool rule was you always watched your friends' jumps. Steph gave me a thumbs up when she reached the edge and settled, and I blasted down the board as fast as I could and bounced into the air. There was nothing fancy about my jump. I didn't strike a pose or yell anything goofy. I just *jumped*, the goal being to propel myself as far as I could, into the stratosphere, into the special brand of pool-air oblivion that began at three metres. I hit the water and sunk, and tried to touch the bottom. It was always out of reach in the diving tank, but I tried. I held my breath until it felt like my lungs would spring a leak, and then pushed my way up, a rush of bubbles shooting from my nose like tusks.

My ears popped when I broke the surface. The first thing I heard was the voice of one of the twerpy kids from the diving board line.

"Nice jump, budger, now hurry up and *move!*"

When I rolled onto my back and looked, all the potential culprits had their heads tilted to the ceiling.

"Zero points for style," Steph said as I joined the group.

"Negative ten points for style," Dylan kidded before pushing further down the wall and climbing out of the pool.

We all headed back to the same line, set to do at least another couple rounds of jumps off the low dive before braving the high dive. While I waited for my next go, I couldn't help but stare at Kyle. As he climbed the ladder for the second time that day, his eyes bright and eager, his smile so permanent it looked like multiple surgeries would be needed to remove it, I was happy to know that he was distracted, or at least as distracted as he was capable of being. That felt like a victory.

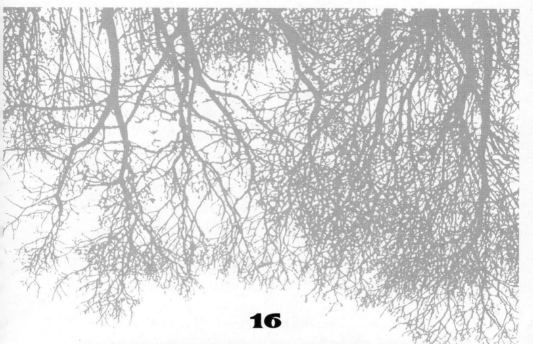

16
EIGHT DAYS MISSING

"YOU'RE DOING IT WRONG. THERE'S NOT SUPPOSED TO BE SO MANY TRI- angles."

With Mom away at an early morning dentist appointment, Dad agreed to go in late for work and hang around the house until she returned. She was fifteen minutes late. I don't think Dad minded, but it had been a while since he'd handled early morning Peter solo, and I could tell my brother was starting to grate on him.

"Peter, shut up," I said. "Just eat your waffle."

"Robin *swore* at me!"

"Shut up isn't a swear."

"Dad, he swore right *at* me. You're not even going to get him in trouble?"

"Robin," Dad said, "don't tell your brother to shut up." And then, to Peter, "Happy?"

Peter considered this for a moment. "Yeah," he said. Then, after further consideration: "Except no, because my waffles are wrong. There're too many triangles. *I can't eat this many stupid triangles.*"

Dad put his coffee mug down on the counter. I don't think he'd had more than two sips yet. And it sure seemed like he needed it. His taking part in the nightly Catherine searches was beginning to take a toll on him. A couple nights ago, he told Mom that he suspected he and the other regulars were being dispatched to far-off areas because the police wanted to prevent them from finding anything. "I think they're worried that with so many of us, we might actually ruin potential evidence," he'd told her. Whether that was the case or not, one thing was for sure: exhaustion meant less patience for nonsense in our house.

Peter pouted about his breakfast once more, and Dad reached over and took two syrupy triangles of Eggo waffle off his plate with his bare hands.

"Problem solved," he said, raising the waffles to his mouth.

"Hey!" Peter protested.

As Dad popped the waffles into his mouth, a glob of syrup plopped off one of them and landed on his freshly ironed work shirt.

"*Dammit!*" He kicked back his chair and stomped upstairs to find a replacement.

Peter picked up his fork and jabbed it into a hunk of waffle. He brought it to his eye level, looked at it like it was a dead salamander, and then took a reluctant bite. Having had about enough of his antics—and so early in the day—I grabbed the copy of the *Herald* at the far end of the table and flipped to the comics page: panel one, Garfield asked Odie the dog to go away. The dog left for the second panel, then returned for the third, and then Garfield told him to *stay* away using his unexplained cat telekinesis. Comedy gold.

Dad came down the stairs with a fresh shirt, tucking it in as he walked, just as Mom came through the door.

"You survive?" he called to her as he transferred his coffee into his travel mug.

"I'll call you at work and confirm once the freezing wears off," she mumbled. Then she looked at me. "Dr. Towne sure is looking forward to your upcoming appointment. You'd think pulling that tooth was the highlight of his career."

Dad planted a kiss on her forehead as they passed each other in the hall, then called goodbye to us and told Peter to watch out for triangles.

As the door closed, Mom said, "Triangles? Peter, did he cut the waffles wrong?"

Peter bowed his head and nodded in way that was so defeated you'd think he was confirming a *National Enquirer* doomsday prophecy.

× × ×

The plan was agreed upon by all parents. My mom would drive Steph, Kyle, and I to Dylan's house. We'd spend the afternoon there and be driven back to our respective homes by my dad before dinner. I didn't know then that it would be the last time we would ever hang out together again.

As Mom turned onto Saddler Mews, it occurred to me that this was the third time in as many days I'd been to Kyle's house. Yesterday after the pool, Mom said that if my gang and I, as she lamely referred to us, were getting together the next day, that we should invite Kyle. I didn't like the idea of being forced to hang out with someone, but Kyle was okay. I never had anything against him to begin with, even *before* his sister went missing. Given a little time I might have even come up with the idea of asking him myself.

"He's lucky to have a friend like you," she said as she pulled to a stop at the curb in front of Kyle's house. "You're a good kid."

"Could you stop making a big deal out of it?" My words came out clipped. Was Dylan's attitude starting to rub off on me? "Sorry. It's just ... I'm not trying to be a good kid or whatever. I—*we*—don't mind hanging out with him, okay?"

Kyle hopped in our van, crawled past Steph and I, and claimed the back seat. We listened to music on the drive over, and anytime a song ended I noticed Mom's hand go to the volume knob, just in case. We managed to make it to Dylan's without hearing a single news report. A bunch of commercials, some chatter between two annoying tobacco-voiced DJs, but no news. Thank you, commercial radio. That, and the fact that no cats were killed, made for a pretty smooth trip from points A through D.

"All righty. Remember what we agreed to," Mom said when we reached Dylan's house, really leaning into the word *agreed*. "You guys are staying here all afternoon. If you go somewhere—anywhere—Diane's taking you."

No one protested. Mom waited in the van until we were safe indoors. With the short leash we were kept on, you'd have thought that the kidnapper's tastes had matured overnight.

Steph and I were surprised when Emily opened the door for us. The last time we'd seen her, she'd looked like she was on Death's doorstep. Now, standing before us in her *Beauty and the Beast* pyjamas, her mousy-brown hair a tangled, pillow-frizzed web, she looked like she was only on the sidewalk in front of Death's house.

Before Emily spoke, she turned her head and cleared her throat, producing a sound that reminded me of the noise our old gas lawn-mower made when you yanked its chord. With the obstruction cleared, she was good to go. "Salutations," she said.

Steph clapped her hands together and laughed. She leaned forward, bringing her head down to Emily's level, resting her hands on her bare knees. "Salutations back," she said. "You're looking a lot better than the last time we saw you, little lady."

A blink-and-you'll-miss-it grin came to and went from Emily's lips. I think it was Steph's *little lady* that did it. She motioned for us to come in, and added, "He's coming." As if waiting for his cue, Dylan bounded down the stairs to greet us.

"Your butler's kinda short," I said to him. Emily, halfway up the stairs by then, turned and stuck her tongue out at me.

"Yeah," Dylan agreed, "you get what you pay for."

While Steph and I stepped out of our shoes and swept them against the wall with our feet, Kyle knelt down and untied his. He stood up and took in the house's entrance. It occurred to me that Kyle, as far as I knew, had never been to the Mayers' house before. And while Steph and I, who came from smaller and less impressive-looking homes ourselves, were very much used to the spectacle that was Stately Mayer Manor—its size, its high-end furniture, its spotlessness—for someone who hadn't seen it before, and who'd maybe never been in a house like it at all, it was impossible not to gawk.

Steph and I walked to where Dylan stood at the base of the stairs.

"You're allowed in too, man," Dylan said to Kyle jokingly. "You just need to leave a damage deposit."

Kyle looked at him blankly, then Dylan's words and the fact that he was kidding sunk in. "Sure," he said, smiling, before stepping off the mat and joining us as we walked down the hall.

In the living room, Dylan's new game, *Turok: Dinosaur Hunter*, was paused on the TV. We followed him to the couches and took a seat, Dylan and I sitting on one, and Kyle and Steph on the other slightly smaller couch across from it, the one closest to the mantel with its white-framed family photos and its antique bayonet.

"You guys need to see this game. It's wicked," Dylan said.

"Yeah, but it's one-player," Steph said.

Ignoring her, Dylan un-paused the game. "I keep finding shotgun shells, but I don't have a gun yet. But the bow and arrow and knife are actually pretty bad ass." As he said this, a bearded warrior charged at the screen.

"*Ha!*" Dylan said, as his character stabbed at the attacker, prompting clouds of blood to spurt from him as he crumbled. The blood looked like pixelated jelly. "See?"

"Cool," I said, "but I thought the game was called *Dinosaur Hunter*. Where are the dinosaurs?"

"You kill dinosaurs *and* humans, man. Give it a minute."

Steph yawned loudly and stretched like it was three in the morning and she was ready to call it. Dylan didn't take the hint. Or if he did, he simply didn't care.

"See?" he said, as a raptor appeared on-screen. He pressed some buttons and his character's hands swapped out the hunting knife for a bow and arrow. "Watch *this*." His character shot at the unassuming dinosaur. Blood sprayed from it the same way it had when he'd killed the human a minute earlier. It took one more arrow to the put the raptor down for good.

When the dinosaur died, Kyle nodded politely. All Steph offered was the raising of her eyebrows. I wondered how long it would take, how many dead humans and ancient lizards, before Steph decided she'd had enough. Ten minutes turned out to be her threshold. "Wow, Dylan, this is *so* cool," Steph mocked. "I'm really glad we all got out of bed, got dressed, and came here to *watch* you play a video game."

Dylan pressed pause and shot her an irritated look. His comment from the day before—*Fucking act like you're all mature and shit. You're not Steph*—hovered somewhere between the three of us. Anticipating a pissy remark, I tensed up, but to my surprise, after upholding his stare for a moment, Dylan's face relaxed and he put down the controller.

"Fine," he said. Even though it seemed like he was addressing everyone, he faced only Steph. "We can take turns playing this, or we can play a multiplayer game like *Mario Kart*."

Steph shrugged. "Or we could not play a video game at all."

"And do what?" Dylan asked.

"We could go out—"

"We can't go outside," Dylan said in the sort of tone that might be acceptable if Steph had suggested we try cocaine.

Steph wasn't someone who liked being interrupted. When I saw the fire in her eyes flare, I decided to jump in.

"Dude," I said, "we know we can't go wander the streets or whatever, but we can go kick a soccer ball around in your backyard or something."

"I'm tired of soccer," Dylan said. "It's gay, and my backyard sucks ass."

Before I could respond, Steph shot up from her seat. People who didn't know her very well sometimes thought she had a short fuse. Maybe it was because she always spoke her mind, or maybe it was because she was a bit of a tomboy and people have a tendency to make unfair assumptions about tomboys. But, knowing her like

I did, I can say with total honesty that she wasn't quick-tempered. She had a low tolerance for bullshit, sure, but as far as tempers went, she was one of the most patient people I'd ever known. So watching her stand over Dylan looking like she was ready to deck him, I knew that this was an edge it had taken some serious effort to reach.

And I could see where her frustration was coming from. Something was going on with Dylan lately. When it came to his recent on-and-off pissy attitude, we gave him some leeway. He was our friend, after all. But while we wanted to help him, it can be hard to help someone when you only have blurry notions about what it is that's eating at them. In the last week or so he'd become one giant knot. Who—or what—was tugging on his strings, I couldn't say for sure, but the tightening in him was undeniable.

Through clenched teeth, and with just a hint a of venom, Steph said, "One: how can a sport be gay? That's stupid. Two: your back-yard is practically the size of Saint Phillip's, so don't say it sucks."

For a moment, it looked like she was done. She went to sit down again. But then she shook her head, as if telling herself, *No, thank you very much, I'm not finished*, and stood right back up again. She pointed her finger right in Dylan's face and said, "And you know, at least you *have* a real backyard. If you thought about some-one other than yourself for two seconds, you'd realize it's actually pretty rude to call your backyard sucky when you know at least one of the people you're talking to . . ." she turned her finger to herself now, "has a shitty little brick patio and a single strip of grass that takes about three seconds to mow."

Then she shook her head as she lowered herself to her couch cushion. Once she was comfy again, she added, "So *rude*," in a jag-ged whisper.

Dylan sat there trying to figure out what had just hit him. And Kyle, his mouth hanging open, looked like he was trying to figure out if, as a witness, he'd need to fill out any paperwork. For a long moment silence fell over the room, and then Dylan opened his mouth to speak. *Oh, no*, I thought, certain he'd throw more gasoline on the fire and we'd all be left with no eyebrows.

"Sorry. For real."

And he meant it. I could tell. He usually was sincere. It just took him a while to get there sometimes. My relief was palpable.

A voice came from the doorway. "Uh-oh, trouble in paradise?"

We all gave a little start, especially Kyle, who jolted like he'd just been zapped by some unseen imp. None of us had noticed Mrs. Mayer standing at the edge of the room.

When no one answered, Mrs. Mayer, added in a singsongy voice: "I certainly hope not."

I wasn't sure how much she'd heard, but the playfulness in her voice didn't jibe with the tension that was still only in the earliest stages of evaporating.

A knowing smile on her lips, she let her eyes move from Dylan, to me, then to Steph, where she lingered a second before shifting to Kyle. When none of us responded, she walked into the room and half-sat, half-leaned on the back corner of the couch that Dylan and I had claimed. She was like a vixen in a shimmering dress lying on the lid of a piano in an old movie. In one hand she clutched a black coffee mug with a lipstick mark—so fresh it throbbed—staining the rim. I couldn't say for sure that there wasn't *any* coffee in there, but from where I sat, the dominant smell coming from the mug definitely didn't make me think the best part of waking up was Folgers in her cup. It made me think of my dad's oldest brother, my uncle Curtis, who'd been to rehab twice and wasn't allowed near the punch at family gatherings.

"We're fine," Dylan mumbled.

Mrs. Mayer didn't acknowledge her son's reply.

The quiet grew awkward. Seconds dripped by slower, like someone had added flour to them to make them thicker. With my back against the couch, I could only see a slash of her in my periphery—the tanned skin of her bare shoulder, a piece of her sleeveless black blouse, a dangling tendril of her brunette hair dipping into frame—but what made my palms sweat and the almost invisible hair on my arms stand on end was the way that I could *feel* her lounging right there. Right behind me.

I looked across the room at Kyle, who was full-on gawking at Mrs. Mayer like he had when he'd ogled the girl in the bikini at the pool. I could almost hear his boner *bo-oi-oing-ing* into existence. I honestly couldn't tell if the guy was shameless or clueless. He stared at Mrs. Mayer with a weird mix of awe and confusion on his face, like he was trying to figure out if he'd spotted a famous person on the street.

"Kyle." She said his name with a note of pity in her voice. As she eased off of the back of the couch, her hair brushed across the back of my neck. Everyone watched as she tiptoed over to the other couch, sipping from her mug and moving to some unheard music—a slow song, by the look of it. This time she took a seat on the arm. Her spell on Kyle increased in power as she sat closer to him. And he stared at her even more openly.

"Welcome, Kyle," she said, practically cooing his name. "I'm Mrs.—" She stopped herself, smiled, and shook her head, then raised a shushing finger to her lips, like she'd said something embarrassing. She took a sip from her mug, swallowed, and spoke again: "I'm *Diane*."

Steph always wore a face of both attentiveness and politeness in the presence of an adult, but when Mrs. Mayer said *I'm Diane*, Steph's eyes bugged a little. She was quick to regain her composure, but I saw the crack in the foundation. It was unmistakable.

Mrs. Mayer saw it too. She snickered, again to herself. Always, it seemed, to herself. She was in on the ultimate inside joke, so exclusive it could never be shared. Then, reaching past Kyle, she gave Steph a playful nudge. "What?" she said. "Are you surprised I have a first name? Am I *allowed* to have a first name?" Speaking into her mug, she added, "I don't know why we have to be so formal," emphasizing *formal* like it was the ultimate dirty word. "Ken's that way, but I've never really cared about formalities."

Steph smiled and raised two surrendering hands. "Oh, I wasn't surprised, I was—"

"Can you stop being weird?" The interruption came from Dylan. For a second I thought it was directed at Steph. Her mouth clamped shut; she clearly thought the same thing.

But that confusion was cleared when Mrs. *Diane* Mayer said, "Excuse me?"

"We're just figuring out what to do," Dylan said. "You don't need to, like, check on us."

"Honey, I'm not *checking* on you," she said with a chuckle. "I'm saying hi. Saying hi to our company." With one broad, sweeping gesture, she confirmed that we were the company. Then she turned her attention back to Kyle and smiled down on him. There was a glassy shine to her eyes.

"You know what?" Dylan said. "Soccer actually sounds good. Let's go in the yard and play soccer." He shot up from his seat and walked right past his mom. She didn't acknowledge him. Once he got to the kitchen, he turned around and with his eyes urged us to follow.

"Yeah," I said, nodding, "soccer sounds good?" Uncertainty laced my words, making them sound more a question than a statement.

Steph and I stood up in unison and joined Dylan in the kitchen and did just as he did: observed from a safe distance. Mrs. Mayer carried on with Kyle as if the two of them were alone in the house.

"Oh, sweetie," she said. "Are you . . . How are you holding up?"

Kyle's eyes fell to his lap. His cheeks flushed, so red and hot that if we had a pack of Jet-Puffed Marshmallows and a few wire coat hangers, we could've made s'mores from where we stood.

"*Mom*," Dylan said. "He's fine and we're going outside to play soccer." He raked his fingers through his hair and whispered, "*Fuck's sake.*"

Mrs. Mayer ignored her son's words, audible curse and all. Kyle ignored him too. It was as if the three of us had become ghosts, only able to observe but not interact with the living, like Scrooge watching the Cratchits on Christmas Eve. I looked over to Dylan who stood with his arms crossed, shaking his head, helpless, frustrated.

"I want you to know you're welcome here," Mrs. Mayer told Kyle. "We're glad to have you." She took a sip from her mug, swallowed. Whatever was in there inspired another thought: "And you make yourself at home," she said. "Okay?"

Kyle nodded, but apparently that wasn't enough, so she repeated, "*Okay?*"

This time, Kyle echoed, "Okay."

With her free hand she reached over and messed his hair. The gesture was more than a little condescending, but what came next was worse. She leaned close to him and in an almost conspiratorial voice said, "And I mean it. Help yourself to anything. Raid the pantry. We've got the good stuff here: Fudgee-Os, Doritos, Snack Packs. You're not in Saddler."

With that, she stood up, gave Kyle's shoulder a poke, and walked toward the hallway. When she passed us, she said, "You be nice to him," in a whisper that wasn't really a whisper, then left down the hall, humming.

Mortified, Dylan was the one with campfire cheeks now. Except his blaze was too much. Our marshmallows would have melted off their wire sticks, fallen in globs, and burned out of existence.

× × ×

We placed a plastic street hockey net at one end of the yard. At the other end, we used two upside-down flower pots. In order to ensure there was no griping, we used the most advanced methods available to ensure the width between the pots was the *exact* same as the width of the street hockey net: we eyeballed it and then double-checked by counting out paces.

In what I'm sure was a gesture of goodwill, Dylan claimed Kyle as a teammate right away. While the two of them walked to their end of the impromptu field to strategize, I heard him say, "Sorry about my mom being weird." Kyle's response was too quiet to be heard. Things seemed okay. And if they weren't, he was too polite to say so.

I looked to Steph, who was watching both of them with interest. When she felt my eyes, she turned to me. Our glances mingled for a second.

"What the hell was up with Mrs. Mayer?" she whispered. "Or is it *Diane?*"

"I don't know, but it was, like, hard to watch."

"No shit."

"I think she was *drunk*," I whispered back. It still felt too loud, and my instinctual reaction was to turn around and look at the house to make sure Mrs. Mayer wasn't standing at the window with headphones on and one of those parabolic spy microphones pointed at me.

Steph shook her head. "Unbelievable," she said, her tone that of a school teacher gearing up to give her class of misfits the "I can't leave this room for one minute" speech.

Dylan beckoned us to the middle of the yard, the ball cradled under his arm. "Robin, we're not going easy on you guys. Might want to lose those glasses for now."

"Har-de-har-har," I said.

"*Har-de-har-har,*" he mimicked.

I opted to keep my glasses on, but throughout the game, any-time the ball came off the ground, instinct brought my hands to my face. I could hear my mom's disappointed voice bouncing off every hard surface in my mind.

Having Kyle in the mix made for a more exciting game than I was prepared for. I'd made the dickish assumption based on the what I'd seen at the pool that he'd be a weaker soccer player than me. He wasn't. The normal hierarchy was Steph on top, and then Dylan and I tied for either second best or second last, depending on how you wanted to look at it. Having Kyle on his team elevated Dylan's level of playing, and that afternoon I was definitely the worst one. Kyle was methodical. He made very calculated movements. At times, he seemed like he was moving too slow for soccer, which would prompt me to rush at him. But then he'd deke around me and leave me stand-ing clueless, like a total goon, while the action pushed on without me. If there were any spectators present, our meetings on the field would look like a graceless Neanderthal charging at a samurai warrior.

When the burning August sun reached its peak and every slice of shade in the yard had been shoved against its will to the side of the house, we decided to call it. We'd stopped keeping score long before the end, but the last numbers had been thirteen and six, with at least two of the six being pity points.

We crashed into the kitchen and descended upon the fridge like a gang of thirsty teenage raiders. Four carbonated hisses sounded as we cracked the tabs of our Pepsis and headed back to the couches. I heard footsteps from down the hall a second later, and in came Mrs. Mayer. Her eyes were less glassy, and she looked more like her usual self. But something was still off. It might have been that her hair was a bit dishevelled on one side—had she been napping?. Or it might have been something else, something I couldn't put my finger on.

"And what's the plan now?" she asked.

We all looked to Dylan, who didn't give much in the way of a response.

"Do you want me to take you guys to Blockbuster?" Mrs. Mayer offered.

Dylan looked up. He shrugged and nodded at us and we shrugged and nodded back. We'd done the outdoors and were ready to hunker down with the modern luxuries of VHS and refrigerated beverages.

As we made our way to the door, Steph added one condition. "No horror, though, okay?"

"Sure," I told her. "You can't watch horror during the day anyway."

× × ×

Leaving the video store, it was noticeably hotter than it had been when we entered. The sun—hovering in a sky that was clear and blue, save for a few streaky jizzstain clouds—blared down on us as we walked across the parking lot. Movie in hand (*Mars Attacks!*— Steph gave a convincing enough sales pitch that craftily avoided mentioning that her celebrity crush, Pierce Brosnan, was in the movie) Dylan beelined it to the family's red Windstar ahead of everybody else and stood waiting for the door to be unlocked. Emily, who had been permitted to wear her pyjamas outside shielded her eyes from the sun's glare. On the drive over Mrs. Mayer told us that she wasn't supposed to be out of the house long because she was still getting better, so we had to choose fast. I wasn't so sure that the twentyish minutes we'd spent in Blockbuster could be called fast, but neither Emily nor Mrs. Mayer had complained.

When everyone was in and belted, Mrs. Mayer twisted the key. She checked the rear-view, then let her eyes fall from it as she put the car in reverse and stepped on the gas using a little more force than usual.

The sound of the slam and the impact arrived like thunder and lightning. So sudden and loud and powerful that it yanked us like rag dolls as far as out seat belts would allow. We all screamed at the real-life jump scare. Emily's scream, so shrill and piercing, lasted twice as long as everyone else's and had a phlegmy depth to it. The van had come to a dead stop, but she kept on going, a one-note banshee blast. When she didn't let up, Mrs. Mayer reached over and clamped a hand over her daughter's mouth. She shushed her, pushed her hair back, and looked her over. Then she turned to us. Her wide eyes were misty and she wore a sort of desperate smile on her face. "Are you all . . ." She didn't finish the sentence, but her stare panned across each of our faces like a roving searchlight. Our expressions must have given her the answer she wanted, or maybe we just looked okay, and that was enough. She exhaled a shuddery breath and made a noise that wasn't quite a word but sounded like maybe it was supposed to be.

From outside, voices.

"Sir! Are you all right?"

"Someone check the van!"

"I'll use the phone inside."

"See if they're okay first."

"Wendy, you always call 911 first."

"*No*, you check and see if there's a reason to."

"*He's bleeding*—that's a reason!"

The hit had caused the front of the car behind us—an old sedan—to swivel outward. We'd hit with the driver's side, and from where I sat, I could see the man sitting behind the wheel. He looked young, maybe in his early twenties, but it was hard to tell with all the blood. It poured diagonally across his face from somewhere on the other side of his profile, and he kept reaching up and dabbing at it with his fingers, then bringing his fingers to his face and looking at them, and then dabbing again. He seemed like he was trying to make the sign on the cross, but he was stuck in a loop and couldn't get past the first step. *In the name of the Father. . . In the name of the Father. . . In the name of the Father. . .*

I realized then that something was off. My brain, operating with a serious lag, located the source of the strangeness: it was my left hand. And it felt weird because it was being held—clutched, really. I don't think Steph even knew what she was doing, because as soon as she noticed that I noticed, she pulled away like she'd just touched a burner on the stove. She quickly tucked the burnt hand against her side.

A couple people came to the side of the car we'd hit. One of them, a lean man in a striped polo shirt with sunglasses resting on his balding head, knocked on the passenger-side window of the car.

"Buddy, I'm gonna open this door, okay?"

Before we could hear what the driver's response was, a woman appeared outside Emily's window.

"Yeah, Barry, there's kids in here," she called. She peered inside and added, "Yeah, they look okay."

Mrs. Mayer popped her door open and stepped out.

"Hi," she waved at the lady with a shaky hand. "Hi, yeah, we're fine. We're all good. Thanks for going—thanks for coming to . . . to check on us."

"Are the children all right?" the woman asked. She had big hair streaked with highlights and looked like she'd just come from a vacation somewhere hot.

"They're . . . yeah. They're fine," Mrs. Mayer said. Then, poking her head back inside the vehicle, she checked: "You're fine, right, guys?"

We all confirmed that we were. A seat belt unclicked behind me, and a moment later Dylan crouch-walked past me, opened the door, and stepped out. Kyle followed, then Steph, then me. The car we'd hit had its door open now, and the bloodied driver sat hunched forward with his legs resting on the ground outside the car. My first viewing of his bloody face had been filtered through two windows, which, I realized now as my legs began to dissolve, had dampened the shock. Seeing someone bleed from the head wasn't the same as seeing blood come from someone's nose or lips. Nosebleeds were gross, but they happened. You got used to them. Same with split lips. I'd seen them happen during some of the tamest schoolyard fights. Split lips actually looked kind of cool. But seeing someone bleed from the head was something else. It happened in movies, but not in real life. Never in real life. Your head . . . that's one of those places you're *definitely* not supposed to bleed from. I followed one drip as it fell onto the asphalt, and when I noticed how many other drips it was joining I had to lean on the van for support.

We all watched as Barry, the balding man, took off his polo, balled it up, and knelt down in front of the hurt driver. He pressed the shirt against the driver's cut and slowly eased him into an upright sitting position. Once the driver was sitting on his own, he took the shirt from the man and held it in place himself.

"Wendy," Barry said to the woman with the highlights, "come sit with him. I'll run inside and call an ambulance."

Emily climbed out and joined us. She went and stood with her mother and brother a few steps from the van. Mrs. Mayer's cheeks were wet with tears, but it didn't seem like she was crying, more like the tears had just spilled out, maybe from carelessness, or because there was an overflow and she'd tipped her head too far one way. She had one arm around Dylan and the other around Emily, an unframed portrait that wouldn't make the mantle cut. One of her hands shielded Emily's eyes from the messiness in front of them. At best, it was a PG-13 mess, and she was capped at PG.

The injured driver's voice made him sound even younger than he appeared. "I don't think it's as bad as it looks," he said.

"You can't be sure. An ambulance is on its way," Wendy replied.

The driver nodded, cleared his throat, then spat a stringy, bloody gob onto the asphalt.

"*God,*" Steph said, covering her mouth.

The driver looked at her and smiled reassuringly. "Don't worry," he told her, "I'm pretty sure that's just from somewhere inside my mouth. Doesn't feel like it came from anywhere deeper than that. Not as . . . bad . . . it looks."

Steph let out an uncertain laugh and then came and leaned against the van with me. I heard sirens in the distance.

Mrs. Mayer exhaled loudly. I watched as she took her hand-shield away from Emily's eyes and wiped the tears from her cheeks. Then, with purpose, she stepped over to the driver.

"What the *fuck* is wrong with you?"

Everyone looked at her. The driver—clearly baffled—didn't respond. She repeated the question for him.

"Huh? Did you hear me? What the fuck is wrong with you? I-I have children in the car!"

The driver's face slowly morphed from an expression of innocent confusion to one of anger. "What the hell are you—*you ran into me, lady!*"

"Oh!" Mrs. Mayer threw her head back and laughed. "Oh!" she said again. "That's how it is! I see. This is all *my* fault. Christ, you were tearing through the goddamn parking lot like a lunatic! How fast were you going? Fifty? Sixty? And you say it's *my* fault. *My* fucking fault that you appeared out of nowhere and endangered the lives of the children in my vehicle!"

The driver raised his hand, maybe to shush her, maybe to indicate that it was his turn to speak. The hand was ignored.

"My God," Mrs. Mayer fumed. "Un-be-fucking-lieveable! *My fault.*" She looked him up and down and shook her head. "How old are you? Are you even old enough to drive? Is this even your car?"

"You're fuckin' nuts, lady," the driver said. He looked over at Dylan and Emily. "If those are your kids, I feel sorry for them."

Mrs. Mayer scoffed. She bent forward, and stuck her finger in his face, her eyes narrowing to slits. "Don't you *talk* to them. Don't you even *look* at them."

Barry, sitting crouched on his haunches, opened his mouth to speak, then thought better of it and inched back a few steps. Good call, Barry.

Taking a chance with the crazy woman, the bloody driver said, "We should exchange insurance information before the cops get here." He leaned back and reached for his glovebox, one hand still pressing the loaner shirt to his forehead. Mrs. Mayer looked on with a scowl. When he found what he was looking for he offered it to her. There was a smudge of blood on the corner of the paper card he was holding out. Mrs. Mayer took one look and then turned and walked to the front of her van. She plunked her purse down on the hood, muttering as her hunting hands churned through the bag.

As the sirens in the distance grew louder, something in her shifted and she looked like she was about to break down. But she didn't. She blinked it away, and the expression that replaced it was rigid. She flipped her purse upside down and dumped everything out onto the hood, sending change and lipstick and everything else falling to the ground. Some of it landed by her feet, some of it rolled under the car. A few of her many cards—her Visa, her Safeway Club Card, her Blockbuster membership—slid off too. Instinctively, Steph walked over and picked them up, carefully placing them on the car's hood. Kyle followed her lead and picked up some loose change and a tube of lipstick. Everyone else, myself and Dylan included, just watched as she shuffled through the contents again.

"*Fuck*," she said.

The wailing ambulance pulled into the far end of the parking lot. Behind it followed a police car. Its blue and reds flashed, but its siren was already switched off.

There were two paramedics, a man and a woman. They were both blond and wore similar pairs of Oakley sunglasses. The woman went to the driver of the car we hit. Barry, the Good Samaritan, stood up and began giving his medical assessment, but she politely shut him down. Then she took the balled-up polo from the bloody driver's head and asked him his name and his address. She seemed satisfied with his answers, if not a little impressed with his calm, clear responses. A swoop of hair was pasted to his forehead with drying blood. With delicate, gloved fingers, the paramedic unstuck the wave and brushed it to the other side of his head where there was less blood.

"Let's get a look at that gash."

The other paramedic came over to us. Mrs. Mayer introduced herself as Diane and assured him that all the kids were fine. The paramedic told her that was good, but we were all going to get looked at anyway. When he knelt down in front of Emily, Mrs. Mayer explained that she was getting over pneumonia.

"We weren't out of the house long," she said, "maybe fifteen minutes."

The paramedic knelt down and looked into Emily's eyes and asked her if she hit her head.

"No," she said.

"Are you sure? Your head doesn't hurt at all? Because sometimes these things happen so fast and we don't even realize that we've bonked our heads on something until way after."

Emily considered this. She poked at the perimeter of her skull and, once she'd done a full lap with her fingers, told the paramedic, "No, I'm okay."

He looked her over and I wondered if she'd get best in show and be awarded a blue ribbon. When he was content, he moved onto us older kids. One by one, he asked us questions about our heads and necks while he gazed into our eyes, his stare deep and unblinking, as if he were reading our minds. I didn't like the invasive feeling, didn't want my mind read. That wouldn't have been good at all.

When he finished with us, he went to Mrs. Mayer. He asked her the same questions about her head and neck, and I noticed then that Wendy and Barry were talking to the police officer who had arrived right behind the ambulance. They both took turns speaking, and both of them were dramatic hand-talkers. The officer, who looked like a caricature with his aviators and tree-trunk neck, nodded along with all the emotion of an oil pumpjack. He jotted down some notes in a pocket notebook and went over to the driver, who was now bandaged up and looking much less icky. There were still traces of blood on his head, face, and neck, but looking at him didn't make me queasy anymore and I found I could stand without the support of the van.

The driver spoke to the police officer in a whisper. And while we couldn't hear his words, the faces he made, which alternated between expressions of disbelief and anger, and the constant pointing indicated that he hadn't gotten over Mrs. Mayer's accusations, and he had no intention of shouldering the blame on this one.

I glanced at Mrs. Mayer, and even though I hardly turned my head, she somehow felt my eyes.

"You . . . you're all right, Robin?"

"Yeah. I'm fine."

"That's good," she said, her voice untethered and floaty, as if coming from some in-between plane.

The officer approached and planted himself at what I judged to be about one finger-length from her face. As I took in their profiles, I wondered what it was like for her, staring at twin versions of her uncomposed self in those two shiny black screens he wore in front of his eyes.

Watching them speak was like watching a guilty child with a baseball bat explain a broken windowpane to a skeptical parent. The officer listened as she, teary-eyed and frantic, told him about how she had checked all three mirrors, and then turned and looked over her shoulder as she eased out of her parking spot, slow, so slow, never taking her eyes off the asphalt behind her. I'd never seen her so worked up. It hurt to watch her, and it hurt to watch Dylan even more.

"I—he was, he was going *fifty*! *At least* fifty!"

"Ma'am, now, I'm gonna need you to calm down, ma'am. Deep breaths. Ca—"

"*I am fucking calm!*"

Silence.

"Ma'am . . ."

"He was speeding. He came out of *nowhere*."

"The couple eyewitnesses I spoke with tell it differently."

"They probably didn't even see it happen. I don't remember seeing them anywhere in the parking lot. I . . . I had children in the car."

"I understand. But I'll need you to fill out an accident report. I'll need to see your driver's licence, insurance, and—"

"Why do I have to fill out an accident report if I didn't cause an accident?"

"That's not how it . . . Ma'am, I'm being very patient here, but I am going to need to see your documentation right away."

Deflated, Mrs. Mayer slowly turned to the hood of the van, where some of her many cards still lay. She shuffled through them, and when she didn't find what she was looking for she groaned and raised a fist like she was going to slam it down on the spotless candy-red hood. She didn't though. She took a deep breath, opened her fist, and lowered her arm, then reached into her purse and pulled out her wallet.

"Here," she muttered, handing the officer her licence.

"Thank you. And I'll need the insurance and registr—"

"I *know*."

She went back to the purse and pulled out a little plastic CAA folder. The officer plucked the folder from her hands and walked away, flicking at it absently while he surveyed the scene. Black boots crunching broken glass into asphalt, he walked over to the other driver and asked, "How's the noggin, Jared?"

Jared gave a him a thumbs up that wobbled like the needle of a wonky pressure gauge. I guess the officer decided that an iffy thumb up was better than a downward one, because from there he moved to his cruiser.

The sound of laughter was out of place among the blood and bits of glass, the tears, the curses, and the accusing fingers. So it took me a moment to register what it was. I traced the sound to Emily, who was covering her mouth with her hand. Her laugh, like her brother's, was giddy and couldn't be contained. Kyle knelt in front of her. He wasn't laughing, but his smile was bicoastal.

"No, no, no." Emily giggled, shaking her head for emphasis. "Alvin's the *worst!*"

"Alvin's the *coolest*," Kyle said. "He has a cool hat and he plays electric guitar. Nobody likes *Simon*—yuck!"

"Uh-huh," Emily said. She pointed at herself with two aggressive indexes and got right in Kyle's face. "*I* like Simon."

"Why?" Kyle asked, like he'd just been told her favourite food was liver and onions.

"Because I like blue, and because he has glasses and I want glasses."

"Why would you *want* glasses?" Kyle asked, his voiced rife with the special brand of enthusiasm people have on reserve for conversations with little kids. "Nobody wants glasses. If you had glasses you'd look like a nerd." He cranked a thumb at me.

Emily studied my face, then turned back to Kyle. "Robin looks like a nerd, but some people look good in glasses. I'd look good in glasses."

"*Hey*," I said, "I'm a cool dude."

"Ooo-kay, Robin, whatever," Emily replied, blasting her point into the bleachers with a huge eye roll. It was just hammy enough to get a laugh out of Kyle, and then me.

"Maybe," Kyle said, "we should talk about a different show, because I can't talk *Chipmunks* with anyone who thinks Simon is number one." He thought for a moment, then offered a new show for her to weigh in on. "What about *Madeline*?" he asked.

Floored, Emily said, "*You* like *Madeline*?" When Kyle answered with a shrug, she added, "But *Madeline* is a girl show!"

Another shrug from Kyle, then: "Yeah, I don't know. Maybe. My sister likes it, so I watch it with her. And I like the house they live in. The old one with the vines all up it. It looks cool."

"Maybe you'll get to watch it with her again soon."

"Thanks," said Kyle. "I hope so."

They stared at each other, their mirroring smiles having a glow-off. It seemed for a second like I was witnessing the only two people in the world experience something pure and I guess beautiful, but something that I felt very much separate from. Like I was looking in on them through a pane of dirty glass.

Their moment came to its end when the officer walked past us, back to Mrs. Mayer.

"I'll need you to take a breathalyzer for me."

He held a little black gadget. It looked like the lovechild of a TV remote and the Casio calculators we had at school. The only feature it didn't inherit from either of its parents was the little straw that poked out from one corner, which must have been one of those genetic traits that skipped a generation. Maybe grandpa was a Slurpee cup. The officer pressed a button on the side. He confirmed something on the screen and handed the device to Mrs. Mayer.

"Deep breath, and don't stop exhaling until it beeps at you."

She looked at the stony cop as if waiting for him to say, *Just kidding! I'm just messing with you!* Or maybe, *Smile! You're on Candid Camera!* When he didn't, she asked, "Why doesn't he have to take one?" gesturing with a nod to Jared, who was standing against the front of his car, watching her while he tried to work a kink out of his shoulder.

"He will," the officer said. "I'm starting with you. If I had two straws, I'd make you both go at the same time. You could be like Archie and Betty sharing a milkshake. But I don't have two straws. So, it's ladies first, 'cause that's how I was raised."

Mrs. Mayer looked down at the straw and made a face like she was being asked to verify the flavour of a piece of gum that had been found in an alley.

"This is clean, I assume?"

"Squeaky."

She closed her eyes and blew out in a long steady stream, and when, finally, the thing beeped, the officer retrieved it from her. He tipped his aviators down the bridge of his nose when he looked at the screen, and then it was his turn to exhale.

"Hmm, .038."

Mrs. Mayer let the number sink in and said, "That's below the legal limit. The limit's—"

"The *limit's* .08. But you don't want to be at the limit, do you?"

"Of course not," she answered, making no attempt to hide how insulted she was.

"Technically, we can impose a penalty for anything over .05—"

"In which case I'm *still* well under," Mrs. Mayer snipped.

"Yes," said the officer, "in which case you're still under. I don't know if I'd say you're *well* under. And being under the legal limit is one thing, but, if you ask me, having any booze in your system when you're carting a group of kids around is . . . questionable to say the least."

He removed his aviators, revealing a pair of blue eyes that had an electrical charge to them. Slowly and silently, he scanned over each of our faces, snapping a mental polaroid of one before moving onto the next. I wondered about the number of faces that lived in a cop's brain. Were they added to a series of revolving wheels, like the symbols on a slot machine? Row upon row upon row, forever spinning until something clicked and the right faces lined up, glowed, and then—*jackpot*?

Once he'd taken his last mental image, he addressed Mrs. Mayer. "Ma'am, how much *have* you had?"

At first she scoffed at the question. She folded her arms across her chest, crowding her breasts against her body, and shook her head. For a second, I wondered if she might try to flirt her way out of it, like you see in the movies. If anyone could pull it off, it was her. But why would she? The things you see in the movies only happen in the movies. Most of them, at least.

"I had a couple drinks earlier in the day. *Much* earlier in the day. It's been hours and I feel perfectly fine."

"What did you have?"

"I had a tiny bit of whiskey in my coffee."

"And what time was that?" he asked.

"It would have been around ten this morning," she told him matter-of-factly.

With that lie, I could feel Steph's eyes on me. We were both thinking the same thing: it had been later than ten. Much later. Maybe she meant she *started* at ten.

The officer rotated, getting another panorama of the mess. When he'd finished his cycle and was back facing Mrs. Mayer, he passed his verdict. "You're under the limit, and I'm not going to charge you with anything," he said.

"You *can't* charge me with anything," Mrs. Mayer told him.

This amused him. "Well, I don't know if it's a good idea telling me what I can or can't do right now. I said I won't charge you with anything, but that doesn't mean there's not a list of things I *could* charge you with if I wanted to. You're lucky I don't want to. And believe it or not, my decision has nothing to do with your charming personality."

He continued, "I don't know if you're aware, but this town has bigger problems right now, and I feel I've wasted just about enough of my time dealing with all this. So you're not getting charged, but that doesn't mean you won't get taken to court if our friend over there"—he nudged a shoulder at Jared—"has any serious injuries. I'm also not going to let you drive any of these kids home," he said. "I'm fine with you transporting yourself once you fill out a report—and I'll be sure to escort you to make sure you get there all right—but you're not taking any of them. Understood?"

Her mask was firm. There was no trembling lip, no pouting. But her eyes gave her away. The wetness welled up, and each bottom lid became a tiny canoe with a hole in it, water pushing its way in, making everything heavy. The wetness held for a second, then spilled over.

Yes, the eyes gave away everything.

× × ×

We called the pay phone outside Blockbuster the Sucker Phone, because whoever used it obviously didn't know about the free courtesy phone inside the store, only a few steps away. And if they did know about it, didn't they want to save a quarter? One quarter got you a play on over half the machines at the arcade. Or a Jumbo Sour Soother at Perry's Pantry. The only times Dylan and I would use the Sucker Phone was when we worked up the nerve to make a prank call, or when we dialed 1-800-WET-GRLS, a phone-sex line that Dylan heard about from Adam. Of course, we never spoke to an actual person on the 1-800 line, but if you called the number, you got to hear the steamy pre-recorded sales pitch before they asked for your credit card number.

Mrs. Mayer stood in front of the Sucker Phone, nervously rubbing a shiny quarter between her fingers as she stared at the keypad like its buttons were teeth. I didn't think it was a phone for suckers then. You'd have to be pretty heartless to call someone so scared looking, so rattled, a sucker.

She lifted the receiver and popped the quarter in, and the phone produced that slide and clink that gave you just the faintest idea of what its guts might look like. She hesitated before she punched the first digit.

"Dylan, do you guys want to go back in Blockbuster while I call your dad?" Her voice sagged.

Dylan told her sure, and we all added a "sure" or a "yeah" for support. Except for Emily, who didn't say anything. Dylan took her by the hand and led her toward the door of the Blockbuster, and the rest of us followed them in, leaving Mrs. Mayer to face her husband.

For a second time, we wandered the aisles, Steph, Kyle, and I roaming free, Dylan and Emily sticking to the kids' section. He didn't let go of her hand.

× × ×

We passed our time at the Mayer house watching *Videoflow* on MuchMusic while we waited for my dad to come get us earlier than planned. Steph would have to catch her celebrity crush in *Mars Attacks!* later. During a commercial break, I headed to the bathroom. On my way there, I caught a glimpse of Mrs. Mayer sitting in the front room in the same spot Steph and I sat a couple days earlier. She was sipping coffee. This time, if the coffee was spiked with anything, it was cream. When I passed her a second time on my way back, wiping my still-wet hands up and down my jeans, she looked at me and forced a smile. I forced one back, and I wondered whose looked more fake.

Mr. Mayer had shut himself away in his office. Like his wife in the living room, it was easy to forget he was in there. But when my dad's brakes screeched to a stop outside the house, I heard sounds of movement from inside the office—the swivel of Mr. Mayer's leather office chair, footsteps on carpet, the clearing of his throat. He slid the door open and stepped out. We all turned and looked. He didn't force a smile to us.

"Hey, Dad," Dylan said.

His response was toneless and flat. "Hi," he said, without looking in the direction of his son's voice.

It was the first thing I heard him say since we'd returned to the house a couple hours earlier. He'd picked us up from Blockbuster after the accident. When he arrived, Mrs. Mayer had tried to greet him first, but he pushed past her—actually physically moved her aside, as if she were nothing more than an obstacle—and came right over to us kids. He gave Emily and Dylan a hard hug and asked each of us if we were all right. When he went to his wife, she buried her face in his chest, and he held her. At first I thought he looked sort of detached, but then I looked closer and thought maybe that wasn't the case. More like he was trying real hard to hold something back. Sadness, or something worse. His shirt was blotted with her tears when he walked back over to us and said it was time to head home.

He joined his wife as she opened the door for my dad. Dad knew about the accident. That it happened and why it happened. Mrs. Mayer had called him at work to tell him pretty quickly after we got back to the house. I told her to call him instead of my mom because Mom was at an appointment with Peter, but that had been a lie. If she had called my mom, she would've sped over here and unleashed a storm. I'm not saying that I thought Dad would take it well, but I knew he'd take it better than Mom would. While she spoke with him on the phone, I did my best to tune out her voice. When they finished their discussion, Mrs. Mayer came and handed me the cordless, and I spoke with my dad and assured him of what I had already assured so many other people that day: that I was okay.

Mr. and Mrs. Mayer couldn't get a hold of Bruce at work. And after calling my dad, I heard Mr. Mayer say it was best to deliver the news in person, so Steph and Kyle would get the VIP package: a lift home and a personal visit. I'd hate to be a fly on the wall for either family, especially for Kyle's mom who already had someone she loved missing, possibly hurt, or even dead. I'd seen enough adults cry in the last few days to last me a lifetime.

Dad and I met eyes as I neared the door. He wasn't one to wear his anger. When he was truly pissed—and I'd only seen this maybe three times in my life at that point—every bit of emotion would drop from his face, leaving him totally blank. Which was some-how more terrifying than any angry expression could've been. I had trouble meeting his eyes, so I looked away, feeling for some reason as though I was the one who had done something wrong.

Mr. Mayer offered his hand. Dad looked at it for a long second before he took it.

The four of us kids were all asked to wait in the front yard while my dad and Mr. Mayer spoke. Wordlessly, we slipped on our shoes and obeyed, like the lowly townspeople who hustle out of harm's way before the final shootout in a Western. It was cooling down outside. We were still a ways away from autumn, but its promise of bright colours and decay lingered somewhere in the beyond. The air was thick. Tension coiled itself around us like an invisible band, forcing us to stand sandwiched together in a tight, silent circle. I thought we'd have to wait longer than we did for the adults to finish talking. I also thought we'd hear yelling, but we didn't. The door opened after about a minute. We all watched my dad walk out. Mr. Mayer stood behind him resting against the frame. He looked like he was off somewhere else, like whatever words had been exchanged between him and my dad had cut a part of him loose.

Dad pulled his keys out of his pocket. "Let's go." By the time he reached his door it occurred to me that I wasn't standing on a conveyor belt, and if I wanted to get to the car some effort would be required on my end.

I parted ways with my friends without saying goodbye.

17

MY PARENTS WERE FIERCELY LOYAL TO CO-OP, SO WE ALWAYS WENT THERE
even though there was a Safeway closer to our house. We needed a
few groceries (at a glance, I saw zucchini and spaghetti scribbled on
the Post-it Dad took out of his pocket when we entered through the
store's automatic *Star Trek* doors). But the real reason for the stop
was to pick up Peter's prescription. He'd been off Ritalin for a couple
months because it messed with his appetite and sleep, but with the
new school year creeping up, my parents wanted him to give the
little white pills another go. There had been a few behavioural issues
last year when he took a break. His doctor suggested he start back up
on a lower dose, and Mom and Dad decided that the end of August
would be a good trial run before school started up again.

Dad put a few items in his red basket as we walked through
the produce section. Two zucchinis, some tomatoes on the vine. He
tested the firmness of four avocados. When none of them passed
his test, he decided the whole pile was no good, so we moved on
without them. We turned the corner and ended up in front of the
butcher's counter, where a trio of men, who all looked like smokers,
sawed meat and weighed meat and arranged meat on sliding metal
trays. They all wore white coats, like scientists, which I thought
was an odd choice given the blood they had dotting their cuffs and
sleeves. I thought of how the blood from Jared's leaking head hadn't
stood out on his dark t-shirt and wondered, why not red coats?
Or a rust colour, if that was available, so the blood would blend in
when it dried. Then I realized all three of the butchers were white
and looked to be between twenty-five and thirty-five and my mind
drifted to Catherine Hillerman. Two of the men had a build that
I'd classify as medium (the third was a generous medium-plus), and
both mediums had dark hair and stubble. My eyes moved again
to the flecks of blood on their coats, and in the span of about two
seconds a feature-length horror movie was born in my mind.

Dad asked me something, but I didn't clue in that I was being spoken to until he finished his sentence.

"Huh?"

"Don't say 'huh.' You'll never get a girlfriend if you go around saying 'huh.' I said, Peter's prescription will probably take at least ten minutes." He gestured to the pharmacy, which was tucked away in the back corner, opposite us. "Do you want to go look at the comics while I drop the script off and finish getting the last couple things?"

"Yeah," I said. "Sure."

As I cut down the cereal aisle, he called to me, "If you see one you want, you can get it." Then he added, "As long as it's not one of those hologram covers that costs as much as my mortgage payment."

I gave a thumbs up and continued on my shortcut toward what Peter and I called the "fun section."

The fun section had things that weren't groceries, so really, it was only fun by comparison. There wasn't an upside-down rollercoaster or a big-screen TV with a game system hooked up to it. Nothing like that. But its selection—racks of comics and magazines, shelves of paperbacks, VHS tapes, cassettes, and CDs—was actually pretty decent for a grocery store. I picked up a copy of *Betty and Veronica*. Cartoon characters or not, they were hot, and I had no qualms about gawking at cartoon women. The cover of the August issue had them both standing on a fishing dock. Veronica—who looked like a younger Mrs. Mayer if you had an imagination—stood in her skimpy red outfit next to her catch: a swordfish. Betty, wearing painted-on denim overalls, stood next to hers: a very stupid and very horny-looking Archie.

Ba-dum-chh! Oh, that Archie.

A new issue of *The Uncanny X-Men* sat on the rack next. I wasn't into comics as much as I was when I was younger, but if either of my parents offered to buy me one, I wasn't going to say no. This issue guest-starred Spider-Man. On the cover he was being attacked by Marrow, an X-Man who could shoot bones out of her skin. She was leaping at him, flinging a handful of bone darts. She also had white bones poking out from her wrist, and exploding from her chest, right between her boobs. She had one of the grosser mutant powers out there, but of course, they still drew her to look hot. Comic book artists must be lonely guys, I thought as I flipped through the issue.

The issue looked like an all right read, so after checking the cover price wasn't too high, I decided I'd go with it.

My gaze was then drawn to a different section of the fun area. To a different kind of fun. As was the case in most stores, the men's magazines sat by themselves in the back pocket of the shelf. They didn't sell *Playboy* or *Hustler*—or any real porn—but they did have *Maxim* and *FHM*. Dylan, who had a pile of both magazines at the bottom of his sock drawer, called these "tease porn" because even though the women were sometimes nude, the important stuff was always covered. By a hand, or a leaf, or a carefully folded pair of legs. Your imagination had to do some work. I did a quick shoulder check to make sure no one was watching, then stood on my tiptoes and snagged a copy of *FHM*. The cover girl wore black underwear and a long black cardigan, sleek like a bat's wings, with only one button, which held on for dear life over her chest. The way the light hit the fabric offered the faint suggestion that a couple nipples existed somewhere below.

"You look like you're gonna cream your fucking pants, Daredevil."

I rushed—practically threw—the *FHM* onto the shelf in front of me, its back cover facing out to avoid further embarrassment. With the magazine out of my red hands, I turned around to face Louis Duss.

His balled-up Ecko hoodie under one arm, he reached past me and flipped the magazine around the right way. "*FHM?* I pegged you for a *Playgirl* type," he said, a wormy smile on his lips. He hung his hoodie on the edge of the *Archie* rack and yanked the magazine off the shelf and started flipping through, his head ping-ponging from side to side as he judged its contents. He muttered, "Not bad, not bad . . . I'd fuck her."

The kind of guys who said that were the type who'd fuck a honey cruller if you left them alone with one for a couple minutes.

205

A Co-op employee, probably on her way to the break room, walked past us. She looked at us like we were up to something.

Louis pointed at my crotch. "Clean up, aisle seven!" he shouted. "Bring the mop!"

Five bucks an hour meant that policing shithead teens was above and beyond her pay grade. She shook her head and kept walking.

"Dude," I said, feeling the needling heat of embarrassment beneath my cheeks.

Having the Co-op lady deny him the type of reaction I knew he wanted, Louis brought his attention back to me. He looked at the comic in my hand. "Oh," he said, "there's the real spank material."

When it came to guys like him, I'd long since learned you could do one of two things: you could struggle, which, like in quicksand, would only cause you to sink faster, or you could move slowly and deliberately and hope either a branch or a jungle vine would present itself to you if you kept your head on and wished hard enough. Sometimes option B meant that while you waited for your deus ex miracle, you had to let yourself sink a little.

"Nah," I said, placing the comic back on the shelf, "the real spank material is right over there." I pointed at a copy of *Martha Stewart Living*.

My words took a couple flips of the hourglass to load, but once they did, Louis threw his head back and emitted a thick, ugly laugh. The sound had the same consistency as puke.

"Fuck yeah," he said. "Stuffing turkeys with Martha." Then, in a flash of inspiration, he pointed at me and said, "Stuffing *Martha's* turkey!"

I laughed nervously, trying to act like we were just a couple of buddies yukking it up. It felt real for all of three seconds, then he wiped his hand down his face and returned to the reality we both occupied, one where a predator and his prey didn't joke around together. About banging Martha Stewart. About anything.

He looked from side to side, shoved his hands in the pockets of his baggy, wide-leg jeans, and stepped in close. "Last time I saw you, you and your pals were in quite a hurry to get away from me and Connor."

I nodded, sucked air through my teeth.

"Yeah," he said. "You and your fuck-buds were running to the ravine to dodge a beating. And it was a well-deserved beating too, wasn't it, Daredevil?"

Daredevil. Fuck, I wished he'd stop with that.

I didn't respond, so he punched me in the shoulder. "Huh?" he said. "Wasn't it a well-deserved beating? Weren't you guys asking for it?"

I shrugged. "I don't know," I said, shifty-eyed, mumbling.

"Well, *I* do," he said. "And I think you were. I mean, never mind Steph not sharing her soccer ball. I don't even give a shit about that, actually. And I don't even care about your pussy friend calling me an abortion, believe it or not."

Silently, I committed to not. He'd certainly seemed to care at the time.

"What I was—what I'm *still* pissed about," Louis said, "was what you did. You fuckers telling the cops that you'd seen us at the mall. They let slip that two *individuals*," he added heavy air quotes for emphasis, "had seen us before we ran into Kyle and his sister. Connor's got a buddy who works at the arcade and he said you guys snuck away right before we got there. That was fuckin' low, Daredevil. That caused us a lot of problems."

My mind whirred back to that day in the park. What Louis had said: *My dad had to come home from work. He was fuckin' pissed.*

It all boiled down to a minor disruption. That's what really wound him up. A little girl was missing—maybe dead—but the real tragedy was that his dad had to come home from work early. *That* pissed Louis's dad off. He'd had to come home from work so that his shitbag son—who, in all likelihood was at least part of the reason the little girl had gone off wandering around by herself in the first place—could be questioned by police about her disappearance. So that his shitbag son could maybe, I don't know, offer some insight, some help, a piece of a puzzle that was mostly voids. A garage-sale jigsaw that no one could complete, because maybe pieces had already been lost forever. But one piece could make a difference, could matter, if it was the right piece. Coming home from work early for *that*? What a horrible, unforgivable disruption. Definitely the kind of thing you get pissed about. I decided then that I didn't have to know anything else about Louis Duss's dad to know what kind of a person he was.

Unfortunately, I didn't have a choice in that matter. I'd known the apple for years. The tree, it turned out, was only a couple aisles away, his ropey roots unfixed, heading in our direction.

"You know," Louis said, looking rather offended, "for a little bit, I thought you might actually be all right. That afternoon when we let you hang with us, I thought maybe you weren't a little fagmo, and you might actually—"

And then, just as his words began to scrape at the tamped-down soil in my mind with frantic fingers and bloody nails, like a hungry EC Comics ghoul in a graveyard, Louis was cut off. The voice that did the cutting was thunderous and severe and somehow familiar. It sounded like it bounced out of a deep, concrete tunnel. It was Louis's own voice, forty years and eight thousand packs of Lucky Strikes later.

"Lou! The hell kind of light bulb was it?" the senior Duss barked from the end of a nearby aisle. A red Co-op basket, stuffed full—pop, Tostitos and salsa, Milk Duds, and lots of KD—dangled at his side. The way he held it, two-finger grip, and low enough to knock his shins, you'd think he was embarrassed by its contents, or maybe for having to carry it at all. He had wild, vine-like blond hair tied into a sloppy ponytail, and a cannonball gut that tested the endurance of his Stampeders T-shirt. Maybe it was on the verge of attaining hand-me-down status too, like the famous bouncer shirt he'd given his son. It was no antique bayonet, but an heirloom is an heirloom.

Nervous was a new look for Louis. Or maybe it's fairer to say it looked new to me. He held it for a second, then blinked it away and came back with a scrunched scowl.

"I 'unno."

"Christ," his dad said. A couple steps behind him, a man who looked like a walking Lands' End catalogue page waited to be noticed so he could be given space to get by. It looked like he might be in for a long wait.

"Forty watts or something." Louis shrugged in a not-my-problem way. "Maybe more."

Duss Senior exhaled. "You shoulda wrote it down," he said.

"Dad, you said to just remember it."

"Well, you did a hell of a job with that."

The Lands' End man gave up. He turned around and took the scenic route to wherever he needed to go.

"Sorry," Louis grumbled, a note of defeat in his voice. The father of the year then turned his palms up, held the pose for a second, and waved his son over with a hand motion similar to tossing a piece of litter over his shoulder. Louis jogged to him. Just before he disappeared down the aisle with his dad, he turned to me and rasped, "You and your friends are fuckin' dead next time."

I waited for a nervous moment before breathing. I don't know precisely what I was nervous about—it could've been Louis's threat. But the promise of death at the hands of him and Connor wasn't really anything new, so I doubted that was it. Maybe I worried that his dad would return and demand in his monster voice that I join them on their quest for a light bulb.

Once my legs unthawed, I turned back to the comic rack and snagged my *X-Men* issue.

But before I went to look for my dad, I noticed that Louis had left his Ecko hoodie hanging on the other side of the rack with Archie and the gang. My eyes fell to the big pouch on the front of the hoodie, and upon noticing it, a thought hatched in my mind. It was kind of an awful thought, but when it came to me, I smiled. I understood then how the Grinch felt when he got his wonderfully awful idea. Like most men's clothes, the hoodie was extra baggy. And Louis, like a lot of kids, bought his already-designed-to-sag clothes a size bigger than he needed to. I eyeballed the pouch and estimated that it was so big that I could've fit a dictionary inside it. What I was thinking of putting in there was much smaller than a dictionary, though. Much lighter too.

On the edge of the fun area was a small bin of cassettes. The whole bin was mostly the lighter side of top forty and what my parents referred to as adult contemporary, which meant bland. U2, Celine Dion, Hootie and the Blowfish, LeAnn Rimes, Toni Braxton—that kind of boring shit. Vanilla ice cream for the ears.

The selection didn't matter, though. What mattered were the little white tags that each cassette had stuck to its packaging, the ones that, if they weren't deactivated at the till, sent a signal to the sci-fi security gates that sat at every store exit. Mom had one go off on her once. The cashier had forgotten to rub her millionth copy of Nat King Cole's Christmas album on the mysterious deactivation pad, so when we left the alarm sounded. She blushed, I froze, and Peter cried because he thought we were all going to jail for life.

I took a quick look around to make sure no one was watching. A full three-sixty, doing my absolute best to look nonchalant. A chill rippled through me when I realized no one else was around, because with that realization came another one: that I was actually going to do it. The thuds of my staccato heart rattling its cage, I stepped to the bin, and in one quick movement, nabbed a cassette from it. I held it loose and low against my leg, so that anyone walking by wouldn't see it as they passed, and did another quick scan of my surroundings. No one. I hurried over to the rack with Louis's stupid Ecko hoodie on it and carefully slipped the cassette into the gaping pouch.

A trembly breath skittered out of me.

Look casual, I told myself. *But don't think about looking casual, because then you won't look casual. Breathe. People look less suspicious when they're breathing.*

When I felt I had backed a safe distance away from the crime, I did my best to take an objective look at my work. Could I see the shape of the cassette? No. No, yeah—I could. Kind of. Well, not really. Not unless I looked for it. And who would be looking for it? And if it did look suspicious to someone, did that matter? I mean, wasn't that the point?

The aisle I fled to was dedicated to vitamins, tampons, and pads. The Flintstones, the Jetsons, and their kin—fellow chewables, golf ball-sized capsules whose bottles rattled like maracas if you shook them, multivitamins that turned your piss into a neon laser—looked across at shelves populated by packages that were strange, mysterious, and more than anything else frightening to me. The things in those boxes were mythical. They had wings and were ultra-strong. They could carry litres of unoffensive blue liquid, and made long-term commitments, promising their wearer: *Always*. When my mind called up the elevator scene in *The Shining*, I hustled like hell to another aisle.

At the pharmacy, the fluorescent lights from the overhead lamps cast a circular glow on the scuffed linoleum floor. The glowing pools moved as I walked, following me in rigid, straight lines, like ghostly UFOs.

Dad wasn't where I thought he'd be. Recalling the few items I'd glimpsed on his list, I figured my best bet was to head over to whatever aisle they kept the pasta in. I wondered if Louis had gone back for his hoodie yet, or if it was still hanging on the rack with horndog Archie. Would he notice my gift, ditch it, figure out it was me? Or, would I soon hear the robotic pulse of the security gates summoning the store's guard to come bust him? My wondering came to a screeching halt when I passed the frozen food section and met eyes with someone I hadn't seen in a long time.

As is often the case when you see a person you know in an unfamiliar context, even though the recognition is instant, it takes a second for you to place each other. I'd known him since I was six. He'd given me noogies, mounds of unsolicited advice, and as a parting gift, his seat at the dinner table. His hair was longer than when I'd last seen him, and the trick-of-the-light goatee Dylan and I used to laugh about now resembled the real deal. The most out-of-character detail was his red Co-op vest, but his name tag, which was almost eclipsed by the leaning tower of Hungry-Man frozen dinners in his hands, confirmed it was him.

"Adam?"

He smirked, shaking his head in the condescending way most older kids do at younger kids they know, like there's something we just don't get. Once he shoved all the Hungry-Man dinners onto their freezer shelf, Adam wiped his hands on his pants, walked over to me, and gave me one of those high-five handshake combo things that I assumed would become instinct when I cleared fifteen. His hands were cold from the freezer. We both laughed as I fumbled my way through the greeting.

"Holy shit, Rob Goblin, weren't you like three feet tall when I saw you last? I haven't been gone *that* long, have I?" His eyes always had a twinkling brightness to them, like the little Christmas tree lights they sold at Canadian Tire. They were the same shade of blue as his dad's, but his shone brighter.

"Uh, I'm five-four," I told him. "I think I grew like three inches since Christmas."

"Are you taller than my brother yet?"

"No, Dylan's taller."

"Really? He seems to only grow sideways." He took a step back and scratched at his goatee, which made a sandpapery sound. I wondered if it actually itched, or if he just scratched it because he could. He regarded me for a second then shrugged. "So, whatcha doing here? Shopping for the family? You married yet? Wife? Kids?"

I laughed. "Oh yeah, I got married a long time ago. Me and the wife have three little ones back at home. They're all brats."

"Well, congrats on that," Adam said. "And tell Steph I said hi."

In a blink, my face went tomato red. Adam threw his head back and laughed again. "Okay, wow, take it easy. You wanna step into the freezer for a bit and cool off?"

I shook my head, and he gave me a punch in the shoulder. "Lighten up," he demanded, then added, "But a goofy-looking kid like you could do a lot worse."

"What are you doing here?" I asked him, eager to move to on to a new topic.

He looked down at his name tag, gave his vest a tug. "Guess."

"Yeah, but, when did you start working here? I thought you were living in Calgary."

"Newsflash: it's August. I've been off since April."

A horde of follow-up questions rushed to get to the front of the line in my head. First come, first served, I started with the pushiest and most obvious: "How come Dylan—how come no one said anything about you being back?"

He busied himself by rubbing his neck while he searched for a response. "I don't know what to tell ya," he said. "I'm not exactly on the best terms with everyone at home right now, but I figured Dylan would've said something. I saw him a couple weeks back. Me, him, and Emily all went to Fioretti's for pizza. Of course, that was before Emily . . ."

"Got sick."

"Yeah," Adam said, "before she . . . before all that. My dad called me about it. I went and saw her in the hospital the morning after she was admitted."

I took a second to digest his words, trying, as I metabolized them, to wrap my head around why Dylan wouldn't have at least mentioned his brother being back in town. It certainly wasn't earth-shattering news, but it was the sort of thing you'd think he'd at least bring up. I asked question number two before I had time to consider whether it might be rude, or the sort of thing that wasn't really my business.

"You're not living at home?"

"No," he said. "Like I said, not on the best of terms." He shuffled back and forth on his feet. "It's not like they asked me *not* to stay," he said. "They didn't kick me out or anything. I just opted to crash at my buddy Bryan's place for the summer. I figured that'd be best for everyone, at least until things are good again." He laughed to himself, but not a happy laugh. Something else. "*If* they get good again."

I wasn't the best at offering sympathy. Most people at thirteen aren't. But that didn't stop me from trying. "Sorry, Adam," I said, the words wobbly and awkward on my lips. "I, like, didn't know anything was wrong. That's shitty."

The twinkling lights of Adam's eyes shone a little brighter. "Hey," he said, punching me in the shoulder again, "watch your fucking language."

"Pardon me," a voice from behind interrupted. I turned as Adam greeted its owner.

"Yes, sir," Adam said. "What can I help you with?"

The old man shuffling over to us wore a mesh ballcap that said World War II Veteran in bold yellow letters and had thick black glasses that rested on the lowest point of his hilly nose. I thought about something Steph had told me once, about how the only things that keep growing throughout a person's life are their nose and ears. Shifting my gaze to the old man's ears, which looked big enough to pick up cable TV signals, I considered that it might be true.

"Can you tell me where . . ." The old man held up a torn piece of notebook paper and pushed his glasses back up the hill. The instant he took his finger away, the glasses began their slow slide back down. "Can you tell me where I'd find oatmeal," he said, splitting the last word in two and giving each half some wiggle room: *oat . . . meal.*

"For sure," Adam replied, in what must have been his customer service voice—perkier, bordering on excited. "I can go grab it for you. What type of oatmeal are you—"

The old man waved away Adam's offer like it was a bad smell.

"I can get it myself. I asked where it is."

"For sure. Oatmeal's gonna be in aisle eight, down that way."

In a slow panning motion, the old man's eyes followed Adam's finger. "Eight," he confirmed. "Down that way. I hang a left."

"That's right."

"Is it right, or is it left?" the old man said, a note of irritation in his rickety voice.

"Sorry," Adam said. "It's left. I was saying—"

Again, his words were fanned away. The old man smiled. "I'm messin' with ya, son," he said, then turned and began his trek.

We both stood and watched him leave. Once we had the frozen section to ourselves again, Adam spoke. "This fucking place. It's not bad, but sometimes . . . I tell ya. I'd love to quit. But what am I gonna do? Calgary's a pricey city, at least compared to Haddington Springs. My dad's still helping with tuition, but I need cash to get me through the semester."

"Totally," I said, as if the world of tuition and rent weren't as completely foreign to me as the tampons and pads I'd seen in the other aisle.

Adam looked down and scraped something that could have been nonexistent off his name tag. "How are they?" he asked.

I shot him a confused look.

Adam clarified. "How are my little bro and sis doing?"

"Good," I told him. "Emily is doing better, definitely *looking* better at least. Your mom said she's still recovering, but she felt good enough to come to Blockbuster with us today." His face scrunched a little. Maybe at the thought of Emily leaving the house while she was still on the mend. I decided then it was best not to mention the car accident.

"And how about Dylan?" he asked.

"He's good too. We went to Tollcross yesterday . . . that was cool."

Again, a nod. "Yeah, you two probably see each other every day." He laughed. "I remember that's how it was the last few summers, at least. It was like every time I woke up, I'd roll out of bed to get breakfast and, boom, there you were. You were like that old *Cat Came Back* cartoon, the one with the guy playing tuba. You'd leave, and I'd blink, and there you'd be again."

Noticing my expression droop at being compared to a cartoon about a pesky cat who won't stay away, Adam quickly clarified, "Not that we didn't *want* you there. Obviously. You were just always there. You're like the fourth Mayer kid."

I nodded. "You know, me and Dylan go back and forth between houses, but we always seem to end up at yours more. Your house is . . . cooler, I guess. There's better stuff. And your mom always lets us get good junk food."

For a second time, his face scrunched, this time into a full frown. I'd clearly struck some sort of nerve. "In summer we're always outside anyway," I continued. "Or at least we were before the whole . . ."

"Missing kid thing?" Adam said.

"Yeah. Before the whole missing kid thing."

He looked around to make sure no one else was around, no boss to tell him to get back to work. "That shit's so fucking awful," he said once the coast proved itself clear. "I never knew anyone from that family, but once I saw them on the news, I recognized them right away. I've definitely seen them around. The dad comes in here sometimes."

"Probably, yeah. The brother of the girl who vanished is in our grade. He hangs out with us sometimes now."

Adam continued as if I hadn't spoken. "Can you imagine? A girl that age—Emily's age? Some sicko taking her? Shit, man."

"It's legit scary," I said, realizing as the words left my mouth that they felt wrong. Inappropriate. An understatement. Horror movies were *scary*. This-is-your-brain-on-drugs PSAs and the STDs we learned about in sex ed were *scary*. Catherine Hillerman—a real person, snatched away—that was something else altogether.

He shook his head in disgust. "I probably don't have to tell you what usually happens to kids who get abducted," he said. "What they get . . . used for."

The way he said it made my stomach turn. *Used for*. Like they were a thing. Like batteries. Like tires. Use them until they're no good anymore and then throw them away. Replace them.

While the two of us stood in silence, dwelling on something I'd tried so hard not to think about over the last several days, I felt suddenly that I should tell Adam about what had happened in the Blockbuster parking lot. I'm not sure what compelled me. Maybe there were too many secrets bubbling inside me.

"You should know . . . something happened today when we were out with your mom—"

"That woman is not my fucking mother," Adam snipped, his words sharp and dangerous, shards of a broken mirror tossed carelessly in the air. I flinched.

"What do you . . ."

He shook his head and knotted his arms tightly across his chest. "I mean *Diane* isn't my fucking mom. She's—let's just say she's one of the main reasons I don't want to live in that place right now."

That couldn't be right. Mrs. Mayer, she'd always been, she had to be, she *was* . . .

Adam looked right at me. His eyes were still bright, but their twinkle looked too hot now. They didn't just shine—they burned. "She's Dylan's mom, and she's Emily's mom," he told me. "She's not mine."

"But you've always . . . She's always been your mom," I said, wondering if this was what it felt like speaking to someone who woke up with amnesia, explaining a person's own life to them.

Adam raised an eyebrow, as if I were the one who wasn't making any sense.

"You call her *mom*, Adam. What do you mean she's not . . . ?"

He stepped in close. "My mom died when I was three. Head-on collision on the Trans-Canada. I barely remember her. And the stuff I do remember, I don't even know if I really remember it, or if the memories just came from the few photos I've seen. Like maybe I saw them and grew memories from them."

He looked at me then, his face pained and angry. And as I stood in front of him, numb with confusion, I felt like I had opened some sealed off door that was best left locked. It suddenly made sense why Mr. Mayer had been so quiet after picking us up from the parking lot. Another car crash . . .

"*Diane* . . . I called her mom, yeah," he said bitterly. "I was raised to." He paused for a moment, shrugged. "And you know, she wasn't ever that bad to me. She didn't love me like she did

Dylan and Emily—*her* kids—but she was never really awful to me. I didn't mind calling her mom sometimes. I didn't mind her being my mother. Sometimes. But when I found out what she was . . ."

His hands clenched into tight fists.

"Fuck, man, when I found out what she was . . ."

"Does Dylan know?" I asked. "Does he know about . . . whatever you're saying she—"

"Well, I couldn't *not* tell someone. I couldn't keep it all to myself," Adam interrupted, defensively. "And Dylan's old enough. He should know."

What she was.

"Know what?" I asked.

For a second, it looked like he might tell me more. But I could see the change of heart on his face. "If Dylan wants you to know, he'll tell you."

Some of the tension in him began to loosen. "You can probably see why I'm not living there anymore," he said, looking at me sideways. "It's a big house, but some things . . . they have a way of making a place smaller. That place was a shack when I left."

A beep, followed by a crackling voice over the intercom: "Courtesy to cash, please. Courtesy to cash."

Adam pointed to the ceiling. "That's me," he said. "See ya, Rob Goblin."

I nodded. "Yeah."

Before he left, he pointed at the comic in my hand. I hadn't noticed I'd done it, but at some point during our conversation, I'd rolled the comic up, and my fingers had worn their sweaty impressions into its cover.

"You haven't outgrown that stuff?"

"I guess not," I said.

"Good for you," Adam said.

× × ×

My dad's luck choosing a checkout line matched the luck he always seemed to have choosing a lane during a traffic jam. The second he committed, another car would trap him, and every other lane would suddenly unclog and start to move twice as fast, the universe flipping him the bird. So naturally the cashier we were stuck with moved with the urgency of a drifting continent.

During our wait, while I continued to process Adam's words, Louis and his future self appeared two registers down from us, Ecko hoodie tied tightly around his waist. While he and his dad waited for some space on their conveyor, Louis's eyes landed on me after a few seconds of wandering. But when he noticed me, he looked away quickly, almost embarrassed. His muted reaction excited me almost as much as it scared me. The cassette had to be in his pocket still. If our cashier continued moving at the rate he did, I was in for a show.

As Louis and his dad began unloading their basket, I stole a glance at the conveyor of their checkout and saw that by putting their heads together they had found their light bulb. Forty watts of brightness between them. I realized it was best that I look away—I didn't want to seem suspicious. I turned my attention back to our checkout, where there was almost enough room for my dad to place a few items on our belt. By the time the cashier started ringing us through, Louis and his dad, who I could just barely see in my periphery, were paying for their stuff. My heart escalated from a jog to something closer to a sprint when I heard, over the ambient grocery store clamour—bleeping scanners, the rigid *shhhkk* of paper bags being forced into shape, the clang of shopping carts being brought in from outside and pushed into rows—the cashier wish Louis's dad a good evening.

When it happened, everyone stopped what they were doing and looked up. The alarm, that throbbing robot rhythm, was loud enough to make a few of the people around us press their hands to their ears.

"Chrissake," Duss Senior groaned, stopping in his tracks, his arms cradling two brown bags. A frizzy-haired woman who wore a blue cardigan over her Co-op uniform walked around from behind the customer service desk and motioned for father and son to come over.

She apologized to them as they placed their bags on the counter for her inspection.

In case any of the spectators didn't know that his time was being wasted, Duss Senior let out an elaborate sigh. Louis plugged his hands into his pockets and took in his surroundings with shifty eyes. It took the frizzy-haired woman a matter of seconds to go through all four of their grocery bags.

"*Hrmph*. Nothing in here that would set it off," she said. "Do you mind going through again?"

They picked up two bags each. Duss Senior walked through first. No alarm. He shrugged at the woman from the other side.

"That good enough for ya?"

Ignoring his question, the woman motioned for Louis to walk through.

The robot rhythm pulsed again, somehow louder than the first time. Everyone who'd lost interest was suddenly brought back.

"*Hrmph*." The woman motioned for Louis to walk back to her. The alarm sounded again when he went through, his face blushing like I'd never seen.

The woman placed the two bags Louis was holding on the counter and started looking through them again. A man in a GardaWorld security uniform came from around the corner. The woman gave him a look and gestured with her head at Louis. The man nodded.

"Can I have you walk through again, son," he asked Louis. "We'll try it without the bags this time."

Louis looked at his dad on the other side. Something had tightened in his dad's face. He didn't move, didn't even blink. Louis turned to the guard and nodded, then went through again, this time without any bags.

He hadn't even stepped all the way past the threshold when, again, the alarm blasted.

"What the hell?!" Louis said, stepping backwards.

Duss Senior stepped back into the store now too. He thumped his bags down on the ground. Everyone was watching. This was must-see TV happening in real life. I was thrilled.

The in-store Sherlock looked Louis up and down, then said, "Mind if I see the sweatshirt?"

For a second Louis looked like he didn't understand the guard's request. Then he looked at the hoodie around his waist, pointed at it, and asked, "This?"

"Yes," the guard replied.

As Louis undid the knotted arms of his hoodie, the guard turned to Duss Senior. "Do you mind if I . . . ?"

Duss Senior, whose face looked like a pot about to boil over, made a be-my-guest gesture.

Louis handed over his hoodie and the guard walked to the security gate and swung it through. The alarm sounded.

A couple people gasped—*what a twist!* All the hot red drained from Louis's face. His dad's eyes widened.

The guard moved his hands through the giant hoodie like someone trying to find a balled-up pair of socks in a duvet cover that had just come out of the dryer. After a moment, his hands stopped. He reached into the front pouch and pulled out the cassette tape I'd put there. Billy Ray Cyrus. Talk about insult added to injury.

Duss Senior sucked a deep breath in through his flaring nostrils. I wondered if there would be any oxygen left for the rest of us. Louis's mouth hung open. He made a whimpering noise that could've been the beginning of a protest, but before he got any further the guard pointed at the pockets of his baggy cargo pants and said, "You mind emptying those as well?"

"My pockets?"

"Yes," the guard said, "your—"

"Empty your damn pockets, Lou!" Duss Senior barked, causing Louis to jump at the sound of his voice.

"I didn't . . ." Louis practically sobbed.

"Let's go!"

Tears crested his eyes as he reached into his pockets and revealed the rest of his hidden score—the score he actually knew he'd stolen, and that I certainly didn't. He pulled out a king-size Twix, a four-pack of Duracell double-A batteries, a package of M&Ms, and four loose cigarettes, which he'd probably lifted from his dad.

The frizzy-haired woman sighed and tut-tutted like she knew it all along. The guard nodded and asked Louis and his dad to come with him. Duss Senior, his mouth a tight seam, didn't say a word. He glared at his son with eyes like craters.

Doing all I could to supress my smile, I thought, *It's sure not a good day to be Louis Duss.*

18

AFTER DINNER THAT EVENING I SNUCK OFF TO MY ROOM WITH THE CORD-
less and called Steph to fill her in on everything. I expected her
mind to be blown by my story about Adam. For her to go full
Nancy Drew and start talking a mile a minute, her raw thoughts
flowing so fast I'd barely be able to keep up. She did find the story
interesting, and certainly *weird*—she told me that much—but she
wasn't nearly as thrilled as I'd expected her to be.

"What if Adam is lying?" she said. "I mean, he's always been the
black sheep."

This was true. There were times when Adam was a blemish on
an otherwise picture-perfect family. He got in trouble often and
had never really been the best role model to Dylan. He was the
brother who'd been suspended from school for getting caught with
weed at the year-end dance. The brother who was banned from
having girls over for "study sessions" after getting busted fooling
around behind his closed bedroom door. The brother who, Dylan
once told me, ruined Christmas dinner when he asked his very
Catholic grandmother if God at least paid for Mary's dinner first.

I agreed with Steph: maybe Adam was just flicking a match at
gasoline for fun, to see if it would spark. But something else nagged
at me. I thought back to the day Steph and I had been looking at
the photo of the Mayer family in front of the Christmas tree at
Edmunds Park, after Emily was rushed to the hospital. Just before
we were interrupted by the mystery delivery, I remember thinking
how Adam looked like the spitting image of his dad, how there was
virtually no trace of Mrs. Mayer to be found in his face.

When I pointed this out to Steph, she mulled it over for a
second, but then reminded me, "Sometimes that's just the case. It's
like one parent's genes just take over. Like, Jeremy hardly has any of
my dad in him. He practically looks full Chinese—he's like a young,
male version of my mom."

"I don't think so," I told her. "I can see your dad in Jeremy."

"Well, then maybe it's all a matter of perspective. Maybe to us, Adam looks identical to his dad, but someone else might be able to spot features from his mom."

"Yeah, I guess."

A few seconds passed with neither of us speaking.

"It's really bothering you," Steph said.

"Yeah."

"Why?"

"I don't know. I guess there was something about the way he said it. He . . . he seemed like he was telling the truth. You know when you get a feeling like that? When you can just tell?"

The phone was quiet for so long I thought for a moment Steph might've accidentally hung up on me.

"Yeah, I do know what you mean," she finally said.

"Do you think we should ask Dylan about it?"

She sighed. "Well, *you* can."

"What do you mean?"

"Robin, my dad was *so* mad when Mr. Mayer told him about the accident. He told him everything—about Mrs. Mayer and the breathalyzer, about the guy being injured—and my dad was *ticked*. Like, more ticked than I've seen him in forever. I honestly thought he was going to punch Mr. Mayer in the face." She paused for a beat. I heard the sound of what I was pretty sure was the dishwasher door closing, followed by a couple beeps. Steph was never just on the phone. She always seemed to have it wedged between her ear and shoulder so her hands were free to do other things. "I'm not allowed to go over there anymore," she told me over the hum and buzz of the dishwasher beginning its cycle. "When I asked my dad for how long, he said, 'Until I say so.'"

I now understood why she'd seemed so much less enthusiastic than I'd expected when I told her about everything.

"That's shitty."

"It is indeed shitty," she agreed.

In the background I heard Jeremy's voice. "You swore!" he shouted.

A loud clacking blasted from the receiver into my ear: Steph dropping the phone. I heard her, distant but loud and clear: "Jeremy, if I catch you spying on me again I will call the friggin' swear police and tell them you said the F-word eight-hundred times, and they'll believe me because I'm older and more credible, and you'll be hauled off to swear jail for the rest of your stupid friggin' life!"

She returned to the line and I told her about Louis Duss getting busted, which I thought she'd get a kick out of. It cracked her up a little, but it seemed kind of put-on. I was going to save the big reveal—that I was the one who'd put the cassette in his pouch, the mastermind behind it all—for the end, but by the time I got there her damp response had left me deflated, and I decided to keep that information for another time when it might be appreciated more.

Before we said our goodbyes, we made arrangements to hang out soon.

After that, I called Dylan. I definitely wasn't going to tell him over the phone about my surprise talk with his brother, but I wanted to tell *somebody* the director's cut version of the Louis Duss story. I gave up after seven rings (two more than my mom had told me was ever appropriate), wondering if there was actually nobody home, or if no one at the Mayer house wanted to pick up. Before I put the receiver back in its cradle, I imagined what they were doing. Four people in four different rooms. Emily up in her bedroom, still in recovery mode. Dylan parked in front of the TV, probably playing Nintendo. Mr. Mayer cooped up in his office, shutting himself off from his family. And Mrs. Mayer, where was she? (*When I found out what she was.*) Was she still sitting alone in the dark by herself?

× × ×

The walls of my room were painted a dark shade called Indigo Batik. I knew the name because I choose the colour myself. Before

Peter was born, we lived in a townhouse on Sixth Street. When my mom, her womb five-months-full with a baby who we'd soon learned wasn't willing to stay in much longer than eight, explained to me that we were going to move to a new house, I didn't take it well, at all. My parents refer to the tantrum I threw as The Great Aggression. I cried for days. For multiple nights, I refused to eat my dinner, and when my parents tried to force me, I'd throw my food or smack it out of their hands. I fake ran away from home twice (only going as far as the playground at the end of our street, where, both times, I was found sitting on the jungle gym pouting). At the height of it, I even threatened to kill myself by jumping off a cliff (which Haddington Springs was very short on). Mom got *very* angry with me when I said that. She grabbed me by the arm and yelled at me like never before, but while she yelled, she was crying too. "You have no idea what you've just said," she'd told me, her hand raised to slap me. She didn't actually follow through, but I think it's fair to say I deserved a good whack upside the head. *I* would have wanted to hit me too. I mean, a new home? A nicer house with more space and a real backyard. On a street with other kids, instead of the weirdo single-and-ready-to-mingle neighbours we had on Sixth Street. What the hell was my problem? For whatever reason, the thought of moving terrified me. The thought of *change* terrified me. I've always hated change.

After many attempts to reassure me, followed by an attempted bribery with a Ninja Turtle action figure, my parents appealed to me by telling me I'd get to choose what colour my room would be. Whatever colour I wanted. I'm not sure why—maybe it was the feeling of making a grown-up decision—but that did it for me. We went to the hardware store the next day, and I got to take a bunch of swatches home. Mom said I took one of every colour available, but I think that's an exaggeration. That being said, I do recall having *a lot* of options. When we got home, I fanned my many maybes out on our living room floor and in a matter of minutes settled on Indigo Batik, probably because it was a similar colour to Batman's cape and cowl. My parents didn't hear another peep out of me about moving after that. A deal was a deal.

I loved the colour, but I soon came to realize that it made for one dark room. In addition to the ceiling light and a small lamp on my nightstand, I had a night light plugged into the outlet by the door. It wasn't so much that I was scared of the dark. It was more like it was nice to have a reminder that I was in a room, in a home, on planet Earth, and not floating in a formless void, which was how it felt on nights when the moon, whose warm milky glow usually shone through my window, was stuck behind a bandage of clouds. When I got a bit older and I felt a night light was the sort of thing a little baby had in his room, my parents got me a package of glow-in-the-dark stars and planets to stick to my wall. The stars were the cliché five-point shapes kids draw on their duotangs at school. And except for the two with rings around them, which were my favourite, the planets were all just circles of varying sizes. I put five stars and all nine planets (at the time, Pluto still counted) in a cluster on the wall opposite my window, my logic being that they'd get a charge from the sun and, when it was bright enough, from the moon as well. But I was quick to learn that most of the light they sucked in came from the electric light of the room. Even with a good charge, their glow would only last about ten minutes, but I liked having the stars and planets there. There was something soothing about watching them fade. When I climbed into bed, I'd fade with them.

Eventually, like their night light predecessor, I decided that glow-in-the-dark wall decorations were a bit childish. I took them all down when I was twelve but never threw them away. The whole galaxy now resided somewhere at the bottom of one of the drawers in my nightstand.

That night, before I started reading my new comic, I climbed out of bed, pulled the drawer open, and after digging through a mess of old birthday cards, loose Pogs, and other childhood relics, I retrieved Saturn and two stars. I took them out and placed them right under my lamp so they could get all charged up while I read about mutants and spandex-clad, radioactive wall-crawlers.

When I finished the issue, I put it on my nightstand, then grabbed Saturn and my stars from their charging station. Standing on the edge of my bed, I pressed them against the wall as hard as I could with my knuckles. With the bit of adhesive on the back of each piece of plastic, I just had to force them to stay put.

I waited a second to make sure they didn't fall from their sky and got back under the covers and clicked off my lamp. Saturn and the stars began glowing right away, and watching them felt like it used to. It was like I had turned the clock back entire years. For the ten or so minutes that their glow lasted, I was no longer thirteen.

But unlike when I was younger, I didn't fade as the glow-in-the-dark did. When the stars and Saturn died out, I still lay there awake in the darkness. Alone in the void. With nothing but my own thoughts to keep me company, it occurred to me that if that old night light of mine hadn't been humming away in in Peter's room right then, I'd have popped it back into my socket without hesitation. It was one of those nights where I could have used a little extra glow.

Laying there in the dark, I tossed, turned, and remembered. . .

19

SITTING ON THE BENCH BY THE PLAYGROUND AT SAINT PHILLIP'S PARK BY myself, I was sipping a Mountain Dew Slurpee, squinting up at the clouds because I didn't have anything better to do. The clouds weren't the puffy eruptions I was used to seeing in late July. They existed in thin smears, like someone had tried to scrape them off with a trowel once they had already begun to set. I looked for shapes, but for the most part all I saw were ghostly abstracts. I know it's a lazy day thing people are supposed to enjoy doing in summer—sitting and watching the clouds go by, not a care in the world and all that—but let me tell you, when you have an attention span like mine it gets pretty damn boring after about two minutes. Steph was babysitting Jeremy and couldn't hang out until even later than usual because her dad was stuck working a double. Dylan and his family were visiting his grandma. He wouldn't be back for another couple days. He'd called the night before, and after he finished telling me about what he'd been up to in Calgary—the big, busy city, with its zoo and minor league baseball team, and its wave pool that had two slides and a kiosk that sold Texas donuts with sprinkles—he told me about the stash of quarters he'd scored from his grandma. "Robin, we'll *own* every high score list in the arcade." He'd sounded like a scheming Bond villain.

Even the Blockbuster was a no-go. I owed ten dollars and fifty cents in late fees and didn't have enough to pay the fine and rent something. So I left empty-handed and meandered to the nearby 7-Eleven to drown my sorrows in syrupy slush with the remaining two bucks I had to my name.

When you get to the last bit of a Slurpee, the name makes sense. The spoon-straws they give you are great if you want to take ten years to scoop your treat out one millilitre at a time, but if you're a normal human and try to suck through the straw, you end up tilting, shaking, stirring, and more than anything else, *slurping*.

Between all my slurping and a lingering brain freeze from a few reckless seconds when I'd forgotten my mortality and tried to chug the remaining neon green at the bottom of my cup, I was almost too distracted to hear them coming. Louis and Connor had rounded the corner of the school before I noticed. I had a decision to make, to stay still or run. If I moved, they'd notice me right away. I'd have a head start, but they'd know I was avoiding them, know I was afraid, and that would make me even more appealing to a couple of dickheads who loved nothing more than a struggling victim. I was quickly weighing my options when another factor hit me: there's nothing more dangerous than a man with nothing to lose. I forgot where I'd heard that. Probably from a movie. Even though I'd never been accused of being dangerous, it occurred to me as Haddington Springs' resident teenage goons cut across the asphalt, that between my near-empty wallet and near-empty cup, I had *next* to nothing to lose. What were they going to do? Grab me by the ankles, turn me upside down, and shake the nothing out of me?

Plus, there was nobody else around. They didn't have an audience. No one to impress or shock. I'd be lying if I claimed not to be scared at all, but compared to other times I'd run into them, the stakes were pretty low. My pulse began to level. I opted to try my luck and stay put.

Connor noticed me first. As they passed below the basketball hoop, he jumped to take a swing at the dangling, shredded net that clung to it like a doomed cliff-hanger. When he landed, his eyes fell on me. He nudged Louis, then gestured my way with his head. Louis scanned, found me, and smirked. They quickened their pace.

"Look at this guy," Connor said as they approached.

Louis, a couple steps behind him, was trying to look disinterested. He kept his smirk, but as his comrade-in-arms addressed me, he stretched and fixed his gaze somewhere in the distance, like he was expecting something more interesting to come along any second.

"Hey, man," I said, surprised at the firmness of my voice. I had expected mud but got concrete. This concrete needed a few more hours to set—you could still write your initials in it with a stick—but it was still firmer than I'd expected.

Connor repeated me in a mocking nasal voice. "*Hey man. Hey maaaaaan.*"

While Louis did his best to maintain his cool detachment, Connor stared at me with an unsettling look of intrigue. "Where are your fuck buddies?" he asked.

I imagined myself saying, "You mean your mom and sister?" And in a flash saw the outcome on the screen in my mind. Deciding that I didn't want Peter to grow up an only child, I replied, "One's out of town, the other's babysitting."

"So, you're a loner," Connor stated.

"Don't be a loner, talk to your boner," Louis chimed in. Both of them laughed.

Connor sat down on the bench next to me. He stuck his finger in the top of my Slurpee cup and angled it so that he could see inside.

"Aw," he said, pouting at its emptiness, "I'm actually really thirsty."

"Sorry."

Connor sighed and shrugged. "I guess the only solution is you treat us to Slurpees now. That's fair, right? I mean, don't you remember being told not to bring it if you don't have enough for everyone?"

I explained to them that I was broke, that I barely had enough left for my Slurpee. When I finished, the two of them exchanged a look. I figured they'd for sure ask me to empty my pockets and hand over my wallet for inspection. But they didn't.

"Man, Robin," Connor said after a stretch of silence. "You're not as fun to fuck with when it's just you."

"Sorry," I told him again.

Connor pointed to his temple, then pointed at me and snapped his fingers. "I know what," he said. "You can help us out with something." It was like a lost horror movie victim pulled into a motel on a rainy night; a navigationally inept idea had somehow stumbled into his mind.

Louis stepped closer. His face took on a serious expression. He looked back and forth between Connor and me. Eventually something clicked.

"Aw, man," Louis groaned. "Him? *He's* gonna help? Why, man?"

"Because," Connor said, answering his friend but keeping his eyes on me, "this way is more fun. And besides, he'll be good at it, Louis. I mean, can't you tell? Robin here is a real daredevil. He's *the* Daredevil."

Louis pointed at me. "Are we talking about the same guy? He's a wuss, man. He'd probably piss his pants before we even got there. Run home crying for his mommy."

"I'm not a wuss," I said.

Both of them seemed startled by my words. *I* was startled by my words. I don't know why I blurted it out. It came out like projectile vomit.

Connor flashed his sadist's grin. "There. Did ya hear that, Louis? He's not a wuss. He told us so himself." Then Connor reached into his back pocket and pulled out a folded piece of notebook paper.

"We're playing a little joke on someone," Connor said. "You know him."

"Who is it?" I asked.

The two of them shared a look. It ended in Connor nodding and Louis shrugging and shaking his head.

"Hillerman."

"Oh. Yeah. I know Kyle."

"You're friends," Connor told me.

"Not really." I shrugged.

"You know where he lives?"

I thought for a moment. "Yeah." I hadn't been in his house, but I knew where it was. When you're young, you only know where a handful of people live. Pretty much every house is just a stranger's, but the ones you know, they stick in your head.

"What is it . . . ? What are you guys gonna do?" I asked.

"What *we're* gonna do"—Connor jabbed at me with the paper in his hand—"is drop off this note for him. It's nothing too bad, we're just gonna fuck with him a bit. Don't worry, he deserves it."

Hearing someone like Connor say that a person deserves something gave me a queasy feeling. "Why? Why does he deserve"—I lowered my eyes to the note, still pressed against my chest, it's pointed edge folding against me—"whatever this is?"

"Because he's a snitch," Louis chimed in, adding a hand gesture I was sure he'd stolen from a rap video.

"He ratted on us at Perry's Pantry," Connor said. "We were in there at the same time as him and his little sister—his *only* fuckin' friend—and he saw us looking at the pornos they keep on the back shelf while Perry was distracted ringing someone through."

"Now we're banned!"

"Shut the fuck up, Louis. I'm telling it. You don't know how to tell it right." He inched a little closer to me and continued. "We weren't even going to steal anything. We were just looking at the cases. They show *everything* on the cases. So we're looking at the back of *Skank Sorority Part Five* or some shit, and Kyle comes around the corner with his stupid sister. They both practically drop their candy when they see us back there. She gasps, and he goes, 'What are you guys doing?' Like he's the Pantry Police or something. But that gets Perry's attention. He blows a gasket! Comes running around the counter and right for us, all 'What the hell do you two think you're doing?' He was so pissed I thought his old ass was gonna have a heart attack. Louis drops the tape and we run like fuck out of the store . . . He didn't catch us or anything, but—"

"But now we're done going there!" Louis cut in. "Basically banned for life. Now we gotta go all the way to 7-Eleven, or the Mac's by the fire hall. Like a thousand miles away. And we weren't even doing anything. We were just *looking*. Like that's illegal? I could've swiped it if I wanted to, but I didn't." He crossed his arms and kicked at something on the ground. "Fucking snitch," he pouted.

Connor snapped his fingers in my face and I brought my attention back to him.

"All we need you to do," he said, "is take this letter and drop it off at Kyle's house."

I took the paper from him. He nodded, indicating that I could open it, so I unfolded it. A big red heart took up most of the page. Its curves were asymmetrical. Its colouring—done with a marker long past its prime—was wild and erratic. In the middle of the heart KYLE + CATHERINE was written in blocky letters that looked like they aspired to be 3-D. Flying above the heart on the sloppiest banner I'd ever seen: SNITCH BITCH!!! INSEST-ER!!! It took me a minute to register the final detail, but once I did, my heart sunk. It wasn't cupid's arrow piercing the valentine heart, but it did have a shaft. The dick was gross and glossy and real. It wasn't a sloppy drawing done with the dying leftovers of a Mr. Sketch marker set. It was an actual photo, cut in half and craftily positioned so it looked like it was poking its way through the top of the heart and coming out near the bottom. This terrible valentine probably took more effort from its creators than any school project they'd ever handed in.

"Look at him stare at it, man. He's gonna want to keep it for himself."

Connor waved a shushing arm at Louis. "Artistic masterpiece," he said. "Louis tore it out of one of his dad's magazines."

Defensively, Louis let me know, "It wasn't a *Playgirl* or anything. My dad's not fucking gay. It was only in there because it was being used on a chick."

I folded the paper back up.

"Why this?" I asked once I found my voice.

"Because he doesn't have anything better to do with his time than narc on people and hang out with his little sister," he answered. "But mostly because it's funny."

I nodded, although it didn't really make sense, then asked my next question: "Why me?"

Connor punched my shoulder. "Because you're our guy. You're *the* Daredevil. You seem like you can run fast, and—"

"And you know where he lives," Louis said.

"Yeah, you know where he lives. We know the neighbourhood, but we don't know what house."

Connor stood up. I felt I should too, so I did. Once I was standing, I put my foot on the bench and fiddled with my shoelaces, like they needed tightening. It was the best improv I could come up with to buy myself some time. While I tugged on the bows of my Gazelles, I recalled every peer pressure PSA I'd seen in school or on PBS. What was I supposed to do again? How do you say no without sounding like a loser and warranting a beating?

With my two feet back on the ground, I gave it a shot. "I'm good, thanks. I gotta go."

Connor and Louis looked at each other, then back at me.

"You're *good?*" Connor asked. "The fuck is that? You're not *good*, and you don't *gotta go* . . . You're coming with us and you're doing this. Once you're done you can go home, but not until it's done."

A spark of challenge flashed in his eyes. I met his stare, held it for a moment, and then looked away.

× × ×

At Kyle's house, once the coast looked clear, I made quick work of it. With Louis and Connor crouching in the alley across the street, I crept up the steps, not knowing at the time that I'd be back there again in a matter of weeks, carrying a casserole my mom made. The mailbox creaked as I lifted it open. The sound was probably nothing—with the rumble of cars from the highway on the other side of the concrete noise barrier, the creak was surely no more than a drop in the sonic ocean that surrounded it—but at the time it felt like the only sound in an otherwise mute world. The valentine had been stuffed into a torn and creased used envelope of Connor's that looked like it had carried a telephone bill in its first life. Hurriedly following the instructions I'd been given, I flung my hand out and smacked the doorbell. Hearing the instant *ding* from inside, I leapt off the top step. I landed rough, rolling my ankle. It hurt like hell, and I went right down to the sidewalk, but I somehow found it in myself to spring back up and haul ass across the street and into the alley. Louis and Connor had already started running. With each step, a bolt of pain forked from my ankle. I ignored it and pushed harder, following the curve of the alley toward the sharp bend where it turned, frantic to get out of sight of the house. Was anyone home? Had the door been answered? Who would've taken the letter in? I didn't dare look back. As soon as I made it around the bend, I saw Connor and Louis. The distance between us had grown. They were so big. There was no way I'd catch up with them. They laughed as they ran, which you'd think would've slowed them down, but if it did it wasn't enough for me to get any closer.

"Fuckin' Daredevil, baby!" Louis called back in celebration, the distance between us swelling.

× × ×

Kyle's run-in with Louis and Connor on the day of his sister's disappearance sent him over an edge. The way they followed him through the mall, poking fresh cuts with cruel words, pushed him to a point where he forgot about his duty as a big brother and told his kid sister to just get the hell away. Since Catherine had vanished, I'd been thinking a lot about edges, and how in order to go over one you need to get right up to it first. Something's got to force you there, push you to a point where you can peer over and see the drop. I don't know for sure if the valentine from hell I delivered was the thing that brought Kyle to the brink before Louis and Connor pushed him past it at the mall that day. I can't know for sure. Maybe it is. And maybe is enough to keep me awake at night, enough to haunt me. Enough to crush me. Slowly, deservingly.

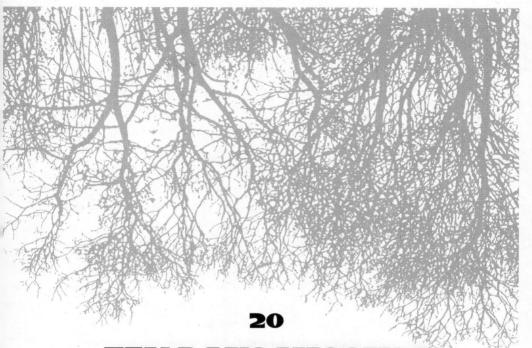

20

TEN DAYS MISSING

IT WAS HARD TO FOCUS ON THE EVENING NEWS ON DAY TEN FOR A COUPLE reasons. The first, and lesser of the two, was that my hidden baby tooth was giving me trouble. I'd eaten a carrot and forgot to chew on the other side for a total of one bite, and man, did it ever hurt. The carrot had nudged the already loose tooth a little out of position, but not enough for it to come out. The little bastard wasn't willing to exit my mouth without the help of a professional, so it looked like my upcoming appointment with Dr. Towne would remain unbroken.

The second reason I was having trouble giving Trish Nadel and Ray Huang my undivided attention was because my parents had had a big fight just as we were finishing dinner. While plates were being cleared from the table, Mom offhandedly mentioned that she had picked up a new brand of coffee earlier that day, and that she'd make sure to put some in a thermos for Dad so he could take it with him on the search after the news. That was when Dad dropped the bombshell: he wouldn't be joining the search that night. He was running himself ragged, and had a shit day at work, and said he felt like he was coming down with something. Well, you can imagine how well *that* went over. Mom asked him to join her in their room while Peter and I finished cleaning up. They may as well have stayed in the kitchen with us, because we heard everything. Her reprimand was swift and brutal. "You think you're feeling *rough*—what about the Hillermans? How can you think of yourself at a time like this? She's a little girl, Bill! They need all the help they can get. If you don't go, I will." And then the one that probably stung the most: "Would you take a night off if it was one of our kids?"

In Dad's defence, I don't think he was being lazy. He wasn't that kind of person. He was always a hell-or-high-water guy when it came to anything that needed to be done. But he'd gone out night after night, walked into dead end after dead end. No, it wasn't laziness. He was just running a little short on hope. And I couldn't blame him. I was, too. I think everyone was.

They had cooled down enough by the time the news started, having agreed to go search together—*date night*, Mom snidely referred to it, sitting curled up on her end of the couch like her cushion was an island. But the tension between them hovered. My parents didn't fight often, so when they did it really got to me. Peter too. Maybe even more.

I was surprised they were okay with us being left home alone, but I took it as a sign, and not a good one. The way I saw it, if my parents were loosening up it meant things for Catherine Hillerman weren't looking good. The only new shred of information I took from that evening's news came from an interview with Detective Hennig. Her hair tied into a tight ponytail, as it had been the day I was interviewed, she stared intently at someone off camera and said that while the police were not ruling out the possibility, they had no reason to believe Catherine Hillerman had been taken out of province. Behind her, Detective Purser stood by a sawhorse with Police Chief Kitrosser and two uniformed officers. He looked as tired as ever, nodding along as one of the officers spoke. It had been nine days since I spoke with them. It felt so much more distant than that. More a dream than a memory.

× × ×

"Hello?"

Mr. Mayer's voice threw me off. I guess it shouldn't have. It was, after all, his house, so him answering the phone wasn't exactly beyond the realm of possibility. But he usually wasn't the one who picked up. And normally when I called Dylan's house, the phone rang more than once before being answered.

"*Hello?*" he repeated when I didn't respond right away, sounding almost desperate.

"Hi, is Dylan there?"

Mr. Mayer sighed. "Yeah, Robin, I'll grab him. One sec."

I heard him call Dylan and tell him to pick up. A few seconds later the beep of the kitchen phone sounded.

"Hey, man," I said.

"Hey, what's up?"

"My parents went out on the search, so I'm at home with Peter," I told him.

"Okay," Dylan said, a hint of irritation—or maybe impatience—in his voice. I wondered if I had interrupted something.

"Uh, yeah, so, how is everything?" I asked, my words clumsy, rushed.

"Everything?"

"Yeah, you know, everything. Is your mom okay? Did—"

"My mom's fine," Dylan snipped.

"Okay. Good."

In the dead air that followed, I considered going against my better judgement and telling him I ran into his brother. But just as the yea side of me and the nay side of me picked up the rope, planted their feet, and started the tug of war, Dylan came along and cut the rope in half at the middle, sending both competitors staggering onto their asses.

"Emily's sick again," he said.

"*What?*"

"Yeah. Well, not sick *again*, she was always sick, but she was getting better. Now she's worse though. Or at least worse than she was when you last saw her."

"How?" I asked.

"Don't know."

I told him I was sorry and asked if there was anything I could do, which probably sounded like a superficial gesture because it probably was. Dylan told me it was fine, and then, as I was about to ask if he wanted to hang out the next day—to get back into our routine that had been shaken up, and that I missed so desperately, that feeling of *normal*—he told me that his parents wanted him to stay home and help take care of her. Whatever that meant.

"They just want me around right now," he told me.

"That's understandable," I responded, surprised at how grown-up the words sounded coming out of my mouth.

I then told him about the Louis Duss Co-op incident, mainly because I thought he'd get a kick out of it and that it would cheer him up. But I also wanted to see if my mentioning Co-op would prompt him to say anything about his brother working there. He didn't bite, but he did love the story. "Christmas in August," he called it. By the end of it, his laughter fizzling, any traces of irritation had vanished. I felt relatively safe from scrutiny when it came to Dylan, so I came clean to him that it was me who hid the cassette in Louis's hoodie. Dylan praised me for it. I was *the man*.

"But you won't tell Steph about that part, right?" I asked.

"No, man, I won't narc to Steph, don't worry," he assured me. "Geez, that's too good," he said, his laughter sputtering to life again. I could picture him wiping tears from his eyes with the knuckle of his thumb.

We said out goodbyes shortly after. Dylan's phone beeped when he left the conversation. Before I hung up, it struck me that for the first time since this whole thing started, I wouldn't be able to see either of my best friends. I started wondering, almost in a panic, how I'd fill the day. When you're older, boredom is usually a luxury, but as a teenager, you fear it. And I sure feared it then. With summer nearing its end, my mind began a frantic scroll through potential prospects for the next day. They were scarce. My wondering was interrupted by a soft clicking noise in my ear. I realized that I hadn't hung up the phone yet. And until just then, neither had Mr. Mayer.

× × ×

It was around eleven when my parents came home. I was sitting on the couch trying to watch TV, but failing because all I could think about was what Mr. Mayer would say, or do, after listening in on our call. I had the volume low on the TV so I didn't wake Peter, who was out cold in the Tartan chair, snoring lightly, a blanket draped over him. The look on Mom's face when she entered the room told me there was news, and it wasn't good.

"They found something," she said as our eyes met.

Any thoughts of Mr. Mayer fell from my head. I pulled myself up from the melty slouch I was in.

"A hair elastic," she said, calling to mind the pigtails Catherine wore. "They're pretty sure it's one of hers."

As she stepped closer, I noticed the puffiness around her eyes. She'd been crying. Probably just minutes ago. Dad came in behind her, shaking his head, one hand resting on the back of his neck.

"Where did they find it?" I asked Mom.

She spoke without looking at me.

"The ravine."

× × ×

The idea came to me around two in the morning, which, I've noticed, is pretty much the typical time that most crazy ideas tended to present themselves. The sort of things that occur to you late at night, after hours of being held hostage by your own thoughts, are the kind that would never reveal themselves during the day. They're strictly nocturnal, and they crawl out of sewers, and skulk out from behind dumpsters, and lumber from thick, dark forests. Sometimes they're so crazy that if you remember them at all the next morning, they feel less like a thought and more like a nightmare that some-one—or *something*—placed into your head. But really, they came from you. From inside you.

Looking back, I blame my idea on a lot of things, but more than anything else I think it was guilt. Guilt can't stay underground forever. When there's enough of it, eventually it makes its way to the surface. Sometimes it seeps up. Other times, something—like maybe a hair elastic—causes it to break through and spray like a geyser of oil, showering everything beneath with its gooey blackness.

I took a pair of socks from my dresser, unballed them, and pulled them on. Then I fumbled my jeans and my old Canucks sweatshirt on over my pyjamas, plucked my glasses off my nightstand, and tiptoed to my bedroom door. I took a quick look at where Saturn and the stars were pasted to the wall. They had faded hours earlier, and I couldn't make out their outlines. That was okay, though. There would be plenty of stars for me to look at outside.

The night air had that late August dampness to it, the kind that felt like wearing a shirt taken out of the dryer before it's done. I took a quick look back at the house, to make sure of I don't know what, and then started walking, doing my best to avoid the pools of light cast by street lamps. The last thing I needed was some nosy night owl telling my parents they saw me out at this hour, walking down the block in a daze, with a steak knife in my hand.

I don't know how long it took me to get there. Time seemed to be operating the way it does in a dream, fluid, pouring on in too many directions at once. Seeing the pointed tips of the ravine's trees gave me a chill. But once the trees were in sight, I found myself quickening my pace, almost rushing to them. I reminded myself then about the ravine's invisible currents, how the little marmalade cat we hit seemed like it was trying to escape from it. The ravine lures, it tugs, it drags. That's what was happening to me. And as much as I was scared, I was also ready, because the magnetic pull felt right. I ran to it.

Just as it had been on the day when we hid from Louis and Connor, the atmosphere changed once I pushed through the trees. It was cooler, and the air on the other side of the border felt somehow different on my skin, in my lungs. It had a taste to it. Wood and dirt, pine needles and secrets. I turned my gaze to the tangled fortress of branches that reached high into the sky, blocking so much of the moon's glow, which only managed to leak in through a few of the cracks between limbs. For a second I wished I had brought a flashlight, then I realized I didn't actually *want* to see whatever else was in here. Taking a few steps in, stumbling over roots and rocks, I began worrying that I might trip and accidentally stab myself in the guts with the steak knife. I decided it was best not to go in too far.

I got down on my knees and touched the ground with my free hand. Dirt. I scraped some up, then poured it back onto the ground. This spot would do. I set my knife down close by and began to dig feverishly with my fingers. The tiny hole must have been about two inches deep when I finished. Of course, I couldn't see it, but it felt like it was that deep. I thought digging a hole would be the best way to put what I needed to into the ravine. The way I figured, it was like the difference between eating a vitamin and rubbing it on your skin. What I needed to give the ravine wasn't a topical medication. It needed to be placed inside, consumed.

Choosing a spot for the knife took a while. It wasn't only that I was afraid of the pain (and believe me, I was), but also that I needed to choose a spot that would allow me to bleed easily and that wouldn't be visible to anyone the next day, especially my parents. So wrists, hands, and arms were all off limits. I decided it would be best to cut my leg, since I could probably get away with wearing long pants until it healed, and if I had to wear shorts or swim trunks, a bandage on my leg would be easy to explain. After some deliberation, I settled on my left calf. It probably had enough meat that it might not hurt as much as, say my ankle, which was basically a twig wrapped in skin.

Rolled up below my kneecap, my jeans and the pyjama pants beneath them created a tight band around my leg. I recalled the couple times I'd had blood taken, how the nurse had wrapped a tight plastic thing around my forearm, and I decided having my leg noosed by two pairs of pants would help me get what I needed faster. Placing one hand in the hole to situate myself, I wiggled until I was as certain as I could be in the dark that my primed leg was in the right spot, and the blood could just pour right in. And then, before I had time to change my mind, I positioned the knife on my calf, right away feeling the pokes from its pointy little teeth, which were made for sawing into meat. I guess that's exactly what they'd be doing. In one swift motion I pressed and sliced. It did hurt, but not in the way I expected it to. The feeling that came with opening myself was like a sting and a burn at the same time. It blazed. The blood came immediately and spilled onto my hand before I had time to move it out of the way. Breath heavy, my heart-beat in my ears, I lowered my leg so that it was practically a lid over the hole. I sat there bleeding for a minute, knowing that what I was doing wasn't tidy, and that it wouldn't all make it in the hole, so I needed to give it time in order to ensure that I got the most bang for my buck.

Once I felt enough time had passed, I shifted to my knees, groped around until I found the hole, and stuck my fingers in. The wetness went deeper than I thought it would, and when it clicked that it was my own blood, I felt lightheaded and pukey. On shaky legs, I pulled myself up and found a sliver of moonlight. The blood that had spilled right after I'd made the cut was already beginning to dry. It painted my hands in runny, spidery streaks. The fingers I stuck into the hole were wet up to the knuckle with a mix of blood and dirt. I'm not sure how long I stood there examining my hand in the moonlight, but the feeling of wetness on the back of my leg broke the trance I was in. I bent forward and swatted at a sneaky mosquito helping himself to a free meal, then rolled my doubled-up pants back down, pressed against the wound with my palm and held it there, I guess hoping that my pyjama pants would act as a temporary bandage. While I waited, more mosquitos came to me. They went for my neck, my face, my hands. Like Kong fending off airplanes, I did my best to keep them away, but in the end it all came down to a numbers game. Anyway, I suppose I was in a giving mood that night.

Before I left, I closed my eyes and whispered a prayer. It wasn't a prayer to God. I was talking to the ravine.

"Please give her back now."

The ideas that find their way to you late at night would never reveal themselves during the day. As I hustled back home—bloody steak knife in hand, a slight limp on one side, and a dark patch that I wouldn't see until later on the back of my jeans like Jupiter's Great Red Spot—it didn't occur to me at all how bizarre my idea was. It seemed like the right thing to do, the thing that made the most sense. I had given the ravine a blood sacrifice. All I wanted in exchange was Catherine Hillerman returned safe and sound. And I wanted summer, or what little was left of it, to be summer again.

21

ELEVEN DAYS MISSING

THE KNOCKING WOKE ME UP. MY SLEEP WAS DREAMLESS AND DEEP, AND coming out of it was like being pulled out of a diving tank, as if there was actual physical distance that I needed to travel before I woke.

"I know you're a teenager, but I draw the line at noon," Mom said from the other side of my bedroom door. "Come have some lunch. We need to talk."

At first I was totally oblivious about what we could possibly *need* to talk about, but once I swung my feet over the edge of my bed and stepped on my jeans, which lay in a limp pile on the floor, one prospect came rushing at me.

"Oh, *fuck*."

The blood spot on one leg of my pants confirmed what I already knew. The stain was darker than it had been when I'd undressed and climbed back into bed much earlier that morning. It had changed to a murky brown colour, but from the right angle and distance, it kind of blended in to the dark denim. It was still there though. Very much real.

As if on cue, the back of my left calf sent a blipping signal to my brain. I pulled the leg of my pyjama pants up as far as I could before the congealed blood that had plastered the fabric to my skin forced me to slow down. Then, with an icky tug that made a sound like old Velcro, I pulled it up past the wound so I could assess the damage.

It was messy, but it wasn't the massacre I expected. A few splotches of rusty brown stood out against my pasty skin. It could've been worse, though. The cut itself had scabbed over, but I'd torn off some of the scab when I pulled my pyjama leg up. I'd need a shower and a bigass Band-Aid. Maybe some Polysporin too, I thought, noticing the throbbing redness of the skin around the slit.

"Robin! This food's going to expire before you get here!" Mom called from the kitchen.

Shit—had it been five minutes?

Not wanting Mom to barge in, I took off my dirty pyjama pants, and dug a backup pair from a drawer and put them on. I threw on a fresh T-shirt too and opened the door and walked down the hall toward the kitchen, just as I had hours before in the pitch dark.

I took a seat at the table across from Peter, fearing whatever questions Mom had in store for me. I couldn't come up with anything remotely close to an acceptable reason for sneaking out at night. If she asked me, I was screwed. While I waited for the hammer to drop, I picked up one of the grilled cheese halves waiting on the plate in front of me and dunked it into the bowl of Campbell's chicken noodle that had been set out with it.

Mom stood at the stove, her back to me. The pot and pan she'd used to make us lunch was already in the sink, soaking in soapy water. Chewing nervously, I watched as she did what she always did before walking away from the stove: she held her hand over each burner until she was certain no heat was coming from them, because apparently you couldn't trust a dial.

"I need a favour," she said, pulling out a chair for herself and taking a seat with us.

I hadn't expected the conversation to start that way. I couldn't remember the last time either of my parents had asked *me* for a favour.

"Okay," I said, somewhat relieved, but still wary.

She stared intently at the table's wood grain for a long moment, running her finger around the rings of a knot shaped like a drop of water. After a couple laps, she finally looked up at me and spoke. "When they found that hair elastic last night, Robin . . . I can only imagine how the Hillermans feel right now. I talked to Barb this morning. She sounded awful. She puts up a strong front, but her voice, the way it sounded . . . all this is wearing her down.

"I asked her if I could bring them anything. But they're already up to their eyes in casseroles and cakes. So she asked me if we could take Kyle for the day. He had such a good time with you guys at the pool and at Dylan's—she didn't even mention the accident—and that it was good for him to be able to get out of that house and feel like a kid for a little bit. His dad's going to drop him off in half an hour, and I'd like you to do whatever you can to distract him. I can give you guys a bit of money, and I'll take you anywhere you want to go. I just need you to try and cheer him up and get his mind off all this terrible—"

"*Mom*," I said, holding my hands up like a crossing guard, "it's fine. You don't need to, like, convince me. I don't—it's not like hanging out with Kyle is a chore or something. I like him." I wasn't sure if that was true entirely. Everything had gotten muddled. Maybe I liked him. Maybe I just needed to be absolved of the guilt I had about what I'd set in motion. I pressed my leg back into the wood of the chair, hoping the pain would distract me.

Mom's lips drew into a smile. She reached across the table and touched my shoulder. "Thank you," she said. "You're a good kid, Robin."

Without correcting her, I finished my sandwich and soup and went off to shower.

× × ×

Standing in our front doorway wearing a Flames hat and backpack slung over one shoulder, Kyle gave off the impression he thought we were going on a hike or something.

"Hey, man," I said. "What's with the backpack?"

"I brought some games and stuff."

"All right."

He stepped out of his shoes and placed them against the wall. When he stood back up, I heard the unmistakeable rattle of board game pieces coming from his bag.

"What did you want to do?" I asked, then added, "I'm good with anything," secretly hoping he'd at least brought something cool, like Risk.

Kyle stepped off the island of tiles we had inside our front door and onto the hardwood with me. He looked around in a way that reminded me of a cat taking in a new space. Once he was satisfied, he turned to me and said, "I'm good with anything too."

I told him that if we wanted, my mom could drive us somewhere. Kyle once again asserted he was fine with whatever. If I'd had more notice that he was coming over, I would've called and told him to bring an opinion with him. Maybe there was one hidden in his backpack. After a bunch of overly polite hemming and hawing, we decided to go downstairs and play *Mortal Kombat 3*, which Kyle had said he'd always wanted to try. Before we could make our way down, Peter materialized.

"Can I come?"

"No," I told him. "You're not allowed to play *Mortal Kombat*. It's mature."

Peter glared at me, probably thinking about whether or not to let slip that I'd let him watch me play a few nights back. "You're not mature," he finally said, accusingly. "Just because you get pimples doesn't mean you're mature."

"I'm more mature than *you*, dweeb."

Kyle found this quite funny. I got the sense he wanted the show to go on, but then, before Peter could get in another word, Mom called him from the kitchen.

"Peter, come help me in here."

"I don't want to," Peter moaned, swinging an arm and stomping for emphasis.

"Do *not* stamp your feet like that," Mom said. "I'm making cookies. If you want any of them, you'd better get in here and help me make the dough."

Cookies. Mom was really pulling out all the stops for Kyle.

"So, your brother's not coming down here, right?" Kyle asked when we got downstairs.

"No," I said. "I mean, he shouldn't. Why?"

"Just checking," he said.

I pressed the PlayStation's power button. The disc started its jittery whir. In the background, the load of laundry Mom had thrown in before Kyle came slapped around in the washing machine. After a minute of waiting in silence as the game loaded, a bell sounded and "Midway Presents" flashed on the black screen. The game's cryptic theme music began playing as it cut to the title screen, the *Mortal Kombat 3* graphic imposed over a pile of skulls and bones, looking like something out of *Raiders of the Lost Ark*. I heard the zipper of Kyle's backpack being tugged open. I turned. He was taking out a board game. Monopoly. Could be better, could be worse, I thought.

"Oh. Did you want to play that instead?"

Kyle didn't speak. He looked up at me and smirked, the brim of his hat casting a burglar's mask shadow over his eyes. Then he manoeuvred the game out of his backpack and placed it on the ground between us.

"Want to see something crazy?" he asked, grinning.

"In . . . there?" I pointed to the Monopoly box.

"Yeah," Kyle assured me. "In here." He tapped the box. "It's not *Monopoly*—well, it is, but it's not *just* that."

I glanced past him at the stairs to make sure Peter wasn't spying on us, then shrugged and said that yes, I did want to see something crazy.

With eager fingers, Kyle worked the lid off the box. It made that kind of groaning animal sound that board game box lids make when they're on too tight. I inched a little closer, my bandaged calf throbbing as I shuffled, and looked in. What I saw was about as crazy as I'd expected from Kyle: a Monopoly game board. Yep, maximum crazy. Definitely one for the books. Call Arkham Asylum.

"Yeah, man," I said, laughing. "Sure is—"

"That's not it," Kyle said, shaking his head. He then removed the game board and tossed it aside, revealing what he'd hidden underneath.

The only actual porno magazines I'd seen before were the ones that poked up from the back of the magazine shelf at Perry's Pantry. They were high up, and their covers, just like the video cases that Louis and Connor got busted looking at, were mostly obscured by a guarding row of white cardboard, placed so that you could only see the titles. The pictures I had for myself were crappy inkjet-blurry photos, torn from the many times they'd been unfolded and folded again. I'd bought them from a kid at our school for two bucks a piece and had them stashed away in the pages of a *Green Lantern* comic.

The magazine looking up at me from Kyle's Monopoly box was in decent shape for how old it was. The date, written in white right below the bold yellow *HUSTLER* that dominated the top of the cover, said August 1981. The girl on the cover was wearing a yellow sun visor, matching yellow wrist bands, and nothing else. She was bent forward slightly, her back to me as she straddled a tennis racket, looking over her shoulder with a shocked expression, like she couldn't believe I'd just caught her playing nude tennis.

Kyle's grin climbed to new heights.

"Man, my mom would freak if she knew you brought this," I told him.

Kyle said, "Open it up." His tone was more demanding than I was used to from him. I did as he asked.

"Go to the middle," he said.

Again, I did as he told me, hurrying as I felt my palms getting sweatier. The pictures I flipped past were almost too much for me to process at the speed I was going. More graphic than anything I'd ever seen, even in R-rated movies. The close-ups gave me mixed feelings of excitement, curiosity, and horror. There was a political article on a thing I never heard of, and another article called "Death by Orgasm." I stopped when I reached a page with the cover girl on it, noticing right away how women from the 1980s looked different—maybe more real—than the ones I had upstairs in my *Green Lantern*.

"You're going too slow," Kyle said, annoyed. He took the magazine from me, turned a few more pages, then handed it back. Hidden inside was a folded piece of glossy paper.

"Is this the centrepiece?" I asked.

"Centre*fold*," Kyle corrected me. "And no, that's a few pages back. This," he said, something behind his eyes catching fire, "this is something way better."

I took it out and opened it. In the centre stood a woman with piercing dark eyes and a head of thick dark hair, teased to oblivion. She had nothing on but a skimpy pair of underwear and was doing her best to cover her nipples with her fingers.

At the top of the photo, a banner in neon-sign-style printing read, "Hush-Hush Holidays."

At the bottom in the same print but smaller: "KISS ANDREA UNDER THE MISTLETOE."

My eyes crawled up and down her body a couple more times before resting for a moment on her heavily made-up face. Smoke-streaked eyes, blushing cheeks, thick, red lipstick on her pouting O mouth. But it was unmistakeable. I knew who she was.

Mrs. Mayer stared up at me. Into me.

22

STEPH'S PUPILS JITTERED LIKE MOLECULES AS SHE SPOONED HERSELF mouthfuls of Mint Oreo Blizzard. Occasionally, she would pause and frown at something going on behind her eyes. She was a detective, hurriedly swishing puzzle pieces around on a table in her head, everything connected to everything else. Start with the edges and work your way in, in, in.

These were the edges I'd given her: I'd told her about my phone call with Dylan. About how Emily was sick again, and about how I was almost entirely sure Mr. Mayer had been listening in on our phone call for some reason. I'd reminded her about my running into Adam, what he said about Mrs. Mayer not being his mom.

And, of course, I saved the best for last.

"You. Are. Fucking. Kidding me."

"Nope." I shook my head. "I'm serious." Jeremy, enjoying a Blizzard at the booth behind us, as per Steph's orders not to be seen with us, appeared not to have heard his sister curse.

She splayed her fingers on the table and leaned forward, extending her long neck.

"Robin, you're *positive* it was her?"

I nodded.

"Do you know if she has a sister? *Ooo*—maybe she's a twin. You know how there's always a good twin and an evil twin?"

"Maybe." The possibility of a sister hadn't occurred to me. I considered it. I closed my eyes and visualized the picture. "No," I told Steph after a quick examination. "I mean, I guess it's possible, but I'm pretty positive it was her."

Steph took a second to absorb my words. "So she, like, makes pornos?" she asked.

"I don't think it's technically a porno," I said. "Kyle's pretty sure the poster came from a strip club his dad went to before he was born, when his parents lived in Calgary."

255

"So a souvenir from a *stripper*," Steph said. "Do strippers even have merchandise?"

"I don't know," I said. "I mean, I saw it, so I guess so."

Steph mulled this over. And those pretty brown eyes of hers, they couldn't stay still. When, after a moment, something clicked, Steph responded with a shiver and vomit-face combo.

"What?" I asked.

"The fact that Kyle's dad not only saw her dance naked, but felt the need to keep the poster. Gross. Do you think he still gets *boners* for her?"

"As much as I don't like to think about it," I said, "he probably does. I mean, he didn't throw it away."

Again, Steph made the vomit face. Her Mint Oreo Blizzard, morphing into a radioactive green and black soup, wouldn't be getting any attention from her any time soon.

"And his *son* found it. God, that's so gross. Can you imagine? Why are guys so gross, Robin? Even the good ones."

I didn't have an answer for her. In the momentary silence that followed her question, I scrolled through a list of every guy I knew—myself included. Pretty much everyone that came to mind was, in fact, kind of gross. At least on some level. And the ones who weren't, I wondered if they were just better at hiding it.

"Steph?" Jeremy had appeared at the side of the table. With one hand he tugged at his sister's shirt sleeve, with his other, he absently scratched at his throat while his gaze floated around the Dairy Queen like an astronaut in zero gravity.

"I thought I said not to bug me, Jeremy," Steph snipped.

"Can we go?" he asked.

"What? No, not yet. We can't leave until Dad picks us up. You know that." Steph looked over her shoulder at the booth Jeremy had taken for himself. "You didn't even finish your Blizzard," she said. "Go eat it," she demanded, too enthralled in our mystery to pay her brother much mind. "You promised you could eat a medium. Dad'll be ticked if I tell him you wasted money."

Jeremy let his hand drop from his sister's sleeve. He stood for a moment, still scratching at his throat with his other hand, staring off at nothing in particular. After a few seconds he went back to his booth and resumed work on his ice cream. I glanced at the clock behind the cashier. It was 6:40. Bruce had told us he'd be back from the grocery store by seven at the latest. He'd surprised us by granting permission to go to Dairy Queen unattended for half an hour, but had made us promise we'd stick together and stay away from the bathrooms. His willingness to loosen his supervision restrictions reminded me of my own parents letting me watch Peter a couple days earlier. If things were returning to normal, did it mean that Catherine had officially become a one-off vanishing act? And what did that mean for her? The ravine hadn't answered my prayer yet. But it seemed reasonable that cosmic deals took longer than twenty-four hours to transpire.

"Well?" Steph asked.

"Well, what?"

"You didn't answer."

"Answer what?"

"Why are guys so gross?"

I raised my shoulders, then let them fall. "I don't know."

"Ah-*ha*!" Steph pointed a pinning finger at me, like she'd caught me at something. "So you *do* agree that guys are gross? All of them?"

"I don't know," I said defensively.

"Yeah you do. I just asked you why guys are so gross, and you didn't say, 'They're not all gross.' You said 'I don't know.' Which means you agree you're all gross."

"I wasn't—I mean . . . like, what's your point? Did *I* do something? Does this have anything to do with the shit we're trying to figure out? Because if it does, I'm lost."

She considered my question, then shook her head. "No, I guess it doesn't. I just want to know if you—a guy—would agree that guys are gross. I mean, if Kyle's dad—who seems like a decent person—has a pervy picture of Mrs. Mayer, does that mean even the good ones are still kind of sickos? Like, when I'm not around, do you and Dylan go ogle women and talk about pervy stuff? Or are you the same as you are when I'm around?"

There was no answer I could give her, or more accurately, none that I wanted to give her. So I waited her out. And eventually Steph spooned herself a drippy mouthful, shook her head. "Man, I still can't believe it. You're *positive* it was her?"

"The name didn't match, but there was no way it was anyone else."

"Name?" she asked.

"Yeah, at the bottom it said, 'Kiss Andrea under the mistletoe.'"

Steph dropped her spoon and slammed both hands down on the table. "Are you kidding me? *Andrea?* That's her name?"

"Yeah."

"Robin—*think.*"

It clicked for me, and it stopped mattering. Because then something happened. Something that made pretty much everything else not matter.

The noise that came from behind Steph was a shrill, raspy rattle, like someone sucking on a kazoo filled with tiny pebbles. In one lightning motion, Steph, recognizing the sound for what it was, spun around in her booth towards Jeremy. She gasped and whispered a panicked curse. When she rushed to him an instant later, giving me a clear view, I understood why. Jeremy had made a real dent in his Blizzard since Steph had sent him back a couple minutes before. There were streaks of Oreo crumble and green ice cream down his chin, and his lips looked to be lined with the stuff. But his lips! They were a painful, throbbing shade of bright red and had swollen to nearly double their size. His throat, which he'd been scratching at when he came to our booth, was stained with a splotchy rash.

"Jeremy—*fuck*—where's your medicine? Where—where's your EpiPen?"

Jeremy produced another raspy wheeze. He looked at his sister with wide, frightened eyes, and when he opened his mouth to speak a glob of thick drool bungeed out and landed on the table.

"I forgot it . . . in the car," he gasped.

By then, I was out of the booth, standing behind Steph, who held her brother by his shoulders. "It'll be okay," she told him, "You'll be okay." But the way she said it sounded more question than fact.

"Stephy," Jeremy said, "my mouth is making too much spit."

Steph looked around the restaurant. "Does anyone have an EpiPen!?" Her voice was met with startled looks from the staff and the few other diners who sat scattered across the room. There was an elderly couple, a cluster of teenagers a bit older than us, a father and daughter team working their way through their own Blizzards. When none of them answered, Steph repeated herself. I don't think I'd ever heard her yell so loud. "*I need a fucking EpiPen! He's having an allergic reaction!*"

Some of the other patrons started to close in. They all looked shocked, but apart from that they weren't doing too much. Jeremy breathed another of his wheezy breaths. A cashier flipped the hinged counter and ran toward us. Steph stepped in between her brother and the encroaching spectators. "He doesn't need a cashier, he needs medicine! A doctor! He needs . . . He needs a . . ."

"*Ambulance!*" I yelled, my voice breaking like chalk. My eyes found the phone on the wall behind the front counter. "Call 911!" I charged toward the register frantically shouting, "Call 911!" at the other cone slinger. It took a second for my command to sink in, but when it did, he sprang into action.

I stood listening as he said, "Yes. Ambulance. There's a boy having a . . . an allergic reaction. He needs a . . . a . . ."

"*An EpiPen!*" I shouted.

"He needs an EpiPen," he repeated into the receiver. "The Dairy Queen . . . the one on—shit, I don't know the address! It's the only one in town, man. The fuckin' Dairy Queen!"

I looked over my shoulder at Steph and Jeremy. She had her arms wrapped around him, whispering something in his ear, and he nodded along, breathing his rattling breaths with an open mouth that was glossy with drool. The teenagers in the far corner looked on like they were watching a horror movie, one of them licking away at his chocolate dip while the scene unfolded. The elderly couple had gotten up from their seats and were standing a few feet from Steph, the woman's hands folded into a praying position. And the father stood at his table with his daughter held tightly against him, turning her away, I guess because one kid shouldn't have to see another kid die.

× × ×

I cried when I told Bruce what happened. He cried too. On the drive to the hospital, barely slowing down as he ran through two stop signs and gunning it through a stale amber light, he kept whispering, "Please, Jeremy. Please, Jeremy. Please . . ." to himself over and over. I'd never seen him—such an unshakable person—rattled like this. It felt wrong.

He parked diagonally between two fading white lines, and from there bolted for the front entrance of Haddington Springs General, forgetting to close his door behind him. I ran around to his side of the car, slammed it shut, and sprinted to catch up. The woman at the desk was quick to give us the information we needed. She stood up from her swivel chair and pointed to a hallway marked East Wing.

"Past the elevators, then hang a right. You can't miss it."

Bruce thanked her and gave me a tap on the shoulder. Then the two of us ran like hell down the hall.

A nurse with a clipboard met us when we got there. She had volcanic red hair, big round glasses, and a constellation of freckles across the bridge of her nose. She looked younger than the few other nurses who were chatting and flipping through charts and zipping around in the background behind her.

"You must be Mr. Sheldon?" she asked, consulting her clipboard.

"Yeah," Bruce said, eyes wide, breath short.

"Jeremy is in room twenty-three. I'll take you." She smiled and motioned for us to follow her down the curve of the hallway, which looked like it circled all the way around.

"Is . . . is he . . ." Bruce began as we walked with the nurse.

Without stopping, she spun around to face us. "He's going to be fine," she said. "He didn't go into anaphylactic shock, but EMS did administer an EpiPen. He's stable now," she assured. "The doctor will be by to give you the full rundown shortly."

Bruce breathed a sigh of relief. I probably would've too if I didn't feel so completely dumbstruck by the whole experience.

"Oh—" the nurse added, turning back around, "your daughter's with him as well. She's been great."

Bruce, barely holding it together, laughed. "I'm sure she has," he said.

We continued around the curve, passing rooms with patient names written on little whiteboards outside them. Noises—beeps and blips, snoring, coughing, Darth Vader-like mechanical breathing—floated out from the open doorways. When we reached room twenty-three, the nurse stopped, stepped aside, and gestured for us to enter.

"He'll be a little dopey, but he'll be fine. The doctor will be by soon."

Before Bruce could get a thank you out, Steph came charging out of the room and attached herself to him. He picked her up off the ground and said something to her I couldn't hear. Then the waterworks started for both of them. They stayed like that for a few seconds, suspended in time, before Bruce set his daughter down, planted a kiss on her head, and stepped past her into the room.

I heard him say, "Hey, bud," and then his words melted and all I could make out was his low register as he spoke to his son.

Steph—negligent sitter, negligent sister who'd forgotten to make sure there were no silver bullets rattling around in her brother's ice cream—took a step toward me. Her red, misted eyes were enough to get me going. I felt a tear canaling down my cheek. For a second, it looked like she was going to break, but then she exhaled a jittery breath that reminded me of an old car sputtering to life, and laughed.

"Robin . . . this summer . . . What the fuck?"

"Yeah," I said, barely managing the word.

"I mean, can things please be normal again?"

She didn't give me time to answer, which was fine, because I didn't have any words in me just then. She wrapped her arms around me and squeezed, and I squeezed back. We held each other, our bodies pressing together so tightly, leaving no room between us, not even for air. I felt her heart beat against me. This is a moment I've kept. A snapshot framed behind glass, safe from time, safe from everything.

× × ×

The nurse wasn't lying when she said Jeremy was dopey. The kid seemed like he was on another plane of existence. He mumbled a bunch, and nodded off a few times, and then he'd wake up with a start and look around the room all confused. The doctor said he'd be fine, but that whenever someone has an allergy attack like Jeremy's, they keep them for observation because traces of the allergen are still in their system and they needed to be sure before they let him go.

Jeremy perked up a little when I said my goodbye. He thanked me for helping save his life (his words, not mine), pointed at me accusingly, smirked, and said, "You *cried*."

"Yeah," I said, "way to make me."

The magma-haired nurse told me I could use the phone at their desk to call my parents for a ride. She could tell Steph and Bruce were there for the long haul. Before I left, Steph said she'd call me the next day. Then I got and a bone-cracking handshake from Bruce, who told me to remind my parents that they did a good job with me.

I wasn't so sure about that, but I told him I would.

I left the room and followed the curve of the hallway. An old man who looked like a tortoise said good evening to me as I walked past him. He was taking baby steps down the hall, his feet never fully leaving the ground. A loopy IV was plugged into his arm, and he was holding onto his pole for dear life. I said good evening back and wondered if he was supposed to be walking around on his own. I noticed then that the front desk I was heading for seemed to be a lot farther away than it had on the way in. I looked at the white-boards outside the rooms. The names were all different than the ones I'd noticed on the way in. I must've taken the circle the wrong way. I considered turning around and going back the way I came, but then I realized, *duh*, it's a circle, and decided to keep going. I took in the new whiteboard names as I passed them: Harrison . . . Mazurek . . . Sparks . . . Mayer . . . Hofner—there was a teacher at our school with that name . . . Bergman . . . Lander . . .

I stopped.

Mayer?

No, that couldn't be right.

I took a few steps back to confirm.

Lander . . . Bergman . . . Hofner . . .

And there it was: *Mayer.* Block letters written in green marker. Room thirty-two. M-A-Y-E-R. I stood there staring for a while, scrutinizing the letters, first individually, and then as a group, once, twice, five times to make sure my eyes weren't messing with me.

They weren't. So, I did the only thing that made sense. I walked in.

Stepping from the hallway into the room felt like dipping my head underwater at the pool. I could still hear traces of what was going on outside, but the new quiet—thick enough to slow me down—muffled everything beyond the room into a distant, abstract hum.

There was someone in the bed. From where I stood, I could only see a pair of feet pointing up like a little tent beneath the blue hospital blanket. My ears registered the soft sound of breathing, laboured but steady, the metronome rhythm of a person sleeping. I took a quick look over my shoulder to make sure no one was watching me from the doorway, and then, with a surge of confidence that came from parts unknown, tiptoed toward the bed.

From the feet grew the form of legs, and from the legs, the form of a small blanketed body, lying on its back. Moving closer, I saw that the body had a head. And the head belonged to Emily Mayer.

Standing next to her, my shadow draped over her like an extra blanket thrown on for good measure, I had to push away the urge to lift the loose strand of hair that had fallen across her forehead and hooked itself under her nose. It blew up with every breath she released; it seemed like the kind of thing that would wake a person up. One of her hands poked out from under the covers, revealing the hospital bracelet around her wrist. I leaned in to get a look at it, and at this new, closer range, I could feel the feverish heat radiating from her, could see the clammy pallor of her skin, could smell the musty scent of her sickness. Her name was printed on the bracelet (last, then first) along with DOB: (01/03/1990), and beneath that, the date she was admitted: (21/08/1997)—yesterday's date. From there, my eyes moved up her little neck, and back to her face, where they met her open eyes.

"Robin?" she asked in a croaky whisper, so thin I wouldn't have heard it if I weren't leaning right over her.

"Hi," I whispered back.

She stared at me, probably wondering if I was real or just a remnant from whatever fever dream I had pulled her from. "Why are you here?" she asked.

"I . . . I was just walking by and saw your name on the board outside the room. I thought I'd visit."

She blinked hard and said, "I'm sick again," making no attempt to hide her disappointment in herself.

"I'm sorry you're sick," I said.

"Yeah. Me too. I thought I was getting better, but then . . ." The sentence floated off and didn't return. A new thought took its place. "Did you see my family today?" she asked.

"No," I told her. "Doesn't your family come and visit you here?"

"They do." She nodded. "My mom is here all the time. And my dad came after work yesterday, and before work this morning. Dylan visits, too. He came with my mom last night. But he didn't come today because he had to babysit."

"That's good," I said, ignoring her confused remark about Dylan picking up work as a babysitter.

She nodded, then turned her mouth to her pillow and coughed. It was the sort of cough that sounded like it burned, gravel and fire blasted through an old metal pipe. She turned back to me. "I just don't get to see *all* of them," she said.

"You mean Adam? He doesn't come by?"

She shook her head, as if frustrated by the stupidity of my question.

"No, he came to visit. He was only here for a bit, and not at the same time as Dylan and my mom and dad—he plans it that way. But he was here." She coughed again, swallowed, then looked up at me with sad eyes and said, "I mean my sister. I don't get to see her."

"Sister?" I asked. Her confusion made me recall a couple Christmases back, when Peter was fighting a flu that came with a fever so high it caused him to hallucinate. He thought the magpies in the tree outside his room were threatening to poison him. "You don't have a sister, Emily," I reminded her.

"Yes, I *do*," she told me, her eyes narrowing in an irritated glare. "I just got her, and we were just becoming friends, and now I'm stuck *here*." She lifted her arms and let them flop down by her side, then crossed them into a pouty knot across her chest. "Dylan gets to see her, but I don't. It's not *fair*, Robin."

× × ×

I picked up where I'd left off with the circle, leaving Emily, who'd fallen asleep while I was wishing her a speedy recovery. The young nurse who'd taken Bruce and I to Jeremy's room was waiting for me at the desk.

"There you are. I thought you'd vanished."

I told her I got lost trying to find the bathroom, and she brought me to the side of the desk and told me I could call my parents.

"Dial nine to call outside the building, and then your phone number."

I nodded, picked up the phone and started dialing. When the nurse looked away, I pressed the switch down to hang up before it had a chance to ring, and then mustered every drop of acting ability I had in me to have a fake conversation with my mom, whose part was played by the dial tone.

"Yep. I'm fine. Okay, I'll meet you downstairs. Okay, I'll go wait now."

And . . . *scene.*

× × ×

My quarter clanked, slid, clanked again, then stopped. The dial tone sounded in my ear. I punched in Dylan's number, which came so natural that if anyone were to ask me what the seven digits were, I'd actually have to stop and think about it.

One . . .

Two . . .

Three . . .

"Hello?"

"Hey, man."

"Robin? Hey, what's—where are you calling from? There's a different number on the caller ID."

"Yeah, I'm at the mall with my parents."

"Oh."

I jumped to it before he had the chance to ask me what was so urgent it warranted calling from a pay phone.

"Can you hang out?" I asked.

"*What?* No, man. I told you, I can't. I mean, I want to, but I have to stay home. Emily's sick and my mom wants me to be here with her."

A stretch of silence followed, then Dylan asked, "Is everything okay?"

"Yeah, man," I assured him. "I just forgot you couldn't hang out. I forgot you were watching Emily."

"Yeah . . . I can't hang out. My mom's still kinda off from the accident, too."

"I bet."

More silence.

"I gotta go, Robin. I'll call you soon."

"Okay," I said. "Tell Emily I hope she feels better."

He told me he would.

"Talk to you later."

"Yeah."

He hung up first. When the dial tone returned, I hung up too, and then started on my way to the Mayer house. My focus narrowed to the scope of a thread: I was far beyond caring if anyone saw me wandering the streets alone.

The blurry jog from Perry's Pantry to Chester Street, and from there toward Wyckham Road probably took longer than it felt, but I was too busy trying to untangle the cluster of knots in my head to pay much attention to time. The sky was a swirling swell of bruises, purple and grey mostly, with the odd void where a puff of highlighter pink poked through like a hernia. As I turned on to Wyckham, it occurred to me that I was taking the route Catherine Hillerman was said to have taken before everything happened. A sharp stitch jabbed me below my ribs. I tried to fend it off by pressing against it, and kept my pace, pushing forward.

Steph should have been with me. I knew she'd want to be, but she definitely had her own problems to deal with right now. And I was sure, sitting in the hospital with the little brother she'd made sit in another booth and told to finish his Blizzard, that she had plenty to think about not involving the Mayers and all the *weird* that orbited them. I hoped that she wasn't too angry with herself, but I knew her well enough to know it was wasteful to spend much hope on that.

The stitch in my side throbbed. I didn't slow down. I tried stretching my torso as I ran but all that did was allow the stitch to spread its crampy little self out inside me. With this pain came the sudden awareness of all the Blizzard rolling around in my belly. Thinking of it summoned a hot acidic fizzling at the back of my mouth. I kept going, my jog escalating to a run.

The sun came out from the bottom of a mass the of clouds and got stuck in the branches of the ravine's messy sketch of treetops. It stayed there for a while then freed itself and continued its slow descent, rolling the dimmer dial on the sky. Probably seeing how much fun my stitch and my ice-cream-tub stomach were having messing with me, my self-inflicted leg wound sent a buzz of pain to my brain. This was all the proof I needed to know my body was conspiring against me. I needed to rest for a second and catch my breath. I stopped on the grass outside the ravine and bent forward, resting my hands on my knees. A blast of Blizzard puke sprayed from my mouth and nose onto the ravine's turf, another sort of offering, I guess. It burned and stung and came so fast and hard that it made my balls hop up to the top of their bag. And just when I thought it was done, having dropped to my hands and knees, a second blast came. This one got better distance than the first. It spouted from me in a messy rainbow arc, rocketing from my face with such force that once it was all out, I felt as if my neck had been throttled.

I stayed there on the grass, catching my breath, letting the aftermath drip from my nose and mouth as I waited for the disorientation to pass.

Swish of feet on grass, then: "You're fuckin' disgusting." The voice came from behind me.

I sat up and took my hands off the ground but stayed on my knees, still catching my breath. A sniff triggered a sneeze, which expelled a little hunk of Oreo from my nostril. I wiped my mouth and nose on my shoulder and shuffled around so that I was facing whoever was speaking to me. I craned my neck up to meet Connor Monaghan. Fists clenched at his sides, face tugged into a tight frown, he towered over me, casting a shadow that had a weight to it. I started to pull myself up to my feet, but I didn't get very far before he booted me in the chest, sending me backwards onto the grass.

Lying there, breath kicked from my lungs, it took a second for the pain of the blow to arrive. But when it did, *man*.

I knew that showing him I was hurt would just provoke more punishment, but I couldn't help it. As the pain spread across my chest, I felt my face crumble into an expression of agony. I rolled onto my side. Connor jumped on the opportunity. He stepped over to me and gave me another kick, this one in the ribs. I whimpered and held out a pleading hand. He stepped on my plea, pinning it to the grass.

"*Fucker*," he said through gritted teeth. "You are such a little fucker, you know that, Daredevil?"

When I didn't answer, he put all his weight on his foot. I screamed, and that got me another kick in the side.

"Shut up," he demanded. "If you scream again, I'll kick you in the head, get it?"

I nodded, took a deep, shuddering breath, and did my best to stay still. He didn't move his foot off my hand. I could feel my fingers being pushed through the grass and into the dirt. That awful, evil ravine dirt that I'd already given my blood to. *What more did it want?*

"Do you even know what you did?"

I shook my head, not trusting myself to speak without puking again. Connor didn't like that. He put more pressure on my hand and repeated his question. "I said, 'Do you even know what you did?' Use your words, dipshit."

"*No*," I said. "*No, I don't know*."

"See," Connor said, looking up at the darkening sky, "the problem is I don't believe you, because I think you're a little snake. You lie and you sneak, and that makes you a *snake*. Maybe that's why you look so good on the ground." He took his foot off my hand, my fingers tingling. "Yeah," he said to himself. "Not a daredevil—daredevils have *guts*—but a sneaky, backstabbing little snake."

He walked to my other side, using my back as a stepping stone. The pressure of his weight forced a wheeze from me that sounded like a squeaky floorboard in an old house. One foot stepped off, the other replaced it, then it stepped off, and Connor sat down next to me.

"Do you know why I'm alone?" he asked.

I shook my head and sat up. Connor surprised me by resting his hand on my shoulder like we were about to have a real heart-to-heart.

"I think you do," he said. "I think you know I'm alone tonight because my best fuckin' friend is in some serious shit. And I think you know it's because of you." It might have been my imagination, but it sounded for a second like his voice almost cracked when he called Louis his 'best fuckin' friend.' He dug his fingers into my shoulder like he was applying a Vulcan nerve pinch. I struggled and he applied more force to keep me still. When I gave in, he eased up.

"It didn't take Louis long to figure out who put that cassette tape in his pocket," Connor continued. "He's not the brightest guy, but he put two and two together. Tried explaining to his dad it wasn't his fault, but his dad didn't buy it. His dad *never* believes him. Louis told me they spent almost an hour with the manager and store security. The cops came and everything. At the end of it all, he ends up with a for-real court date. And that's not even the worst part."

He moved his hand to the back of my head, grabbed a handful of hair. "His *dad's* the worst part," he said. "Man, he went *off.*" His voice showed more cracks, enough for me to know I wasn't imagining them. "One eye's black, the other one's swollen shut. He's talking all funny—slurring. Probably fucked up his jaw. And he's limping around like a fuckin' gimp."

I considered for a moment pointing out that the cassette wasn't the only item Louis had been busted for shoplifting, but figured that wouldn't do me any favours.

"I told him I was going to call social services—for real this time—but Louis made me promise not to. He *begged* me. Made me swear I wouldn't. Said it'd ruin everything." He looked at me again. His eyes were wet, but they had a blankness that sent a chill rippling through my body. "So, here I am with you, Robin," he said. "Because someone's got to pay for what happened to my friend."

He stood up and guided me to rise with him. Once we were both on our feet, he repeated, "Someone's got to pay for what happened to my friend." It was as if he had to remind to himself that whatever he was about to do was necessary. Then he started marching me forward, to the ravine's wall of trees.

× × ×

"I'm sorry Louis got hurt. I didn't mean—"

"Shut up." Connor gave me a boot in the ass, which sent me stumbling forward. I tripped over a crooked root. He caught me by the shirt and steadied me with a hard tug that was accompanied by the sound of ripping cotton.

"I don't want to hear that you're sorry. I don't care about sorry. I told you to keep walking."

I kept walking.

It was much earlier than it had been the last time I'd been inside the ravine, but somehow it was just as dark. My glasses, smudged with fingerprints and flecked with tiny dots of Blizzard puke, felt about half as useful as they should've been. Wind shook the high branches. Their rickety tremble sounded like rattling bones. Some of the leaves on the trees were already turning yellow and stood out like bright loonies among their still-green peers. A tear slid down my face and dropped off my chin. There had been a lot of crying already that day, with more to come.

Connor commanded me to stop. "Here," he told me.

I turned to face him. The scant light that filtered through the trees made his face into a broken stained-glass window.

"What now?" I asked.

"You don't wuss out and you give me a few good shots, maybe I get my fill and decide to call it a day before you look like Louis. You make this difficult for me, I'm just gonna get more pissed and probably—"

I couldn't let him finish. I lunged at him, fist cocked, which got him to raise his fists in defence, then—hoping that was enough for a fake-out—swung my foot, going for a field goal with his nuts. He got a leg up in time to block it, and my foot smashed into his kneecap. My toes cracked, but the blow seemed to hurt him more. He screamed and yelled *fuck*, and hopped backwards, tripping over a rock or a root or something. Wasting no time, I turned and started running back in the direction we'd come from, pushing past branches, twigs jabbing me, scratching at my arms, neck, face as I hopped over the uneven ground. But any delusion I had of a successful escape lasted only as long as it took to buy in.

The menacing grip of Connor's hand clutched the back of my shirt. He yanked and swung, and I spun and staggered and then crashed into a tree, sending scabs of white bark fluttering from it. Before I could get my hands up, he flattened my nose with his fist. Immediately, my second gusher of that summer started up. As the sting sunk in, I felt my legs giving up. My back pressed against the birch behind me, I melted to the ground, feeling blood drip down my chin, its coppery taste in my mouth, on my lips. I looked up to see Connor was charging at me. It was his turn to go for a field goal. I got my knees and arms up just in time to block his foot, which was swinging for my face. My arms took most of it. But the impact was strong enough to fling my head back against the tree, which cradled my skull about as much as you'd expect a piece of solid wood to cradle anything. I hardly had time to think before he landed another one.

"Snake!" Connor huffed. "Sneaky little shit! See? That's what I'm talking about. Cheap shots, tricky shit—that's what you do." He reached down and slapped me, then backed up a little, readying himself for a third kick.

"Wait!" I yelled, holding my hands up. "Please, wait!" my voice, a nasally gurgle.

Connor paused. I wasn't sure he was capable of showing sympathy, but his hesitation made me realize how pathetic I must've looked.

"I'm sorry about what happened to your friend," I told him. "I wanted him to get in trouble. Because I felt guilty about helping you guys deliver that fucking letter. And because . . ." I spat out a mouthful of blood. It was thick and couldn't travel far, so it landed on my shirt, adding to the mess that was already on there. "Because . . . mostly because you guys are always such dicks to us." I sniffed wetly and continued. "Honestly, man, if I'd known his dad would beat the shit out of him, I wouldn't have slipped that cassette in his hoodie . . . I don't know though. That might be a lie. So, I'm sorry, but at least one of you deserved to get in shit. Just like maybe I deserve this right now. I don't want you to keep hitting me. But maybe I've had this coming for a while, and even if I don't . . . I don't know how to make you stop."

A silence blanketed us. I wondered if I actually might have gotten through to him. Then he looked up at me—his eyes somehow even deader than normal, like rounded tips of dull pencils—and asked softly, "Are you fucking done?"

I covered my face with my hands. Sobs began to shake me.

"I'll take that as a yes."

Waiting there on the floor of the ravine, I did my best to brace myself for the beating of a lifetime. Maybe one to *end* a lifetime. While I waited for Connor to drop the hammer, I thought how even though I wanted longer, thirteen years was an all right amount of time, and that I was grateful, because not everyone gets that much. I thought about my parents and Peter, and how they'd get along without me. I thought of Steph and Dylan, and Kyle and Catherine, and how I'd die without ever knowing for sure what happened. And I thought . . . I thought . . .

I thought I *heard* something.

I took my hands away from my face and opened my eyes.

Connor was still standing in the same spot. His back a straight line, his ear cocked to the sky. He'd heard it too. We shared a look. Nothing. Nothing. Then, there it was again: a low groan accompanied by the snapping and crunching of twigs and branches. Steps. Big, lumbering, coming from somewhere behind him. Growing closer.

I pulled myself up and even moved slightly toward Connor. He'd turned his back to me as he stood in anticipation of whatever was coming our way. My mind was a messy smear from the blows.

I forced myself to focus. The steps continued, but the groaning had been replaced by heavy, huffing breathing. I could feel my heartbeat in my ears.

The shape appeared a second later, trudging through a net of branches on an incline not far in front of us. All I could make out was his form. It—he—was a man. Or had the shape of a man. He groaned again and Connor and I both screamed like the kids we were. My legs were cemented to the ground, but Connor was gearing up to haul ass out of there. He was faster than me, which left me in a bad spot but kicked in my self-preservation instinct. I leapt at Connor and shoved him forward with all my remaining strength, into the lumbering shape that had just reached the top of the incline and stood only a few strides away.

Connor's screams sounded like they came from someone else. They were the screams of a scared little boy who could do nothing *but* scream. That shrill, terrified noise was all his body was capable of in that moment.

I turned around and ran like hell, his cries following me through the trees.

23

IT WAS MOSTLY DARK WHEN I GOT TO THE MAYER HOUSE. A GLOWING SHAFT
of light from the rising moon glazed the edges of the concrete
pathway that led up the vast painting of a lawn. I had walked up
and down those steps so many times in my life. That night would
be the last time.

The door was unlocked. I finally found it in me to enter without
knocking, just like Mrs. Mayer—or had she always been Andrea?
Andy?—said I could. The house was dead quiet. As I closed the
door behind me, I caught my reflection in the mirrored doors of
the front closet. I looked like roadkill. Dirt streaked on my forehead, arms, clothing. My nostrils, rimmed with dried blood, were
enlarged by the ratty wads of Kleenex I'd stuffed up there on the
walk over—my mom, a firm believer that a person should always
have an emergency Kleenex on them, would have been proud of
that, at least. There was more dried blood on my chin and throat
and, of course, plenty of it on my shirt, which with its Blizzard
splatters and newly stretched-out collar was its own disaster altogether. I hardly recognized myself in the mirror, and I wondered
what Dylan and his family would think when they finally saw me.

I looked up the stairs, where I could see the landing at the top
and a bit of the connecting hall that led to all the bedrooms. It was
mostly dark, but there were a few small slashes of light that had
found their way up from the main floor. Not knowing where or how
to start, I tiptoed down the hall to see if anyone was around. I could
hear the soft murmur of the TV in the living room; it sounded
like it was tuned to the news. I moved a bit closer and stopped
when I saw the kitchen, where not that long ago I'd sat down with
the Mayers for dinner. Looking past the table, I saw Mrs. Mayer
standing outside on the deck. She had her back to me and had one
arm wrapped around herself. In her free hand she held a glass of

red wine, and she was staring off at the night sky as if she expected something from it.

I glanced at Mr. Mayer's closed office door. The lights were off. He could've been somewhere else in the house, or out. I hoped for the latter.

Tiptoeing out of the kitchen, I went back to the front of the house. At the foot of the stairs, I looked up to the landing. Each room had a soft glow coming from the crack beneath its door. I knew I had to go up. A sick uneasy feeling had parked itself in my stomach. Part of it came from thinking of Connor, who I'd thrown into the clutches of that awful ravine thing. For all I knew, he was being eaten at that very moment. Connor was a garbage person, but he didn't deserve that because no one did. The bulk of my uneasiness came from everything else: seeing Emily in the hospital, the poster with Andrea, my conversation with Adam at the grocery store. So many things I thought I knew, it turned out I didn't. Everything was wrong. As I stepped onto the first stair, I found myself hoping that the whole summer had been a dream. One long, fucked-up, lucid dream. I wanted it to be the end of June. The last day of school. As soon as I woke up, I'd think, *that was strange*, and I'd get dressed and eat breakfast and rush out of the house. I'd meet Dylan and Steph at our usual spot by the portables and tell them about what I'd dreamed, but I'd leave out the part about Dylan's mom, because I wouldn't want him to think that I thought of her that way. And they'd both think the dream was hilarious, but also *weird*, and Steph would try and analyze it and would talk about my subconscious because she'd read a book about that stuff once and she only got so many chances to flaunt it. And in class later, you know what else I'd do? I'd become better friends with Kyle. I'd try and get him to join our group, because he's not an awful guy and three's a crowd, so four is . . . better. No, three's a crowd and four is *even*. Balanced. And balanced is better.

If only.

I was about halfway up the steps, heading toward Dylan's room, when her voice stopped me.

"*Robin?*"

I turned around in a slow-motion spin, my limbs, my neck, every muscle rigid, tensing in unison.

"You startled me," Mrs. Mayer said, not yet taking in my dirty and beaten self. "I heard something. And was worried . . . I didn't know . . ." She was looking at me with the same sort of relief a person has after determining that the suspicious noise that stirred them was just the wind. Or a kitten. Something harmless and ultimately laughable. Her gaze moved to the surrounding darkness before returning to rest on me. "But it's only you," she said. "All by yourself. All alone."

I could pinpoint the instant her eyes adjusted enough for her to get a proper look at me. Any idea she might have had about rushing me out of the house evaporated then. "Jesus, what happened?"

I wanted to respond, but a lump of ice that might have been my heart had lodged itself in my throat. The lump got colder when, a second later, the click of a door opening came from upstairs. I looked up to see Dylan on the landing, staring down at me.

"Robin? What the hell, man? Why are you . . . ? You can't be here." Then: "Why do you look like that?"

The most I could manage was a strained exhaling noise that sounded like a shorting light bulb. I was thankful when Mrs. Mayer, seeing my distress, chimed in.

"I'll get you fixed up. Come downstairs. Both of you."

× × ×

She put one finger underneath my chin and tilted so I was looking up at her and into the light of the chandelier that hovered behind her head like a halo.

"I got in a fight," I said. Then, realizing there was no sense in sugar-coating it, corrected myself: "Actually, it wasn't much of a fight. I got beat up."

"By *who*? Who did this?"

"Connor. He found out about that thing I told you about." I gestured to Dylan with a twitch of my elbow. "How I got Louis in shit at the grocery store. I was on my way here and I ran into him at the ravine."

At the mention of the ravine, Mrs. Mayer gave a little start. Something in her shifted. She was quick to settle back in place.

"How long have these been shoved up there?" She pointed at the wads of Kleenex plugging my nose, which I'd gotten so used to I'd forgotten were even there.

"I don't know. A while. I kind of lost track of time." My voice was nasal and flat.

"Do you taste blood? Can you tell if it's still leaking into your mouth?"

I let my tongue roll around. My teeth had that rough, grimy feel that came with puking. There was a lingering penny taste of blood, but it wasn't as bright as it had been right after I'd been slugged.

"Not really," I told her. "Only a little."

She hesitated, then got up and left the kitchen, stopping to finish off her wine on her way and telling Dylan to turn the kettle on. She returned with a wet cloth and pulled a chair up in front of me. As she lowered herself into it, my heart rate climbed and my eyes moved over her body. She tugged the Kleenex loose from my nostrils, handling them with the careful hurriedness reserved for only the ickiest of icky, then took off my glasses and wiped my face with a washcloth that was much hotter than I was ready for. Her face near my face: the image of Andrea—smoky eyes, teased hair—flickered on and off in my head like something connected to a switch.

When she finished, she sat back in her chair and took me in with a nod, content with her work. The kettle had started its rattling *shhhh-hh-hh-hh*, like a bunch of needles were being swivelled around and around inside its metal shell. Mrs. Mayer disappeared to the laundry room to get rid of the washcloth, then came back to the kitchen and got to the kettle just as it began its scream. She took the hot chocolate powder out of the pantry, spooned some into a couple mugs, and added hot water. Before she brought our drinks over, she paused in front of the microwave clock and scowled at it, for some reason unimpressed with its report.

"Robin, you said you were on your way over here when you ran into this . . ."

"Connor," I said.

"Yes, Connor. He's from your school?"

Both Dylan and I nodded. "I honestly thought he was going to kill me," I said. "He made me walk into the ravine with him and told me I needed to be punished for what happened to his friend. He just pushed me around a bit at first, but I tried to fight back and that got him really pissed. He punched me in the face and kicked me a bunch of times, and I think I hit my head on a tree, and . . ."

"How did you get away?" Dylan asked me.

"This . . . thing showed up."

"A *thing*?" Mrs. Mayer asked, raising one of her calligraphic eyebrows.

I told them about the shape, how it lumbered like Frankenstein's monster, how I was able to shove Connor into it, and how Connor was probably being digested as we spoke.

Mrs. Mayer folded her hands like she was about to pray before cupping them over her mouth. She whispered something into them, then took another look at the microwave clock.

"Why did you come *here*?" Dylan asked.

"Because I know you're hiding something. I don't know what it is, and I can't figure out how it all fits together, but I know something's wrong. If Steph were here, she'd back me up. She probably would've even figured it out by now. But I haven't. I just know—I think I know—*this*," I waved a hand, gesturing at nowhere in particular, "this is the middle of everything. It has to be. There's been too much weirdness going on here for it not to be."

If my accusation stirred anything, it didn't show on Mrs. Mayer's face. Her elbows on the table, her delicate chin resting on her fists, she looked at me with the same unbiased indifference a second-grade teacher has when they're hearing out a tattle-tale. Then, she got up and disappeared into the dining room. I heard the stubborn door of the liquor cabinet groan open then force shut. She reappeared a few seconds later with a bottle of what I was pretty sure was whiskey. She got herself a new glass and poured a liberal amount and then brought her new drink and the bottle over to the table with her.

I noticed her staring at me from across the table with a look of impatience. She wanted me to continue. I wanted me to continue too, but I didn't know how. I wished Steph was there, but she wasn't. I was alone. To move forward, I needed answers. And the best way to get those seemed to be to tell what I knew. There was no point in holding anything back. The fastest way down is never the stairs— it's the ledge.

"When I saw Louis and his dad at Co-op, I ran into Adam. I didn't know he was back." I turned to face Dylan. "Why didn't you tell me he was back?"

"Dylan doesn't have to tell you everything," Mrs. Mayer said on her son's behalf.

"I know." I held my hands up in defence. "I didn't say he needed to tell me *everything*. But his brother being back? That's the sort of thing you tell your best friend."

"Families . . . every family . . . has things that they keep between them," Mrs. Mayer said. She took a drink then plunked the glass down on the table and levelled her eyes with mine. They were beginning to get that shine, the one they'd had the other day.

"I don't know what he told you, but Adam"—she said his name with a sort of disdain—"has been a very . . . *difficult* young man these last couple years. He's been—I might as well call a spade a spade—an entitled brat. We thought going away to school would help him grow up, but that hasn't been the case. When he came back home in spring, Ken refused to pay Adam's university tuition. Go figure, there are consequences to failing all your classes and being placed on academic probation. Adam was livid. He can't take not getting his way. He stayed with us for a few days before we had to ask him to leave.

"We couldn't take him right back—he was *awful* to us. After all we've done for him, he still found it in himself to be so . . . cruel." She sighed and ran her fingers through the deep-water waves of her dark hair. "Kicking your son out is a hard thing for a mother to do, but he needed to go. Tough love. Taking responsibility for yourself is part of growing up." She helped herself to another mouthful of her drink and added, "I blame myself."

Her testimony confused me. "Adam told me that Mr. Mayer was still paying his tuition."

"No," Dylan said, shaking his head elaborately to make it more of a *hell no*. "That's not true. My dad cut him off because—"

"He was being a little fuck-up," Mrs. Mayer snipped. "He was cutting class, and lying to us, and wasting our money—and his brain cells—on pot and God knows what else." She snapped her finger and pointed at Dylan. "I told your father that if we didn't do something, Adam would end one up of those deadbeat kids living in a dumpy apartment in Saddler with a bunch of loser roommates. Pissing his life away." She turned to me then, placing the splayed fingers of her free hand on her chest. "Do you think I want that for any of my kids?"

"Except he's not your kid," I said. I shocked myself by saying it, but once it was out, there was no taking it back. The impact of my words was almost instant. She leaned into the table and pushed her head forward, her eyes crackling fierce.

"*Excuse me?*"

"He . . ." My voice cracked. I coughed into the crook of my elbow and tried again. "He isn't your son. That's what he told me when I saw him. He said he couldn't live here because he found out what you were. That's what he told me." The words rushed out of me, smashing and crashing into each other like cars with summer tires on an icy hill.

"You don't know what you're talking about," Dylan told me.

I pushed on. "And what about Emily?" I asked, my voice growing louder, out of my control. "You're lying about her too. I know she's not here. I know that even though you're making Dylan lie about having to babysit her, that Emily's really in the hospital." I shot up from my chair. I knew I had to get it out—all of it—in one go. I pointed an accusing finger across the table at Mrs. Mayer. "And you. Who are you even? *Why can't you people stop lying? What can't*—"

"Don't talk to my mom like that, you fucking dick!"

Dylan's eyes were brimming with tears, but they held a wild charge. I could tell what was coming. I pushed my chair back, began to inch away, but he was on me before I finished my first step. He grabbed me by my shirt and yanked me toward him like a pitcher bringing his arm back for a windup. Then with both hands, he shoved me backwards with a force that immediately reminded me of the size difference between us. I went down on my right side, my elbow and hip banging the hardwood, before I slid and smacked the side of my face on the base of the counter. Cutlery from inside the drawers rattled. My jaw lit up like an arcade machine. Dylan stood over me with an expression of shock that probably came pretty close to matching my own. He looked like he'd woken up and his mind couldn't process what was happening in front of him. Then his mom grabbed him by the arm, tugged him close, and gave him a crisp smack on the back of the head. But before Mrs. Mayer could say anything, the creaking of a floorboard announced the entrance of a visitor. We all turned and looked.

She had a purple shiner around one eye and a little gash on the opposite cheek. The gash had scabbed over but wasn't yet ready to peel. There were bruises on her wrists and forearms. Blooming splotches of purple and yellow. But despite all she'd gone through—whatever it was—she still seemed like the same girl I'd seen at the mall with her brother. She was wearing what I recognized to be an old pair of Emily's pyjamas.

Emily. *My sister. I don't get to see her.*

"Hi, Catherine," I said, wincing at the sharp pain in my jaw.

She smirked. At first it was that of a shy child: sheepish, reserved. That part held for a second, and then it gave way to its successor: a playful grin that had a trace of whimsy in it.

"Hello, *dah*-ling," she said.

I guess she remembered me.

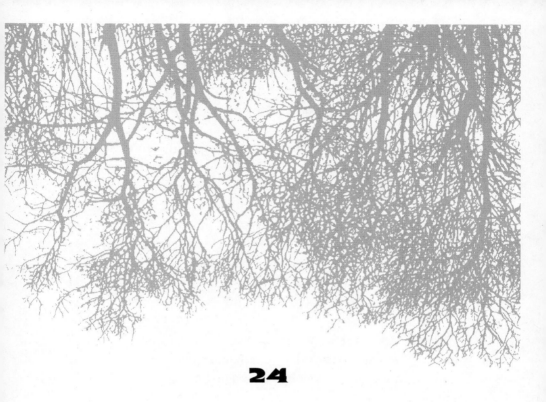

24

MRS. MAYER KNELT DOWN IN FRONT OF CATHERINE HILLERMAN. SHE PUT
her hand on the little girl's shoulder and smiled a smile that looked
like it took a lot of effort. She held it like a weightlifter trying to
break a world record.

"Miss Diane?" Catherine asked.

"Yes, sweetheart?"

"I can't sleep."

"You can't? Well, would you like some hot chocolate like the
boys are having? I can put some warm milk in it. That might help
you sleep."

Catherine was on board with that.

"All right," Mrs. Mayer said. "I'll make you some, but you've
got to promise to go right back to bed after. You've got a *very* big
day tomorrow."

Catherine nodded and leaned against the wall, smiling in anticipation of the treat on the horizon. And Mrs. Mayer got right to it.
She got a mug—a purple one that, like the pyjamas, I recognized to

be Emily's as well—and spooned in the powder and got the kettle going again. We all waited, the only sound between us the kettle creeping its way to another boil. I took a sip of my hot chocolate and learned that the act of opening and closing my mouth was one that came with little lightning bolts of pain. I recalled every coach and gym teacher I ever had invoking the expression *walk it off*, and decided I should apply that time-tested method to my jaw. I opened it and closed it. It hurt. I opened it again and closed it again, then again, then again, then again. The fifth repetition ended with a pop. It was a good pop. The popping of something being worked back *into* place. I let my tongue probe around my mouth to see if the collision between my face and the counter had done anything else.

It had.

At the back-right corner of my mouth, my tongue came across a tooth. A molar whose exit was a couple years overdue. It had already been loose, but now it was hanging by what felt like a single nerve.

The kettle reached its boil, and Mrs. Mayer poured the water into Catherine's mug and added quite a bit of milk in hopes it would help carry her off to dreamland.

"Can I drink it in my sister's room?" Catherine asked.

"Of course, dear. But then right to bed. Big day, remember?"

Catherine nodded and then waved and told us goodnight, her wide eyes staring at me and Dylan while she took a furtive sip from her mug. Mrs. Mayer gave her a pat on the head and ushered her down the hallway. Dylan, not wanting to waste the opportunity that presented itself when his mother left the room, reached for the whiskey bottle and poured some into his hot chocolate, then mine. His portioning aptitude was clearly a hereditary trait. I lifted my mug and sniffed its newly infused contents. Wood and turpentine. I took a sip. It burned its way down and took very little time moving to my already-foggy head.

Mrs. Mayer returned and we all listened to the soft whispers of Catherine's feet on the stairs followed by the distant clicking of Emily's bedroom door being pushed closed.

"All right," Mrs. Mayer said with a sigh of resignation, "we might as well get to talking." Again, she looked at the microwave clock. "I've got to do *something* to pass the time while I wait for your father to come home."

She—Mrs. Mayer, Diane, Andrea, Andy, whoever she was—downed the rest of her drink then pushed the empty glass as far away as her reach would allow, as if she were trying to indicate to an invisible bartender that she was ready for her bill and didn't want to be tempted further.

"We're not the bad guys here, if that's what you're thinking," she told me. "Quite the opposite, actually. This whole . . . mess started because someone was trying to hurt *us*. Hurt our family. This person—or these *people*, I guess . . . I'm not really sure if it's just him—wanted to ruin us. They nearly did. And somewhere along the way, other people got hurt too. That's what we're trying to fix right now, why we have Catherine here with us tonight."

She bowed her head and rubbed her hand back and forth over the back of her long neck like she was trying to work out a kink, or maybe console herself. When she looked back up, her eyes held a pained, faraway look.

"The first letter came at the end of July. An envelope, blank except for the names of the people it was addressed to: Ken and I. No house number, no stamp. It clearly hadn't been dropped in our box by our mailman. The way our names were written on it—two messy scribbles in pencil—I thought at first it was a note from a child. Was I ever wrong about that. I almost fainted when I opened it up."

She bit down on her lip. "That seems silly now, because really, I'd been dreading this arriving at our home for years—not quite *expecting* it, mind you, but I knew it was possible . . . one day. The only thing written on the note was a phone number and a dollar amount. Fifty thousand dollars, written in the same idiot scrawl our names were written in on the envelope. The amount shocked me—fifty thousand dollars is a lot of money—but it didn't frighten me the way the rest of it did."

She eased back in her chair and let her eyes drift over our heads as if to watch a movie playing on a screen that only she could see.

"Those photos brought back memories. Mostly bad ones, but . . . not all. I'd be lying if I said they were all bad. There are one or two that still have some glitter on them. I wish I could keep those and get rid of all the rest, put them in the firepit and throw a match on them and watch them crisp and curl and die. But memory doesn't work that way, does it?" She shook her head, maybe in disappointment, maybe answering her own question. "I was so young. So naive. How could I have known there would be so many wolves out there?"

She placed her elbows on the table and folded her hands. Telescoping her neck out, she opened her mouth and, with the air of a someone telling a midnight campfire story, said, "But there are wolves here too, aren't there? You've probably seen some of them. Yes, there are the stupid ones who make no point of hiding what they are. But the smart ones? The smart ones know how to stay hidden. They know how to disguise themselves. And they . . . are . . . *everywhere*."

Dylan, I saw in the corner of my eye, was ringing his hands together and squirming like he had to pee. He froze when he noticed me looking.

"*What?*"

"Are you okay?"

The gears got moving again. His hands, his squirming body. "No, I'm not *okay*," he said, glaring at me. "I'm fucking sick of this. Sick of hearing about it, of being part of it." He smashed a fist on the tabletop, pushed his chair back, and stomped out of the kitchen. A door slammed shut.

"He's doing his best," Mrs. Mayer told me. "I keep telling him, 'We're almost there, honey, just a couple more days,' and then 'Just one more day—I can see the finish line.' But it's taken such a toll. And really, could I say anything to make it easier on him? Words are just words."

I cleared my throat. "What happened with the letter? You said there were photos? And . . . *wolves?*"

She chuckled in a contained way. "Oh, yes. Photos and wolves. In this case, the wolf who wrote the letter had somehow gotten his hands on those photos. I don't know who he is or how he did it, but he did . . . He's the reason we are where we are."

Again, she looked past me.

"I wasn't born here in Haddington Springs. I did a lot of my growing up in a little house down in Saddler, but I was actually born in Saskatoon. We came here when I was two, my mom and I, and stayed until I was fifteen, but then we moved to Calgary. That's where I went to high school. Class of 1978. Can you believe it? It seems like a lifetime ago." She pumped her fist with mock excitement and said, "*Go, Griffins!*" but her fake enthusiasm was quick to dissolve back to seriousness. "Once I graduated, I started working at a bar downtown called The White Hat with a girlfriend of mine. The waitresses there were either fresh, like Mel and I, or lifers. You *had* to be one or the other at The White Hat. Either a young girl lured in by the prospect of making big tips—which you never did, everyone who drank there was a cheapskate—or a miserable old hag who knew that dump was the best she could do. I remember the building had this *smell* to it, like you were inside a rotting lung. It'd hit you the second you walked in, and it would bother you just as much at hour nine of your shift as it did at minute one. It was one of those smells you never got used to. Ever.

"Mel and I had been working there around a year when one of our regulars, a man named Ricky, who had hair like Elvis and the sort of godawful mustache you never see on anyone anymore, approached us. 'You girls want to make some *real* money?' We did." She shrugged, then sunk a little in her chair. "*We were so young,*" she whispered.

I'd never had someone talk to me like that before, open up and put themselves on display like that. It bothered me, but I think on some level I was grateful too. I took a long drink, draining my mug to its bottom third. The whiskey sent its glowing liquid warmth down into my stomach and made my cheeks flush. When I returned the mug to the table, Mrs. Mayer continued.

"He told us he was co-owner of a place called Hush-Hush, a so-called gentleman's club that, I can assure you, never had a single gentleman pass through its doors. I didn't know that then, though. Ricky told us everything we wanted to hear. He did his best to paint a respectable picture of the place, luring us with the money we would make, the lifestyle that came with it. How we'd be *adored*. He made it all seem so glamourous. All we needed was an audition. It sounds ridiculous now, but at the time . . . Well, I didn't think that way at the time.

"Mel and I went to audition," she said, adding heavy finger quotes to the word *audition*, "where we learned that Ricky wasn't a co-owner like he told us. He was the bartender who'd been there long enough to feel like he owned a piece of the pie. I guess the name Ricky should have been a clue—what kind of respectable man goes by a name like that? Ricky? Billy? Teddy? If you don't drop the *y* by eighteen, *that* speaks volumes.

"Apart from Ricky, four other men were there. One of them, a man named Wayne Vick, introduced himself as the owner. The other was a photographer, which Wayne assured us was normal for auditions. And the other two? I have no idea who they were. Probably bartenders or bouncers who were in tight enough with the boss to get a VIP invite to the fresh meat panel. They gave us some drinks to loosen us up and put on some music. You know, I have to change the radio station every time 'Fame' comes on? It's a shame because I've always loved Bowie . . . I can't stand that song anymore.

"Once we were liquored up enough, they told us to start 'having some fun,' giving us pretty clear instructions of what kind of 'fun' we should be having. We went with it. Of course, we had been expecting *something* like that. The photographer had his camera going the whole time. Once it was all done, when the bottles were all empty and all the music had been played and Mel and I were getting to fastening straps and buttoning buttons, I remember thinking that I'd just crossed some sort of threshold that there was no coming back from. Of course, I had no idea how many other thresholds were waiting beyond that one, but I remember it all feeling so final at the time. Like that was the farthest I could ever go."

She stopped speaking for a moment. The reel to her memories had to be switched, or maybe the projector lamp burned out and needed to be replaced. In any case, the pause gave Mrs. Mayer time to turn and steal another look at the microwave clock.

"Mel didn't last long, but I made it work. After a few months entertaining at Hush-Hush, Wayne, the owner, tried to sell me on an *under-the-table* business the club had going. Girls paid to keep men company. *That* was his pitch. As if there wasn't anything more to it than grabbing a bite, maybe a drink or two, and having a nice conversation. I remember thinking he was a nice guy to offer. Like he was doing me a favour out of the goodness of his heart. How messed up is that, Robin? The crafty ones," she said, raising a cautionary finger, "they can fool you like that."

"Is that when you became Andrea?" I asked, interrupting her unspooling.

She measured me with her eyes and asked, "Who told you that name?"

A boulder in my throat sealed off any words I might've had.

"It's all right, you can tell me."

Like a magnet to metal, the tip of my tongue nudged at my loose tooth, making my words sound garbled. "I . . . someone I know, their dad has a picture."

"Who?" she asked. Her tone was inviting, friendly even, but somehow the word felt like a threat. Three letters that served as a secret code for *you better tell me, or else.*

"Kyle Hillerman. His dad had a poster hidden away somewhere. Kyle found it and showed me."

Mrs. Mayer smiled knowingly. "Wolves, Robin. They're everywhere." Then with a snort of laughter she added, "I suppose you won't need to resort to sneaking around the house if you want to get a look at me."

My face burned.

"I always liked the sound of Andrea," Mrs. Mayer mused.

I heard something then. Muffled by distance and the wood of the bathroom door and maybe even something more . . . a towel? The sound of Dylan crying. Mrs. Mayer didn't seem to notice. She was too wrapped up in telling her story. Stories can do that to you, I've since learned. The best ones—the ones shelved away with the thickest layer of dust on them—are a rush to tell. Even when you know you shouldn't, once you start, it's impossible not to finish. The right thread exposes itself, someone asks the right question, giving it a tug, teasing it out just enough, and the next thing you know you can't stop until the whole thing has unravelled in your hands.

The picture Mrs. Mayer painted me was a portrait of a young woman caught in a storm. A mother ripped away by illness at the worst of times. A forceful boss with a surplus of empty promises. Far too much of some things, not nearly enough of others. As she told it, I could practically see the drowning pools swirling in her pupils. But that changed when Mr. Mayer came into the story.

"Ken was everything I never knew I needed." Her eyes flashed a spark at the mention of her husband. "A buddy of his booked me for him. I think it was supposed to be some sort of backwards attempt at therapy. See if I could help melt some of the ice in his veins, you know. Ken had been a widower for a few months at that point.

"Of course, doing what I did, I had men making me offers pretty regularly. I felt I'd already been offered everything under the sun by the time I saw him sitting on the edge of the motel bed, fidgeting like a nervous little boy. I'd had men say they would give me cars and jewellery. I'd had men propose to me, or offer to take me on vacation with them. The thing is, the ones who make those offers, most of them can't back up what they're trying to lure you with. The ones who can? Well, they're so"—she groped for the word, found it—"*unpleasant* that you don't want their gifts. It's a lose-lose. When Ken came along, he didn't offer me anything extravagant. After, laying there in the dark—his friend paid for an hour, and we still had about fifty-five minutes of it left—Ken asked if he could take me for dinner sometime. That was a question I got all the time from 'nice guys,' or guys who like to think they're nice . . . I can't say for sure what made him feel so different. Maybe I pitied him because he was a widower and had a kid to raise on his own."

"Adam."

She confirmed with a nod. "He seemed like the real deal—an *actual* nice guy. It definitely helped that he was good-looking. Clean too, which set him apart from a lot of the men. And he seemed to have his head on straight. But I think that more than anything, he came along at the right time. He wanted to take me away at a time when I actually *wanted* to be taken away. I slipped him my phone number. Lo and behold, a couple nights later, I got a call."

While I sat there, letting the information sink in, Mrs. Mayer got up and grabbed the bottle she'd poured from earlier off the counter. I guess it wasn't past last call, because she added a controlled splash to the glass she'd pushed away earlier.

"So the photos that were in the letter you got, those were . . ."

She wiped her lips with the tip of her finger, then nodded. "There were two photos from my so-called audition in the envelope. When Ken called the phone number on that letter, a man said he had prints of everything and the negatives. He said if he didn't get his money, he would start distributing the 'worst of the worst' to everyone we knew. Friends, family, our children's teachers, Ken's staff. *Everyone.* I knew exactly which shots he was talking about. The flyer Gil Hillerman has is nothing. I was mortified.

"We ponied up. Fifty grand. We don't have that sort of money just lying around, but we managed to scrape it together. We cleaned out our savings and Ken had to sell some stocks, but we did it. We followed all of this awful man's rules: unmarked bills, suitcase, no cops. You'd think this guy took all his cues from the movies. But once he got the money, he fucked us. Ken did everything he asked, and this son of a bitch fucked us. He left an envelope with the prints and negatives in it for Ken at the exchange spot he'd been told—we burned everything that very night in our firepit—but then we got a call a week later, just as we were getting used to the idea of having this leech off our back. He said that he had one more set that he'd be happy to part with for the right price."

She rubbed her arms as if a chill had suddenly found its way to her.

"I think our mistake was paying him so quickly. We thought that if we were co-operative and gave in right away, he would just . . . piss off. Take the money and leave us alone." She shook her head. "Nope. Not that easy. Nothing in life is. He came back for more, and Ken tried to keep it from me at first. He's always been like that—protective. I found out eventually though. When things got dangerous, he had to tell me.

"It isn't as though we *couldn't* have gotten more for him—our savings might have been depleted, but we could have always taken out a second mortgage or come up with some excuse and borrowed the money from Ken's family. It's that we *refused* to pay him again. That didn't go over well. Next thing you know there's threats being thrown back and forth, him to us and us to him, on and on. And . . . I broke. I wanted this man out of our lives, so I decided the hell with it. If he actually had this *supposed* second set of prints, he could do what he wanted with them. I love living in Haddington Springs, but if these pictures got out . . . well, there are other towns. Know what I mean? You just can't let shame control you, Robin. Ever."

Glass in hand, she got up. I was positive she was going to knock it back, but I was proven wrong when she dumped the whiskey down the drain and replaced it with tap water. She didn't return to the table, but leaned against the counter and sipped intermittently.

She continued, "After we said no, he threw a new threat at us, a much worse one than the photos. He . . ." She covered her mouth shut her eyes. Tears leaked from the corners. "The bastard said he was going to take Emily. It wasn't just blackmail anymore, now we were dealing with a ransom threat. Oh, God . . . my little girl."

She held her head back and forced her eyes wide open so they could get some air and she fanned herself with her hand, compelled to finish telling; the thread demanded it. "Ken called me in a panic. He said this guy told him he'd d been watching us, that he knew what we did, when we came and went. He knew Emily by sight and had just grabbed her off the street by the ravine. Ken said he even put her on the phone for proof. 'Say hi to Daddy,' the man said, and then Ken said he heard Emily cry for him. Ken was so worked up, so frantic, that he had me convinced she'd been taken, even though Emily was playing in our backyard right in front of me. I was watching her through the window. I doubted my own eyes. It took me a second to calm down, and then to try to get Ken to realize that yes, this monster had grabbed a little girl off the street, only he—"

"Only he didn't grab your little girl," I said. "He grabbed the girl who's sitting upstairs now."

"Yes," Mrs. Mayer took in a long breath, releasing it slowly. "The girl who, in the moment, looked enough like Emily and who happened to be in the wrong place at the wrong time."

× × ×

The moon had found its way into the kitchen window. A sliver of its pockmarked face hovered in its frame above the sink. The digital clock, which Mrs. Mayer seemed to have given up on, told me it was 9:33 p.m. I should have been home by then. I wondered if my parents were worried, or if they thought I was still with Steph and her family. Surely, they'd tried calling her house by now, but no one would've picked up. Would that cause them to panic? Or would they figure that I'd be safe and sound? If they'd somehow gotten in touch with Bruce and found out I wasn't with him—maybe he'd called from the hospital—they'd definitely be freaking out. I imagined Mom standing by the living-room window nervously wringing her hands together as she stared intently down the street in hopes I'd materialize on the horizon. Or Dad, driving through the neighbourhood, grilling anyone he passed. If he were doing that now, it'd probably look like he was up to something, behaving the way Catherine's abductor was said to have. Something obvious occurred to me then.

"Wait. Why is Catherine here and not with the kidnappers?" It wasn't my intention to sound accusing, but I didn't know how not to.

"It's such a mess, Robin," Mrs. Mayer said in a way that made it sound like she couldn't believe it herself. "When the kidnapper figured out that he'd taken the wrong girl, he still tried to use Catherine as leverage with us. I'm not sure if it was because the Hillermans couldn't pay what he wanted, or maybe to keep things as contained as possible, but whatever it was, the son of a bitch threatened to do all kinds of things to her. At first his angle was 'Do you want that on your conscience?' But then he got a little pushier and escalated, threatening to kill her and frame us for it. We had to do something. There was a lot of back and forth, but he and Ken came to an agreement the other day."

"What was it?"

"More money," she said. "A little girl's life was on the line. What else could we do? We agreed to another fifty thousand." The beginnings of a smile formed on her lips then. "But, Ken, he *knows* how to negotiate when he needs to," she said with a little swell of pride. "He got the guy to agree to something I never thought he'd be able to. But . . . lo and behold."

She told me how her husband had sold the guy on the idea of handing Catherine over first by telling him they'd need a couple days to get the money together and they wanted to make sure she stayed safe. "I thought it was too risky and that it wouldn't work." She shook her head and again checked the time on the microwave before continuing. The kidnapper was reluctant at first, but Mr. Mayer pointed out how the case already had so much attention— everyone in Haddington Springs was on the lookout—and the longer he kept Catherine, the greater the chance he had of getting caught. It sounded like Mr. Mayer spun it like he was doing the guy a favour. The detail that won him over was that, if the Mayers didn't pay up, the guy could throw them under the bus by calling the cops and giving an anonymous tip. *You know that the little girl the whole city is looking for? I know where she is.*

"So that's it?" I asked. "You paid up?"

Mrs. Mayer gave me a look like I should have known better.

"It's going to *appear* that way, but Ken has a plan. He . . . I'm expecting him back any moment." I didn't know if she was assuring me or herself.

I noticed something move on the floor. The long tip of Dylan's shadow stretched across the hardwood and nudged my foot. I turned to see him standing at the edge of the room, leaning against the wall where the hallway and kitchen met. His eyes were blood-shot. We locked on each other for a second, then he looked away, so I did too.

Turning my attention back to Mrs. Mayer, I asked, "You don't know who this guy, the kidnapper, is?"

She shook her head.

"Ken did some detective work. We only had a few prospects, but we crossed each one off the list in one way or another. Ricky, the guy who brought me to Hush-Hush in the first place, died in 1988. Cancer. And morally, I wouldn't put it past Wayne, the club owner, to try something like blackmail. But Ken learned that in addition to the club he now has his fingers in commercial real estate too. So it didn't seem like Wayne would *need* fifty thousand dollars. Not that that crosses him off completely, but it's unlikely. The only others I could think of were the actual photographer. I don't remember his name but he seemed to be on the older side back then, and I can't imagine him being physically up to the task now. And the two unknowns who were present for my audition. For the life of me, I can't remember either of their faces, but I do remember that they didn't seem . . . capable of a plot as elaborate as this."

Something in my mind began to stir, just far enough back that I couldn't quite get to it no matter how hard I reached. Like a climber trying to close his hand around a hold he couldn't see. I'd graze the thought, scrape at it, but no matter how far I stretched it always seemed like it didn't want to be touched and was somehow inching away from me. Something said, or maybe something seen. I could almost . . . *almost* . . .

Lights flooded into the house. The soft purr of a car pulling into the driveway. "There he is," Mrs. Mayer said, relieved. Feet pounded against the concrete steps outside and sent tiny tremors through the house that I could feel quivering up the legs of my chair. Mrs. Mayer, Dylan, and I all came together and peered down the hall at the front door. As the steps grew nearer, I noticed the uneven, clunky rhythm of each footfall. Doubled up, but out of sync: there were two sets of feet. The sound of a frantic fist hammering on the door came next. But whoever was on the other side wasn't very patient, because a couple seconds after that came the scrape of a key being shoved into its hole. Twist and *click*. The door flung open, so hard that the handle bashed against the inside wall. Two people stepped inside: Mr. Mayer—hunched forward and covered in dirt and damp, his face paper white, his hand clutching at his chest— and Adam—wide eyes bugging in his sweat-slicked face, his arm wrapped around his slumping father, holding him up.

The instant they crossed the threshold into the house, Mr. Mayer's legs buckled. He fell forward onto his knees, taking Adam halfway down with him. A stream of blood spilled from his chest. The blood leaked through his fingers and splashed onto the floor with a rainy patter. He tried to prop himself up with his free hand, lifted his head and looked down the hall at us, his gaze fixing on his wife as his face twisted like a screw in a block of wood.

"He needs help!" Adam yelled.

Mrs. Mayer screamed. We all did.

25

THE SADDEST PART ABOUT WATCHING HIM DIE WERE HIS LAST WORDS. OF course, everything that led up to what he said was heart-wrenching: Mrs. Mayer kneeling at his side, pleading for him to please just hang on, *please!*; Dylan hyperventilating in the corner, a fountain of tears streaming down his face, over his quivering mouth; Adam pacing in circles muttering to himself (*"It wasn't supposed to be this way . . . It wasn't supposed to be this way"*); and Catherine Hillerman, drawn out of Emily's room by the commotion, whimpering at the top of the stairs as she watched a scene from a horror movie unfold before her eyes. But his words left the strongest imprint on me. They're what I think about most. That and what Dylan did.

In a city as small as Haddington Springs, it didn't take long for an ambulance to arrive. Time moves differently in a crisis, but no more than five minutes could've passed between Mrs. Mayer calling 911 and the ambulance ripping into the driveway, its flashing blue and reds splashing through the windows. Unfortunately for Ken Mayer, just like the growing puddle of blood that had pooled on the floor, five minutes was something he just didn't have in him anymore. Before we even heard the sirens approaching, he squeezed his wife's hand, found the strength to lift his head off the ground in order to look at her as levelly as he could, and then stuttered his final words.

"I-I . . . I'm so sorry. I d-d-didn't mean f-for . . ."

And that was it. He trailed off and his eyes rolled back. Both of his sons rushed over, but before they got to him, his neck gave up and sent his head lolling back to the floor, where it landed with a bony thud. His chest rose and fell a couple more times, and then he spasmed like he'd touched a live wire, and that was it. His body relaxed and he was completely still. His last words on this earth were the beginnings of a broken apology.

That just makes me so sad. It's such a waste.

The paramedics would still have plenty to do when they got there though.

After his dad had breathed his final breath, Adam crawled into the corner by the door, covered his face with his hands and continued to sob his new catchphrase. *"It wasn't supposed to be this way . . . It wasn't supposed to be this way."*

Dylan, still hyperventilating, stepped out of the corner, his hands shaking. He walked past his brother, his mom, his dad's body, brushed past me, and disappeared down the hall.

"It wasn't supposed to be this way . . ."

In hindsight, it was a blessing that Adam's hands were already covering his face. Because when Dylan came charging down the hall at him a second later, his grandfather's bayonet in his hands swinging in a motion that somehow reminded me of shovelling heavy snow, he needed them ready.

Yeah, it definitely wasn't a wasted trip for the paramedics.

26

I'D NEVER HAD SO MANY ADULTS STARE AT ME AS WHEN I WAS ESCORTED through the police station that night. I felt like a celebrity. Officer Langmann ushered me through the crowded network of desks, with set after set of curious eyes following me with each step. He brought me to a room at the far end of the station, opened the door, and gestured for me to enter. Noticing my hesitation, he smiled and reminded me that my parents had been called and would be there any minute.

The interrogation room was dingier than the ones in *Law & Order*. Cement block walls painted two different shades of green. A false ceiling with a couple of fluorescent lights humming inside it. Totally empty except for a wooden table and two chairs. Just looking at them made my butt hurt. Officer Langmann was clearly in possession of some level of telepathic ability, because as soon as I thought that, he went and got me a different one with thick wooden legs and a cushioned seat. He asked me if I wanted anything to drink.

"Water? Milk? Tea? Hot chocolate? I can see if I can wrangle up a Coke if you give me a minute."

I told him that hot chocolate sounded good and he nodded and told me I'd made a great choice and that he'd be right back. Before he left, he let me know that the door to the room would stay open so I didn't feel like a "bad guy." He kind of talked to me like I was a little kid, but other than that he was all right. While I waited, I wondered if I'd get to talk to Detective Hennig or Purser again once my parents showed up. They'd both pulled up in front of Dylan's house shortly after the two uniformed police who'd arrived with the paramedics. Before I left, I saw Catherine get in their car. I wondered if they took her right home, or if she was somewhere here at the station too. Maybe they brought her to the hospital to get checked over. She probably needed that.

Officer Langmann came back in with a steaming Styrofoam cup that had one of those little brown plastic stir sticks poking from it. I didn't even really want hot chocolate, but I figured it would mask any lingering scent of alcohol on my breath. I wondered if Officer Langmann could smell it on me.

He disappeared for another second then returned with a different chair for himself, one with wheels on it that probably came from his desk. He brought in a drink for himself too, the smell of coffee wafting from the Robin's Donuts travel mug was strong enough to caffeinate me by proxy.

"Don't want to feel left out," he said as he sat down in his chair. He started to tell me about his son, who he said was a few years my junior. Apparently his son wore glasses too, and he hated having to wear them under the cage of his hockey helmet because they weren't comfortable and he couldn't wear contacts because he was allergic, but that's about all I got before I started to zone out.

"Hey," Officer Langmann said, snapping a finger, "you still with me?"

I immediately nodded. I don't know why I nodded as eagerly as I did. Maybe because he was a police officer and I felt I had to.

He smiled at me, and something in his smile told me that, yes, this man is definitely someone's dad. Then he started to explain how I was still processing what I had seen, and I might have some delayed symptoms of shock. He didn't get much farther before another officer came in the room, tapped him on the shoulder, and gave him a shrug-and-point gesture that meant nothing to me. Officer Langmann then turned back to me and explained that my parents were here and they'd like me to talk to a detective now. Before he left, he said that I was brave and got me to give him a high-five, which was cheesy. But, like I said, he seemed all right, so I didn't really mind.

My parents walked in with Detective Hennig a minute later. Mom started crying right away. That got me going, but I didn't have much left in me, and maybe Officer Langmann was right that I might be in shock. I figured my real-deal tears would come later.

Dad even started up, but he never really got going either. He kept knuckling at his eye like there was something stuck in it.

Once everyone was in the room, Detective Hennig closed the door behind her. With her hair hanging loose instead of tied into the ponytail I had memorized, and dressed in casual clothing—jeans and a navy-blue MRC sweatshirt—she looked like a Bizarro version of herself. Like seeing a teacher on the weekend. I figured her and Detective Purser must have rushed from their homes as soon as they got word that Catherine Hillerman had been found.

Mom took a seat in one of the reject chairs. Dad went to sit, but stopped himself halfway down and asked if Detective Hennig wanted the chair. She told him she preferred to stand, so he lowered himself the rest of the way. She pulled a tape recorder from her purse, placing it on the table in front of us, just as she had nine days ago. She pressed play and record at the same time, and I watched as the fat supply reel fed its black tape to the skin-and-bones take-up reel.

"This is Detective Amy Hennig. The date is Friday, August 22nd, 1997, and the current time is 11:16 p.m. The interview being conducted is with Robin Murphy, age thirteen. Both of the subject's parents are present at this time and have consented to their son taking part in this interview."

I told them everything. Almost.

EPILOGUE
SEPTEMBER 1997

APPROACHING THE SCHOOLYARD, TEETERING SOMEWHERE BETWEEN CON-fident and uncertain thanks to my new back-to-school shirt being a slightly brighter shade of blue than I would normally wear, the first thing I noticed was how many other kids I'd forgotten existed. Younger kids scampered like lemurs around the playground. Kids my age and older clustered in the field or in conspiratorial packs on the asphalt tarmac. And every face was someone who'd been wiped from my mind at the beginning of summer vacation.

Like Curtis Goddard, who was in my grade. He'd bleached his normally dark hair and was experimenting with slicking it straight back, giving everyone a fleeting glimpse of the douche he'd one day become. He'd go on to sell real estate in Calgary and I wouldn't be able to walk through my neighbourhood without seeing his smug face peering from a bus bench ad.

Or Lizzy Alston, one year my junior, whose claim to fame was puking on the kid in front of her during a Christmas concert. She was growing into her teeth nicely and had decided to start the new school year by taking the jump from overalls to jeans. Lots of kids were taking risks on new fashion and hair, in fact. For some, the risk would pay off, and they'd be catapulted into an elite realm of coolness few ever got to experience. Others—*most* others—would simply be crucified for daring to try to be anything other than what they were.

The more of these new looks I noticed, the less self-conscious I felt about my own appearance. Not just my shirt, but the fact that I was starting eighth grade with a missing tooth. I decided my mom was right. No one would see it anyway. Not unless something made me laugh or smile real big, which was unlikely. I wouldn't be saying "Pepsi" on picture day.

There were also faces in the throng I couldn't have recognized, because these kids weren't just new to the school, they were new to Haddington Springs. Something had actually *brought* them here. I felt an echo of the ravine collecting its blood debt. But I pushed that kid-thought out of my mind and returned to the newbies. I'd always wonder about these kids on every first day of school, but their presence that September was especially weird to me. After all the national attention our little city had gotten, I found myself looking at their excited faces and thinking, *Why here? Why now? Don't your parents love you?*

I walked down the line of dirt that existed between the field and the asphalt tarmac that bordered the school. I turned before the basketball courts, which opened onto another smaller field and the portables where some classes were held. This was where Dylan, Steph, and I had met pretty much every morning for the last couple years. One of my friends was waiting for me by the portable stairs. My other friend, I knew, would not be.

Steph had her hair down. She was wearing jeans and a new green-and-black polo shirt that looked like a European soccer jersey. When she saw me, she smiled like she was nervous, but not for herself. As I got closer, she slipped her backpack off her shoulder and let it fall to the ground, then she took a few steps to close the gap between us, stopped in front of me, and gave me a long hug, squeezing me tighter that her frame suggested she was capable of. A few people around us called, *Ooh la la* and *Hubba hubba*, but I didn't care and neither did she.

We got to the elephant in the field right away. It would be weird without Dylan and neither of us knew how we would get along without him. I told her what my parents had told me: that he and Emily—who had beat the pneumonia and pleural effusion that followed it—were staying with their grandma and would probably come back once things settled down. Steph told me her dad had said the same thing about them staying with their grandma, except he didn't think they'd come back.

"What do they have to come back to?" he'd asked her.

I didn't want to believe they were gone for good, but it made more sense than what I'd been told. I guess part of growing up is accepting things you don't want to be true.

We tried to cheer each other up by running through a short list of Dylanisms, his greatest hits reel. We talked about his Mickey Mouse laugh and the time he said that winning a pie-eating contest was just another way of starting a shitting contest. But the highlights felt forced, and soon we both fell quiet. It was like we were reminiscing about a friend who had died. Plenty of *Hey, remember the time...?* Like the last two mourners sitting in a funeral parlour after the service.

Steph knew as much as most people did about that night because it was all over the news. She'd have known that Diane Mayer had been taken into police custody and was waiting to be tried for her involvement in the abduction of a child, even though she maintained she hadn't abducted Catherine, that she had helped get her back and was hours away from returning her to her family. Steph would have known that Adam Mayer was facing charges for extortion, child endangerment, and kidnapping. He hadn't been present for the actual abduction (if he had, the right kid would have been napped) but his involvement still remained, which meant he was in on it, and in *for* it. He was in police custody, which in his case meant a cop sitting outside his hospital room. The news said a full recovery was expected. But I knew that before Mrs. Mayer had torn the bayonet out of Dylan's grip, he had given his brother a puncture wound to his chest that would require at least two surgeries. Adam would have to face his charges alone because his partner, the alleged mastermind—although that was a stretch based on my only encounter with him—was on the run. He had a lot more to run from than Adam did, because he also had a murder on his hands, which Adam swore was never part of the plan. I believed him, because I saw the way he looked that night, pacing in a loop while his dad bled out. *It wasn't supposed to be this way . . . It wasn't supposed to be this way . . .* The night before school, the news reported the other guy had been spotted at a gas station somewhere near the Montana border.

And, of course, Steph would've known that Ken Mayer was dead. That he'd gone to meet someone in the ravine and tried to pull off something he couldn't. And how that had gotten him killed. But Steph didn't know the whole story, so, being Steph, she asked me point blank.

"The bell doesn't go for seven minutes," she said, consulting her new digital Casio. "Fill me in."

I did my best. I told her about seeing Emily at the hospital, and about Connor and the ravine and Diane Mayer's other life, and what it was like to be interviewed by police. When I didn't give details about seeing Mr. Mayer die, she didn't push with questions.

The school bell rang. The grade ones, twos, and threes all entered from the front of the building and their shrill screams floated over the roof to us. One of life's universal truths is that it's impossible to move a large mass of young children from one point to another without their volume at least tripling. I had no doubt that Peter and Jeremy were contributing to this racket. On our side of the building, the grade fours, fives, and sixes all hauled ass to get to the doors, not being experienced enough to avoid the inevitable bottleneck. Us older kids—the sevens, eights, and the almighty nines—all hung back until we could drift in casually. Like the cool kids we were all trying to be.

Steph and I were waiting on the edge of the crowd when I noticed a bunch of kids turn their heads, whisper, and point at someone coming our way. I stood on my tiptoes and saw Kyle Hillerman making his way to our end, his eyes fixed on some far-off point, ignoring the walls of kids gossiping at his sides. When Steph noticed, she waved him over. I gave him a reassuring smile, even though I didn't know if he'd want to talk to me. I had, after all, taken something that was his, something he had shown me in good faith. It was stuffed in the middle of an *X-Men* comic. I still look at it from time to time. I can't bring myself to get rid of it.

The three of us inched toward the school's double doors without speaking, keeping the same zombie pace as the rest of our peers. I wanted to ask Kyle how Catherine was doing, but my better judgment intervened. He'd talk about that when he wanted to. I still feel guilty about the valentine. Guilt doesn't dissipate once the blood's cleaned up. It doesn't lose its potency, or spoil like food, warping fuzzy and green, unrecognizable in its container at the back of the fridge. It retains its form, its purity. And I don't know if it's forever, but I do know that if it has a shelf life at all, I haven't reached it yet.

Before we passed through the doorway, I caught someone moving in the corner of my eye. Connor Monaghan. He was pacing back and forth at the edge of the school grounds, watching the masses enter the building from a safe distance. He had this anxious, hurt look on his face, and for a second, I felt kind of bad for him because he was all alone. His one and only friend, Louis Duss, had gone to live with an aunt of his in Edmonton. He had to go because his dad had split. Like I said: last seen on the run in Montana. The former Hush-Hush bouncer wasn't as incapable of masterminding an extortion plot as Diane Mayer had figured. I'd place a bet that at Louis's new school, he wouldn't be proudly sporting his dad's old work shirt. I wondered if father and son were keeping in touch at all. Maybe not by phone—that would be too risky—but they both had a passion for sending secret messages by mail.

I couldn't feel sorry for Connor though, for two reasons. First, he was a category-five asshole. He'd made it his life's mission to make as many people as he could feel like shit. He'd terrorized Kyle and Dylan, and along with Louis, had suckered me into delivering that awful note and, most recently, he had beaten the shit out of me. Second, he was alive. He hadn't been killed and eaten by the ravine monster, because the ravine monster was only a man. A dying man who was just trying to get back to his house, to his family, before the knife wound in his guts put him down for good. So, given everything that had happened, Connor Monaghan got off pretty easy.

But so did I.

My stare must have gone on too long, because Connor had stopped pacing and his eyes locked on me. I couldn't know for sure what his look meant, but I could hear Diane Mayer's voice echoing in my mind.

Wolves. They're everywhere.

Steph punched me in the shoulder.

"Don't stare," she said, grabbing me by the collar of the shirt and tugging me inside the school with her. "They view that as a challenge."

ACKNOWLEDGEMENTS

HEARTFELT THANKS TO EVERYONE AT NEWEST PRESS, A PUBLISHER I'M privileged to work with. There are so many great people on the board of directors and staff who make the press as great as it is. Special shout out to man-with-the-plan Matt Bowes; to Christine Kohler and Carolina Ortiz for their work in office administration and marketing, respectively; and to the brilliant Jenna Butler. Thank you, Claire Kelly, who, in addition to her role as Marketing and Production Coordinator, also edited this book. You brought so much to this story and I can't overstate how much I appreciate your insight. It was a blast working (and talking *X-Men* comics) with you.

Writing is such a solitary gig. I'm fortunate to have friends who, while not in the same boat, are certainly in the same waters. "Hammerhead" Guru A.J. Devlin, co-conspirator Randy Nikkel Schroeder, Druid-from-another-brood Mike Thorn, and Jason "I'm-going-for-the-Margherita-Pizza" Wall are always kind enough to take breaks from their own journeys to help me out. Whether it's reading a draft, lending their assistance in untangling plot knots or talking me through uncertainty, these authors have helped me keep my head on straight during this marathon of a novel. Thank you also to fellow pulp peddler Philip Elliot, the voice from the *Void*, for the magazine real estate he was willing to give after the publication of my first novel.

Thank you to the very talented Michel Vrana, for the wonderful design of this book.

A huge debt of gratitude is also owed to my friend Jaclyn Arndt, who lent her editorial prowess to an early draft and helped me get the story straight before sending it off. Doctor Ola Czyz and Constable Nathan Rogers let me pick their brains about all things medical and law enforcement. Thank you to you both. Any details that are off in this respect come from me directly ignoring their words for the sake of making things work within the narrative.

Thank you to everyone who's ever featured me on their radio show or podcast, and everyone who's written an article or blog about my work.

I'm so fortunate to have the support of my family and friends. Thank you to Mom, Dad, Mariann, Claire, my kick-ass extended family, and the friends who have encouraged and indulged me over the years. There are too many of you to mention in this short section, but you know who you are. I am way too lucky to have you all in my life, and your support means everything to me.

Lastly, and most importantly, thank you to my wonderful wife Alicja, for her love, patience, and inspiration. And to my son Rory, who's staring at me while I type this and, I think, is expecting a mention here.

NIALL HOWELL LIVES IN CALGARY, ALBERTA WITH HIS WIFE, SON, AND PETS.
His debut noir novel *Only Pretty Damned* was shortlisted for the
Kobo Emerging Writer Prize for Literary Fiction and is a part of
the Nunatak First Fiction Series. *There Are Wolves Here Too* is his
second novel. His short fiction has been featured in *The Feathertale
Review* and *FreeFall*. He can be found on Twitter @niall_howell.